M000117801

THE
MIDDLE
STEP

To Marj,
Thanks for
the support
and hosting
the book club!
Enjoy!
Denise Pattiz Bogard

The Middle Step

By Denise Pattiz Bogard

High Hill Press

This is a work of fiction. Names, characters, and incidents are products of the author's imagination or are used fictitiously and are not to be construed as real. Any resemblance to actual events, locales, organizations, or persons, living or dead, is entirely coincidental.

COPYRIGHT © Denise Pattiz Bogard
All rights reserved

Published by High Hill Press, Missouri
No part of this publication may be reproduced in any form without the prior written permission of the author. The book in its entirety may not be reproduced without written permission of High Hill Press.

HighHillPress@aol.com
www.highhillpress.com

ISBN: 978-1-60653-097-9

First High Hill edition: 2015
10 9 8 7 6 5 4 3 2 1
Cover Image provided by Robert Bogard
Cover Design by High Hill Art Department
Library of Congress Number in publication data.

For Robert,
my husband and my best friend.

And in loving memory of my parents,
Gene and Lucille Pattiz.

HELP WANTED:
A woman to live with and care for four teenage girls in a residential home, to serve as foster mom and guide the girls through the academic and emotional challenges of high school. Master's in Social Work preferred.

St. Louis Post-Dispatch

CHAPTER ONE

Lisa Harris arrived ten minutes early and then sat in the car for fifteen, trying to quiet her anxiety. The house appeared more dilapidated than she'd dared to imagine, though no more rundown than those surrounding it. Even from the curb Lisa could see the curled strips of paint peeling from warped clapboard. An upstairs window was boarded and taped, the lawn overgrown with patches of thick weeds and brown grass. Sitting in her new silver Camry and feeling conspicuously out of place, Lisa nearly turned the key and drove away. This was pure madness!

Instead, she checked her hair once more in the rearview mirror—badly in need of a haircut and dye job, but passable enough—double-checked that the car doors were locked, and climbed the house's three porch stairs, stumbling on the loose step.

Before she could ring the bell, the door was swung open by an overweight, jet-black-skinned woman, who thrust out a hand for a hearty shake. "So glad you found the place. Come in, come in. I'm Sheila Johnson. I work down at the school." She pulled a crumpled handkerchief out of the inside of her short sleeve and loudly blew her nose, then offered an apologetic shrug. "Summer allergies. Watch your feet. We haven't cleaned the place up just yet."

Small black pellets Lisa might not otherwise have noticed were scattered across the porch floor. She shuddered and raised her eyes to the level of Sheila's broad backside as they entered a long stifling hallway that opened into a dark dreary area that appeared to be a den or small living room. She stood for a moment to survey the room. Drab green curtains hung in uneven folds over grease-smeared windows, blocking out the sunlight and partially obstructing the tepid air sputtering out of an old air conditioning unit. The walls were bare with chunks of missing plaster. Ashy gray carpeting was badly stained and tattered. The place was even grimmer inside than out. She caught Sheila watching her, taking in her obvious

1

dismay, so Lisa forced a wide smile. "I can't wait to hear about the job."

They sank onto two metal folding chairs and began to talk. Lisa explained that she had seen the help-wanted ad in the *St. Louis Post-Dispatch* for a residential house mother and while her resume didn't exactly reflect her social work degree, she was extremely interested. Sheila Johnson offered a curt nod before launching into a broad description of the position. If hired, Lisa would need to live full time in the "GIFT House" to provide stability and support to four teenage girls no longer with their own families. She would assume the role as guardian, a foster mother of sorts, responsible for their safety, schooling and medical needs, as well as their emotional well-being—in exchange for room, board and a small stipend.

"GIFT stands for Girls In Family Trouble," Sheila explained. "And I'm not talking babies, I'm talking serious trouble. Every one of these kids has endured situations that warrant them leaving their families to live here."

Lisa found herself bobbing her head throughout the interview, her emotions swinging from excited to unsure, confident to terrified. There was one bad moment when Sheila leaned in close, too close, and with intense dark probing eyes asked the obvious: "Why do you want this job?" Lisa had rehearsed the answer in front of the mirror, yet now found herself at a loss for words. Her eyes welled with tears and after several awkward beats of silence, Sheila sat back and sighed.

"If you can't answer that, this is not the place for you. But I'll ask you something else, and give you a minute to collect your thoughts. Why should I want to hire you?"

That Lisa could readily answer. "I have a lot of love to give."

Sheila snorted. "You do realize that moving in with girls of this kind of background is a little more challenging than simply giving 'a lot of love.'"

Lisa felt an instant clutch of fear, could hear a small sane voice telling her to get out now. But she shook the voice away. "Of course. And as to your other question, I want this job for the same reason I hope you will want me. I have a background in dealing with adults in need and now I want to help children. From what you've told me, I think this is a good match."

The response seemed to satisfy Sheila. She immediately switched her tone, describing logistical details usually reserved for an employee. At one point Lisa's stomach began to rumble. She felt it before she heard it, and in a panic she talked louder. She'd skipped breakfast, thinking if she felt thinner she'd project more confidence. When the gurgling outshouted Lisa, she began shifting in the metal chair hoping the squeak would disguise the noise. Not soon enough. Sheila raised a bemused eyebrow but said nothing. It was this, perhaps as much as anything—the suggestion of Sheila's sensitivity—that caused Lisa to immediately say yes when twenty minutes later she was "provisionally" offered the job.

Sheila placed several files into Lisa's hand. "Study them closely and even then you'll know only a fraction of what you've gotten yourself into." She smiled to soften the words, but there was no humor in her eyes.

Lisa opened each of the folders and skimmed the first page of the three girls already approved; a suitable fourth candidate had yet to be selected. Danesha Davis, kicked out of foster care, sent back home and then turned over to the GIFT House. Brianna Jones, abandoned by her entire family. And Coreen Thomas, a victim of multiple moves, schools and upheaval. All three girls would be entering ninth grade the following month at the partnering Stone Charter High School, where Sheila served as school social worker.

"Understand," Sheila said, "this is not just a new job. It will become, in many ways, a new life."

The words were magical—a new life—yet when Lisa spoke she couldn't keep the concern out of her voice. "I really want this but now that I know all the details, I wonder, maybe I'm not qualified?"

Sheila balled her hand into a fist and socked it against her thick, full chest, making the sound of falling into a pillow. "I go by this, and this tells me you're the one." She then gave a sheepish smile. "Plus, you're the only one knocking on this door."

Lisa slapped shut the files. "May I look around?"

There were four small rooms and a bathroom on the second floor and one even smaller bedroom and bathroom downstairs, which would serve as her own. The first floor bathroom's toilet lid was cracked and the sink had rust spots bleeding orange from the dripping faucet. A small washer/dryer unit was shoved into a pantry-sized closet behind the kitchen, which was narrow and dark, though all the appliances appeared to be new. The entire place was uncomfortably warm and had the closed rank smell of an unloved house in a neighborhood where it was safer to breathe in mold than open the windows. Every room needed a fresh coat of paint, new carpeting, window treatment. And even then...

She re-entered the living room as Sheila stood to leave. "You'll need to go through all the channels—background screening, fingerprinting, references. We'll set you up for the training program, but don't worry, it's only thirty hours. You can knock that out this month. And if all that checks out," Sheila's smile was wry, twisting her lips into an S-shape, "you can move right in."

This time as Lisa slid back into her car the leather seats felt slicker, the air-conditioned inside clean and crisp. She drove slowly down the street, one house after another in some form of glaring disrepair, as she tried to imagine living in this neighborhood. Living in that filthy run-down house. Living with those girls. *Actually living here.* Again, she felt a rising sense of panic that tasted of bile. She pulled over to the curb, put her car in idle, turned on her cell phone, then halted, just inches away from calling Sheila Johnson. For long moments she sat still, staring without seeing. She lowered the car window, inhaled several hot humid breaths. A new life. She placed the phone in her purse and put the car back in drive.

The first person she called was the last person she wanted to tell.

"Hey, Mom, I got the job. And I, uh, already accepted."

"Tell me you didn't," Jeanette retorted.

Lisa could have replied in any number of ways, each of which would likely have upset her mother. She opted for silence, knowing she'd get no credit for what she *didn't* say.

"Was the place nice, at least?"

How cathartic it would be to unload, to be able to admit to the one person she wished would support her unconditionally. *What if this is a huge mistake?* But she knew how her mother would react—in fairness, how any reasonable mother would react—and Lisa didn't want to hear it. So she answered, "Yeah, it has a lot of potential. The girls each have their own bedroom upstairs and I'll have my own room and bathroom on the first floor. I didn't see much of the neighborhood but it might be cool. Kind of an adventure, you know, urban living. From what the social worker tells me, the girls are all going into ninth grade and..."

"Are you insane?" Jeanette interrupted. "*This* is what you're choosing? Seems a bit extreme for an almost forty-year-old, don't you think?"

"You're the one who told me 'untested, unknown.'"

Jeanette harrumphed, a guttural sound that carried her disapproval across the three states separating mother and daughter.

Lisa glanced around her studio apartment. It wouldn't take more than a few hours to pack her belongings and with any luck she'd find someone with a van or truck to help her move. A half day, at most, to trade this life for the next. She'd spent more time selecting a new purse.

"How's Daddy?"

The pause lasted too long.

"Mom?"

"To be honest, he's driving me crazy. He's gotten so forgetful. He doesn't pay attention when I tell him things and then he insists I never told him."

"You know Dad. His head is always in a different room than his body." When Jeanette didn't respond, she added, "Are you worried?"

"I don't know. I'm trying not to worry. I'm trying not to clobber him either."

Lisa chuckled, picturing her mother's face, the feigned exasperation that nearly but not quite concealed the expression of tenderness. She suddenly missed Jeanette with a powerful longing. It had been almost a year since she'd been back home.

"Well, I wanted to let you know about the job," Lisa said. "I hope you can be happy for me."

"Oh, honey. You had the entire world in your hands and you're throwing it away," Jeanette squeaked, her voice breaking with a sound of grief as she hung up the phone.

"No, I didn't throw it," Lisa whispered soundlessly. "It threw me."

Rumbles of thunder erupted every ten minutes or so, just often enough to play into Lisa's fear of bathing during a lightning storm. It was only four a.m. Three more hours until her former neighbor arrived with his van to help her move, and she was out of tricks. The Benadryl hadn't knocked her out, the rerun of *The American President* hadn't calmed her nerves and now she couldn't even take a bath.

She flipped on the light and scanned the room. Everything packed away into a small grouping of boxes, nothing on the dresser or desk or walls. Truthfully, it didn't look all that different from the past three months of living here.

"So now what?" she muttered, as much to see if her voice still worked. It had been days since she'd spoken to anyone, the last conversation being the one in Dr. Berger's office. "I don't know what I would have done if you hadn't taken me on," she'd said, attempting to express a gratitude that ran so deep she had no adequate words. He'd flushed with pleasure and false humility. Clearly they were words he'd heard many times before, yet his appreciation was also genuine.

"You did all the hard work," he said. "I just posed the questions."

She'd reached for a tissue but didn't bother to use it, allowing the tears to trickle down her cheeks and splash onto her lap. "Do you...do you, oh this is so hard." Her eyes traveled the familiar room for the last time and resisting the urge to plop back down onto the couch, to beg him to schedule her for next week, next month, for as long as it took to feel whole again, she forced out the question. "Do you really think I'm ready?"

"Yes."

They'd hugged good-bye, she clinging tight while he held professionally still.

Startled, she realized that that was, in fact, the last time she'd used her voice. Just one of the many aspects of her daily life that was about to dramatically change. Her whole body was tingling with nerves and excitement. It had been almost two months since her job interview and now, after a month of training and waiting, finally this time tomorrow she'd be in a new bed in a new house with three new "daughters." She needed to sleep or she'd be a total disaster on her first day. She dug her head deep into her pillow, pulled the blanket up to her chin, turned from her side to her stomach to her other side, then kicked off the blankets . "Forget it," she shouted into the silent room and then picked up the phone.

Bonnie answered on the sixth ring. "Lis? You okay?"

"I know it's late. But I can't sleep. Will you talk to me?"

There was a long pause and Lisa could nearly see, so vivid was the image in her mind, Bonnie groping for her glasses as she quietly slid from the bed and tip-toed out of the room in order not to wake Jerry. Lisa waited until she heard the rattle of the side door open and shut as Bonnie stepped out onto the porch, before she asked, "What if I'm not ready? Berger said I am, but this isn't pretend anymore. I mean, I'm going to have to take care of those girls. How do we know I can?"

"Piece of cake. After what you've been through, this will be a walk in the park. A stitch in time, a clean slate...."

"Enough!" They both giggled, the two-hundred miles distance and time of night dissolving as they instinctively slipped into a pattern, two decades old and so over-used they often didn't need to say anything before one or the other would begin to laugh.

Lisa shoved a small box aside and stretched all the way out on the couch, feeling her spine give way. Bonnie's voice was the balm she'd needed.

"Lis, seriously. You've been to hell and back. You're a survivor. Berger's right. You're ready."

"My mom doesn't approve."

"Of course not. Your mom has common sense. This job's crazy. But that's why you'll be perfect for it. Just remember what you've learned and stay on your Zoloft."

Outside a car skidded, followed by loud laughter and the slamming of doors. Her downstairs neighbor coming home drunk again.

"I hate to ask. Have you told Nate?"

Lisa hesitated then admitted, "I'm sort of hoping he doesn't find out. At least for a while."

"This isn't a prom date we're talking about."

"I'll call him in a couple of weeks." When Bonnie said nothing she added, "Just support me here, please. Even if I'm wrong." She glanced at her left hand, at the bare ring finger with its thin tan line and slight indentation of skin. "His friend Alan posted something on Facebook that made me think Nate may have gone on a date with someone. Can you believe that?"

"No, I don't believe it. Anyway, all of this is just for now. You guys will figure it out later."

She clasped her hands together until it hurt, hoping it would keep her from crying. She would have thought she'd run out of tears by now.

"Look, I know you're shaky. I hear it in your voice. But I think you're going to love those girls and they will go nuts for you. Call me immediately after you meet them."

Lisa managed to sleep for an hour before waking with the sun, groggy and only mildly panicked. She brushed her teeth, swallowed her Zoloft, poured her coffee and waited by the window for a sighting of the gray Toyota van that would take her to The GIFT House.

CHAPTER TWO

Lisa studied the faces of the three teenage girls who had just become "her children." They were so much more *real* than the photos and files and case studies. Pitching her voice low to cover her panic, Lisa scanned her notes and said, "I need to make sure you understand, we expect each of you to get a part-time job when you turn seventeen. Then you'll contribute a percentage of your earnings to rent. For now, I'll buy everything we need from our GIFT money. It's a small budget but I think it's adequate. I mean, if you really need something that isn't covered, the..." She stopped, suddenly realizing she was talking too fast, too loudly and had absolutely no idea how to end the sentence. Not that it mattered. The girls had already heard variations of the spiel several times before and they weren't even trying to hide their indifference.

"You'll check in with Ms. Johnson, the social worker, once a week and we'll meet together with her once a month. I know some of you haven't met her yet, but I think you'll really like her. I liked her," she said as her voice cracked with what Nate had always called her "nervous laugh." The girls barely responded with a nod.

Lisa continued. "You'll be assigned weekly house chores. We can put a new household-duties worksheet on the refrigerator every Sunday. Okay?" The heavy one, Coreen, nodded yes. The other two didn't offer even that much.

"All right then, and every afternoon for one hour and at night from seven to nine will be quiet homework hours down here or in your own room. Absolutely, no phone, no stereo, no Internet during that time...."

The pretty one lurched forward. "That's bullshit! What if I need the Internet for homework?"

"Check with me first, Brianna." The girl whooped in laughter. "Oops, I mean Danesha. And, please don't use that kind of language."

Her answer was a scowl, so Lisa continued, "It goes without saying, I'm sure..."

"Then why you sayin' it?" Danesha murmured.

"No boys will be allowed in your bedrooms. Absolutely no use of drugs or alcohol. Your curfew will be eleven on weekends. I'll need to meet anyone who drives you somewhere and you can never, ever be alone in the house without an adult. Follow these simple rules and I just know we'll get along fine. Questions?"

Again nothing. Lisa scrounged her mind for some sage advice she'd learned during her brief training. She could feel beads of sweat dripping down the back of her neck and between her breasts, but forced herself not to draw attention by wiping them away. "How about if everyone tells a little something about herself," she said, adopting the falsely perky tone she always hated in others. "Who wants to go first?"

"Wee, let's play show 'n tell," Danesha boomed, her mouth stretching into a clownish grin.

"I'll start," Coreen said. "My favorite color is pink and my favorite animal is cats. Don't ask my middle name 'cause I hate it. I've got three brothers on my Mama's side and one sister, and on my Daddy's side I have four brothers, no, five counting the one from my Daddy's first wife, and two sisters."

"Girl, no wonder you came here. You ever get a chance to piss in the shitter? Or shit in the pisser?" Danesha slapped her hand against the table like she'd said something hilarious.

Coreen shrugged her broad shoulders and sank into her seat.

"Please, we really need to be respectful of one another," Lisa said, sounding as ineffectual as she felt. She turned to the littlest one. "And what about you? Care to share anything?"

Brianna hugged twig-like arms tight against her midriff. "No, thanks," she said, her voice barely above a whisper.

Lisa decided to try another tactic. "Danesha, you looked upset before when I was explaining about house chores. Do they seem unfair?"

"No, ma'am. I'll do whatever I'm supposed to." She curled her lip into a sneer.

"Brianna?"

She shook her head ever so slightly, more a tic than an acknowledgement.

"Coreen? Any questions? Suggestions?"

She shrugged, her face impassive.

A sigh escaped from Lisa's lips like a long, lone whistle. This wasn't going at all how she'd hoped, where the girls would immediately decide Lisa was a loving and cool "mother" and within minutes would be opening up about boyfriend problems and questions about make-up. Yesterday she had bought three identical pink teddy bears she'd planned on giving to them as she tucked them into bed tonight—if they even went to sleep rather than huddle together for an all-night slumber party.

Instead, three hardened pairs of eyes were staring at her with obvious distrust, as if waiting for her to say the exact wrong thing. She dared to stare back, at each of these strangers she had committed to living with *every single day for the foreseeable future.*

Danesha was more striking in person than her photo. Her skin was so dark it was nearly blue black. She had straight, bright, if slightly too-small, teeth. Her tongue was the rosy pink of a puppy and her eyes charcoal gray. Unlike most adolescents, all of Danesha's features already seemed to fit. If she could relax the tightness in her face and turn the grimace into a smile, she would be stunning. As it was, her beauty was disturbing, inappropriately provocative, even as she slumped against the back of the chair and folded her arms across her chest. Her pasted-on, low-rise jeans and form-fit shirt were in themselves no more suggestive than what most teens wore. But her hooded eyes and sideways smile were sensuous beyond her fourteen years.

Brianna was a wisp of a child, easily ten pounds underweight, the bones of her face and the bones on her wrists and hands skeletal, giving the impression of fragility. Her smile, though timid and tight-lipped, showed just enough teeth to reveal the buck-protrusion of a late thumb sucker. Her nose was broad and flat, oversized on her small, angular face, her ears large, sticking out beyond the corn-roll braids. Brianna's skin tone was light brown, and she shifted her hazel eyes around the room as if in fear they might latch onto another person. It was puzzling, given that her file indicated until this past year she'd been raised with love and security.

Everything about Coreen was thick. She had full thick lips, thick shoulders, a large shelf-like bust, pudgy hands, a roll of fat around her waist, wide hips. Her hair was clipped short, a style particularly unflattering to her moon-shaped face. Her eyes were the same flat brown tone as her skin. She was the least attractive of the three and the only one willing to make direct eye contact, though her expression was unreadable, neither inviting nor rejecting any connection.

As she studied them, it struck Lisa she was likewise under scrutiny. Her pale white skin and unusual eyes. The dark roots of her bottle-blonde hair. Her pudginess and her cleavage sagged beneath a too-dressy silk blouse. She should have worn jeans instead of linen pants, taken the time to get to the hair salon, not slathered on her vanilla-scented lotion, a sudden and unwelcome reminder of Nate. She'd spent an hour this morning trying to figure out an outfit and had managed to get it all wrong anyway. Sheila had warned her about the girls' sixth sense and Lisa suddenly felt transparent, as if everything she'd been through, her reasons for being here, were laid bare.

She leaned forward, lowered her voice. "I'll be honest, I'm excited for us to create a new family. But I'm a little bit scared. You probably are too. So we'll just have to figure it out together, okay?"

"We're all down with that," Coreen said.

"You ain't my mouth," Danesha muttered. She tilted her chair back until it scraped the newly painted wall.

"What'd you say?" Coreen taunted.

"I said, *you ain't my mouth.*" The flimsy material of Danesha's shirt stretched tight against her chest. She glanced down, then arched her back in what seemed a practiced move.

Coreen shrugged. "Whatever."

"Why do you do that?"

At Coreen's puzzled look, Danesha shrugged her shoulders with wild exaggeration. When Coreen didn't respond, Danesha leaped up and blurted, "Know what? All these stupid ass rules. You think I care where I stay? Well I ain't trippin' offa any of you."

She shoved her chair and stomped out. Lisa could hear her climbing the stairs to the bedroom, hear the door squeak open and slam shut, and minutes later came the blast of her stereo.

Lisa's mind raced through the scenarios they'd role-played. Should she sprint up the stairs and into Danesha's room to demand an apology? Or threaten new and tougher rules, making it clear she was the one in charge? Or maybe she should tread lightly, grasp the child's hand and calmly talk one-on-one about "appropriate responses."

Instead, Lisa sat, the music above their heads so loud the ceiling practically trembled. Out of habit, her right thumb and index finger traveled to her left ring finger, searching for something to twirl. Finally she was able to summon the forced cheerfulness to ask, "Do you two have any ideas for decorating the house? If you brought something from home, we could certainly hang it in any room you want. Or we could go shopping together to pick out some posters. This is your house now."

Coreen started to shrug, then visibly stopped herself. "Naw, I don't have any ideas about that. Whatever you want, Miss Lisa." Brianna immediately nodded in agreement, her eyes begging not to be asked.

Lisa's sigh seemed to linger until eventually both girls left the room. She sat alone for several minutes, listening to the rumble of Danesha's rap music, to the echoes of rage. Had she really bought these girls matching pink teddy bears? She squeezed back tears of disillusionment as she suddenly remembered Sheila's comment that Lisa was the "only one knocking on this door."

In fairness, Sheila had certainly tried to warn her. As they'd left the house that first, interview day, Sheila took Lisa's hand and probed with eyes so brown they nearly disappeared against the woman's dark, round face. "Trying to become a family could be the toughest challenge you've ever faced."

Lisa had almost laughed out loud at the irony, but she'd kept her expression neutral. Her past finally could belong to another life. A clean slate.

Clearly, it was her present and future she now had to worry about.

CHAPTER THREE

There was so much Lisa didn't know or understand in the early weeks at the GIFT House. How could she? She was given three thin files and told by Sheila, "Be careful as you read these that you don't turn the children into a cliché. Forget the *individual* and you forfeit any chance at success."

Through letters and reports Lisa gleaned the basics. Danesha Davis had been pulled from her home after her drugged-out brother had attacked their drunken mother. Subsequently she was kicked out of her foster home after being discovered in bed with the nineteen-year-old neighbor boy. Mom went through rehab, took back Danesha, then gladly relinquished her the following month. Brianna Jones had been abandoned by her entire family—an absent father, a mother who continued to send empty promises from Florida, and the sudden death of a beloved grandmother. And Coreen Thomas had never stayed longer than two years with any relative, switching schools every time she went to live with mom or dad or auntie or grandma or mom again or even dad's distant cousin whom he barely knew. All three girls had been turned over to the privately funded GIFT House program with barely a second glance beyond their mothers' signatures.

Lisa's own background could not have been more different, marked by a quiet childhood of careful plans and few surprises. Jeanette and Albert had recently celebrated their fortieth anniversary in the same house to which they'd brought baby Lisa home from the hospital. She and her younger sister Kate grew up in an all-white suburban Minneapolis neighborhood where nearly everyone they knew, themselves included, was Jewish, educated, and earning a steady middle or upper middle class income. As children, the only violence Lisa and Kate witnessed was on the television shows they watched when their parents went out on Saturday nights.

Still, Lisa had expected she would fit right into the rhythm of the house. As a college student, she'd chosen social work because even at age eighteen she had a passion to help those less fortunate. Since finishing grad school, she'd worked as a debt-counselor for destitute mostly African-American clients, and on slow weekends she and Nate had volunteered for Habitat for Humanity. She had been damned good at her job, too. Her approach fostered trust and her carefully honed skills had saved a number of clients from disaster. She'd had no reason not to imagine those qualities would automatically transfer to kids. Yet, as she was quickly discovering, working eight hours a day at a desk with adults who had actively solicited her help was *not* preparation for living with troubled, suspicious teens of a different race, religion, culture, economic level and mindset. Lisa found herself continually second-guessing everything she said and did. Like a woman in a cocktail dress at a party where everyone else is in jeans, she often felt as though there were a set of instructions she'd yet to receive.

Sheila came around every several days to check in. One afternoon she stopped by during what was already becoming a routine power play between Danesha and Lisa.

Danesha had arrived from school and immediately announced she would need to go over to a friend's house to study.

"Do I know this friend?" Lisa asked, a ridiculous question, since she'd yet to meet any of their classmates. But it seemed like something a "mother" should ask, which was the one guiding force Lisa kept trying to rely on.

Her eyes opened wide in mock surprise. "Why, Miss Lisa, I don't think you do." Her voice was dripping with sarcasm, and before Lisa could respond—with patience or anger, she was struggling to decide which way to lose the battle this particular time—Danesha turned her back, put her headphones on and blasted her music.

Lisa reached to pull the headphones off as Danesha swung around and hurled the hand away so fast Lisa jammed her thumb against the table.

"God damn that hurts!" she screamed, stomping her foot in pain and frustration just as Sheila came walking in the door.

"What's going on here?" Sheila asked.

Danesha quickly shut off the iPod and yanked her earphones down around her neck. "I'm trying to do my homework, Ms. Johnson."

Sheila and Danesha both turned to Lisa. Seizing what she hoped was a moment to earn Danesha's gratitude, Lisa said, "Everything's fine. Danesha, how about if today you study here until I find out more about your friend? Maybe you could go over there tomorrow?"

"Then I won't do the fucking project. You happy?"

"Whoa there." Sheila grabbed hold of Danesha's arm. "You want soap in your mouth? You apologize right now and then I'm giving you three minutes to retrieve your backpack and assignments and get back down here or you're looking at your last hour of freedom. Maybe ever."

"Yeah, sorry," Danesha muttered, her lips curling around the word, before she scurried out of the room.

"Wow, she actually obeyed you without a fight." Lisa rubbed her throbbing thumb and with a whine added, "I thought I'm supposed to be the one in charge here."

"You thought or you know?"

"Huh? I'm telling you, Sheila..."

"Shh," Sheila raised her finger to her lips as Coreen and Brianna approached from outside and Danesha re-entered from the hallway, lugging a tattered book bag behind her, headphones again on and music spilling into the room.

"Ms. Johnson!" Coreen squealed.

"Girl, you are *so* loud," Danesha shouted over her own music. She dumped the book bag on the table and made a big show of searching for the assignment sheet. "See," she said, pointedly turning her back to Lisa. "It says we gotta work with a partner. Only how am I supposed to do that when *she* won't even let me?"

Before Lisa could respond, Coreen piped in. "You're such a liar. I have the same science teacher and we don't even start that project for two more weeks. You're a liar and a cheat."

"You *don't* wanna be clickin' on *me*," Danesha hissed.

Coreen pulled the chores chart off the refrigerator. "Look at this." She waved the paper in front of Sheila, pointing to a

17

line visibly smudged. "This was Danesha's week on dinner dishes and she erased her name and wrote in Brianna's."

"You a lying bitch." Danesha stepped toward Brianna, "Did I do that to you?"

Brianna's chin trembled as she shook her head back and forth.

Coreen's mouth dropped open. "Brianna?"

"Girls, girls," Lisa said, clapping her hands together, "we can work all this out. Everyone just wants to be fair to each other, right?" Her voice rose to a squeaky pitch, which was immediately mimicked by Danesha, humming under her breath in sing-song. Lisa placed a hand on Danesha's shoulder. "Come on. Admit what you did. We're a team, remember?"

Danesha shrugged off her hand and began to walk out.

"Oh no you don't." Sheila was up and blocking the doorway with speed that belied her heft. "Shut that thing off or I'll take it away. Go sit over there," turning to Coreen, "and you get your sorry self in that chair," and to Brianna, her voice softening only slightly, "get out of the corner and sit your butt down too. Now..." her eyes blazing, "let's get to the bottom. And I don't want to hear excuses or lies."

Danesha audibly gulped. "Yeah, I changed it. But you can't blame me. I ain't no house slave. At home I never had to clean this much."

Sheila shot her a contemptuous look before responding, "Well, this *ain't* home, girlfriend, and around this house you do your chores and you do them with a smile. Unless, of course," she paused for emphasis, "you'd rather go back into foster care."

Danesha's dark skin flushed.

Sheila turned to Coreen, who blurted, "I know, Ms. Johnson. I need to do better with Danesha. I'll try."

Brianna nodded and in a soft voice echoed, "I'll try too."

Again, Lisa clapped as though they'd achieved a great victory. "Hey, this is progress. Now, how about if you go do your homework, and then tonight we could do something fun together?"

All three inched their way toward the door. "Just hold on," Sheila boomed. "There's one more thing. I want to hear from Miss Lisa next time I come that you have been giving her proper respect. Or there *will* be consequences. And they won't be pretty. Get your pitiful selves upstairs and do what you're supposed to do."

Within moments came the sound of bedroom doors opening and closing. Lisa waited to see if Sheila would say anything, and when she didn't, said, "You're amazing."

"I'm not amazing. I'm just not afraid to let them know I'm in charge."

"You mean the way I let Danesha cuss? You've told me not to 'major in the minors' and I think compared to so much else, this one..."

Sheila cut Lisa off with a flick of her palm. "Let me ask you a question, and try to answer me honestly. One mother says to her child, 'Honey, isn't it time for your bath?' Another mother says, 'Boy, get your rusty behind in that bathtub, and I mean *now*.' Which mother is likely to get the best result?"

"Why does this feel like a trick question?"

Sheila smirked but didn't answer.

"Okay, I think the first mother. Obviously."

"Obviously?" Sheila raised a single eyebrow. "Lisa, our children expect an authority figure to act with authority. When a teacher or parent or other adult tries to be a friend, the message sent is that this adult is not in charge." Sheila drummed her fingers against the table, seemingly lost in thought. When she spoke again, her voice was softer, but its undertone challenged dispute.

"I'm going to let you in on a little secret. I happen to believe that the second mother, let's assume she's a black woman, has the better approach...at least for our kids. If the mother were to ask, 'Isn't it time for you to take your bath?' she would be offering a true alternative." Sheila paused. "When you *ask* the girls to do what you *expect* them to do, you confuse them. Frankly, it would confuse me. Danesha, especially, sees you as not being in command. And, regarding the cursing, personally I wouldn't put up with it. But what's important is that *you* establish the rules and *you* follow through with the consequences."

Lisa nodded. "I can work on that. But I still don't understand why they resist me so much."

"Look, we knew it would be difficult. This job certainly isn't for everyone. We'll give it 'til spring and then re-evaluate." She heaved herself up from the chair, standing for a moment to regain her balance. "I need to get back down to the school. I never intended to stay this long. And don't go apologizing either. Sometimes you're as bad as that little Brianna."

On impulse, Lisa squeezed Sheila's hand. "Thanks. For everything. But, Sheila, what if I don't know how to be a mother to these girls?"

"Don't try to be their mother. They each have a mother."

"Yeah, mothers who signed them away."

"That's right. And don't think for a moment they ever forget that fact. Maybe even, in some convoluted way, they blame *you*. Don't try to be their friend either. Just be in charge." Her eyes traveled across the room. "As soon as we get more funding, we'll hire a day assistant to fill in so you can have some time to yourself. That will help. Meantime, let's see if things improve over the next months."

The pointed reference to her probation status hung heavy in the air, weighing Lisa down as she stared out the grimy front window, watching as Sheila pulled away, her old green Dodge with its grumbling muffler a much better fit for this neighborhood than Lisa's new and shiny silver Camry. What an idiot she was. Why would she admit her insecurities to Sheila? And that perky voice she'd used, as she actually *clapped her hands together*. With a groan, she trudged up the stairs, stopping halfway to lean into the stairwell wall. She shook her head repeatedly, then heaved her shoulders back, nearly a shrug but not quite, and climbed the stairs to the second floor. All of the bedroom doors were closed and the hall was uncharacteristically silent. She wanted to knock on a door, as if she would know what to say if someone invited her in.

Be patient, Dr. Berger used to remind her, *change is slow and difficult and often confusing*—a maxim so obvious, so trite, yet so hard to actually live.

Their bathroom was at the end of the hallway and like their bedrooms, its upkeep was the girls' responsibility. It was a jumble of mess and chaos. Wet towels on the floor, jeans behind the door, unopened jars of "kink-out" hair gel, bottles of lotion that promised to get rid of ashy skin, a plugged-in flat iron dangling near the sink, dark purple eye shadow and deep bronze blush-on. The trash can was overflowing with tissues and candy wrappers. Three damp bras hung from the shower curtain, as varying in size and style as the girls themselves—red lace, stiff white and stretchy sports bra. Lisa breathed in a tart, musty odor, feeling the intimacy and the alienation of all this black adolescent femininity.

There was a timid knock on the door. "Is someone in there?"

"It's me, Brianna. I'll be right out."

"Sorry," she said, followed by the sound of quiet padding down the hall and the click of a closing door.

Lisa lifted the toilet lid and grunted in disgust. One of the girls had her period and hadn't bothered to flush. Lisa flushed, then flushed again, until the water swirled back completely clear. Without bothering to remind them of the twenty-five minutes left in homework hour, she walked down the creaking steps and into her own small room. She plopped onto her bed and stared at the ceiling, fighting the dizzy sensation of falling backward. Even when she closed her eyes she couldn't erase the image. That bowlful of blood—not her own—bright red blood. She didn't try to fight the tears of self-pity that streaked the sides of her face as she clenched both fists to her stomach, rolled over and burrowed her head into the pillow, powerless to staunch the memory.

You're pregnant?" Nate had sputtered. "You're not thinking of keeping it, are you? We're not ready for a baby."

Lisa had surprised them both by nodding yes. Ardently pro-choice, she was choosing life.

They fought as never before. Nate needed more time, more money, more marriage—not parenting, but marriage—before becoming a father. If ever. "We're so happy, Lisa. Why would we change that?"

Lisa had her own misgivings too. For seven years she and Nate had reveled in their time together. She loved their cocooned world, had not wanted anything to change. Starting a family felt like a conversation they weren't ready to have.

Yet, here she was. Pregnant.

Each morning began with a battle and each evening ended with a chilly separation as Nate sulked on the couch and Lisa cried alone in their bed. It was the first true crisis of their marriage and one in which one of them, by necessity, would need to make a fierce compromise.

But how does one compromise about a baby? Lisa explained, "It's not that I won't, it's that I can't." Unhappily, Nate finally gave in. She called her parents and sang into the phone, "Grandma. Grandpa."

The sheer amazement that her body could create and grow a new life burst Lisa's world into full vibrancy. After spending her entire life coloring inside the lines, with everything going according to a scheduled plan—college, grad school, marriage—this was the most glorious *unplanned* occurrence.

Then she began to bleed.

"It's okay to bleed so long as you don't have cramping," the obstetrician reassured.

Then she began to cramp.

The doctor put her on bed rest. She cupped her hands to her stomach, too scared, too hopeful, to talk. Every hour or so, she reread the section in *What to Expect When You're Expecting* describing the women with bleeding and cramping problems throughout successful pregnancies.

But on the fourth day Lisa bled out huge clots. Drops of blood splattered the toilet rim and the floor. She was shaking too hard to even cry. She grabbed her left hand with her right to keep from reaching into the toilet to grasp what she knew was her baby. The baby she'd already held and dressed and kissed in her mind.

Frozen in place, Lisa stood in a daze before pushing the handle, numbly aware the loss she was feeling would be hers alone.

She crawled back into bed, squeezed shut her eyes and buried her face into Nate's chest, knowing this would allow him to hide his expression of relief.

CHAPTER FOUR

The expectation was that Lisa would use the first month to get their house in order before beginning weekly volunteer hours at the school. She still wasn't clear about the relationship between Stone Charter and the GIFT House, only that the school helped to sponsor the house and both received funding from grants, private donors, and in the case of the house, minimal monthly payments from each of the girls' families. As such, Lisa was spared from dealing with the DFS, DYS, CSW, RCST, CSPI, DJO, GAL, etc.—a seemingly unending list of acronyms that all added up to an inefficient system already over-loaded, under-funded, under-staffed and overly bureaucratic. Sheila had alluded to this during a brief meeting, with a promise to offer the background details of the house's origin at another time. "There's time for that story— it's a good one—but for now, just work on creating a *home* here."

There was plenty to do in order to convert the small, filthy two-story house into a home. The living room carpeting was deeply stained and seemed to show every new footprint unless Lisa vacuumed daily. The entire first floor was newly painted mint green, but the old plaster walls grew sticky and soiled unless regularly washed with ammonia. The kitchen linoleum floor had several worn spots and permanent tar-black scuff marks Lisa futilely tried to scrub away. No matter how many times she wiped the kitchen cabinets with bleach, they were perpetually smudged. Some days she spent hours trying to make the place sparkle, but the years of grub and neglect could never be wiped out.

The only progress she'd made was that she no longer had to call her mom to ask what kinds of cleaning supplies to use for various chores, unlike the first week when she'd spent an absurd amount of time in a Wal-Mart aisle squinting to read the minute print on the bottles of Lysol and Clorox and off-brand sprays, trying to determine which one could "cut the grimiest grime" without, incidentally, poisoning the residents. Some days Lisa was even able to take satisfaction in a gleaming surface without wanting to cry at the reality of all she'd traded away. Every once in a while snippets of memory snuck past her guard, memories of a house that shone from the efforts of the weekly maid service that let itself in and was gone by the time Lisa and Nate came home from work. Then she'd forcibly block out the thought. "Stay in the now," she'd command herself, turning the radio up louder to drown out the noise in her head.

The days stretched on interminably while the girls were at school. Alone in the quiet house, Lisa had too much time to think and to remember. In spite of her best intentions, some days she'd give in, go back to bed and cry away half a day. Those were the panic days, when she'd call Bonnie for reassurance or call her mom for distraction. Eventually, she'd rouse herself and anticipate the arrival home of the three girls. Often, though, within minutes of them entering, Lisa longed for the next morning when they would leave again. Dinners were particularly exhausting and uncomfortable as four strangers sat around one small table. Lisa struggled to draw out information about their friends, their classes, their pre-GIFT lives—desperate to forge a connection. Most of her questions were met by silence or mono-syllables. Even Coreen, the friendliest of the three, seemed contained within an impenetrable shell. And not once did any of them ask a question of Lisa. She was there to cook and to leave them to scatter to their own rooms as quickly as possible. If it weren't so pitiful Lisa's initial images of their little sorority-like pajama parties might have been amusing.

Yet, despite the dreariness and loneliness, Lisa spent nearly all of her early weeks locked inside. The GIFT House was located in a section of north St. Louis city where street names were recognizable for their prevalence on the evening news. Clara Road itself was part of an active Neighborhood Watch program, but that offered little reassurance when one block over in any direction there stood abandoned buildings, boarded-up windows, gang sign tags.

"What do you think about this area? Scary?" Lisa asked Coreen.

"It's better than most places I've stayed." She shrugged. "And it ain't bad in the light, Miss Lisa."

To which Lisa had thought, "Maybe for *you* it *ain't* bad."

Yes, she had readily jumped worlds across town when accepting the GIFT House position—had welcomed the chance to travel as distantly away as any fifteen miles allowed. But the longer she lived here the more Lisa realized just how impulsive and naïve she'd been to accept this job. Sheila claimed a handful of older white families lived several streets over, but so far on Lisa's drives in and out of the neighborhood, she'd yet to see any other Caucasian.

She'd lived in St. Louis her entire adult life, sixteen years now, and she well knew that as one of the most segregated metropolitan areas in the United States, where you lived defined you to the extent that when asked, "Where did you go to school?" the answer was assumed to be high school. Each of the various St. Louis suburbs and neighborhoods was characterized by wealth or by level of education or by religion, race and politics.

The "north side," where the GIFT House was located, and neighboring north county municipalities like Ferguson, Normandy and Wellston, were predominantly black, poor and plagued by high crime rates.

Lisa had wanted to escape her homogeneous past with its association of personal pain. But as she was discovering, it was one thing to be a minority at work and then go home to the assumed safety of her suburb. It was quite another to actually live where crime was a daily reality and where her white skin made her feel like a target.

Inside, too, Lisa found herself suddenly, uncomfortably, race conscious in a way she'd never been before. Especially when irritated or frustrated, Lisa saw the blue-black of Danesha's skin before she saw the girl. Coreen and Brianna's brown tones seemed to characterize them as much as their sizes. And she was pretty certain that when the girls looked at her what they mostly saw was white skin and bleached blonde hair.

Of course Sheila picked up on it. "Look, Lisa, their darkness absolutely is who they are," Sheila had recently said.

26

"No sense in pretending otherwise. And," she'd added, cocking her head sideways in an expression Lisa was growing to recognize as barely concealed judgment, "no sense in pretending it doesn't influence how you feel about them or about this neighborhood. It's like acting as if our President's blackness is immaterial. Or denying the incidence of racial profiling. The only true way to shed racism is to acknowledge its existence and move beyond it."

Today, then, she would move beyond. She would go for a walk. It was time to claim the neighborhood. Three times, she changed her clothes, discarding the matching cream-colored workout suit as too rich, then realizing as she was nearly out the door, she shouldn't be walking in red or blue—gang colors. Finally, sporting a pair of faded denim shorts and an innocuous Race for the Cure T-shirt, she carefully locked and double-bolted the front door. Glancing both ways with the intensity of hunted prey, Lisa set out on a walk, her back and shoulders straight, her eyes roaming for lurking danger. Nate would have fit in better with his dark olive complexion, nearly black hair, hazel eyes. She shook away the image. "I have as much right to live here as anyone," she muttered, though even her own ears heard the warble of doubt.

As though reading her lips, the neighbor across the street shouted out, "Yoo hoo. Miss Harris, hello there."

She offered a shy wave.

"It's no day to be inside, that's for sure. Been wondering when you'd come out."

Lisa giggled. *This* is what they meant by "neighborhood watch?"

Up and down Clara Road small, old red-brick houses were piled up on postage-stamp-sized lots. "Our Eyes Are On You" signs were prominently displayed in front windows, including those covered by bars or boards—bright orange signs with bold white lettering and the eye icon in place of the word, lending a tone of frivolity ill-suited for the message and even more so for the neighborhood.

The A.M.E. Church of God took up a large portion of the narrow street corner. Lisa knew from the girls that almost everyone on the block attended this church, but a growing concern was that the pastor of thirty years was out of step with the congregants. Coreen and Brianna had woken up at eight the past two Sunday mornings to go to services and filled the Sunday dinner conversation with church talk.

"It's a sin to take the evil drink," Coreen had mimicked at last night's supper, her voice booming with fire and brimstone. She pointed her fingers at each of them, one at a time. "Jesus sees *every single* sin. And, folks, I know who's sinnin' too."

"I don't know about that pastor, but Jesus sure as shit has better things to do than to go worrying 'bout *every single sin* round *here*," Danesha blurted, causing all three girls to erupt in a rare moment of shared laughter.

Despite their mockery, the church seemed to fill a void for Coreen and Brianna, evoking a sense of calm in both girls for the first several hours after they returned. Lisa wished Danesha would consider going, but she had fumed, "Jesus ain't done squat for me" with such vehemence Lisa didn't push. Particularly since she herself only went to synagogue, at most, once or twice a year for the Jewish High Holiday services.

Just beyond the church was a small, muddy area with a swing set, a slide and a warped, wooden picnic table. She walked around a broken Colt 45 bottle, tempted to throw it away, until she realized much of the park was littered with crumpled trash and broken glass. She kept her eyes straight ahead as she headed toward the swings, determined not to let the piles of garbage deflate her mood.

Gingerly, Lisa sat on the swing. The plastic sheaths covering the rusted chains were cracked and stiff, but Lisa squeezed her fingers tight and began to pump her legs, reaching higher and higher, feeling the breeze as it blew away the sense of despair she'd been wearing like second skin for so long she barely noticed its existence. She closed her eyes and flung her head back, embracing the dizzy wonder of flying.

A memory came rushing back with its simple sweetness. It was Lisa's tenth birthday and instead of the large birthday party her mom always pushed, Lisa opted for a family picnic.

Jeanette had packed a basket full of Lisa's favorite foods. She could still see it. Peanut butter, banana and honey sandwiches on white bread without the crusts, celery sticks with cream cheese, cheesy Doritos and Oreos. Her dad had actually taken a full Saturday off from the furniture store. "Forget the sale, it's my special girl's birthday," he'd said, giving her an uncharacteristic hug. And eight-year-old Kate wasn't crabbing or insisting on being her usual "I'm the adorable baby sister" center of everything. Lisa got to choose playing on the playground equipment and swinging for nearly a half hour before eating and no one complained. She remembered feeling surprisingly empowered, if slightly uncomfortable, to be in the limelight of her family when her usual role was to step back. As she years later told Nate, "I think that's when I first realized I didn't have to be pastel. I could be more demanding, start expressing my own opinion," to which he'd quipped, "Yeah, my luck."

At the sound of low heckling, Lisa opened her eyes, immediately transported back. A group of dark-skinned teen boys were huddled together at the other end of the park, palms outstretched then quickly hidden. Lisa felt an instinctive bubble of fear as she allowed her legs to droop and the swing to slow. Two of the boys glanced over and murmured something, which caused several others to hoot and walk toward her. She stiffened her arms to stop the swing as quickly as possible, then jumped to the cement. Her knees buckled as she pitched forward, stumbling into the air and barely righting herself from falling onto broken glass.

She took off running and was halfway down the street before she slowed, panting, heart pounding. Fearfully, she looked over her shoulder, and seeing no one, felt a relief so palpable she nearly collapsed. Those outstretched palms. Were they exchanging drugs? Did they have a gun? Why weren't they in school? Why were they laughing when they looked at her?

She picked up her pace, continually glancing back and then downward until she reached Clara Road. Across from the GIFT House, the same woman still stood on her porch.

"Did you have a nice walk?"

Lisa nodded her head, hoping her face gave nothing away. She stumbled on the loose stair, pushed down the rusted lock and gratefully entered the GIFT House. Immediately, she drew the drapes in the living room and closed the blinds throughout the first floor. She should be feeling shame—admit it, Lisa, if those boys were white would you have run?—but all she could feel was a choking sense of claustrophobia. What the fuck had she gotten herself into?

She sank onto the sagging couch and stared vacantly, listening to the noises outside the darkened room as she waited for the three girls to come "home."

CHAPTER FIVE

The fourth spot was filled. Eva-Lynn Fox. Lisa skimmed her records, then read them more carefully, after leaving them to sit for half a day. With so many adolescents in dire situations, why select such a disturbing, obviously inappropriate girl? She called Sheila.

"Can I refuse Eva-Lynn?"

"No."

"What if saying no is right for the other girls?"

"She needs us, Lisa. Maybe most of all."

Lisa studied Eva-Lynn's photo. Pierced eyebrows, nose, lip, her entire outer ears. The girl's face would never pass through airport security. She wore heavy black eye liner, had two clownish red cheeks that stood out from her pale white skin, and covered her lips with purplish-black lipstick that extended beyond her actual lip line. Her teeth were crooked and appeared dingy yellow, though that might have been the contrast with the dark lips. Her hair was cropped short, spiky, and dyed orange.

Lisa closed the file, engulfed in a sense of dread. As she dusted the living room she found her mind continually traveling back to the image of the fourth candidate, of the slathered on make-up, the dramatic hair.

She had just put away the cleaning supplies when the phone rang.

"Miss Harris?"

"Yes?"

"My daughter thinks she's comin' to live with you all, but I've got some questions to ask."

The woman was talking too loudly, her voice shrill.

"Who is this?"

A high-pitched laugh. "Oh, of course you wouldn't know. I'm Sheri Fox, ma'am. And, see, my husband and me, we have some questions for you."

Lisa waited.

"We was wonderin', see, no one really explained the program to us, or if they did it sure weren't clear, and we was wonderin' if you all pay us to let us give you our Eva-Lynn for a while."

"Excuse me?"

"Well, you know. We thought since we lettin'..."

Lisa did not attempt to hide her disdain. "Mrs. Fox, you've got this all wrong. In fact, you need to pay *us*." She paused. "But maybe you'd rather Eva-Lynn didn't come here?"

"Oh, no. I'm sure she'll be better off with you all. We just thought that maybe... Anyways, can I ask you something else?"

"Okay..."

"You aren't colored, are you?"

No, but I'm a *Jew*, she almost, but didn't say.

"You don't talk colored." The sound of gulping, liquid going down, then the husky dropping of the woman's voice as though burned. "You see, we don't much care for coloreds. Neither does our Eva-Lynn."

Lisa held the phone away from her ear, shook it as if to shake the woman herself. "This is a special home for girls who can't live with their families anymore. Someone's skin color has no place in this conversation."

"Yeah, well, so long as you ain't a nig, I mean colored."

"Mrs. Fox, every one of the other girls is African-American. *Everyone*."

The woman's tone changed to ice, all chumminess gone. "I see. We didn't know that. Maybe..."

Lisa held her breath.

"I think your little home just ain't right for our girl. You tell that Ms. Johnson, please. She colored too?"

"Oh, yeah. She is colored. The neighbors are colored. Even the roaches are colored." Lisa slammed the phone down, trembling with outrage. What a horrible woman!

She stepped out onto the porch. Dark clouds covered the sky. A thunderstorm was predicted, which meant Lisa would need to pick the girls up from school in a half hour. She leaned against the post, inhaling the sticky humid air. Jesus! Coloreds? Who used that word anymore?

Back inside, Lisa gathered the file to lock it away and as she did so she reached for the photo, tempted to rip it to pieces, but found herself studying the image once more. The piercings, the hair dye, the clownish make-up. Eva-Lynn Fox would be a caricature of a rebellious teen but for the eyes. Crystal blue, eyes too old and too sad to ignore in the face of a fourteen-year-old child. And then there were the hints of yellow and purple on her collar bone, bruises that never quite heal before new ones appear.

Lisa sank into a nearby chair, feeling the swallow of remorse. What had she just done to this girl?

CHAPTER SIX

Every time Lisa thought about the conversation with Sheri Fox she re-experienced a wave of queasy disgust—as well as a sense of pride. "Even the roaches are colored," she'd think and giggle to herself, having responded for once with the perfect rejoinder at the perfect time. Yet—and the irony was not lost on her—that didn't keep Lisa from staying cocooned inside because of her own continuing uneasiness with the neighborhood. Sheila had been too busy to interview candidates to serve as GIFT House assistant, which allowed Lisa the daily excuse to shutter windows and hunker down. But today the autumn sky was cloudless and a soft shade of blue St. Louisians only saw a handful of days each year. It was simply too beautiful not to go out.

On Clara Road there were few trees to glorify the brilliant reds and oranges of the season. What little grass there was had turned mostly brown from the merciless heat of summer months and the absence of expensive chemical treatments that kept suburban lawns, including her own previous lawn, gleaming green. This time the porch across the street was empty, as was the park. Turning the corner, Lisa again came upon a group of teens loitering on the street corner. She cast her eyes away, watching her feet as she slowed her pace and hunched her shoulders, trying to be as inconspicuous as possible. She could almost hear Nate's voice telling her *fear is as much about perception as reality*. She exhaled a deep breath and realized she was slightly more at ease than the last time she'd walked down this street.

"Hey! You in my space."

Lisa looked up into the clean-shaven, angular face of an older teen, who leapt aside with exaggerated motion as if she might plow him down. The gold of his topaz-colored eyes gleamed against the deep rich brown of his skin, offset by the burnished red of his soft leather jacket.

"Sorry," she stammered. "I guess I wasn't paying attention."

"Ain't no drama." His laugh was deep, calculated and practiced, clearly a laugh to woo adults. "You just walking or..." he flashed a bright metallic smile, revealing a front row of gold-capped teeth. A status symbol and a sign of gang membership. Lisa fought a wave of panic that was quickly disarmed by his wink. "Or you looking to buy?"

She felt herself blush. "Actually..." she glanced past his shoulder and saw the yellow brick façade of Stone Middle and High School. She hadn't realized she'd walked so far. "I'm going to visit my girls' school."

He lifted his eyebrows in question.

"Well, not *my* girls, but the girls I take care of."

A rumble of a laughter sounded in his throat. "You Miss Lisa."

"How do you know me?"

"I'm Devon, king of this corner, and I know every game goes down here. Need me to take you in?"

"Oh, no. I mean, but thanks anyway." She felt his eyes travel her flabby backside as she walked away, holding herself stiff, uncomfortably aware he was sizing her up as if selecting from a menu.

At the front stairs, she paused to catch her breath. Lisa's visit to meet the teachers and begin volunteer work was long overdue, though not unusual in a school of low parent participation. Still—and she could hear Sheila's echo as she pushed open the solid heavy door—Lisa was supposed to be different, to be a model of what a parent *could* be for these girls.

An overpowering stench of cleaning chemicals assaulted her as she entered a cavernous area brimming with noise and heat and chaos. Students were shouting over heads to one another, throwing paper balls, banging lockers, pushing, hugging, laughing. The sudden rush of such hormonally charged energy immediately lifted her spirits.

"Fight!" came a screech from down the hall and the crowd dispersed to another part of the building, leaving Lisa standing alone in a large space whose quiet was as startling as the roar of moments before. She searched for a front office but finding none began wandering the halls.

A bell had rung, insistent and shrill, and except for a few stragglers, everyone had disappeared into classrooms. Then her eye caught a familiar shape sneaking just past the last locker toward a side exit.

"Danesha!" Lisa shouted and knew by the stiffening of her spine she heard, even through her headphones. "Where are you going?"

Danesha gave a toss of her mane of braids, yanked open the door and ran across the asphalt away from the school.

"May I help you?"

Again, Lisa looked up to a stranger, this one as plain as the other was striking. He had a long, pale face, thinning light brown hair, and a medium-sized doughy build. But his smile was welcoming, and he exuded a mix of approachability and authority, in part because of his "uniform"—khaki cords, a tweed jacket, a powder-blue golf shirt—and in part because he was the only other adult in sight. He stuck out his hand, large and strong, and said, "I'm Ron Stone, school principal. And you are...?"

"Lisa Harris."

"Oh, yes, Ms. Harris. From the GIFT House. I've been wanting to meet you. Can you come into my office to chat for a few minutes?"

She glanced once more at the disappearing figure of Danesha. His eyes followed. "Actually, that's one of the things I want to talk to you about. I hope we're on the same page."

Ron Stone's office was surprisingly plush. An over-sized, dark walnut desk and deep green leather swivel chair were surrounded by three over-stuffed chairs whose burgundy and green striped fabric complemented the small couch along the side wall. It looked more like a decorator's vision out of *Architectural Digest* than what Lisa might have expected in an urban high school.

Ron motioned for her to take a seat as he retrieved a file from the side drawer. "Are you aware, Ms. Harris, that Danesha Davis has been absent from class nearly as much as she's been present?" Without waiting for a response, he launched into an accounting—times missed, times tardy, assignments not turned in, teacher write-ups. A brief pause, then, "And how is Danesha's behavior at the house?"

Lisa debated between honesty and dignity. "She's a bit defiant."

His brow furrowed. "I imagine so. Has she talked to you about how she's doing here?"

"Not really. But she doesn't share much." Lisa raised her palms in a gesture of "we're on the same page" futility.

"Well, like so many of our children, Danesha has had many challenges in her young life. Some of these kids are quite defensive. But you know..." his expression softened, "I would anticipate she will improve with more time of nurturing and consistency. Of course, you have to be firm too. I'd be especially vigilant about homework hours. Check their work with them each night; that one-on-one attention is huge. Remember, these girls have never had this kind of structure before. And it might not be a bad idea if..."

Lisa struggled to listen. She was hoping he'd have some easy solutions. After all, he *was* the principal. But all her ears seemed to catch were "should" and "must" and "if not." Eventually, Ron scribbled some notes in Danesha's file and with a wave of his hand dismissed Lisa with an invitation to look around "her school."

It had been years since she'd walked the long, wide hallways of a high school, and as Lisa passed the rows of lockers and peered into the glass panes of classroom doors, she was thrust back to those heady days of promise and possibility, when her biggest worries were her SAT score and GPA, both tickets to opening doors to even wider doors.

A burst of laughter sounded down the hall, where she spotted Coreen in front of a class waving her arms in dramatic pantomime. The other students were clapping and cheering her on. Lisa crept in, sliding against the side wall. Immediately Coreen's face brightened. "This is my house mom," she announced, and proceeded with her dramatic rendering.

Lisa stood and watched in amazement. She could never have imagined Coreen in front of a class, much less commanding such enthused attention. The girl was good, too, mimicking what must have been a character's voice, her expression so animated as to be nearly unrecognizable from the flat affect she projected at home. Lisa soaked in a sense of pride that made her arms tingle. She waited until Coreen sat down, then offered a thumbs-up and slipped back out.

It took another five minutes of wandering the school peering into classrooms before she found Brianna, slouched low in the seat farthest from the teacher, shoulders hunched and her head bent. The class was in an uproar, girls sitting on boys' laps, kids talking on their cell phones, no one even pretending to listen to the pink-cheeked young teacher standing in front of the room visibly struggling not to cry. "Come on, Brianna, look up," Lisa muttered to the window, to no avail.

Lisa walked the now empty halls, past the office and pushed open the door, her first official visit to the school finally behind her. Standing on the front steps, she peered around the side, half expecting and somewhat dreading to see Danesha, but the school yard was empty except for a tall, thin man raking leaves. As she passed by he stopped his task, leaned against the wood pole of the rake, its shape a twin to the man's own lean frame.

"Mrs. Rothman?"

She froze, rooted to the spot.

"Ike Green." He tipped his head. "You don't remember me? I sure won't ever forget you."

Lisa's hand flew to her mouth. "Oh my gosh, Mr. Green. I'm sorry, I guess out of context...of course I remember you. How are you doing?"

He grasped the rake in both hands. "I'm living me a new life, ma'am. It ain't much, but it's a lot better than it would of been if I'd never met up with you."

She shrugged off the compliment, sputtering how anyone could have helped him, she was just doing her job.

He held up a hand. "No, Mrs. Rothman. You've got a way about you. It wasn't just the loan that did it, ma'am. It was how you made me think I *could* do it."

When she didn't respond, too stunned even to respond, he resumed raking, talking now with his back to her. "When I went in for my last appointment at Credit-Solutions and you was gone, I hope you don't mind, ma'am, but I asked about you. I heard from some of the folks you had your own troubles, so you left. Whatever they was, I sure am sorry."

She dug her nails into her palms.

His face loosened in empathy. "Life's full of surprises, ain't it?"

She nodded, unable to trust her voice.

"So, you work here too, Mrs. Rothman?"

The name sounded alien on his tongue, undeserved and ill-fitting. "Uh, as you said, I've kind of gone through some changes." She waved her hands in self-deprecation, feeling the heft of every one of her newest extra pounds and the raggedness of her overgrown hair. "I'm not Mrs. Rothman anymore. I took back my maiden name and...well, I'm *Miss* Lisa Harris now."

"That's fine, ma'am. You visiting someone? I sure didn't expect to ever see you 'round here."

"You know what, Mr. Green, I never would have expected it either. I've been acting as a resident mom over at the GIFT House for some girls. At least for now. I'm not sure I'm the right person for it."

"I bet you're perfect."

"Far from perfect. But thanks."

She extended a hand for a shake and was surprised and pleased when he wrapped both of his hands around her own and squeezed. "I learned something special from you, Mrs. Roth. . . Miss Harris. I learned not to give up. It's good to remember that, you know. Real good."

She blinked away tears, resisting the urge to fold herself into his concave chest. He turned back to his rake and Lisa walked on, dragging her feet at first and then nearly running the entire way to the GIFT House.

Of all people, Ike Green, whose three-year-old daughter was killed when their house burned to the ground. Ike had no insurance, no job, no house, and now no family; his wife left him after the fire. The first time Ike came to Credit-Solutions, he'd put his head on her desk and bellowed loud, shuddering sobs. Lisa had never heard a man cry like that before, with such depth of despair.

What a young, clueless woman she was then. Mrs. Lisa Rothman. So clueless she actually imagined she understood what her clients were going through. She would come home from work and tell Nate about her day, sometimes picking his brain, sometimes simply using his ear to work through her quandaries about how to best assist her clients. They would sit on the plush love seat in their comfortably furnished den, grateful for the seeming certainties of their fortunate lives. They weren't wealthy but they never had to worry about paying their bills. They had their work. They had their home. They had each other. They assumed they had their future.

She could feel it starting, the stabbing pain that quite literally made it hard for her to breathe. No! She would not go there. Not anymore. Deliberately, she closed her eyes and willed herself to go numb, standing motionless in front of the porch steps until she was able to force her mind blank. There was still an hour before the girls would leave school. Just enough time to start tonight's dinner.

CHAPTER SEVEN

D anesha continued to disappear from school. Lisa would get regular calls from Ron Stone and Sheila Johnson, then from the teachers themselves. She dreaded answering the phone. *What do you expect me to do?* she wanted to say, but each time held her tongue, gurgling an encouraging *hmmm* and *of course*, so all could pretend Lisa was in control.

In truth, there was a desperate need for house moms, with many more candidates for residential care than there were caretakers or funding. All Lisa had to do was recall the ease with which she was hired; the position offered during the first interview hour. But the GIFT House was Sheila's responsibility, her "baby," and clearly the home was to be nothing less than a glowing example, hence, Lisa's probation status. Added to her general frustration with Danesha, Lisa also resented that the girl's actions potentially jeopardized her own job security. It may not be a job she wanted to keep or should keep—but she sure as hell didn't want to be fired.

Even after six weeks of living together, Lisa felt like she didn't know much more about Danesha, or really any of them, than she did in the beginning. And that was part of the problem. So one day, sure no one was due home for hours, Lisa went snooping. She looked through all of Danesha's drawers, in the closet, through school books and notebooks. Danesha would go insane with fury if she knew, but it was worth the risk if there was new and useful information to be found. She had just discovered a thick pocket folder stuffed inside a dresser drawer when she heard a noise downstairs. She froze, waiting, heart pounding. How would she ever begin to explain herself to Danesha? Then the noise again, and Lisa exhaled with relief. It was only a wind-blown branch knocking against the window.

She pursued her hunt in earnest, but in the end discovered nothing. Everything sterile and remote as if the room of a brief visitor. Clothes almost obsessively folded into crisp neat piles, nothing on the floor or under the bed, nothing of note in the desk drawers and nothing on the desk—the signs of a girl who'd spent most of her life hiding herself from a volatile mother.

Lisa had read Danesha's file, had read all the girls' files repeatedly during her frequent insomniac nights. Lisa knew that the year before, Danesha had cowered in the kitchen corner, helpless as she witnessed the violence that landed her mother in the hospital and her brother Jerrell in prison. Lisa also knew with an alcoholic mother and absent father, Danesha's brother had been her protector and best friend, and his removal from her life was the root of the girl's daily rage.

Yes, she knew all that. But what Lisa didn't realize—what she couldn't imagine at the time and would need to forgive herself for later—were the reckless measures Danesha was willing to take to get her brother back.

That day Lisa first saw Danesha running out of Stone Charter and across the school lot, she was meeting up with, of all people, "king of the corner" Devon. Danesha first met Devon when she was leaving Ron Stone's office and banged into the chest of a tall, older boy. She immediately recognized the sweet smoky smell of weed on his leather jacket and for a moment let herself sink against his body, craving her brother Jerrell with a pain that nearly made her cry out loud. She pulled back slowly and looked up to see his topaz eyes. He gave a slow wink then scooted around her and into the office of the man Danesha had as little interest in as she did all white folks, only to hear this fine Hershey-skinned boy shout, "Yo, Mr. Ron, my man, thought I'd step in to see what's doin' at old Stoner High."

For the next three days, Danesha eyeballed the halls and playground, even in one weak moment going to the principal under a pretense so piss-poor she would have been shamed were she not desperate to find the boy whose fine looks and druggy scent reminded her of Jerrell.

On the fourth day she skipped out of math class and was heading in no special direction across the asphalt basketball court when she saw him leaning against a tree. She stopped and watched as his hand made its way from hip to lips, as his chest puffed out then deflated. Dang! The brother was smoking pot on school grounds.

She walked her walk, shaking so her ass looked bigger, 'til he looked up and coughed out smoke. The whistle he let out told her all she needed to know.

Within a week she had him right where she wanted. Some days she made him wait 'til last hour, other times it was instead of breakfast. But every day she helped him remember who was his new boo. She got high, he got head, she went back to class.

For a while, the thrill and the weed were enough. But then Devon wanted more. He wanted her "love," he claimed, pinprick pupils narrowing as he would lean in close and fill her nose with stinking breath. No one knew she was a virgin, stupid really to keep her black cherry, like who was she saving it for anyway? But it was about the only thing she had to claim as her own, and she was keeping it on lock until *she* was ready. She was too smart to give it up for nothing.

Only Devon was smarter. "I got somethin' you want, boo. You buying?"

Danesha struggled not to frown. She didn't even like Devon. He'd turned out to be pretty much a hobo, just older and better weed. Still, she enjoyed the game. So she slanted her eyes as she inhaled from the damp tip of the joint. "Yeah, what's that?"

He dug his heel into the dirt, stalling.

Shit, he really did have something. She made her voice go low and mashed her boobs against his chest. He groaned, pushed his body into hers, but she backed off and asked again, "What you got for your boo?"

"I've a buddy who knows someone who's in the same pen as your brother. He says he can run messages back and forth, maybe even sneak in something to make the bruh's days hum."

Danesha felt her eyes sting with the surprise and had to clamp her palm against her lips to keep from shouting. "You gotta get me in to see him."

43

Devon was looking down at his feet now. She knew saying "no" shamed him, so she'd help him say "yes." Reaching out, she grabbed the rock in his pants, squeezing once. "I'll do you so fine."

"Girl, you are making me one hot mess." His eyes rolled back and he slumped against the tree. "You know I can't get you into no prison. Not without an adult relative."

Abruptly, she turned on her heel and dashed toward the school.

"Wait! Don't trip offa me. I'll do it," he shouted clear across the school yard.

She kept walking but slowed her pace, her head held high, hips swaying, her ass wiggling like an open-house invite. At the door she turned once and slowly licked her lips before offering a wet sideways smile, the same one she offered each day as she lowered the zipper of his jeans.

CHAPTER EIGHT

Devon was good on his word. Several days after making his promise, he picked Danesha up at the corner of Goodfellow and Delmar in a borrowed truck during the middle of a school day morning. They rode the two hours in near silence; Danesha too excited to talk, Devon focused on how he was going to make her pay on *her* promise.

She waited in the parking lot while Devon slung her a "guardian," slipping a twenty into the palm of the mother of an inmate.

"Danesha, meet your Auntie Janetta Olsen," Devon said, reaching into the truck for his cigarettes and iPod. There was a single tall tree he planned on leaning against where he could eyeball the moment she came out. "Ain't no rush. I'll be right here."

She shot him a quick look of thanks, trying to ignore her shakes as she turned and followed Miss Olsen's silky hot-pink dress up to and through the first set of steel doors leading into prison. "Keep moving, girl," "Auntie" Olsen hissed against Danesha's neck, "this ain't no party."

There were nearly thirty people crowded into a room for half that number. Other than Danesha and a couple of snot-running kids, everyone was older and mostly women. With no shame she studied them—even in jeans (and a new yellow knit shirt she'd snuck out of Brianna's closet that pulled tight against her boobs)—she looked finer than anyone. Finer than all the fat grandmas already wiping their eyes; or the young, sexies dressed in heels and tight low-cut blouses like some black ghetto Barbie; or the trucker women in men's T-shirts, tattoos all over their ashy arms, stinking as if they hadn't showered since their man got locked up.

Uniformed guards stood at each corner, packing clubs and pistols. They stared blankly into the center of the room, barely blinking, seeming to see everything and nothing. Danesha swallowed a kind of scared that tasted like spoiled cheese, but she kept her eyes on Miss Olsen's hot-pink ass and allowed her body to be pushed forward, through the next room, down a skinny hallway as another steel door clanged and locked behind her, where she was again signed in and patted down, until finally she entered a large gray space filled with small metal tables.

The visitors were told to stand against the wall, and as the guards walked up and down in front of them, silver walkie-talkies gleaming against dark brown pants, a group of new guards let in a row of handcuffed guys, all dressed in orange, heads down but eyes hunting the room. Danesha felt sweat pouring out of her armpits and between her thighs.

And then he entered. Danesha screamed out, a cry of joy that filled the whole place, causing a guard to rush to her side, and Jerrell, sweet wonderful Jerrell, to burn red with embarrassment. But she didn't care none. It was Jerrell!

As soon as she sat across from him, Danesha grabbed his handcuffed hands and started smothering them with kisses. Right off she felt the connection that took her back to her entire childhood, to all those moments when only Jerrell could save her from her life. She couldn't stop kissing his hands until he laughed and she saw his two front teeth were rotted brown. Without warning, she began to cry.

"Oh, Nesha, don't do that."

She tried to smile but she couldn't get her lips to move that way so she covered her face with his sweet warm palms until she could look at him without crying. "Are you okay? Do you miss me? I miss you so fuckin' much."

"Me too, lil sister." He was grinning like a fool, so happy to see her that suddenly his bad teeth didn't look so bad.

She leaned in and whispered, "Can we bust a u-turn out of here?"

"Nesha! That ain't funny to joke about, girl. You'll get me sent to isolation."

She studied him, the way his face caved in at the cheeks, the cuts all over his hands. "Jerrell, Mama weren't worth it."

He spoke fast. "Don't waste our time hatin' on her. Tell me everything about you."

She was hesitant at first, holding back, then it all came pouring out—the loneliness from living with a bunch of strangers and going to a school full of goons; about Miss Lisa and Brianna and Coreen; about her hobo teachers. And the whole time Jerrell's sweet face kept changing to angry, funny, happy, sad—all for her. She loved him so much she didn't even care if he was faking some of it.

If she focused on his face, she didn't notice the orange scrub shirt with the number stitched on the front, or the brown uniformed guards, or the other guys, dressed the same, handcuffs and shaved heads like they were dogs instead of men. If she squinted, she could almost pretend they were back in the hood, sitting on top of Jerrell's car, drinking down some cokes and eating White Castle onion rings, hot summer afternoon, grease and sweat slippering their fingertips.

Finally, she told him her plan. How she had this new boyfriend, Devon, already out of high school by a couple of years, and he knew someone who could get her a modeling job soon as she turned fifteen. She'd seen enough skanky girls in her magazines to know she was more hella-fine than any of them. She was gonna use the good looks God gave her and go to New York. Devon said if she was still his boo then he'd take her, even help her make enough money to buy the best lawyer in the entire universe to prove that what Jerrell done was the only thing anyone living with their piece of shit ma coulda done.

She was talking so fast she kept spitting and twisting her fingers together, trying to ignore how Jerrell's face was growing darker. And darker.

"Stop! Girl, slow your mouth down."

"What?"

"Quit frontin' like you don't know what. That's a plenty fucked up plan."

She tried to swallow her hurt, but it got stuck halfway in her throat and she could only croak out, "I'm doing this for us."

"You can't drop out of school. You want to be a bum like me? And that boy Devon is running jackshit on you. How old is he anyway? You just fourteen. He ought to be where I'm sitting."

47

She turned from the brown-tooth frown.

"Look at me."

"Why?"

His face had softened, but his eyes still burned anger. "You promise me right now you're gonna stay in school and never see that punk again. And if I ever see him I'm gonna knock him down two feet under his regular height." He mugged a clown face, trying to get a giggle, but she wouldn't give one.

"And promise me you're gonna stay in that house. Getting you in there was the best thing Mama ever done for you. Promise me, Nesha."

Promise me. Yeah, like he was one to talk about promises. How many times had he promised never to leave her? She glanced around the room at the other inmates and their visitors. Seemed like everyone was feeling sorry. She shook her head back and forth, biting her lip.

Abruptly, Jerrell stood, his handcuffs clanging too loud on the metal table. "Guard. I'm done."

She wanted to beg him not to leave her. Again. And she almost said it, his promise, whatever he wanted.

"Girl, you better step your game up," sounding more like a warning than love, and that fast he was gone.

With tears she didn't bother to wipe away blurring everything, Danesha plodded through the steel doors, the next patting down, the streams of orange and brown. Outside on the steps, she stretched her arms and inhaled and exhaled. It was drizzling, cloudy, colder. But it was free not-in-prison air. She could do whatever the fuck she wanted.

Which is why, when Devon tried to wrap his arms around her, his eyes red and his breath stinkin', she shrugged him off and began walking away as fast as she could, ignoring his "Danesha? What the shit?" and ignoring the chance Jerrell was watching her from inside the joint.

She wouldn't tell Devon what had gone down, and she wouldn't let him touch her, not even to hold her hand on the long ride back, and she wouldn't kiss him goodbye or squeeze his cock, even when he screamed as she got out of the car. "You sure was all up on my jock when you wanted something.

You owe me, girl..." His anger carried clear across the street where her nosy neighbor stood up straighter, as if she'd been waiting her whole day for more drama. But Danesha ignored them both, not glancing back as Devon peeled away, with the borrowed truck backfiring like a 20-gauge shotgun. She climbed up the front stairs, shoved the door open and entered the GIFT House. The first person she saw was Miss Lisa, whose face brightened as though she was actually happy to see Danesha, and, without understanding how or why, she found herself falling into her house mom's arms and sobbing so hard it shook not just her body but the body of Miss Lisa as well.

CHAPTER NINE

Lisa lay awake for hours that night, replaying the moments of holding Danesha in her arms. *She's just a child*, she'd thought as she patted Danesha's back, rubbing her palm in wide circles over the bony knobbiness of young shoulder blades, barely resisting the urge to hug her even tighter. As Danesha sobbed and hiccupped, for once Lisa had the sense not to pry or prattle, but to simply be. *I know heartache. I can help you. I can help you!*

Finally, at 5 a.m., Lisa threw off her blankets and tip-toed to the locked file cabinet in the corner of the kitchen. She brewed a cup of herbal tea, a flimsy substitute for the wine she craved right then. Settling into the second-hand recliner, she studied, yet again, Danesha's background, searching for clues to suggest the child's surprising show of vulnerability. There was certainly plenty to cry about, but what could have caused the letting down of her guard?

Every time Lisa reviewed one of the files she was newly appalled by the cruelty and neglect the girls had lived through. It made her crazy those women could call themselves "mothers." But this time these feelings were tempered by the incredulity that *she* could comfort *Danesha*. She hadn't felt this hopeful since her early social work days when she'd discovered her ability to keep clients from declaring bankruptcy. She found herself humming as she locked up the file, with the thought, *maybe everything can work out*, replaying like a favorite chorus.

Her optimism didn't even survive the sunrise. All three girls were running late and rushed to catch the bus without so much as a chin nod for Lisa. As they scurried out the door, Lisa shouted a cheery "have a great day," which was greeted with a brief frown from Coreen, no acknowledgement from Brianna and a cold stare from Danesha. They were all staying after school for tutoring, which meant it would be another slow day for Lisa alone. Not that any of them knew or cared if Lisa had plans. She sank onto a kitchen chair, overtaken by a rush of self-pity. How was it possible for the girls to show *no* interest in Lisa's life? Weren't they a tiny bit curious? Sure, all teens were self-focused, but this was so extreme. Even during her worst—most retreating—teen phases, she'd never been truly disconnected from Jeanette. Yet another reminder that this was not, would never be, a "real" family. The brief connection with Danesha was more likely an anomaly than a turning point.

She picked up the phone to call Sheila and instead of a dial tone heard, "Let me out down there and I'll talk to her while you park."

"Sheila?" Lisa asked.

"Oh, I didn't hear it ring. Listen I'm a minute away. Can I stop in? I have a surprise for you."

Moments later Sheila arrived. "You can thank me later," Sheila sang out, her voice unusually light as she stepped into the kitchen. "I have finally found you some freedom, long over-due. Her name is Vanessa Morrison, she's twenty-four, from Memphis, and I think the girls are going to be crazy about her. She's checked out clean, so you're the final word."

Lisa felt her gut tighten. *The girls are going to be crazy about her?* "That sounds great. When will she be here?"

Sheila laughed. "Glad you're okay with it. She's just parking the car and, oh, there she is. By the way, a couple of those porch stairs feel loose. It's a danger. Remind me to get someone over here to nail them down."

Lisa swung open the door as Vanessa Morrison leaned in to knock and narrowly missed banging her fist against Lisa's chest.

"Oops, don't mean to slug you down," Vanessa said, flashing a toothy smile around glistening red lips. "I'm Vanessa and I'm blessed to meet you, Miss Lisa."

Lisa took a step back and examined the young woman who was to become her assistant. Like herself, Vanessa was carrying extra weight, but while on Lisa the pounds looked like fat, this young woman was lush. *A lot of woman,* she could almost hear Nate say. She was slightly taller than Lisa, about five-six, large busted and thick-waisted, but there the resemblance ended. Vanessa's hair appeared to have been

51

styled minutes before, a head-full of narrow braids pulled tight to show off her rich brown complexion, and an oval face that exuded confidence and the bright gleam of youth. She was dressed in a shiny lime green blouse that gaped at the bust and would have looked flashy in any circumstance, much less an early-morning job interview. Her black pants had the sheen of cheap worn polyester and were too short for the three-inch high heels of her black strappy sandals.

Immediately, a range of emotions swept through Lisa. Did Vanessa truly believe this was the way to dress for a job interview or was this the best she owned? This was the other woman expected to set an example for the GIFT House girls? Sheila was right. The girls were going to adore her.

Lisa studied Vanessa's face as she took in the threadbare worn furniture and dipped her chin in obvious approval.

"Nice place. I bet all y'all love it here, don't you?"

She struggled to croak out a half-hearted, "Yeah," before motioning for Vanessa to sit in the one sturdy chair.

Unlike Lisa's own interview in the room, this conversation lasted less than fifteen minutes. Obviously Sheila had already decided and Lisa's opinion was merely pro forma. Vanessa was putting herself through a master's in social work program at a small school on the other side of the river. Her schedule was fairly flexible and she loved teens. She'd volunteered at a United Way home similar to this for the past several summers. She could start immediately and was prepared to work around Lisa's needs except during the week of finals when she might not work at all—if that was okay with Lisa.

Vanessa seemed too eager, too young, too *something*. Lisa swallowed hard, stalling; Sheila had said hers was the final word. But then Lisa thought of the past weeks, of the way she couldn't leave beyond the neighborhood, and how every single afternoon and evening she was required to be here with no relief. With an assistant, she could try to recapture some of her former life. Call an old friend. Get her hair cut. Join a gym.

With a mental sigh, she shook the warm, plump young hand and went into the kitchen for the calendar to schedule Vanessa's first day of work. She even managed to appear enthused as they established a start date and Vanessa breezed out, shouting back, "Thank you all so much. I can't wait to start."

Immediately, Sheila pounced. "Okay, what's the problem?"

Lisa tried to smile but the result was clearly insincere. "Isn't she too young?"

Sheila tilted her head. "Too young to be responsible? Or too young *not* to connect to the girls?" When Lisa didn't answer, Sheila's voice softened. "Having another set of eyes to watch out for the girls will be a good thing. You need some freedom to be able to live a bit of your own life, and they need the steady influence of someone with whom they can truly relate."

Lisa's voice squeaked as she forced herself to ask, "Do you think these girls will ever connect with me too?" and then immediately, as if to answer her own question, "Hey, I did make a breakthrough with Danesha yesterday. She was crying and hugged me for comfort!"

Instead of nodding with the approval Lisa sought, Sheila asked the obvious. "Why was she crying?" and when Lisa didn't answer, Sheila patted the nearby chair for her to sit.

"Look, I hired you because I believed—and I still believe, by the way—that your background, different as it is from the girls, will serve everyone well. That you'll be a strong role model with expectations that are good for them. But there are details of their lives you've got to understand so you recognize what you're dealing with here."

"I don't know what else to do other than read their files, wait and hope they connect with me. I reread Danesha's just last night."

"Those reports are paper only. And, truthfully, in some ways I'm almost more concerned about the other two. Danesha is so in your face, it's possible you allow her to completely overshadow Coreen and Brianna."

Lisa felt yet again that naked sense of exposure. How could Sheila *know* so much every time?

"So let's start with Coreen," Sheila said, leaning back into the sofa, wordlessly inviting Lisa to do the same.

In an even voice, Sheila began to speak. From birth, Coreen was soft. Soft body, soft disposition. Her grandmother wrote about her, "If you take our girl, you won't be sorry. She's the easiest person anyone knows, maybe the only easy person I know." Grandma Thomas had written this on the back of a Shop 'n Save receipt, clipping the grease-stained paper to the GIFT House form filled in by Coreen's mother.

According to her file, Coreen was nearly sixteen, but at the time of her recommendation to the GIFT House she was still in eighth grade. Throughout elementary school she was earmarked as "special," and was eligible for government-funded tutoring that she never received. In second grade she knew only a half dozen letters of the alphabet. At age eleven, she was reading at a first-grade level.

Lance Richards, the man who fathered and then abandoned Coreen while he was still in high school, wrote on her application, "We all just thought she was retarded." He re-entered his daughter's life when she was eight. During those years Coreen was tossed around like everybody's afterthought, living with her mother, her grandmother, two aunts and one of her mother's boyfriends. Once Lance re-appeared, she stayed with him for two years, before beginning the spin cycle all over again. Altogether, Coreen had moved in and out of twelve places and had attended six schools before entering Stone Charter Middle school, where Sheila witnessed Coreen reciting word for word a Langston Hughes poem she had heard for the first time in class hours before.

Sheila arranged for a battery of tests that measured intelligence and analytic thinking rather than knowledge. To everyone's amazement, Coreen not only did not test "retarded" but actually scored above normal. She was still years behind her grade level in reading and math, but surpassed in IQ many of her peers at the charter school.

"Coreen Thomas is an ideal candidate for our new GIFT House program," Sheila later stated in her request to Candace Thomas and Lance Richards to relinquish custody of their daughter. When Sheila received no response to the written appeal, she went to meet in person with Coreen's mother.

"You ain't taking my daughter away from me," Candace had retorted when Sheila calmly explained the purpose of her visit.

"Miss Thomas, we're not 'taking her away' from you. We simply want to offer Coreen an opportunity to get the best education possible. To live in one place and go to one school for all of her high school years."

Candace had thrust out her chest and scowled. "You saying I can't raise my own girl?"

Sheila kept her expression impassive. She well understood the threat she posed, though she would not be daunted when it came to doing right by the children. She took Coreen out for an ice cream cone. "Do you understand what this is about?"

Coreen shrugged. "Yes, ma'am. You want me to stay somewhere else and my mama don't want me to go."

"How do you feel about it?"

Again a shrug. "Don't matter much to me. I been moving my whole life." Coreen's indifference reminded Sheila of all the teacher reports describing the girl as "dull." This child needed to be able to live in one place long enough to develop roots, those tender tentacles that lead to attachment.

With renewed determination, Sheila went back to the parents, drawing upon her arsenal of influence. Eventually—because frankly neither parent cared all that much—Sheila got both Candace and Lance to agree to release their daughter.

Sheila narrowed her eyes on Lisa. "In many ways Coreen is the reason the GIFT House exists." Lisa recalled the surprising scene of Coreen standing in front of her classmates, pantomiming a scene from the book the group was reading, and she felt a smile spreading across her face. "I think she's gaining some self-confidence. Don't you?"

Sheila granted a curt nod when her mind was clearly elsewhere. She looked at her watch, pulled her cell phone out of her purse and called the school to tell them she would probably be another half hour or more.

"Now Brianna," Sheila said, continuing to speak in the same steady tone. "You must have noted that originally I recommended that the GIFT House not accept Brianna and then, obviously, reconsidered and admitted her into the program. Even knowing that she might be pulled out of town at any time."

Unlike the others, Brianna's childhood was marked by stability. Although Lenore Jones was only fifteen when she had Brianna, and no one knew the whereabouts of the father, the girl was raised by a loving grandmother, aunt and mother. Grandma Jones and Aunt Billie watched the baby all day, enabling Lenore to graduate high school and attend a two-year community college program, before taking a full-time position as a receptionist in a downtown law firm.

Brianna sailed through elementary and early middle school years with strong grades and few problems. Though shy and quiet, her teachers consistently remarked on her helpful nature and her ability to get along with everybody. Then, nine months ago, the law firm split up, taking among its casualties Lenore's job. Three weeks later, during a family dinner, Grandma Jones gasped once and slumped over into her plate of food. She was revived by the EMS workers but pronounced dead upon arrival at the hospital. Aunt Billie took a job in Florida, and Brianna suddenly found herself living alone with a mother who spent most of the days and nights weeping in bed.

As the weeks turned into months, Brianna retreated further and further into herself. Her grades dropped, her weight dropped, her attendance dropped. The eighth grade principal's calls home went unanswered so many times that she eventually drove over to the house. According to the report she filed—which was later expanded upon after a series of interviews conducted by Sheila—dirty dishes were piled high in the sink and scattered throughout the kitchen. The pantry and refrigerator were nearly empty; soiled clothes littered the floor, and Mom was in what appeared to be a stupor, possibly drug-induced, possibly severe depression.

The principal found Brianna slouched in a corner, clutching a tattered blanket to her chest. She pulled the child up, helped her gather a few belongings and sent her out to wait in the car. Then she turned her attention to Lenore. "Miss

Jones, you have a daughter to take care of. If you can't get yourself together to act like a mother, you're going to lose her."

Breaking a personal and district rule, she brought Brianna to her own house for one week. On Saturday morning, she drove Brianna back home and knocked on the door. A fully dressed, smiling Lenore Jones flung the door open.

"My baby," Lenore squealed, hugging Brianna into her arms, allowing the screen to slam against the principal's face. "I have wonderful news. Auntie Billie has found me a job. Girl, things are looking up, up, up."

"Wow, Ma. Doin'what?"

Lenore pulled back. "Brianna Jones, you are looking at the new receptionist for the biggest Chevy dealer in all of Jacksonville, Florida."

"Florida? We're moving to Florida?"

Lenore rolled, then unrolled, and then rolled again the sleeves of her good white blouse. "Uh, we can't both move, baby. Not yet."

"What do you mean, Ma?"

Lips twitching, eyes roaming everywhere but on her daughter, Lenore explained how Aunt Billie was staying with a friend and the place was already crowded so Lenore would have to sleep on a couch until she saved enough to get a place all their own. But they'd be together again before Brianna even noticed she was gone. And this was such a fantastic job that pretty soon she and Brianna would be living like queens, going to the beach every day.

Brianna shook her head side to side. Her lips were so dry the words were pebbles trying to find their way out of her mouth. "What will I do? Where am I gonna stay?"

This time Lenore looked straight at the principal, tilting her head in unspoken question. Which is how the principal, who had recently met Sheila at an educators' conference, came to tell Lenore about the GIFT House. Lenore wrote a fistful of letters on behalf of her daughter and met twice with Sheila before taking off for Florida and leaving Brianna behind.

Lisa had read those letters, the most poignant: *"I hope you want my girl to raise for a while. She is no trouble at all. She will love to help around the house and she barely makes a noise. You won't hardly know she's there."*

"This is all I know from conversations with the principal and with the families. And now I've got to get back to the school," Sheila said. She pushed against the armrest as she struggled to stand, both knees cracking with stiffness as she straightened her legs. "Colder weather's not far away," she added, reminding Lisa of the original meeting when Sheila pulled out a handkerchief to blow her nose against summer allergies. Even the weather, Sheila seemed to have a handle on.

At the door, Lisa squeezed Sheila's hand. "Thank you," she said, and then Sheila was gone and the house once again was empty, leaving Lisa to process the stories alone. Perhaps the most alarming was Brianna's, the girl who promised to be "no trouble at all."

It's the quiet ones you need to worry about. How many times throughout her childhood and adolescence had Lisa heard her mother repeat this favorite of her Truths—a Truth she alluded to every time she chided Lisa for keeping so much to herself, for spending her free time alone and reading, as if a preference for solitude was a personal failing. "At least with your sister Kate, I always know what she's up to and how she's feeling...even when I'd rather not know," Jeanette mused until she discovered Kate—the "open child"—at age seventeen in bed naked with a twenty-six-year-old woman. The following year, Kate moved a thousand miles away.

Lisa glanced at the clock, startled to see that it was only ten-thirty. The day ahead loomed long and lonely with no distraction. She could go grocery shopping, though her week's food allowance was already gone. Yet another bizarre aspect of this new life—to have money in her own account and then live this poor. But she had decided to rely solely on the GIFT House budget in order to better understand the girls' backgrounds. So grocery shopping was out. She could always crawl back into bed for a nap, but that pattern was a slippery slope she knew all too well. Her mom kept urging her to find a hobby, start knitting again or resume bowling or "something, anything, Lisa, what's happened to you?" Knit for whom? Bowl alone? Years ago she used to cross-country ski, but that was back in Minnesota. For a while she'd been a decent runner. Hell, for a while she was a size six. So it would make sense to go for a power walk, try to lose some of this flabby fat that refused to simply melt away on its own. But those boys at the park, the shooting last week in the parking lot three blocks over. Jeanette just didn't understand. Trying to resurrect former hobbies would require her to imitate the person she once was, and she was no longer certain that the person she could imitate was the person she would want to be.

Instead, she'd discovered a great appreciation for house cleaning. There was something so inherently satisfying about the immediacy of wiping the dust away. If she didn't allow herself to think about how much money she'd spent for graduate school, she could take pride in the tart pungent scent of ammonia in a clean kitchen, a bathroom that shone from bleach, patterned lines in the carpeting. Back in her old life she'd occasionally arrive home from work while the cleaning crew was still there. There was a sense of shame she couldn't quite shake as she watched strangers clean her piss off of the toilet or wash away the grease splatters from her cooking, and she'd rationalize that she was giving employment to people who needed the money. But now she got it—you swipe a dishrag and for that moment you have triumphed over your most immediate challenge.

She pulled out the vacuum cleaner and as she engaged in the soothing repetition of the back and forth motion, stopping every so often to poke the vacuum hose into dirt-filled corners, details about Brianna and Coreen continued to swirl through her mind.

And in spite of herself, she allowed her mind to reflect on her own story.

After her miscarriage, Lisa mourned the loss of their "first child." Unplanned. Mere weeks. A hiccup. But for Lisa, the baby that slipped away created a yearning so deep, so visceral,

59

every prior priority shifted. No longer would just the two of them be enough.

"Nate, let's try for a baby as soon as possible."

Nate was dismayed by her response and her surprising crying jags. For him, the pregnancy was little more than a missed period. And now a chance to go back to life as before.

No one else understood Lisa's pain either, offering well-intentioned, hurtful platitudes. "At least it was early on." "You're young, you'll have others." "It's nature's way." And the worst of all. "It's for the best."

It took a lot of cajoling and pouting, but eventually Lisa convinced Nate to start trying to get pregnant again. "You'll see. It will be good. We'll create a family from our love. And," winking, "think how much fun we'll have making it happen."

But as the year crawled by and Lisa failed to conceive "fun" had no place. She led a double life, marking the calendar by what was and what would have been. "I would be wearing maternity clothes now," she would bemoan to Bonnie. "I would have been six months along now." Or seven, eight, and then nine. As the original due date drew nearer Lisa grew ever gloomier. She and Nate no longer made love. They had sexual intercourse to procreate and abstained from sex to rebuild sperm. Every month dragged while she waited in vain hope and then sank at the first sight of blood. It was hard to remember the last time they'd laughed together.

One Saturday in late spring Nate left the house early and returned an hour later with a sapling in the truck. "We'll plant a tree in memory of the baby we lost and we'll be able to watch it grow alongside our future children." That afternoon, with dirt under their nails and blisters on their palms, they made love, and for the next several weeks they re-experienced a bout of joy. That month, the pregnancy test came back positive.

Lisa sailed through the early weeks with enough nausea and exhaustion to know her hormones were doing what they were supposed to do. She'd let work slip but now delved into her debt-counseling projects with renewed vigor. After years of carefully cultivating a professional distance from clients, she suddenly found herself squeezing hands in comfort and sympathy at the tragic tales.

The day of the prenatal ultrasound Lisa awoke with a strange tingling in her legs and the premonition that something was amiss. The ultrasound jelly was cold against her warm skin and she couldn't still the shaking of her feet in their stirrups. She clenched Nate's hand as they watched the charcoal fuzz become more distinct, gasping as the first—then the second—blinking black dot indicated the solidly beating hearts of...twins!

As Lisa cried with delight and disbelief, she recognized there were moments in every marriage when the world shifts perceptively. Nate turned a startling shade of gray and had to sit with his head between his legs. Clearly this was one such moment.

Immediately, life became twin-centric. Each evening, Nate cooked while Lisa sat with feet elevated. She pretended to listen as Nate relayed details of his day, as though she cared about the new line of dishes he was buying for his party rental business when she was already at the park, each of them pushing a swing, one with a curly-topped, freckled little girl and the other with a rugged, red-cheeked son.

"Nate, can we dress them the same?"

"The plates?"

The first time Lisa bled it was brown, old blood and scant. Of little concern, the obstetrician reassured. Still, bed rest might not be a bad idea, at least until the first trimester had passed. She clung to the couch cushions, struggling not to panic and willing the hours to speed by until her pregnancy crossed into the safe zone.

One week before the end of the first trimester, Lisa woke up to thighs stuck together with bright red blood. Hours later, back at home from the hospital and again on bed rest, she called Jeanette.

"I don't even know how to feel, Mom."

"First tell me what this doctor had to say."

One twin's heart had stopped beating but the other twin was still viable. They would not do surgery to remove the deceased fetus because it might kill the live twin. The decision, for now, was for Lisa to stay off her feet for several weeks and "let nature take its course." Likely, her body would reabsorb the one fetus, and, hopefully, the other baby could continue to thrive.

Surely, her mom meant well when she clucked her tongue and said, "Whatever happens next is meant to be."

Just as Nate was sincere when he said, "We'll get through this. As long as we have each other, that's the most important thing."

Just as Lisa knew some people had real sadness, like so many of her clients, whose entire lives had fallen apart.

And yet none of this was of any consolation as she lay on the couch in front of the muted television, watching flurries of silent action. Days passed and Lisa allowed herself a measure of hope—until the afternoon she stood to make herself lunch and saw the stain of fresh blood. As she calmly dialed Nate at work she was surprised to see her legs shaking and knees knocking together because she could not feel anything. Even after the D&C surgery, during which she lost so much blood she had to stay overnight in the hospital, Lisa felt nothing.

Unlike the first miscarriage, when she'd cried for weeks, this time her grief took on the character of emptiness. She could taste the bitterness, sour and tart, her lips pursed in perpetual frown. She would never have believed she could feel this old, this young.

She returned to work, where she fielded questions with clipped answers, straining not to look at her watch to see how long before she could go home and escape to the couch. Her co-workers were kind initially, but the men clearly didn't understand and the women began to avoid her as if infertility were catching.

Occasionally she considered Nate's emotional response, but she didn't have the energy to prod the difficult words out of his down-turned lips. She pushed his hands off her body and offered a cheek to his lips. She didn't intend to be callous. She simply had nothing to give.

"We can try again, Lisa," he offered, but then went on to add, "This was just a fluke."

A fluke? Three lost babies reduced to "a fluke?" She at least had the wherewithal to turn away before saying something crueler than either of them deserved.

CHAPTER TEN

Loud, hard banging was followed by rapid, impatient knocks. "All right! All right!" Brianna shouted as she stumbled down the hallway toward the stairs. All the bedroom doors were open, the rooms empty. Last thing she remembered was falling her tired self into bed for a minute.

Now a foot was kicking the door, probably Danesha, who was too friggin' lazy to keep her key with her and was about to break the thing down. "Stop your fool bangin'!" Brianna yelled, swinging open the door. "Oh!" she cried out. "My bad. I thought you was..."

Slouching in the doorway, all signs of impatience gone, was the most gorgeous boy Brianna had ever seen. Standing on *her* porch. She stammered, "You must be looking for Danesha? She ain't here."

His grin was slow, as was the nod of his head. His eyes were the color of a wild animal. His teeth gleamed white and gold and his lips were full and soft pink. Brianna thought she might faint right there.

"I'm looking for Danesha if she's here. I'm looking for you if she ain't."

Brianna stepped aside, unable to speak, as he walked in, shut the door and stood so close she could feel his body heat.

"Me and Miss Vanessa the only ones home right now. But Danesha should be here soon. Course, don't really know 'bout her."

"Yeah, you got that." His forehead wrinkled and for a moment some kind of mad clouded his eyes, then he just looked beautiful again.

"You must be Brittany? I'm Devon."

"Brianna."

"Whatever. Anyhows, you gonna give me something to drink or eat while I'm waiting?"

Her whole body liked to hum as she poured him a Coke and got down a near-empty bag of chips. A large, black roach dashed across the cabinet ledge. She slammed the door shut before Devon could see.

"So, now, you the smart one who acts dumb or the mouse turd?"

She jerked back but when he didn't say sorry, answered, "I'm smart enough to let them think I'm a mouse."

Devon laughed with a wide open mouth, his row of gold capped teeth catching the sun coming through the window. "Then you the smartest one of all, huh?"

Brianna said nothing, but her body surprised her by stopping its shaking. She sat up straighter.

"I guess you know me and Danesha been tight?"

She shrugged.

"Yeah, well, Danesha don't talk much around here, do she? She sure don't talk much to me. Don't know how to keep her promises neither."

Brianna sat on her hands so she wouldn't wrap her arms, which she knew made her look skinnier.

The phone rang into the quiet, five long rings before it gave up. Still Brianna sat, not quite staring at Devon, but not looking away neither. When his eyes locked onto hers, the gold softened to butter yellow.

"Anyone ever tell you how hella-fine you are? Seems I been eye-ballin' the wrong girl," Devon whispered, leaning in and running one of his fine fingers across her cheek, down her neck, around her collarbone. His fingertips danced along her arm and to her palm, where they tapped a widening circle.

She forced herself to pull back her hand. "Uh, I need to tell Miss Vanessa you're here. She's in the house office, studying for a test. She musta not heard you come in."

He winked so slowly she was sure it meant nothing until he let his tongue trace the outline of his lips as he again slowly lowered his eyelid as if an entire conversation were taking place without words.

"Except she told me to only bother her if it's important. She's like not doing so good in the class or something..."

He pulled her to her feet and they walked on tip toes up the stairs, his body right behind hers, so close Brianna could hear the swishing of his clothes. He sat on the edge of her bed and grabbed her wrists. He was panting rapid shallow breaths.

She stood completely still as Devon unbuttoned her shirt and let it drop to the ground. He gasped aloud at her braless chest, then put his lips against the pointy dark nubs of her nipples.

She closed her eyes, picturing another time, another place. "Your skin is so beautiful," he used to say, never touching her. No, he wouldn't do that. But he was "in love with" the smooth shine of her light brown tone, "caramel with just a hint of vanilla," like she was some kinda dessert. No, he never touched her, yet his eyes wrapped themselves across every inch, leaving her no secrets except this one, full of shame and excitement, fear and longing.

Devon touched. A smooth palm across her small, new breast, a hurried hand yanking off her shorts and panties, pulling her onto his lap, a long dark finger finding the short curly hairs that recently covered her down there, and then, finding *her*.

He stretched out across her bed and she, naked, stretched out across his body, feeling his hardness, the heat of his skin, wanting to be loved, when Devon whispered, "Danesha," and then quickly hummed, "Brianna, Brianna," but her body had turned cold and she was whimpering and pulling back when he murmered, "Your skin is so beautiful," and her body went slack. He thrust, moaned, shot and then rolled away.

CHAPTER ELEVEN

The week after Danesha visited Jerrell, she arranged to see a lawyer. The morning of the appointment, Miss Lisa was in the kitchen cooking up something that smelled like day-old trash when Danesha came downstairs dressed in her one good skirt and a sweater she'd never worn before.

"Don't you look pretty," Miss Lisa said, stepping forward.

Danesha shrank back. Ever since that hug-moment she wished she could snatch away, the house mom had been acting like they were now besties or something.

"Where you off to?"

"Out."

"Need a ride?"

Danesha paused, tempted, but as Miss Lisa reached out a hand, she quickly shook her head "no."

"I'll take you wherever it is," she smiled.

"I said no," Danesha snapped, but at the door, turned and gave an inch. "Uh, thanks."

She raced to the corner just as the bus was pulling away. "Fuck," she shouted against the exhaust fumes. Now she would be at least twenty minutes late. The secretary who had worked her into the lawyer's schedule warned that if she didn't arrive exactly on time she shouldn't bother to come. She stood on the curb for several moments trying to think what to do and was just about to walk back to the GIFT House and beg a ride when a chopped blue Chevy, belonging to Devon's best friend Quinn, came zipping by. He slowed for her and got her to the appointment by speeding and going through one red light in return for the promise that she'd hook up with Devon.

"That guy's jacked for you, girl," Quinn said. "I ain't never seen him like this."

"Tell him I'm gonna be his boo again," Danesha said and stretched out so her sweater would sneak up and show some skin before she closed the car door and waved him away.

Right off, the surprise was that the lawyer was black. Maybe she should have figured from the deadbeat neighborhood one block over—broken windows, coked-up guys on the corner, mothers wearing nothing but housecoats and rolls of fat. But still she was shocked, once she took the elevator to the fourth floor, that inside the shiny glass office and behind the gold-plated door was a black man, since all the lawyers on television were white and rich.

"You look as though you were expecting someone else." His voice was too low, like he was trying to seem more important. Danesha knew she couldn't afford the good ones, but she didn't want a whack job.

He crossed his fingers and rested his hands on the desk, waiting until she blurted, "Are you really a lawyer?"

"I am certainly not a circus clown." His eyes were cold as they moved across her body, making her suddenly aware of how tight her skirt had become. It was the last thing her mama had bought for her, bright turquoise with pink and black flowers, and a nearly matching rosy pink sweater. The skirt had hung over her skinny hips, the top wrinkled right under the place where boobs should be. "The day you fill this out, the day you start watching out, girl," Mama had hooted when she tried it on. Today, pulling down the skirt over her round hips, yanking the top over her new bra, she'd felt a cry choke her throat.

"And you are?"

"Danesha Davis."

"Yes, well Miss Davis, I *am* a lawyer and I *don't* do pro bono work."

"Huh?"

"Pro bono. Free."

"I can pay!" Then she admitted, "Okay, I don't have much, but I got plans. Fact, I already have a couple things 'bout to go down. What do you charge?"

He peered over his glasses. "Why don't you first tell me about your case?"

She smoothed the wrinkles out of her skirt. "It's my brother. I gotta get him out of prison. He did what he had to do and now they locked him up. I need him out." She spoke so fast her words were running together and she saw in his tilted head the same expression teachers gave when she came to class high.

"What do you imagine I can do for you, Miss Davis?"

"Get him out. I told you that. Our mama had it comin'. He was just protecting himself. Protecting me too. See 'cause of what happened I had to leave home and the whole thing is one fucked up, oops, excuse me, Sir, one frigging mess. It's my mama should be in the joint, not Jerrell."

He nodded his head slowly. "I need specific details about the circumstances."

"You're gonna help me?" She couldn't keep the excitement out of her voice.

"I'm willing to listen." He looked at the wall clock above her head. "I have fifteen minutes until my next appointment."

She began to talk, talked so much she thought he would shush her, but he didn't. She told him about her ma's drinking, and how Mama used to slap Jerrell around when he was littler so that he kept on building up all that anger.

He listened politely, only glancing once at his watch. Finally she shut her mouth and sat quiet, looking around as he wrote out some notes. There were no photos, no knickknacks, nothing to say what kind of man he was, only two framed diplomas, undergrad and law school, both from Howard University. He followed her eyes to the wall, stared for a moment and then sat up straighter in his desk chair. "Is this a first offence?" he asked.

She hesitated, wanting to lie.

His pen hung mid-air.

"The other time weren't his fault. Couple of bums set him up. He got caught, stealing one of them little portable refrigerators. Supposed to be a business deal and they told him to pick it up, already paid for, then he gets slammed. Like why would he even want one of them things anyhow? But that's nothing like this."

He closed the file. "I'm sorry, Miss Davis. I really don't think you have a case. I know you miss your brother. Tough break for you. But I can't represent you." He stood, session over. "Why don't you call your deputy juvenile lawyer for help?"

"Who's that?"

"Your address. It's a foster residential home, right? So the DFS should have assigned a lawyer to you."

She shrugged. "My Mama lets me live at the GIFT House. Nobody pulled me out this time, if you can friggin believe that."

For a moment his face smoothed in something that looked like sympathy but then he mugged a scowl that told Danesha more than his words. She could feel red anger rush to her cheeks and spread throughout her chest. "You're not gonna help me? After I spilled my fucking guts?"

Now annoyance wrinkled his brow. She knew that look—she'd seen it too many times.

She grabbed her purse and stood. "I'll find a way, I'll get him out. Whatever it takes. And I'll get me a lawyer who will help."

He waved his hand. "Good luck. But..." his voice carried so that she stopped in the doorway, turned to face him. "Whatever your *'plans'* are, make sure they make sense, and that they're legal, or you'll wind up under the same roof as your brother. Stay in school and become a lawyer yourself. About that time he might be coming up for parole. That's when you can help him."

Danesha paused and let his words sink in. "You think I'm goin' *hoeing?* That what you think? You don't know *nothin'* about me."

He groaned and it had the sound of exhaustion, like the weight of an entire population in his breath. "But you see, I do know about you. You imagine because you got yourself some pitch dark skin you deserve a break. That you all can run around breaking laws, stealing and shooting, running open-air drug markets and, as you say, *hoeing,* but I'm going to help you? Because I'm the same color? Young lady, I am nothing like you."

She choked back a scream and was about to slam his door when again he stopped her, again waving his hand across the air. "What?" she barked.

"You want me to help? Okay. I require a three thousand dollar down payment toward the retainer. Come back when you have that kind of money."

She stumbled out of his office, fighting tears until she was back on the streets, one block over, back among the shouts and the noise and the filth, back to where one more young girl crying wasn't even worth a second glance.

CHAPTER TWELVE

As Lisa entered the kitchen in search of her keys and purse, she was surprised to find Brianna and Coreen sitting at the table, looking bored. Usually the girls hid themselves behind closed bedroom doors unless forced to come downstairs for meals or chores. "What's doing? And is Miss Vanessa here yet?"

"Wow, looka you. Where you going?" Coreen nodded her head in obvious approval as she took in Lisa's gray dress suit and pumps. It was the fifth outfit she'd tried on and the only one that still fit, though only because her stomach was marginally less poofy from having fasted for almost twenty-two hours.

"Today is an important holiday for me and I'm going to services in the Central West End. Actually, if you're not doing anything and don't have much homework, I could drop you off to hang out for a couple of hours while I'm at the synagogue."

"The sinner huh?" Coreen blurted. "What's that?"

"Synagogue. It's like church for Jewish people. And today is our holiest day of the year, Yom Kippur. I'm not eating or drinking anything until sunset."

"The whole day? Why?" Brianna asked, squeezing her arms around her midriff, as if just the thought was making her thinner.

How to explain that the Jewish holiday she had most dreaded as a child was the only one she observed as an adult. Yom Kippur—the Day of Atonement—in which Jews all over the world fasted from sundown to sundown as they searched deep inside to ask God for forgiveness. Lisa had never been much for "standing in the sin line," as her mom called it. But the idea of *not* observing Yom Kippur always felt slightly more uncomfortable than the fast itself. "Well, we Jews believe..."

Coreen interrupted, "Miss Lisa, you're *a Jewish?*" Her tone was suspicious, almost hostile, and her face had grown ashen. "I didn't know that. I mean, are you really?"

Lisa stalled, chewing her lip as she tried to think through how to respond. But before she could say anything, Coreen's face shifted into a dull flat gaze and with obviously forced neutrality she mumbled, "That's tight. Whatever."

"You seem upset, Coreen. Does it bother you that I'm Jewish?"

"I just never heard you trying to Jew no one down. And you don't have huge diamonds or nothing."

Lisa felt her mouth drop open, and for a moment, in her mind, Lisa gripped Coreen by the shoulders and demanded *what the fuck?* But she reigned in the emotion. She sure didn't need to add to her list of things for which she was about to atone. With effort, she repeated her offer to take the girls to the Central West End, then waited as they ran upstairs for their jackets.

She was searching for a pen to write a note to Vanessa, who was due fifteen minutes ago, when she heard the rattle of the back door and Vanessa's cheery, sing-songy, "I'm here, I'm here. Oh, Miss L, traffic was something fierce. Hey, you look pretty."

Again, that expression of surprise, making Lisa painfully aware of just how dumpy she normally appeared, in whatever jeans she could squeeze her newest ten pounds into and whichever T-shirt she grabbed first out of the drawer. In contrast, Vanessa continued to come to work dressed as if going clubbing. Today's outfit, a low-cut white keyhole polyester-made-to-resemble-silk blouse with the same black high-sheen pants and heels she'd interviewed in.

And as usual, Lisa found herself caught between responses, whether to reprimand Vanessa for being late, *again*, or to keep the interchange pleasant and accept the compliment with grace. Instead, she gave curt instructions— Danesha due home in one hour, put the meat loaf in the oven at five, the three of them expected back by six-fifteen, the lettuce needs washing and that pan that's been soaking all day could use a good scrubbing.

Vanessa's smile grew larger with each detail and larger still when Brianna and Coreen walked back in.

"Miss Vanessa! I haven't seen you in a hundred years," Coreen shrilled, passive personality discarded as spontaneously as a wool coat in summer. She grabbed hands with Vanessa and together they swung their arms as if school-girl chums walking the playground.

"I love your plaits. When'd you get 'em?" asked Brianna.

"And that top. I want one," Coreen said.

Vanessa pulled Brianna close for a hug, no resistance on either one's part. Lisa felt a surge of jealous annoyance so powerful she knew she could only partially blame her thirst and hunger for its strength. Before she could stop herself, she barked, "Girls, I know you're just *so* thrilled to see Miss Vanessa, who *finally* got here. But if you want to come with me we've got to leave *right now*."

They offered another quick hug to Vanessa then dutifully followed Lisa, their moods clearly dampened by her sour displeasure.

Giving Lisa one more reason to atone after all.

Brianna leaned against a storefront window as she tied the sleeves of her jacket around her waist. Sweat drops rolled off Coreen's forehead and large wet spots stained the pits and back of her long-sleeved shirt. She looked even hotter than Brianna. The temperature yesterday had been in the low sixties and today it was near ninety. They were dressed for yesterday.

"Damn it's burnin' up. And Miss Lisa ain't coming for how much longer?" Coreen said. "You got the house cell phone? We need to call and have her get us now."

"You know we can't do that."

"I don't get it. What's that place called she went to?" Coreen's face twisted as if she'd tasted something bitter.

Brianna fanned herself with her hands, not answering. Mostly Coreen was easy going and seemed to get along with nearly everybody, but then she'd suddenly be downright *ugly*.

Coreen slumped against a brick wall and shifted to peer into the storefront window. "Girl, take a look. Them pants is four hundred fifty dollars. Let's go try 'em on. Give that white lady working in there a heart attack. You know she'll be calling the cops minute we walk in and touch that stuff."

Brianna shook her head no and started walking down the street as quick as she could. She could hear Coreen panting behind her, trying to catch up.

"Geez, Bri. I was only joking. Wait up, it's too hot. What's wrong with you today?"

Brianna slowed, barely. Sometimes she didn't even like Coreen, and she was her only friend. But soon it wouldn't matter. Ma had finally written, *My preshus Brianna, things are going great guns here. You best start packing to come down to live with me ON THE BEACH. You can bet you won't be seeing snow this year.* Since it was already October, Brianna figured any day there would be a new letter with money for the bus. Or maybe Ma would send her a plane ticket so she could get there faster.

"Hey, stop here. I gotta get something to drink," Coreen huffed. Her face was red and wet. Brianna flashed to the image of Devon, the way their chests stuck together from all his sweat and how when he grunted he sounded like a *man*. He hadn't stopped by again or called, not even for Danesha. *Seems I've been eye-ballin' the wrong girl*, he'd said. Brianna knew how to wait.

She started to open the door to the Coffee Cartel, then stopped. The only ones in the place were white adults and a couple of little white kids. "Not here."

Coreen shaded her eyes with her hand as she stared through the glass. "Sometimes don't you just hate white folks?"

"That's terrible!"

"Okay, they ain't all of 'em jacked up. But I don't trust them neither. My daddy always said, the day you start countin' on a whitey is the day you quit watchin' your own back."

"What about Miss Lisa? And Mr. Stone? They're both cool. Sort of."

Coreen paused as if really thinking about it. "Mr. Stone's tight. But I bet Miss Lisa will be runnin' out soon. I mean, where did she come from, anyway? And can you believe she's a Jewish and she never even told us?" Coreen started walking again, at her own slow pace. "She thinks cause she's white she don't owe us nothing. She knows everything about us but she sure don't talk about herself none."

Brianna felt like she was supposed to defend Miss Lisa, except what Coreen said was true. But they didn't any of them ever talk about their pasts. Coreen had a thousand or more relatives, so why was she living in the GIFT House? Danesha was always angry about *something*. And even Miss Vanessa, who was near to perfect, sometimes seemed *too* cheerful, like she was covering up. Why shouldn't Miss Lisa have secrets too?

"How come you care about her religion?" Brianna asked, without bothering to correct Coreen's hobo self. *A Jewish?*

Coreen stared at Brianna as if she'd just asked about Miss Lisa having three eyes or something. "For one thing, they don't believe in Jesus, even though they killed him. You know what that means? Miss Lisa won't get no salvation."

Brianna didn't mind if Miss Lisa wasn't with her in the afterlife, especially since she'd be leaving so soon for Florida, and she'd probably never see any of them again. The thought cheered her. She grabbed Coreen's arm and pulled her to the next block, down Maryland Avenue toward the restaurants and bars.

"Think we have time to get something to eat?" Coreen asked, with that whining tone she got whenever she was hungry.

"Yeah, we still got about twenty-five minutes."

Suddenly, Coreen elbowed Brianna and started giggling. Two men passed by, holding hands and whispering into each other's ears. The oldest one cupped his hand around the other guy's butt.

"What's more pitiful than a coupla' ugly white faggots?" Coreen said. "They're everywhere."

Brianna looked in both directions, where nearly everybody out walking just then was older white men, a bunch of them in pairs or with women skuzzy enough to be worse than fags. If Miss Lisa had any idea what the neighborhood was like she sure wouldn't have dropped them off alone.

Then she saw him. She stumbled backwards, caught by a lamppost.

"What the...you all right?" Coreen leaned in, her pudgy face filling Brianna's vision.

"Yeah, maybe I'm just hungry too. Let's get something here." But she didn't follow Coreen into the bakery. She stood as long as she dared, trying to pretend she wasn't staring as he put his arm around the shoulders of a way-young, teeny woman, same light brown color as Brianna and just about as skinny. They were smiling at each other as they swayed from side to side, as if to keep from falling.

Right as Coreen came back out of the shop, her arms loaded with a box of steaming doughnuts and shouting her name, he looked up and seemed to notice her. For a moment she almost ran down the street and into his arms. She would forgive him anything. But then he turned his head and disappeared around a corner.

That was okay, she thought, as she took a sugar doughnut with sweating hands. Now that she knew he was in town, she'd find him again.

They sat on the bench waiting for Miss Lisa. Coreen wolfed down one doughnut after another, as Brianna struggled to swallow the sticky sweetness.

At exactly six, Miss Lisa pulled up alongside the bench and tapped her horn.

"Shotgun," Coreen said, yanking open the front passenger door.

Fine with her. Brianna slid into the back, inhaling Miss Lisa's vanilla perfume that filled the hot car like a cookie left in the oven. Miss Lisa's eyes and nose were red, and damp crumpled tissues took up half the passenger seat. *Don't ask,* she was thinking as, sure enough, Coreen blurted, "You been crying, Miss Lisa? How come?"

Miss Lisa shook her head no, but then sighed a long whispery sigh that seemed to pull her whole head down. "The end of the service is a memorial. I was just feeling sad thinking about...just sad, that's all." She forced her lips into a smile that adults never realize kids immediately know is fake. "Let's go home. I don't know about you girls, but I'm starving."

Coreen filled the car with non-stop chatter the whole drive back, allowing Brianna to disappear into the special secret that belonged only to her. No one knew, not Ma, not Grandmama Jones when she was alive, not Auntie Billie, not Coreen, not even that file locked away in Miss Lisa's drawer. "Your skin is so beautiful," he would whisper. "You are the perfect blending of your Ma and me." No, no one knew that Brianna's daddy had kept in contact with her all those years before he left town.

No one even knew she had a daddy, a wonderful, loving, handsome, white daddy.

CHAPTER THIRTEEN

Sheila happened to pop over as Lisa was futilely trying to scrub away the rust in her bathroom sink with cleanser and a brush. She must have looked as annoyed as she felt, because Sheila grabbed her by the elbow and tugged her into the living room, where they both sank onto the couch.

"You've never lived poor. I recognize that it's an adjustment," Sheila said with the calm with which someone might mention the need to adjust to an electric stove instead of gas. "But you've got to give all of this more time. And, frankly, more tolerance."

"More tolerance?" Lisa countered. "Because I don't enjoy living with rust? I don't mind the cleaning, but rust where I brush my teeth and wash my face?" She could hear the exasperation in her tone, knew she should check it, but just once it would have been nice for Sheila to offer a compliment, or even advice, that wasn't immediately diminished by an implicit "but."

Sheila waved her hand, gesturing aside Lisa's frustration. "Lisa, you take things so personally. I'm not judging you..." she glanced around the room, seeming to see it with fresh eyes. "Let me tell you the background story of the house and school. Maybe it will help you appreciate the miracle this place can be." She paused, and then with a smile added, "Even with the rust."

Ron Stone was thirty years old when he inherited his father's dry cleaners. It was an old family business, founded by his grandfather between the First World War and the Depression. During Grandpa Stone's tenure and for the early years of Dad Stone's management, the dry cleaners was stationed in an all-white, predominantly Jewish area. Then in the early Sixties and throughout the Seventies, whites fled as "Afro-Americans" moved in, bringing with them the perceived threat and eventual reality of lower housing values, diminished schools, drugs and crime. Still Stone Cleaners stayed.

When Ron took over in the early Nineties, the neighborhood was entirely African-American. One block down was a notorious crack house. A street away was the local headquarters for the Crips gang. It was a neighborhood where gun shots were heard, where mothers shooed their children into the house in voices laced with worry and defeat. Grown men loitered on the sidewalks during the daylight hours of unemployment. Teen boys ran their "business" with unabashed daring on the corners as cars lined up three and four deep, windows unrolled by inches, furtive wads of green pushed out as baggies were pushed through.

Ron never wanted to manage a dry cleaners, but it was all he knew. Since age fifteen he'd worked with dirty laundry, from recording pick-up days to applying the actual chemicals, steaming, hanging and processing. To the question of why he stayed in a neighborhood where he had to duck his head as he drove away at night, he would shrug his shoulders with the passivity borne of never having the concern, or the luxury, of wondering what to do with his life. He didn't like the neighborhood, who could? But he wasn't afraid either. A fatalist by nature, Ron assumed he would be safe unless he wasn't. He refused to buy a gun, but he did carry mace. Mostly, he tried to be pleasant and fair to all his customers and he was particularly friendly with the patrolling officers.

Then one day, in a string of such days, when Ron's regular help failed to show up for work, he cajoled several of the teens to come in and work for him. The boys would have laughed at his offer to pay minimum wage—"Man, we get more for one joint than you're gonna pay us for a whole fucking day?"—but it was bitterly cold, with a howling wind and chilling snow flurries. At least the cleaners was warm and dry, and when Ron brought back White Castle burgers and onion rings, with the promise of more tomorrow, he had them hooked. Pretty soon, Stone Cleaners became a hang-out on bad weather days. After a while, the girlfriends started to show up too.

"How come none of you kids are in school?" Ron asked. Though they scoffed, he saw regret and shame on many of their faces. So he started buying and bringing in magazines,

Ebony, Jet, Rolling Stone. A few of the kids flipped through the magazines, but most never even cracked the covers. One day as they were piling out at closing time, Ron nabbed Devon, a leader and a reader, pulling him back by the hood of his sweatshirt. "Why are you and Tamonika the only ones who read the magazines?"

Devon twisted his mouth in an expression Ron had learned was forced bravado to cover up something darkly private. "You shittin' me? You don't know?"

"It's why I'm asking."

"Most of these homies barely read, man."

"But how. . .?"

Devon's laugh was bitter and amused. "You think a teacher wants a kid like Lorenzo or Shontell in her class *another* year?"

Ron went to Left Bank Books, bought a stack of primers and brought them in. During a customer lull, shouting over the boom box, he told the group, now expanded to nine regulars, "I want to help some of the little neighbor kids learn to read. Can you guys go through these books to decide which ones to use?"

Initially, only a couple of teens responded. But after a few dull days during which the howling winds and icy rain kept customers away and the group inside, they started reading the books aloud to one another, mocking the "crackers."

"Listen up to this one." Devon read, "'Mikey was confused. He didn't know whether to get a bright red bike like his best friend or a blue one like his brother. Or, he could get silver, his dad told him, and be an individual.' Poor fucking Mikey. Dude should get the silver one so when we rip it off we have us an *individual* shiny bike for our bru." Amidst the hoots and laughter, the interest in the primers grew.

Ron brought in note paper and pens and challenged them to write a rap. He'd use his connections, he said, to let the winner record in his friend's studio. No promises to produce a demo, but he'd at least open the door. But, Ron warned, only the rap with no spelling errors would even be considered. They could help each other or come to him, but anything with mistakes would automatically be thrown out.

And so it evolved. Certainly not every teen drop-out discovered a spark to learn, and once the winter weather blew through most of them stopped coming in. But the seed had been planted. For the first time in his placid life, Ron Stone had a mission.

He emptied out a portion of the back area by giving away all the clothes that had been stored for two years or more. He bought basic supplies and several tables and chairs from his brother who owned an office furniture supply outlet. And he went back to school himself, taking night classes toward a degree in education.

He put out the word, and the word quickly spread. Ron Stone was "cool" and he was offering free GED tutoring to anyone interested. It started small until Devon sauntered in, wearing a new deep-red leather coat and three-hundred-dollar watch, plunked down on a rickety seat and announced, "You need me to help out, man? I'll get Ada too. That girl read better than anyone."

It took countless meetings, multiple applications, out-of-pocket cash, a lot of sweat, grants, federal money, and donations from BMW-driving liberals. But Ron Stone eventually achieved his dream. Stone Cleaners would become Stone Charter Middle School.

Clothes and racks and machinery were hauled out. Desks and supplies and books brought in. Four teachers were solicited from nearby city schools. A principal was coerced to forego her early retirement. Bricks were knocked out and glass panes put in, walls were built and lighting brightened. The pervasive odor of dry cleaning chemicals lingered, as did the gangs on the corner, but five years after inviting the teens in for burgers, Ron opened his charter school to thirty-eight sixth graders, who ranged in age from eleven to fourteen.

The following year, thirty-two of the original thirty-eight advanced to seventh grade, and forty new sixth graders were added. Sheila Johnson was hired as a full-time social worker and counselor. By year three, Ron Stone had a master's degree in education, and the former dry cleaners building was teeming with one hundred ten middle schoolers and a waiting list. All of the students were on free and reduced lunch. More than half the student body had IEP's, the alphabet soup of educational challenge that portended the highest failure rate. The building was costing double in maintenance what had been budgeted. Staff turnover was high because of the demanding nature of the student body. The standardized test scores were among the lowest in the area and government funding was being threatened.

Yet, Ron continued to look upon his efforts as success. So far Stone Charter had only lost nine students to drop out, only one had become pregnant, only three had been busted for drugs. Those students who'd had their parents hot-lined were kept under close supervision and under the nurturing eye of his staff. Several of his initial teens from the dry-cleaning-primer-reading days routinely dropped by to visit.

So when Ron Stone was faced with the decision of what to do with his eighth graders, who would be going on to high school, he quickly determined that Stone Charter Middle would become Stone Charter Middle *and* High School. He had worked too hard to create a safe haven, to send his kids out into the grim, unaccredited St. Louis city public school system of large classes, under-valued teachers, and poorly educated students.

Ron was in the throes of his usual fiscal and educational challenges when an old friend called. "I have a house I'd like to donate to your cause," he said. The property was in bad shape but in a reasonably safe area, one mile west of the school and on a block with a strong Neighborhood Watch program and tight police control.

Ron's brain began to spin with options—he could house the upper classmen there or hire more staff and expand the total number of students. He was mulling over ideas as Sheila Johnson walked into his office and handed him the file of a new eighth grade transfer student, Coreen Thomas. When he got to the last test score he looked up and shook his head. "Astonishing."

"That girl can *think*. Hell, you should hear the way she

83

memorizes entire poems. But she's never been in one school or one home long enough to learn two plus two," Sheila said, not bothering to hide her scorn. "I don't know whether to cry or celebrate. Though she'll likely be gone to another school and another household before I have the chance to do either."

And in that moment, Ron Stone conceived the GIFT House.

"Now, one year later, here you are, Lisa. You and the girls."

"And the rust," Lisa teased, eliciting a grudging smirk.

Sheila smiled. "Yes, and the rust." She heaved herself out of the chair with a grunt and walked into the kitchen. Lisa heard the cabinet door under the sink squeak open and a couple seconds later squeak shut. Sheila came back in, giggling, and plunked down in front of Lisa an unopened box of steel wool soap pads.

"Did someone call for help? Who says I don't know how to lend a hand to a sister?" Sheila continued to giggle as she left to go back to school.

Sheila giggling? Lisa was struck with the unexpected thought that it would be fun to go out to lunch with Sheila sometime.

She'd never before been called a "sister" except by Kate. Out of Sheila's mouth it was a very nice surprise. She sat for some quiet moments, aware of the smile on her face, then zeroed in on the box and laughed out loud. S.O.S.? What marketing genius had come up with that name?

CHAPTER FOURTEEN

There had been no more word from Eva-Lynn Fox or her mother. Every time Lisa passed that extra empty bedroom she crossed her fingers in hopes Sheila would somehow forget about it or that future candidates would be deemed unsuitable. After being together for two months, Lisa and the three girls had finally forged a web of sorts. And like the web of a spider, their bond was intricate and flimsy, yet potentially strong enough to hold.

It had been decades since Lisa had lived with other females, and she'd forgotten how cyclical the prevailing moods were when hormones shifted dramatically from week to week. As in college dorm days, pretty quickly they all seemed to be on the same menstrual schedule (they never told Lisa, but the girls expended little effort hiding their bodily functions). There were weeks when snarls and glares were the only form of communication. But there were also occasional nights of laughter and music, when even Danesha would join in.

One such evening occurred in mid-October.

As it turned out, Coreen's pantomiming in front of the class that day wasn't an aberration. She possessed a true flare for performance and had a strong, if undeveloped, singing voice. She had been cast with a leading role and a solo in the neighborhood YMCA Halloween musical, sponsored to provide a safe place for children to trick or treat. The theme of this year's show was Motown MoJo. Coreen was to perform a medley as Diana Ross of the Supremes.

When Danesha heard, she took one piercing look at Coreen—who seemed to widen under Danesha's scrutiny—and hooted aloud. "Have they took a look at you? A thick-ass Supreme? They want someone who's got *my* game."

"No, they need someone who can sing, not just bitch. Bitch," Coreen hissed.

"Miss Lisa, did you hear what she called me?"

"Did you hear what she said to *me*?"

"Hey, I'm staying out of this," Lisa said, forcing levity into her tone, as if the antics of the girls were of the usual playful nature of "sisters" everywhere. Danesha glared at her as Coreen visibly shut down.

"But here's the advice my grandmother used to say, 'Words left in your mouth belong to you,'" Lisa quipped, and with obvious exaggeration she stuck the tip of her tongue between her teeth just as Coreen stumbled into her, forcing Lisa to bite down. Hard. She screamed as pain ripped through her mouth.

"Oh, Jesus!" Danesha screeched. "You're bleeding."

"I'm so sorry, Miss Lisa. I didn't mean it," Coreen's voice choked.

Lisa waved her hand as if it were nothing, but she couldn't hold back the tears, so intense was the throbbing.

Brianna raced to the kitchen and came back with an ice cube wrapped in a paper towel. "Here, my grandmama taught me this."

Immediately the paper splotched red, but the cold brought relief and Lisa was able to force a smile and squeeze Coreen's arm in reassurance. "I know it wasn't intentional."

Danesha brought a hand-held mirror, shoving it against Lisa so she might see the gash on her tongue. "Miss L, that's some jack shit advice about keeping words in our mouth, huh? See why I never do it?"

Lisa giggled and Coreen, with obvious relief, tried to laugh, but it came out sounding more like a squawk, causing Danesha to blurt, "Girl, you sure they want you *singing* in that show?"

"Omigod. The show. I've got to practice," Coreen said, sliding back into the center of the room, Lisa's tongue already forgotten. She straightened her spine and then slowly raised her right arm, finger pointed outward, and nodded one at a time at each of them, drawing them in. "I am...the great...the one and only... Diana Ross, and you three," Coreen raised her other arm and thrust forward her hip, transporting them back several decades, "are my Supremes."

"You crazy. I ain't playing that shit," Danesha sneered, but even as she said it she unbuttoned her top two buttons to tuck her shirt into her bra to reveal some cleavage, and she sashayed into the middle, hand on hip, index finger extended. In spite of herself, Lisa snorted, spurting bloody droplets onto the front of her pink T-shirt.

Coreen rolled a magazine into a microphone. She lowered her head, closed her eyes, began to hum, quietly at first, then building in tone, as she deliberately raised her head up, and backwards, and then she belted out in a voice that was so full of gusto, so pitch-perfect, they all stood still and stared. "*Stop! In the name of love...*" And as though they'd been rehearsing for weeks, Brianna and Danesha immediately chimed in with "*before you break my heart.*"

Lisa hung back, smiling with a joy that was so tender it nearly hurt, as all three girls sang the entire song and segued into a medley, playing off one another, swaying to the same tempo, shaking their young hips and pushing out their firm chests.

Coreen grabbed Lisa's hand and pulled her into the center of the room. "C'mon, Miss Lisa. We're gonna help you not be so wacked."

"Coreen, you can't say that," Brianna burst out, causing Lisa to wonder if being "wacked" was even worse than it sounded.

Danesha chimed in, "Hella-yeah, if I gotta do it, you gotta be a Supreme too."

Lisa hesitated for only a moment, then let loose with a full-shouldered shimmy while the girls broke into peals of laughter.

"You're so white!" Brianna exclaimed and immediately covered her mouth with both hands.

"It's true, Miss Lisa, have you got no rhythm?" Danesha asked, whereupon she scooted behind Lisa, put two hands on her hips and pressed close to "feel" the music.

Lisa tried, she really did. She'd always been a clunky dancer—what else to expect from a generation raised on "the robot" and "break dancing"?—and next to these nimble girls, she was suddenly reminded of her last vacation with Nate, the one that was supposed to save their marriage. They had spent a week in Jamaica avoiding *the talk* by slurping down icy glasses of rum punch and making dispassionate love. She would stare in drunken misery at the young Jamaican women, watching how they didn't walk but glided, how they didn't dance but rode the notes, and she'd felt used up and dried out.

But this was different. These were "her girls." Coreen was a surprisingly fluid dancer, Brianna uncharacteristically un-self-conscious, Danesha almost giddy. Struck by the bizarre randomness that she was living this life, experiencing this moment, Lisa stepped further into the center and let them play her, trying to dance as they did, though the more she mimicked the more awkward she became and the fatter she felt. She definitely needed to start an exercise program. Maybe it could be her new "hobby" and get her mom off her back and the fat off her ass. She chuckled at the thought, and then, what the hell, she'd already made a fool of herself, she burst into full-throated song, which sent all three girls into more laughter as her voice squawked high then low.

Brianna, especially, laughed so hard she had to grip her stomach. At one point she ran out of the room, shamefaced, yelling, "I've got to *use* it." She returned several minutes later wearing her Tweetie Bird pajama bottoms, muttering with a giggle that she'd "kinda wet herself."

Fortunately, Lisa thought to capture the moment. After some fumbling, Coreen figured out how to work the remote feature on Lisa's digital camera. The girls wouldn't stop long enough to look at the pictures. They danced and sang until they grew hoarse and exhausted. It was nearly midnight, long past when they should have completed their homework and gone to bed. Instead, Lisa made hot cocoa and popcorn. They sat around eating and arguing about which musicians were "dope" and which were a "tenner."

"A tenner?"

"You know, Miss Lisa, like a ten out of ten."

"Oh. Like Bono."

"Who?"

Finally, they wound down. Lisa followed the girls upstairs and stood outside their open doors as they got ready for bed. She wanted to tuck them in or at least hug them, but she satisfied herself with leaning into each bedroom door jamb and wishing them pleasant dreams.

After all their lights were out, she went down to the kitchen to make lunches for the next day. It felt good to know that Danesha liked a lot of jelly and very little peanut butter, that Brianna preferred butter and cheese, and Coreen would gladly eat anything.

While closing up the first floor, Lisa suddenly remembered the camera. She scrolled through the images, stopping at one. She stared for several moments. There was something about the picture, something remarkable, but what? And then she realized.

As with families in which everyone favors another member just enough so they all wind up looking alike, so, too, did the four of them—each standing with out-thrust hips, pointed fingers, cocked heads, varying skin tones shading one to the next, humor evident on every face. Danesha. Brianna. Coreen. She didn't love any of these girls yet. But for the first time since that long-ago job interview where she'd glibly told Sheila, "I have a lot of love to give," Lisa recognized that she truly *could* grow to love each of them. And that felt like an important step.

She climbed into bed, wearing the blood-spotted shirt, intending for her first waking sight the next day to be a reminder of this evening. As she dropped into sleep, she ran her tongue across her front teeth and winced in surprise at the sharp stab of pain, but still, Lisa fell asleep with a smile on her face.

CHAPTER FIFTEEN

L isa was feeling good. For four mornings in a row, she had waited until the girls left for school and then driven to Forest Park and begun to power walk. She was slow and out of shape, her legs and lungs hurt, but yesterday as she walked she'd actually thought about how much fun it would be to bring the girls with her on a weekend day, maybe rent bikes or this spring rent a row boat. When Lisa called and told Bonnie, she'd quipped, "Wow, Lis, did you just say 'this spring?' Those are some serious endorphins!"

"It's not only the exercise. Ever since that night we danced last week, we've all been kind of good. Like we crossed a line or something and this could work. I'm sort of tempted to stop my Zoloft." Into the loaded silence, she added, "You disagree?"

"It seems too soon. Don't forget what Berger said, how moving forward is rarely a straight line, there's always a zig and a zag."

That was the part of the conversation Lisa later remembered when, as Bonnie described it, "the zig hit the fan."

Lisa was sitting alone in the living room mindlessly watching a late-afternoon television show when the explosion occurred. She'd nearly grown used to the ruckus of urban living—neighbors fighting, glass breaking, sirens screeching, and the rapid back firing of cars that each time made her cringe with fear. This explosion, however, rocked the house and sent her rushing to the porch, with Danesha and Coreen immediately behind.

"Omigod, it's a bomb," Coreen wailed.

"You too much drama," Danesha retorted, but she leaned her body so close their hands nearly clasped.

A second explosion burst through the neighborhood, this one louder, deeper, and followed by a spiral of black smoke that fogged the sky a full block away. Soon the shrill cries of a siren sliced the air.

"I'm going over there. See what's going down." Without waiting for a nod, Danesha scrambled across the lawn.

Flames were shooting higher, sending fiery orange sparks against the trees and rooftops. The air had grown thick and pungent. As more sirens sounded and neighbors shouted to one another—"That the Rimmel house?" "Anybody in that house?"—Lisa slumped against the porch column, frozen by an eerie sense of foreboding.

"You okay, Miss Lisa? It ain't gonna catch where we stay." Coreen's face was calm, the face of a child who had known so much turmoil in her young life that the state of vulnerability no longer felt frightening, but familiar.

Lisa struggled to offer a half smile and slid down to the top step, her legs suddenly weak. She inhaled a deep breath filled with the biting sting of smoke and patted the ground. Coreen sank as though having been waiting for an invitation. She sidled up close, her skin warm and soft. Lisa reached for her hand and squeezed. Coreen squeezed back.

All up and down the street people milled about, excitement drawing them out of their homes. Lisa became acutely aware of being the only white-skinned person outside, and she couldn't stop herself from asking, "So you still think it's mostly safe, living right here?"

Coreen shrugged. "I told you, I've stayed in way more drek than this. Bunch of times."

"What was it like to move around so much? Tell me, Coreen."

Her lips parted, but no sound came out as a drape seemed to fall across her face. Lisa peered into Coreen's brown eyes, inviting her, but the door was closed. "Well, I'm glad you're here now."

Coreen's eyes grew moist and for the briefest moment she allowed her head to rest on Lisa's shoulder, before drawing back up and resettling her expression into mask-like neutrality. Was it possible the girl was as good of an actor off stage as on?

"What about the others?"

Coreen seemed to think before she answered. "Danesha act like she ain't scared of nothing. And Brianna..." as she paused Lisa pictured Brianna hugging herself smaller, trembly and uncertain.

Coreen must have had the same thought because she sputtered before adding, "She says she ain't scared, but anyone can tell that a lie. She's always wanting me to come meet her at the school when she gotta stay late. So she don't walk back alone."

Lisa felt a flush of shame. *She* should have been the one to walk Brianna home.

"Now I did stay one time where it was really ghetto. With Auntie Tiffany. Used needles all over and drunk hobos even in broad day. But she went everywhere with me so it was my favorite place. I cried when I had left there."

An invitation, though if she asked for more, would Coreen shut down again? Before Lisa could decide, Coreen abruptly switched the conversation.

"Miss Lisa, you shouldn't a let Danesha go to the fire," Coreen said. "Someone could be thuggin' blood," and at Lisa's puzzled expression, she added, "Could be bad."

"Yeah, I was thinking that too. I better go look for her." She struggled to keep the dread out of her voice.

"I'll come," Coreen said without hesitation, but just as they stood to go, Danesha hurried forward, her usual sauntering replaced by sprinting.

"Holy shit. It is hammin' over there." She was grabbing her stomach and panting. She reeked of smoke, several braids were unraveling and sweat rolled down her neck, a stark contrast to how carefully Danesha usually presented herself.

"What'd you find out?" Lisa asked.

Danesha started laughing, a high-pitched squeal that matched the sirens in tone. "Somebody blew the house up. The whole fucking house."

"Whoa." Lisa grabbed the step for support.

"Whose place?" Coreen asked.

"You know the one. The empty blue house." Danesha looked straight at Coreen and tilted her head in a gesture that seemed full of meaning. Coreen turned away from Danesha's knowing smirk. Lisa's gut tightened. There was no *good* reason for the girls to know about an empty house in this neighborhood.

Coreen hissed, "Don't be telling me what I know."

Undeterred, Danesha continued, her face bright with excitement, her words rushing over one another. "The whole place is burnin' and first no one told me jack shit, but then this one boy say the Bloods bombed it 'cause of the Crips slangin' in their territory."

"I thought there weren't any gangs around here. Isn't this a 'Neighborhood Watch' area?"

"Miss Lisa, you a hot mess sometimes." Danesha's laugh was hard to read and she seemed about to say more when she stopped, her eyes opened wide. She pointed. "Uh oh, there's that truck again. What's that white dude want from us?"

"Hey, I've seen him driving by too," Coreen piped up.

The tomato-red truck slowed to a stop in front of the house, its engine on idle, and the driver squinted across the yard. Lisa's and his eyes locked, into what she would later describe to Bonnie, as "one of those movie scenes I would rather have been watching than starring in." As she began her slow descent down the creaky stairs of the GIFT House porch, what she felt was not surprise—not even alarm—but a surrender to inevitability. Her soles scuffed the pavement as she made her way to the truck, imagining herself a reluctant child scraping the toes of her shoes to indicate her displeasure even as she does what she must do.

He unrolled the window, clearly uncertain and perhaps afraid. They stared at each other, taking in the changes. Lisa spoke first.

"Hello, Nate. What are you doing here?"

"No, Lisa, the question is what are *you* doing here?"

He looked good. A little too thin, and he needed a haircut, his dark brown hair long enough to curl. He had a fresh scab on his chin; he must have rushed when shaving this morning.

"You may as well come in." She stepped aside as Nate opened the truck door and slid to the ground. Their bodies curved as if in memory. Lisa's was larger, Nate's smaller, but so familiar was their fit that for an instant she nearly let herself fall into his chest.

93

Then Danesha hooted and immediately Lisa jerked away. He followed Lisa through the narrow front door into the living room that suddenly seemed more dilapidated than usual. She motioned for him to sit on the one chair that wasn't near collapse as she shooed the two girls out of the room. "Go on now, upstairs. I need some privacy."

Danesha jutted out a hip. "Aiight, Miss Lisa. Whatever you say."

Nate barely waited for the door to shut before he jumped up from his chair. "Miss Lisa? What the fuck?"

"We need to talk."

"So talk."

"You knew I needed something else."

"But this?" He waved his hand, taking in the broken-down mismatched second-hand furniture, the frayed carpeting, the soiled drapes they'd yet to replace. "*This?*"

Lisa understood why Coreen shrugged in response to life. It was the most succinct non-answer to a question that had too many answers. But as he continued to glare, unblinking with an intensity unusual for Nate, she resisted a shrug, motioned for them both to sit and as gently as she could, she stated the truth, "It seemed like the best possible option."

"Exactly what option is that, Lisa *Harris*?" he snarled.

"How did you..." but the anger in his eyes stopped her short. It didn't really matter how he knew, what mattered was that he did. Lisa felt a wave of her own resentment. "Harris or Rothman? Realistically, isn't it semantics at this point?"

Nate snapped back as if slapped. He breathed in deeply several times. "I'll let that pass. Tell me what the hell you're doing here."

"I'm a house mom now. I live here. It's my job. And *why* are you giving me *that look?*" Her voice caught on the last words, and what she said next came out a choked whisper, full of frustration as much as sadness. "You wanted this separation too."

"I didn't *want* any of this."

"As if I did? Nate, have you forgotten how impossible and complicated everything got? What's changed from that?" She hesitated, unsure about asking a question when she wasn't yet ready to hear the answer, then asked anyway. "Are you...are you dating?"

She'd expected sheepish defiance. Instead, he crumpled, nearly folding in on himself. She'd seen that Nate before. His pain was like looking in a mirror, and she couldn't live it double.

"You know," he said, "I lost those babies too."

Lisa shook her head vigorously back and forth. *Don't go there. Don't you dare. Not when I'm finally, finally, doing better.*

Unhappiness twisted his face into tight lines. "Oh, Lisa." Again, he waved his hand across the room, repeating an entire conversation without words. "Enough is enough. We can survive this. I know that now. And, and...I bet you know it too."

She stood and began to pace, daring him to acknowledge her appearance. Underneath the stained, misshapen T-shirt she was braless and her breasts, previously a source of sensual pride, hung heavy and low, supported only by the round shelf of her stomach, evidence of what her body had learned these past months—it cost way less to eat fat than to eat thin. She wore no make-up, making the moon-shape of her once contoured face appear sallow. She'd neither cut nor dyed her hair since leaving him, the dark roots an unflattering contrast to the dulled blonde shade of the uneven layers that split at her shoulders.

Yet, when she found the courage to stare him squarely in the eyes, she didn't see disgust or pity or disinterest, or even anger anymore. What she saw caused her to gasp back a sob. Nate still loved her. Nate, in his familiar loose Levis and wrinkled denim shirt that was missing a top button—a button she should have been there to sew on—and his grubby running shoes that he wore daily but had never jogged a mile in. Seeing this man she'd loved and slept with, dreamed and cried with, fought with and retreated from, seeing him in this room, created a hurt as if punched into the hollow between the bones.

She slumped into the broken recliner and covered her face with her hands. For long moments neither of them said anything, the only noise was the sound of a siren that grew

95

louder and closer before fading back away. She looked up, not even trying to wipe away her tears. "Why did you come?"

He leaned in and grasped both of her hands. His fingertips were cold against her clammy palms. "Tell me something, Lisa." He squeezed so tight she winced, but he didn't let go. "Do you think if we'd had our baby..." his voice husky with raw anguish, "maybe you wouldn't have quit loving me?"

Without thought, she dropped to the floor alongside his chair, wrapped her arms around his slender waist and squeezed him tight. "I've never quit loving you. And...you still love me, don't you? But," she inhaled, held her breath, fighting for control, then finally sighed, "it wasn't enough for us anymore." And with a softer voice said, "Was it?"

At first he sat stony still, his arms draped by his side. But as she nestled her cheek against his lap, he relented. Very gently, he ran his fingers through her hair, tracing a line along her ears and down the nape of her neck. She heard his intake of breath, of desire, felt it herself, its shape and scent as immediately familiar as falling into one's own bed after a weary journey. She tightened her hug and burrowed her forehead against his thigh. Nate.

Then a soft, squeaky voice. "Oops! Excuse me Miss Lisa."

She pulled back and shot up. "Brianna. You're home early."

The girl was clasping herself and very nearly shrinking into her skin. "They canceled after-school tutoring because there's a fire in the neighborhood. I was...kind of scared it was our place. But I'll go up to my room now."

"No, no, Brianna. Oh, God, I'm so sorry. I was going to come get you and then," she tilted her chin toward Nate. "Uh, this is, this is Mr. Rothman. A friend of mine, who just stopped by for a minute."

"Not Mr. Rothman. Please, call me Nate."

On cue—had she been peeking the whole time?—Coreen strode into the room and thrust out her hand. "Hi. You didn't really meet me. I'm Coreen," she said, pointing. "And this one is Danesha. We all live here with Miss Lisa."

Nate turned toward the girls, now in a group, with Lisa standing to the side. Nodding to Coreen, he said, "Well, that's really something."

"There's just three of us girls now, but somebody else will be staying here too at some point, right Miss Lisa? For all of high school."

As Nate openly scowled, Lisa struggled to keep her own expression neutral, suddenly so worn out she sensed that if she lay down now she might choose never to get back up. Instead, she stepped between Brianna and Coreen and placed a hand on each one's shoulder. "My job, Nate, is to help these girls be the best they can during high school. Which means, you two, go put in your hour of homework before dinner. You know the rules."

"Nice meeting you, Mr. Nate. We'll see you again?" Coreen cocked her head sideways, the implication that clearly he was someone of importance, and also someone whose name she'd never heard before.

A realization crossed Nate's face as a dark shadow of irritation and insecurity. Too many times Nate had met people in Lisa's separate world who seemed startled by him. It was an old wound that still had the power to touch a nerve.

It dated back to their first meeting, when Lisa had looked right through him, seeing only the blue collar of a deliveryman carrying in rental dishes for a Credit-Solutions holiday party. Despite the number of times she'd tried to make light of it, Lisa's initial dismissal had been a ghost throughout their marriage, even as recently as one of their last times together when she'd read aloud a favorite passage from Eudora Welty, then stopped mid-sentence when she realized that of course he wasn't listening and asked, "Am I boring you?"

They both knew when they married that Nate's lack of education would always be a prickly point, at least for him. He'd hated school. After too many years of C and D grades and of feeling lost when teachers gave multiple-task instructions, he'd simply given up. To please his father, he'd stumbled through two mediocre years at the local community college before an irresistible opportunity to buy a floundering party rental business fell into his lap. They had a fancy name and lots of resources for it now, auditory learning disorder—but back then the only label he heard was stupid.

Lisa was a straight-A student, who'd previously only associated with fellow academic achievers. She had a Master's in Social Work degree; Bonnie had a PhD in chemistry; even Lisa's college boyfriend had gone on to get an MBA. Sometimes when Nate and she went to parties and everyone started discussing where they'd gone to college and what they'd studied in graduate school—when names like Tulane, Macalester and Brown floated through the air like satiny pillows of privilege— Nate would quietly slip out of the room and go outside to lean into the bricks and yearn for a cigarette.

The irony was he was a hell of a lot more successful than most of their peers and, to Lisa, much more interesting. How many of them could at age twenty take a failing business and within five years turn it into a financial success? And he would match wits with anyone when it came to keeping up with the news or engaging in discussions about politics.

Yet, there it was, its murky presence invading even this room that reeked of relentless failure.

"Well, Miss Lisa, I'm glad to see you doing so well," he muttered, the bitterness palpable. He grabbed his jacket and headed to the door, where he stopped and pointedly looked around.

Once more she saw the shabbiness through his eyes. But what he didn't see was the night of dancing in a circle when Lisa felt lighter and more hopeful than she had in years. Or the way the girls would come home from school and carelessly toss aside backpacks, hurry to the kitchen for a snack, every so often "joning" one another, sometimes, lately, filling "Miss Lisa" in on a day's story.

"Hold on, Nate." She reached out a hand. He waited. Her arm hung in the air. She had no idea what she wanted to say.

His voice was even, tempered by an emotion Lisa couldn't quite discern. "You asked if I was *dating*? Of course not. I came here to ask you to come home. I know we agreed to give each other more time, but," his shrug wracked his whole torso, "well,

I see now that I was being naïve. House mom? What were you thinking?"

"I wasn't thinking. Or feeling. I...just...skipped breakfast that day and when Sheila pretended not to notice..."

"Huh?"

"Nothing. I don't know. I just found this. You understand?"

Nate didn't turn his head quite fast enough to hide his wet eyes, but his hunched back was a door slamming shut. "I need things too, Lisa. I hope *you* understand."

Stunned, she watched as he shuffled to his red truck and got inside. She continued to stand on the porch, as the lingering smell of smoke covered her skin and clothes. The sirens had stilled, leaving an eerie, unfamiliar neighborhood silence.

She was about to go inside when he opened the truck door and slowly made his way back across the lawn and up the porch steps. For a moment she thought he'd whisk her into his arms and they'd float off into a life of joy, all disappointments and disagreements cast astray, far away from sorrow. The movie scene she did not admit aloud, even to Bonnie.

Instead he stopped just short of touching her. "I will wait through this school year before I file for divorce. But if there's any fucking chance that you actually intend to stay here through these girls' high school *years*...then there's no point in even waiting 'til spring."

He turned in what was obviously meant to be a dramatic exit. Only, instead, he stumbled on the middle step and slid to the ground. Lisa didn't even try to bite back a giggle as she offered a hand, which he refused, awkwardly pulling himself up. She gave him a quick hug. He brushed his lips against her ear. "We could try again. It's your choice."

He pulled away before she could respond and this time when he reached the truck he climbed inside and immediately drove off, either ignoring or truly not hearing her plaintive, "Try *what*?"

CHAPTER SIXTEEN

Nate broke three china dinner plates the day he first met Lisa. He was carrying in a crate of dishes for the Credit-Solutions annual holiday party when from out of the conference room emerged a slim, sleek blonde, walking briskly, pencil behind her ear, frown on her face. She'd looked right through him, but it was enough to startle him into loosening his grip and letting the bottom plate, a holiday Gold Band, shatter to the floor. The woman raised an eyebrow and hurried past.

"Thanks," Nate whispered sarcastically, just loudly enough for her to stop dead on her heel, scowl, then walk out. He found that his hands were shaking as he lowered the stack of plates safely to a table and began to pick up shards of luminescent china. "God damn," he muttered as two slivers implanted deep into his fingertips.

His business partner Alan had picked this week in mid-December, the heaviest week of their party rental business, to vacation in the Cayman Islands. Two of their assistants were out sick and Nate was left to set up for their season's corporate bookings by himself. He'd bloodied a large area of a white linen tablecloth before he realized that his fingers were dripping. "Can I get a Band-Aid around here?" he shouted into the empty room. He retrieved a matching linen napkin from a shrink-wrapped bundle, wound it around his hand, and continued unloading the ninety place settings, all the while cursing his partner who was probably at that very moment seducing an under-aged, bikini-waxed woman who would only learn of Alan's two failed marriages on the last day of the trip.

Nate was carrying in the last carton when she stepped out at precisely the moment he stepped in, their bodies colliding as the pile of fine china teetered and the top plate slid right through her outstretched hands onto the foyer's ceramic floor, breaking into several even parts.

She winced. "Sorry."

As she bent to retrieve the broken pieces his eyes roved up and down the curve of her back, the way her shoulders, surprisingly broad, and her narrow waist formed an inverted triangle, and how her ass swelled at the thighs and then flattened against her lean frame. Nate felt his aching fingers itching to roam her body. When she stood up straight, jagged china pieces filling her long-fingered hands, he was startled to note that one of her blue eyes was half brown, with a pencil-point-sized black spot in the center of the brown. Inadvertently he leaned in closer for an inspection, as she leaned back, though in sync so they resembled a well-rehearsed dancing couple. It lasted only a moment, this startling electricity, but it left Nate foggy-headed and confused.

Normally Nate would have used the hours of actual party time to leave and either relax or check on another booking. This time he stood like an idiot, leaning into the back doorjamb, eyes traveling the room for a glimpse of her. Hours later, as the final guests brushed by him without so much as a nod, he began loading the dirty dishes, over-stacking them into the crate. Salad plates, desert plates, wine and water glasses, and lastly the heavy dinner plates, sticky with congealed sauces and the greasy leftovers of red meat.

He walked out of the building and stood for a few moments on the top step, noting that the snow had thickened into large white slippery flakes. He reached for the banister just as the door opened and a flash of light brightened the dark landing. He felt his back prickle and inhaled, filling his lungs with biting winter air and a sexy scent of vanilla.

"Hi again." Her voice was soft, having lost the earlier snooty tone.

As he turned to her his footing slipped on an icy patch and he briefly stumbled, a mere skid before he regained his balance, but enough for a plate to slide off, where it skimmed the side of the metal banister, clipping a large chunk before falling onto the snow-cushioned ground.

"Oh no!" she exclaimed, and then suddenly burst into laughter. "We sure break a lot of plates. We better not ever live together."

Nate's lips curled into a smile of joy, and in that moment, cold, tired, aching, he realized that he desperately wanted to sleep with her. And Nate, who not only did not believe in love at first sight, but who didn't much believe in love at all, sensed that he could spend the rest of his life desiring this woman.

On the day Lisa moved out, Nate stayed home from work, sat down by the fireplace and calmly proceeded to drink close to a full bottle of Jack Daniels, taking large burning gulps until the room spun so much he could barely weave his way to the bathroom where he puked into the bathtub and onto the floor. Spent, he forced himself to stagger back to the den. He collapsed into the bean bag chair and stared at the ceiling, fantasizing about how it would feel to smash each of their own china plates—moderate Noritake they'd selected together and bought wholesale through the business.

The next morning he called in sick, but the day after, and all the following days, Nate worked nearly round the clock, pouring himself into other peoples' parties until his brain and heart were numbed.

Alan kept telling Nate to accept their separation in stride. "Trust me, man. It's gonna be a hell of a lot harder on her. You can grab yourself a young piece of fertile ass and put all that unpleasant business behind you." Alan had actually smirked when he said it.

Then today, while loading the truck, he'd stumbled and nearly dropped an entire case of china plates. As he regained his balance, he was gripped by a sense of overwhelming and sudden grief. With deliberate care, he placed the crate into the truck before he slumped to the ground, put his face into his hands, and began to cry. Alan came round and squeezed both of Nate's shoulders from behind. "It'll pass, buddy. It always does. It hurts like fucking hell, and then it doesn't."

Nate didn't bother to answer. Instead, he climbed into his truck and drove to Clara Road.

Chapter Seventeen

With a sense of apprehension, Lisa punched the last number and waited during the customary eight rings for her mother to pick up the phone.

"Could you hold on just a moment, dear?" and without pausing for a response Jeanette clicked over to call waiting. Lisa was about five seconds from hanging up when her mom came back.

"Sorry, it was somebody trying to sell me a lifetime of light bulbs. I couldn't get rid of him until I agreed to a six-month trial." Her voice was breathy, a sign her asthma was flaring again.

"We've talked about that. You and Dad have got to stop falling for these schemes."

"The light bulbs sound perfect. Think of it, never having to change a bulb again for the rest of your life."

Lisa cleared her throat to keep from laughing, then immediately felt a pang of regret. There was little humor in her parents if she couldn't share it with Nate.

"You saw Nate?" Jeanette asked.

"How do you know?"

"Just wait a sec, dear." Again, she put Lisa on hold, this time for even longer. Lisa slowly counted backwards from ten, straining to contain her annoyance as she gave her mother time to come up with a reasonable explanation for staying in touch with Nate. Before the separation, Jeanette had always found Nate lacking. Now, apparently, he served a new purpose.

Jeanette wheezed into the phone. "He's still my son-in-law, right?" When Lisa didn't respond, she added, "I know you don't want to hear this, but you're a damned fool to throw away a husband and a beautiful house in order to live with a bunch of delinquents."

Lisa hung up the phone.

Nearly five minutes passed before Jeanette called back. Lisa let it go to voice mail twice before answering. It was an old game, one they should have long since out-grown, but there it still was.

Before Lisa even said hello, Jeanette continued, her voice rising. "Okay, I shouldn't have called them delinquents. That's not right. And God forbid if I refer to the color of their skin, right, Lisa? As you reminded me last week, you're no longer in Minnesota and they actually—let's see, what were your words?—'allow dark-skinned people into St. Louis.' As if I care one iota about something like that. Really! Since when did a daughter of mine become so touchy?"

This was the point in their conversation when Lisa would have motioned to Nate to shout that she needed to get off the phone so they could leave for somewhere, anywhere. Finally, after enough silence to know that Jeanette wasn't going to apologize or relent, Lisa couldn't stop herself from saying, "You were never all that crazy about Nate. So what's the deal now?"

"Sweetie. Nate's fine. He turned out to be a better man than I realized. I've told you that. Mainly I worry about you. Alone." Lisa willed herself not to start crying. She glanced around the kitchen. There was a new chip on the countertop. She flipped off the light switch and had a thought—how would her parents know after only six months if the "lifetime" bulbs were for real?

"So how's Dad?"

"Something is really wrong. Two nights ago I found him about to urinate in the kitchen sink in the middle of the night. And that doctor I told you about won't see him for another month."

"Oh, no, Mom. I didn't realize..."

"Of course you didn't realize," Jeanette snapped. "You're down there taking care of strangers, and your sister is off doing her *thing,* and I'm the only one here."

Lisa pressed the phone closer to her ear, listening past the inflection. Maybe her mother was exaggerating or "too much drama," as the girls would say. After all, didn't a lot of older people get confused at times, especially at night? And her dad had always been spacey. But she let her mom talk, every so often offering a "hmm" or "go on." Clearly her mom needed a supportive ear and the sound of Jeanette's voice in the GIFT House kitchen, despite the words, was oddly comforting. Ever since Nate's visit, Lisa had been restless and dispirited. The ache of loneliness again had a name and a face. She still needed to feel part of a bigger whole, and right now only her mom could do that.

Jeanette finally wound down, exhausted and out of breath.

"Obviously you'll let me know what the doctor says. And, Mom, if it gets worse sooner, then you need to call and make them see Dad right away. Okay?" When Jeanette didn't respond, Lisa added, "I've got to get going. But I'll call you tomorrow."

"Lisa?" Her voice was barely a whisper. "I have something important to say. And I want you to really listen to me."

She stiffened.

"You don't want to grow old alone. Please, honey. Don't be a fool."

Lisa caught back a sob, disarmed by the gentle love in her mother's tone. "I've gotta go, Ma." Her hand was shaking so hard it took two tries to hang up the receiver.

A familiar wave of panic took hold as Lisa stumbled to her room and slid into bed. She pulled the comforter up to her chin and stared at the ceiling, her whole body icy cold, trying to shake off the dread that something terrible was happening to her dad. Every time she closed her eyes she saw an image of her Dad *peeing in the kitchen sink*. When she could no longer resist the pull, knowing she'd be sorry but powerless to fight, Lisa got up, opened the closet door, and retrieved from the top shelf the carefully hidden, half-completed pastel blue blanket. Taking care not to jab her eye with the knitting needle within its folds, she buried her face against the soft yarn and wept.

"Let yourself feel the sadness," the grief counselor advised. "It won't kill you. It just feels like it will."

After losing the twins, Lisa hung on to the counselor's every word. She attended his monthly support groups and occasional one-on-one sessions. She even sought solace in a meeting with the kindly Rabbi Ben Feldman, whose congregation was one mile from their home. "Why would I lose three babies?" she implored, to which the rabbi responded, "The challenge will be to figure that out and find comfort in the answer." She cried, pounded pillows and scribbled in a journal. Then, finally, as promised, scabs formed and Lisa was ready to try again.

Nate had been wonderful—patient, understanding, unusually communicative. He was confident they could create a family. Long gone was the Nate who'd offered to take off work for an abortion.

They turned down an invitation to go out with co-workers and instead spent New Year's Eve alone. By the end of the holiday weekend, the king-sized bed was littered with discarded newspapers, carry-out containers, dirty dishes, massage oil bottles and sticky wine glasses. Lisa no longer felt self-conscious about Nate seeing her naked despite the seven pounds and sagging skin leftover from her pregnancy with the twins. For the first time in over a year, Lisa found herself giggling for no reason.

She vowed it would be different this time. She would continue to focus on work and on her marriage and not count the days until her period was due. But just to be prudent, she began drinking a tall glass of cold milk with dinner and popping the horse-pill-sized prenatal vitamins with breakfast. When the pregnancy test came back positive two weeks later, Nate quipped, "Damn. I was hoping we'd need lots of practice." Yet, he, too, was thrilled. Holding hands as they walked toward the car after the Ob/Gyn appointment, they decided not to tell anyone for three months, nor would they plan beyond the moment.

It was a productive time of helping clients. It was a quiet, close time with Nate. So that when, at ten weeks, they heard the heartbeat, and at sixteen weeks saw on the ultrasound screen that their baby had a penis, Lisa felt a surprising twinge of misgiving that her wonderfully constructed world of Nate and work was going to irrevocably change. But it was only a twinge, and it passed as soon as she heard the joy in her parents' voices when she was finally able to call home and announce, "Well, Grandma and Grandpa, looks like this one is a keeper."

The day Lisa bought her first maternity outfit, she teared up in the store. The night Nate came home with a pint-sized Cardinals baseball cap, she outright cried in his arms. At eighteen weeks, she was sitting in a client meeting when a fish swam across her belly. "Oh!" she exclaimed with dawning realization and astounded joy. The next day Nate and Lisa went crib shopping. They agreed on pecan wood, but decided it might be bad luck to bring anything home until nearer to the due date. Still, they couldn't stop themselves from leaning over the showroom crib rail and bantering.

"I like Sam."

"Too ordinary. What about Seymour?"

"You're joking, right?"

"Solomon?"

"Are you insane?"

The frivolity lasted three more days. Then Lisa went in for a mid-pregnancy ultrasound. The technician kept moving the paddle over the same area and taking too many still photos. When she pardoned herself to go get the doctor, Lisa squeezed Nate's hand so tight she felt his fingers spasm. The doctor's voice had the careful modulation of someone trained to deliver disturbing news.

The baby was too small, with suspicious spots on his abdomen. It likely was nothing, but to be safe, they would run some more tests. Lisa and Nate were sent to another floor in the hospital for blood work and an amniocentesis. It would be two weeks until all the results came back.

At first they told no one, having neither the vocabulary, nor the strength, to form the words. But as the days dragged on, eventually Lisa shared her agony with her mom and Bonnie and even with a couple of co-workers. The following week she shared her delight with those same people as every several days they received a call about another test result. "The baby doesn't have cystic fibrosis." "The baby doesn't have neural tube defect." Nor did their son have RSV or a prenatal viral infection. His heartbeat was strong, all the blood work normal. Every test back but one.

One afternoon Lisa glanced out of the second-story bedroom window and spotted Nate propped against the sapling they'd planted after the first miscarriage, the week of the twins' conception. The tree had thickened and grown taller, but it appeared flimsy beside Nate's broad shoulders.

That night as they were leaving to go out to dinner the phone rang. Lisa let Nate talk to the doctor. As soon as she heard his tone, she walked out of the room and went to bed.

They spent several stressful days exploring options. Nate insisted they had no other choice. Why would they wait to continue this pregnancy knowing that there was a ninety-nine percent chance their son would die in utero, putting Lisa's own life at risk? If the baby survived pregnancy and delivery, he would never go home from the hospital and would not live to his first birthday. "But what if they're wrong?" Lisa insisted, to which Nate replied, "Honey, we know they're not wrong. And I won't take the chance of anything happening to you"—a response that made her love, and hate, him more than at any other time. Jeanette agreed with Nate, as did her obstetrician. Bonnie's response was just as definite. "I love you, Lisa girl. Please don't risk your life." So she called the counselor she'd seen after the twins. "You don't want to do this alone," he said. Beaten, she gave in.

It was a fluke—this time truly—for someone so young to have a baby with Trisomy 18, a fatal chromosomal abnormality usually only seen in older mothers.

The next day Lisa entered the hospital. Because she was nearly six months pregnant, she would need to deliver the baby. The intravenous medicine would induce labor within four to forty-eight hours. She was instructed to ask for anesthesia when the pain became intense.

The hours slogged by. Nurses came in to speak the language of obstetrics. Was she dilated? Had her cervix softened? Were her labor pains increasing?

And there were other questions. Would they hold the baby? Name him? Photograph him? Bury him?

Nate did not leave her side the entire two days until their stillborn baby was finally delivered. Then he bolted from the room. Lisa could hear him bang his head against the wall, slide down to the floor and felt each of his wracking sobs as though he were in her arms soaking her chest with his grief.

Her parents had flown down and neither of them could stop crying. But Lisa wouldn't cry, not yet. She knew too well there would be much time for that later. Instead she found the strength to reach her arms out for the baby, though she needed only the small of one palm to hold him. "Sam," Lisa whispered, as she examined her son with the tenderness and curiosity of any mother cradling her newly delivered infant. The skin on the back of his neck was thick. His fingers were malformed and his ears were too low. His eyes were sealed shut and his mouth was pursed as though about to cry. He had two arms, two legs, a small curved back, and ten little webbed toes. Lisa placed her mouth against his cold forehead and kissed him, the bitter taste of birthing fluid burning her lips and lingering on her tongue.

Lisa had the paradoxical sensation of wanting to thrust the baby back to the nurse and of wanting to never let him go. She could not later say in response to Nate's questions how long she held their son or who took him away. "One moment I blinked and I never saw him again."

They'd decided to donate his little body to science for research, so there would be no funeral. But later that evening, Rabbi Feldman conducted a brief memorial service. "Most of us stumble through our first experience as parents, having no idea how precious and miraculous it all is. This baby will leave for you a lasting gift. You will be better parents because of him."

Lisa knew differently. She could not go through this again. Ever. It was over.

CHAPTER EIGHTEEN

The day after she cried into Sam's blanket was a low day, perhaps the worst since moving into the GIFT House. Lisa got the girls off in the morning, forced herself an hour before they came home to take a shower and get dressed, and otherwise spent the entire time in bed crying. Oh, Sam. So sweet and little and damaged. Hairless, he'd resembled an old bald man with the soft creamy skin of an infant. She opened her palm and could almost feel him filling it. Then she drew a fist and slammed it against her pillow. "Fuck!" she shouted into the empty room. "Sam!"

The next morning she called Bonnie. "911-Girlfriend, I need you. I did a stupid thing yesterday."

"Get your butt to that park right now. I'll try to sneak out for a quick walk at the same time."

"Can you sneak out for three or four days?"

"Ha. I wish. It's this stupid promotion. I can't get away from work anymore." She must have heard Lisa's sniff because she quickly added, "Call when you get there. I should be able to talk for about twenty minutes."

It took nearly an hour to gather the energy to pull on her workout clothes and drive the three miles to Forest Park. But almost immediately, Lisa could feel the fog dissipate enough to clarify what was actually the most nagging question when Bonnie answered her call. "You think I should try to make it work with Nate again?"

"What I really think is you've made a commitment to this job. You owe it to yourself and to those girls to stick it out. At least for now."

"But if I wasn't doing this job? Then what would you tell me?" Lisa leaned down to double knot her laces and when Bonnie still hadn't answered, she began to walk, holding the phone close to her ear with her right hand, swinging her left arm to get the momentum the person in front of her seemed to have

Finally Bonnie asked, "What's changed since you guys split? What would be different?"

Lisa didn't respond and Bonnie granted her the silence as they both walked, two hundred miles apart, the wind in Bonnie's background ringing through the phone on this too-warm St. Louis autumn day. She was grateful for the noise. Hopefully, it helped to disguise her own huffing and puffing. Unlike Lisa, Bonnie had stayed slim and fit, looking just as good as when they met at Carlton freshman year of college in their one required gym class.

On that first day, in a room full of tall slender blondes, Bonnie was the only other Jewish-looking brunette and they both were the only two in old and mismatched work-out clothes. They'd gravitated to one another immediately. The fact that they shared a similar sense of humor became instantly apparent when Bonnie leaned close and whispered to Lisa, "Call me crazy, but did we stumble into a Scandinavian sorority rush?" which caused Lisa to laugh too loudly, at the wrong time, and that fast they became friends.

"Listen, I need to talk about something," Bonnie said.

"Hell no. I've got exclusive rights this go-round." When Bonnie didn't offer an appreciative giggle, Lisa asked, "What's going on?"

"Mom called last night. Her mammogram looked bad, so they had her come in for an ultrasound and they saw a mass."

"Bonnie, why didn't you tell me? You're letting me go on and on about my shit when you've got this to worry about." Without thinking, she touched her own breasts then noticed a young man across the field staring. Immediately she dropped her hands to her side and turned in another direction. "What are they going to do?

"On Friday she'll have a biopsy. I'm going to try to fly out there to be with her."

"You want me to come with you?"

Bonnie hesitated so long Lisa found her mind wandering to what she would tell Sheila and where she'd get the money. She'd saved enough from her previous job, and surely Sheila would give her a few personal days. But before she could take the plans any further, Bonnie said, "Absolutely not. Don't make it so scary."

"Look, the majority of breast lumps are benign. But just say the word and I'm sitting next to you on that plane."

Bonnie's voice choked, "Let's change the subject. I can't cry. I've got to get back to work now. Tell me fast what you did yesterday that was so stupid."

"No, you have enough on your plate."

"Lis?

That same young man was now just steps behind her. Lisa slowed down and waited until he'd walked on and was no longer within hearing distance. "I went through the baby box. And I almost ripped apart Sam's blanket. I could have so easily pulled the needle out and rolled the yarn into a ball. Or better yet, cut the little fucker to shreds."

"But you didn't? See how well adjusted you are."

"Yeah. Sure." She scooted aside as a rollerblader zoomed past on her left and then hopped back to the other side as a bicyclist whizzed by on her right. Moments later, the mother up ahead had to do the same with her toddler, scooping the baby into her arms as if to save his life. Lisa watched as she cuddled the child close, planting a noisy kiss on his head before putting him back down, walking hand in hand.

Lisa plopped onto the nearest bench. She made a decision. "Bonnie, can I tell you something I've never told anyone? Not even Berger."

"Go on."

She pulled her feet up to the bench and leaned into her knees, head down, dropping her voice to a near whisper. "You know how I smoked for a while after the twins? Stupid, I know. Like who starts smoking in her thirties? Anyway, after I tell you this, you have to promise never to bring it up to me again."

"You know I do."

"Well, I had quit smoking, but then, I don't know, I guess I was so nervous about the pregnancy and all... anyway, I smoked for like three weeks right after finding out I was pregnant with Sam."

"Okay."

She held the phone away, shook her head at it. "Bonnie, don't you hear what I'm saying? He had a defect. How do you think he got it?"

"Oh, Lisa. The doctor *told* you. The baby's chromosomal defect was not caused by anything you did or could have done. Sometimes these things just happen and we never know why." Bonnie's voice grew more emphatic, so she was almost shouting, "But listen to me and this is really important. You are having a dip, that's why you're thinking about this. You saw Nate. Your dad's acting scary. *But you are going to be okay.* I promise. It is not like last time."

She popped up, trembling with such a tangle of emotions she couldn't keep her legs still. She started walking faster, neither of them speaking for nearly a quarter of a mile. A rarity but enough space for Lisa to capture her breath. "Thank you, Bon. Really. And that's enough about me. So did your boss finally put in the paper work for your raise?"

Bonnie scoffed. "Yeah. It only took about a hundred reminders. Speaking of which, I'm back at the office. I gotta go. I love you."

Lisa was smiling when she hung up. The walk with Bonnie—something they'd shared in college and all these years and miles later still shared—had revived her spirits. She'd reached the two-mile mark but instead of circling back, Lisa decided to push forward. The park's asphalt path was more crowded today than she'd seen it, no doubt due to what might be the last warm day of the season. Several times she had to jump to the side as more rollerbladers, bikers and runners sped past. It was nice to note the variety of ages, skin tones and ethnicities, something she'd rarely seen in her early-married days of jogging in the suburban park near Nate's and her house. Back then, she never would have considered coming down to Forest Park alone, even in the daylight, knowing that it was on the wrong side of Skinker Boulevard. Ironically, Forest Park now seemed safe and comforting in comparison to her GIFT House neighborhood, and she felt a sudden sense of pride to be part of the diversity, in one of the most polarized city-counties in the country. For the first time

113

in her life, she was not only working her values, but living them too.

She headed back to her car with a renewed determination to make the GIFT House job a success. This was her do-over. She would need to make it work. She would get these girls to love her.

Plus, as Bonnie would have said aloud were they still on the phone, let's be honest here, Lis, you don't have a better plan B.

The day of crying—followed by the brisk walk—lifted a weight off of Lisa, and surprisingly what ensued in the days following was a pleasant sense of floating in a bubble, when Lisa and all three girls actually pulled together. Those crisp-air, leaf-changing, pre-holiday-season weeks were for the most part uneventful, and, as such, special and safe.

Bonnie's mother's biopsy came back benign. At the same time, Jeanette seemed less concerned about Albert—no new disturbing incidences to report, so Lisa decided to hope for the best and not dwell on the potential worst. Nate's visit and the image of his red truck tail lights disappearing down Clara Road continued to haunt Lisa until one morning—after getting all three girls off to school without a single squabble or complaint—she again summoned the ability to throw herself into *this* life and place Nate out of her mind.

The neighbor's house explosion also contributed to the change. In the past, Lisa had very purposefully worked to hide from the girls the extent of her anxiety about the neighborhood. But they'd shared this fear, and for a number of days after the fire, they all hunkered down inside their house, shaky, not daring to go out unless together. Suddenly, there was an *us* and a *them*, with Lisa the center of *us*.

Dinners were pleasant as all four exchanged the day-to-day updates of people who live under the same roof. Mornings were still hectic, but probably no more so than any family. Lisa would stand at the kitchen window and watch the three of them dash for the school bus stop. Though they often walked home at the end of the day, they took the bus in the morning.

They were always running late, but had established a system in which one of them would grab the three lunches while the fastest runner—usually Brianna—would race to the bus stop and dawdle there so that the driver had to hold up for the others. They seemed like sisters then and Lisa, watching with equal measures of amusement and annoyance, felt how she imagined a mother would feel.

After they left, she'd go into their rooms, gather their discarded clothes and do their laundry. She liked how who wore what characterized the girls. The Stone Charter students were required to wear khaki pants and a collared red or gold uniform shirt, but they could cover all but the collar with anything "appropriate." Despite a full closet, Coreen wore the same zippered pink sweatshirt every single day. Brianna rotated several plain sweaters in muted tones. Only Danesha bothered to add flair to the uniform—a turned collar, a blazing red scarf or a jumble of inexpensive necklace chains.

Of course, not unlike the mother of teens everywhere, Lisa had no idea that even as they collectively appeared to be at peace, in truth, each of the girls held her own closely guarded secret. Danesha was continually plotting how to get the money for the lawyer to get her brother out of prison. In her fourteen-year-old mind it was that simple, and that essential. Twice she had written a letter to Jerrell trying to explain how she knew best and twice she tore it into shreds without sending. But that was okay. She would just have to surprise him with her success. Brianna was passing time until her mother sent for her. Or, until she could find her father again. Or, maybe, until Devon realized who he was missing. Coreen was concealing her emotions, as she'd been doing her whole life, putting forth the face that others wanted to see and making sure that no one suspected otherwise. She'd long ago learned that fat girls were invisible, dull girls invited few questions, and when all else failed, babble covered up what she wasn't saying.

The girls continued to meet monthly with a case worker and have weekly counseling sessions with Sheila Johnson. Lisa realized there was much she couldn't know, but she consoled herself that the safety net for each of them held strong. And, for this little while, under their roof, life was mostly sweet.

Together, they went to see Coreen perform as Diana Ross, and their applause was the loudest and most enthusiastic in the room. Driving back even Danesha raved about Coreen's performance. "Girl, you was *ratchet* up there. Where'd you learn all that shit?"

Coreen stopped her shrug just in time and muttered, "Thanks." She seemed to hesitate, and in the rearview mirror Lisa could see Coreen's face open as if a layer were being peeled away. "Well, when I was nine, my mama's boyfriend..."

"Oh no!" Brianna moaned, interrupting as they pulled into the driveway. Someone had smashed the two GIFT House pumpkins, leaving a trail of gooey strands and seeds all over the door, porch and steps. One of their windows was egged and the lone tree in front had been TPed.

They cleaned up the mess, working quickly as a team. Afterwards, Lisa gave them each a large bag of assorted candies, which they immediately set about swapping and bickering over. Even after the girls had gone upstairs, Lisa could hear them trading, harkening Lisa back to the childhood ritual she'd shared with her own sister. On impulse she called Kate but hung up when voice mail answered. They hadn't spoken in months, but leaving the message, "Do you still love Almond Joys?" felt ridiculous.

A cough and sore throat virus swept through the house, sending all of them to bed for several days, except for Lisa, who ignored her own symptoms to tend to the girls' misery. They were just recuperating when one afternoon the furnace died. To wait out the chilly hours before a repairman came, they went to the movies. Lisa didn't notice until they were walking out that she was the only white person in the theater, and then she was too busy talking with the girls to feel uneasy.

The weather began to turn, with a blustery wind that scurried the leaves to the ground, portending the inevitable gloom of winter. Lisa fought against her usual despondency from the waning hours of sunlight by eating more (and, unfortunately, walking less). She imagined Dr. Berger would say that she ate to fill a hole. Or to make herself undesirable so a marital decision could be made *for* her, rather than *by* her. Maybe it was for both reasons, maybe for neither. All Lisa knew was that food suddenly tasted particularly glorious, bursting with flavors in her mouth and warming her insides as it went down. Sweet, sour, spicy, salty—everything was game. As her sweat pants waists stretched to discomfort, she couldn't resist the lure of peanut butter, chocolate cake, potato chips, double portions at every meal. Once in a while she'd dare to study herself in the mirror and wonder that she could become so heavy and shabby and not even care.

Several weeks before Thanksgiving, Lisa did decide to take a personal beauty day. She called and asked Vanessa to fill in for the entire afternoon. Lisa drove out to the suburbs, back to the salon where Robby, her hairdresser of ten years, was unsuccessful at stifling his dismay when he saw what had happened in the months since she'd last been there. Diplomatically, he ignored her size. He didn't, however, resist chiding Lisa for the "disgrace" of her hair. She told him not to touch the color, and after a few exaggerated gasps and clenches of fist to his heart, Robby compromised by reshaping the layers so the roots seemed to blend rather than look like what they were—an ever-thickening dark line of neglect.

Lisa went to Robby because she liked what he did for her hair. More importantly, as most any woman would admit, Lisa went to Robby because she liked him.

That day she sat in the center of the haute couture salon, listening as women complained about their maids, "impossible to find one who really cleans anymore," about their nails, "damn if I didn't chip my polish as soon as I got home last week," about their perfect babies from their perfect bodies, "I just don't know how I can bear another sleepless night," about their cars, "can you even believe how much it cost me to fill my Lexus?" Listening to these conversations she'd been hearing—though never liking—for years, Lisa found herself becoming edgy and light-headed. She shut her eyes to discourage having to make small talk with Robby, but with closed eyes the chirping grew louder. The lousy connecting flights between St.

117

Louis and Europe. The leak in the hot tub that ruined the newly laid ceramic tile. The difficulties of making soccer practice in time when the carpool line at the private middle school was so slow.

The week before, Coreen had matter of factly stated that one of the best parts about going to Stone Charter was that for the first time in her life she now regularly got three meals a day. Danesha had immediately quipped that that was why Coreen was such a thick-ass, but there was a defensive acknowledgement in her retort. The high-fat burger, off-brand macaroni and cheese, and canned peaches were at least something these girls could count on.

Lisa canceled her manicure and pedicure. She no longer had the stomach for such indulgence. She put the haircut, tip and mousse on her charge, totaling ninety-six dollars—the price of an overflowing cart of Shop 'n Save groceries. Driving home to the GIFT House she mused on the girls' near obsession with their hair. The first Saturday of every month Sheila took all three girls to get "styling" at a friend of hers who didn't charge them. Once Lisa asked to go along, momentarily considering having scratchy synthetic (blonde?) plaits braided onto her own scalp and not having to brush her hair for a month. But all four had made it clear Lisa was not invited. "You ain't black, Miss Lisa. It'd just be too weird," Danesha had blurted. "Plus, you don't really care none 'bout your hair anyways." Thinking about it now, Lisa realized she probably wouldn't have been any less comfortable there than she was at Robby's salon, and it was just as well she didn't "care none" about her hair since she didn't seem to fit in anywhere anymore.

With the approaching holiday season, Lisa decided to increase her volunteer hours at Stone Charter. The timing was fortuitous; the Missouri standardized test scores had been released and analyzed and for the fourth straight year, Stone Charter students did not make the grade. In fact, they didn't even come close.

Lisa set up a meeting with Ron Stone and found a very troubled Sheila Johnson also waiting in the principal's office.

"We are in a desperate situation," Sheila said by way of a greeting. She shoved the packet of test results across the desk, and waited as Lisa scanned a report that was alarming even to the untrained eye. On average, the school had scored three to four full grades below standard level, with nearly twenty percent of the student body too low to even register. Of the GIFT House girls, only Brianna was nearing proficient, with the other two above the school average but lower than where they needed to be for ninth grade.

"We stand to lose all our funding if we can't pull these scores up this spring," Ron said, his voice catching. "Or, hell, they could keep the school open but come in and fire us all."

Sheila walked to the glass window that separated Ron's office from the Commons. Students were milling about, enjoying their minutes of freedom between lunch and fourth hour. Sheila balled her hands into fists as if preparing for a fight. "'No Child Left Behind?' What a crock! Half these kids don't know where they'll be staying next week, and they're supposed to diagram a sentence? I know it's an excuse, but it's also reality." She rubbed the side of her head with the ball of her thumb.

"Head hurt?" Lisa asked.

"More of a heartache, I suppose. This school may not be perfect, but I don't know of a better place to send them. As if that matters. No, let's just shut the damn place down. Force the kids out to the streets like a bunch of rats."

Ron had once told Lisa that one of the first tough lessons he had learned was that he couldn't save them all. But he would never give up so long as he could save some. He appeared now as if about to cry. Lisa wasn't sure whether she should pat his shoulder or leave him alone. Then it hit—if the school closed so too would the GIFT House.

"Uh, I'll do what I can to help."

So without any formal agreement, Lisa began volunteering daily at Stone Charter, pulling kids one at a time and in groups, tutoring them, bolstering them, offering whatever tools she could, at times having Vanessa stay with the GIFT House girls so Lisa could work longer hours with other

119

students. She found the work with the teens (the ones she didn't *live with*) deeply satisfying and wondered that she had waited so many months to dive in.

In between sessions she would sometimes hang out in Sheila's office, finding that the more they shared the easier they grew with one another. It was the first new friend Lisa had made in a long time and the potential often left her smiling for hours after leaving the school.

Without consciously acknowledging it even to herself, she was becoming ever more entrenched in this new life.

Then Nate returned, the doorbell rang, and the bubble burst.

CHAPTER NINETEEN

He waited a full month. When he couldn't stand it anymore, overcome by curiosity and by the sense that he needed to save Lisa from herself, Nate loaded up his truck with his toolbox, stopped by Home Depot, and retraced his route to Clara Road.

With grim irony, he again stumbled on the loose stair, jabbing his ribs with the hammer he'd shoved into his coat pocket. He pressed against the door bell and when it didn't budge he knocked, the hollow sound revealing the door's flimsiness. He pounded harder, waited, pounded again, and was turning to go when he heard a hesitant, "Who's there?" as the door inched open and a brown eye peered out.

"It's Mr. Rothman."

"Who?"

He moved closer, trying to see if he recognized the speaker, but as he did so she slammed the door shut. He knocked again, this time more gently, and shouted, "I'm Miss Lisa's friend. We met several weeks ago."

The door swung open. "Oh, yeah, now I remember you. Miss Lisa ain't here," she hesitated, "but I guess you can come in."

The living room was even drearier than he recalled. But the girl's smile brightened the bleakness and Nate felt unexpectedly cheered just to be there. He pulled the hammer and a handful of large nails out of his jacket pocket. "If it's okay with you...Coreen, right?...and with Miss Lisa, I thought I'd fix those front steps. I think I've got a doorbell kit in my truck too. You mind if I replace that old one?"

She shrugged in response, her thick shoulders and large breasts moving up and down. "I need to go check with Miss Vanessa." She disappeared down a dark hallway, and moments later returned, followed by a full-figured young woman, who flashed a glistening smile.

"Welcome to the GIFT House. Coreen tells me you're here to fix up them steps and some other repairs. 'Bout time. I nearly kill myself whenever I come here."

Nate sputtered, "Well, actually. . ." but before he could clear up the misconception, she thrust out her hand for a hearty shake.

"Name's Vanessa Morrison. And you're?"

"Mr. Rothman. No, well, Mr. Nate. Or just Nate?"

Her laugh filled the room. "You got yourself a lot of names," she said, winking. "And, now, excuse me. I've got work to do myself."

Nate couldn't stop his eyes from following as she sashayed away, her youth and curves set to advantage by the fitted black jeans and lime-green blouse. *A lot of woman*, he thought, then noticed Coreen noticing him. "Hey, want to help me?" he asked, heading out the door.

Coreen followed Nate to the truck for his tool box and back to the porch. As he hammered nails into the stairs, she chattered, barely pausing for breath.

"I like being here. I thought it would be worse, you know, staying with strangers. Only it ain't so bad. First time I've got my own room. And only three of us sharing the upstairs bathroom. You probably don't think much about that, 'cept one time I stayed with eleven of us and only one bathroom. See, my daddy's side, he's got seven other kids, and then his wife, she's got four, no, five kids now, but some of them stay with their daddy. Anyway, that was the worst. When I was with my auntie it was just me and my cousin and her baby sharing a room, so that was 'aight. Now I can take a shower whenever I want 'cause Brianna mostly stay in her room and Danesha always gone or hiding to keep away from us. Miss Lisa is real quick in the shower. It's almost like she don't care how she look. Don't you think?"

Nate didn't answer, transported to a steamy lavender-scented bathroom, the hot water cooled to warm, his and Lisa's bodies locked in a soapy embrace, backed against the shower stall wall, her whispers against his drenched ears, "It's *so* good, Nate." His knees buckling and sliding down together as the water continued to beat against her breasts, his thighs, until they pulled apart, laughing as they tried to shake the water out of their ears, standing to turn off the shower, and his legs buckled again. The day they found out she was pregnant with their son.

He snapped back, aware that Coreen was staring with open expectancy. "I'm sorry, what'd you ask?"

That fast, her face shut down. It was subtle, yet he saw suddenly a filming in her eyes that had not been there before. He felt shamed, sensing that the child had spent much of her life not being heard.

"Please, Coreen."

She scuffed her shoes against the ground, head down, and muttered, "Wasn't nothin' important."

He wanted to touch her shoulder. Instead he reached his hand out, beckoning for her to hold the screwdriver for him. But something had shifted and he worked on the doorbell's rewiring in silence. As he suspected might be the case in any project involving this house, the overall disrepair made the challenge greater than it should have been. Finally, he tightened the two small screws and turned to Coreen. "Give it a go?"

She pressed her finger against the doorbell and smiled with delight when the rhythmic chime rang out. She pressed again, and then several more times, until they were both grinning at their shared success, when they heard, "What the fuck. I was trying to sleep." Standing in the doorway, fingers fisted, tousled and scowling, was the dark-skinned girl.

"Hey, Danesha, remember Miss Lisa's friend, Mr. Nate?"

With chameleon-like mastery, her demeanor immediately transformed. She leaned into the door jamb, jutting out a sharp hip and straightening her shoulders to push her chest upward and out. Nate fought to conceal his dismay.

"Why, Mr. Nate. It's so nice to see you again. Did you come to visit us? Or," she raised her eyebrows, "are you looking for Miss Lisa. Because she ain't here. Said she was going over to the school, but who really knows where she goes?"

"Don't be such a jerk," Coreen snapped.

Nate picked up his toolbox to leave, then spotted the third girl, the little one, standing just inside the door, eyes wary. On impulse he asked, "Mind if I come in and rest a while?"

"We got to ask Miss Vanessa first," Coreen said.

Danesha shoved her aside. "Miss Vanessa said don't disturb her 'til she done studying. Anyway, she don't care and she's just down the hall anyways."

He sat behind the kitchen table and was pleased when all three girls took a seat too. "So what's your favorite subject in school?" he asked, throwing into the room the first question he could think of.

They exchanged looks and no one bothered to answer.

"Well, do you have a favorite teacher?"

This time Danesha actually rolled her eyes.

He forced out a laugh, trying to cover his discomfort. Damn! Could he be more lame? But what did someone say to girls like this? He wouldn't dare ask about their families and, as much as he wanted, even he knew not to pump them for information about Lisa. So instead he settled deeper into the chair, trying his best to be invisible as he listened to their idle conversations. They were each different from one another, and they didn't seem to actually like each other. Yet there was a connection between them that made him feel lonely and old. Nate didn't usually spend time with kids. As a younger man, he'd never had the interest. In recent years, it had been too painful, a constant reminder of what had eluded them. But as their banter continued—they were actively disagreeing about the *finest* singers and actors, each claiming that Miss Vanessa agreed with *her*—he glimpsed a first hint at why Lisa lived in the GIFT House. And thinking about Lisa, he also glimpsed possibility.

"Hey, anyone hungry for pizza?" he asked.

Vanessa and the three girls were sprawled around the kitchen table, a large empty pizza box in the middle. And Nate. He was sitting there too. And all of them were laughing together.

At first Lisa was genuinely confused, and then, as she fully took in the scene, she felt a surge of anger and betrayal. "Nate! What are you doing here?" She could hear a shrill in her voice and saw the startled expressions on each of the girl's faces. Even Danesha seemed to fold in on herself. But all of this registered later when she replayed the scene. At the time, she only saw Nate. How the blood drained out of his face. How he sat up rigidly in a defensive posture. How he had the audacity to look to the girls and to Vanessa for support. Coreen shrugged in response to Nate's unspoken appeal. It wasn't her usual avoidance shrug, but a genuine *don't ask me what's wrong* gesture.

Lisa clasped her hands for control so that her tone was even, her words carefully measured. "Well, girls, since you've already eaten without me, go upstairs right this minute and finish your homework."

"Aw, Miss Lisa..."

"And, Danesha, it's your turn to clean up this mess. During your study break."

Brianna popped up and began clearing her plate, as Coreen slowly stood, her face blank. Danesha didn't bother to hide her disgust as she shoved the chair against the wall and kicked the table leg. "*Go upstairs. Do your homework*. It's all you ever fucking say," she sneered. "You can't tell me what to do. You're not my mother!"

"No, I'm not your mother. And look what your mother..." She stopped, choked back the words, horrified by what she almost said. Lisa whipped the air with her hand, a terse "go, go," and watched as Danesha scurried out of the room, cursing under her breath, followed closely by the other two. She waited until all three bedroom doors had been slammed shut and Vanessa had hurried out, muttering that she'd be back on Friday. Then she turned so fiercely to Nate, she wrenched her neck. "What the hell do you think you're up to? Bringing over pizza?"

"Wow, why are you so pissed?"

"Are you kidding? Why am I pissed? The deal was it was up to me *if* I would contact you. And we never, ever, said anything about you being here with the girls." She paused, rubbing her neck. "Jesus, Nate, have you no sense at all?" As he opened his mouth to speak, she snapped, "And don't even try to tell me Vanessa said it was ok. She's not in charge, I am. She should be fired for this. Shit, I could get fired. And you could get arrested. These girls are in ninth grade." *These girls were already laughing with you. They hardly ever laugh with me.*

He sank back to the chair, as the significance of her words hit. When he looked up, his eyes were as mournful as she'd ever seen them.

"Lisa, we're *married.*"

"Nate, we're *separated.*"

He stared at her as though searching for a familiar item among a rubble of ruin. "You're a fool. Even your mother thinks so."

"Leave her out of it."

"Yeah, sure will. And you know what? I'll leave you out of it too. That's what you want? Well, you got it." He shoved his chair against the wall, Danesha style.

"Damn it! Why do you always think you can do whatever you want?"

"*I* do what *I* want? That's a joke."

"This is why we agreed to split. *We* agreed, Nate. Both of us. Remember? So we wouldn't do this."

"Do what exactly?"

"This." She swept her hand across the space between them. "I don't want us to hate each other. And I don't want to hate you for wanting to be in the same room *with someone else's children.*" She didn't attempt to hide the bitter sarcasm and Nate didn't deign to answer.

He brushed by, taking extreme care to pull his body in so they didn't touch in the narrow space. He reached for the front door just as the doorbell chimed. For a moment he seemed to forget himself and brightened with pleasure at the sound of his new doorbell.

The bell rang again and then immediately again. He swung open the door.

Standing there was a filthy teenage girl, smudges of black make-up smeared beneath her blue eyes.

"May I help you?" Nate asked.

A yellowish swell puffed her cheek and a deep-purple bruise covered her chin. The girl was shivering in a muddy t-shirt, torn jeans and sandals.

"Can I come in?" she asked, as Lisa approached, peered over Nate's shoulder and said, "Eva-Lynn Fox."

CHAPTER TWENTY

S he slept for thirteen hours. Slept through the girls' early-morning showers and frantic screaming. "Who took my backpack?" "Have you seen my homework?" "That ain't your sweater."

She slept through Lisa's anxious review of her file and feeble plea to Sheila, "Can I please send her back before the others get home from school?"

She slept through Lisa's phone call to Ron Stone to set up an appointment to register his newest student, the fourth and final GIFT House girl.

She even slept through the nauseating conversation with Sheri Fox, where Lisa held the phone so far from her ear, the whole kitchen was filled with slurred shrieking.

"You think you can handle that miserable whore? You can have her."

"Mrs. Fox, you'll need to sign some forms releasing Eva-Lynn to our care. And she arrived without any of her possessions. When will you drop off her clothes and personal items?"

Her answer, harsh laughter and the slamming down of the receiver.

Sheila was unimpressed. "This barely counts as a challenge. Just bring Eva-Lynn in this afternoon. I'll handle the parents."

She slept through Lisa's vacuuming, continuous peeks into the room. Lisa was just lying down to take a short power nap when she heard footsteps padding to the bathroom and minutes later heard the shower. Lisa couldn't bring herself to go upstairs and give the girl a clean towel or her own bar of soap. Instead, she sat at the edge of the couch, feeling even more uneasy than at her first meeting with the others.

Finally, Eva-Lynn came downstairs, walked into the room, and in spite of herself, Lisa gasped. Without the veneer of dirt, Eva-Lynn's face was a painter's palette, splashes of violet and green against skin so pale it had a bluish tint. Her lip had swollen to three times a natural size around a lip ring. Fresh, painful looking cuts covered both of her hands, as though she'd run through a bramble of bushes. Her eyebrows, nose and entire ears sported an ensemble of cheap posts and hoops. She was wearing the same filthy jeans she'd arrived in and the same thin sandals, but she'd put on a gray hooded Nike sweatshirt, which Lisa immediately recognized as belonging to Danesha.

"S'ok I'm wearing this? I was freezing and someone musta left it on my bed for me."

Lisa felt her body go cold. The girls had all stayed upstairs and then gone to bed early, so they didn't yet know that Eva-Lynn had arrived last night, a moot point anyway, since there was no way Danesha would have allowed anyone to borrow anything of hers. Much less her favorite sweatshirt. Much less a white girl.

"It doesn't have to be this hard," Nate had said last night when she'd walked him to the door, after which she'd cooked and served Eva-Lynn a huge helping of scrambled eggs, five strips of bacon, two pieces of toast and glass after glass of orange juice. The girl refused to answer when she'd last eaten, mumbling, "Been a while, I guess." No one talked much. Eva-Lynn was obviously starving and exhausted. After eating, she stumbled up the steps and fell into bed, fully dressed, and was asleep before Lisa closed the door.

"You got any socks I can borrow?" Eva Lynn's vowels had the sleepy drawl of rural Missouri.

Lisa and Nate had traveled to the "boot heel" once, so-called because of its geographical shape on a map. They'd gone to dinner at the only restaurant in town, a Ponderosa that served iceberg lettuce salads and pre-frozen steak cutlets with soggy garlic bread. When they entered the dining area, all conversations stopped, as the locals shamelessly stared, their eyes blazing the unwelcoming message, *you're not from around here.* Only later did Lisa discover that the surrounding region was home to Confederate flags and garage meth labs. She never forgot the accent, and her association of the flat, slurring Ozark drawl with racism. Hearing it in this kitchen, in this neighborhood, sent a tremor of foreboding through Lisa's body. "Uh, yeah. I'll get you a pair of socks. And, actually, why don't you borrow my sweatshirt instead of the one you're wearing."

Eva-Lynn's eyes slanted in a defensive slit. But she neither challenged nor admitted anything. Lisa walked halfway down the hall, then quickly went back into the kitchen and, as nonchalantly as possible, clutched her purse to her side as she went to retrieve a sweatshirt from her closet.

They rode to Stone Charter in silence for the first several blocks. Out of the side of her glance, Lisa saw Eva-Lynn stiffen as she took in their "colored" neighbor sweeping her porch. But otherwise the streets were empty.

Eva-Lynn whistled as she ran her hand across the creamy leather of the seat. "Nice car."

Lisa kept her focus on the road. She knew when she was being played.

"You mind?" the girl asked, and without waiting for an answer she began pushing radio buttons, changing stations every couple of beats, until she turned it off and exhaled sour breath into the car. "We're going to the school where those others go?"

"Yes, and, look, we're already here." Lisa's voice was pitched high with a perkiness she felt compelled to fake. As they got out of the car, Lisa brushed Eva-Lynn's arm. "Listen, there's something you ought to know about the school..."

"Morning, Mrs. Rothman, nice to see you. Oh, sorry, ma'am. The name is now?"

"Hello, Ike. Please, just call me Lisa. Nice to see you too, but I need to get going." She grabbed Eva-Lynn by the elbow and pushed past Ike Green as he leaned into the rake, a large pile of dried brown leaves at his feet and an expression of near-reverence on his face. Eva-Lynn stared long and hard then sported a smug smile, like she was privy to some secret.

The front hall was empty and today smelled particularly pungent. Eva-Lynn's nose wrinkled and her face stretched into an ugly grimace just as Ron Stone came out of his office, outstretched his hand, introducing himself as the girl's new principal.

"No way!" Eva-Lynn exclaimed. "I'm not going here. I just needed a place to crash for the night."

Ron shot Lisa a look, as Eva-Lynn frantically shook her head.

"No, Eva-Lynn. Your parents signed over temporary custody rights this morning. You've been admitted to our program." Lisa rushed on, "And this is wonderful news for us all."

"So of course you'll be enrolled here too," Ron said. "It's a rule that anyone living in the GIFT House has to attend Stone Charter. And your three new housemates are on their way in to meet you."

Some relationships are decided in a moment. Perhaps if Ike hadn't appeared when he did, Lisa might have been able to prepare Eva-Lynn. As it was, aside from a single neighbor and Ike, Eva-Lynn had only seen white people during the first hours of her new residence and school. Now, when Danesha, Brianna and Coreen came walking into Ron's office, Eva-Lynn's skimmed-milk complexion went deathly pale and then bright red as her head reeled back in visible recoil. They all saw it too—to a girl. Within a blink, Danesha's face flamed pure hatred; the other two looked hurt and defensive. They didn't bother to hide their own disgust either, probing Eva-Lynn's bruises and piercings with eyes that were more than curious. And there Lisa stood, no less horrified than any of them.

"I assume you'll help Eva-Lynn find her classes tomorrow," Ron said as the bell rang and he ushered everyone out of the office and into the crowded hallway. The girls disappeared for their last class without saying good-bye. Eva-Lynn grabbed Lisa's arm, clinging close until they left the building and were back inside the car.

There were no snide comments about the leather this time. She chewed on her lip the short drive back and picked at the cuts on her hands until so many pooled blood, Lisa had to reach into her purse for a packet of tissues.

As they pulled into the GIFT House driveway Eva-Lynn turned to Lisa. "I can't live here," she said, her voice trembling with fear. "They're all monkeys."

Lisa felt pity for the girl, even as she was revolted by the words. "Leaving is not an option."

Eva-Lynn continued to stare forward, her eyes wide in shock or panic. Eventually she opened the door and ran into the house, leaving Lisa to carry in the over-stuffed black garbage bag dumped in the middle of the lawn and marked in large, block letters, EVA-LYNN'S SHIT.

CHAPTER TWENTY-ONE

B ack in her college days, in a science course she was required to take, Lisa had studied issues related to invasive alien species—defined as all foreign organisms that are harmful to an existing ecosystem. It was a concept that meant little to her at the time and one she'd given absolutely no thought to in the nearly twenty years since. Then yesterday, while switching between television stations, she'd happened onto a National Geographic program highlighting the plight of thousands of poor Ecuadorians, who had been booted from the Galapagos Island because their growing population was creating "unsustainable chaos" to the environment. Without apology, some government lackey had callously likened the people to "an invasive alien species," offending Lisa until she had the disturbing realization that Eva-Lynn's entry into the GIFT House had brought the concept home.

The fragile peace of before already seemed an illusion as once again tension crackled in the air when the group was forced to be together. Lisa manipulated to keep Eva-Lynn's job chores totally separate from the others, but they were still required to share a bathroom, a dinner table and a bus ride to school.

Brianna had withdrawn back into herself and Coreen had again gone flat, neither girl engaging with Eva-Lynn, and barely with one another. Not surprisingly, the most rancid combination was Danesha and Eva-Lynn, whose issues, backgrounds and temperaments were just similar and just different enough for them to view one another with complete distrust and repugnance.

Dinners were the worst. Sheila had emphasized the importance of having at least one meal every single day with everyone present. "You'll see, they'll come around, even if it's just to ask for another helping," she'd said yesterday when Lisa called, nearly in tears, and begged Sheila to re-consider Eva-Lynn's presence.

"Sheila, you're not here to see it. If we try to talk to her, she barely answers, and she won't make eye contact with anyone. At meals she pushes her chair as far away from everyone as she can. It's nauseating. And," Lisa added, "I can't get that 'monkeys' comment out of my mind."

But Sheila stood resolute. "She needs us," she repeated, with the detached surety of someone who didn't live there.

Lisa decided to try an experiment. On the second Sunday of Eva-Lynn's arrival, while Coreen and Brianna were at church, Lisa insisted that Danesha and Eva-Lynn sit with her at the kitchen table.

"We're going to do something that my mother used to do when my sister Kate and I didn't get along," she said, ignoring Danesha's rolled eyes and Eva-Lynn's ashen panic. "I need you both to look at each other... yes, I do mean it and...I'm waiting...okay, now I'm going to ask a question and give each of you a chance to answer." Without pausing, she continued, "Name one thing you like about yourself. Danesha, you go first."

"Are you fucking shitting me?" Danesha boomed, slapping the table with her palm as she lurched to a stand. "I ain't doing this bull crap."

"Whoa," Lisa grasped Danesha's slender wrist. With a confidence she neither felt nor had earned, she lowered her voice and calmly stated, "This is not negotiable."

For suspended moments, Danesha continued to stand, shoulders thrown back, her body stiff. In her mind, Lisa summoned the voice of Sheila—*just be in charge*—and as Lisa quietly counted backwards from ten, scrambling to consider what she would do when she reached zero, Danesha slowly sat down on the edge of her chair, keeping her back ramrod straight, and exhaled an exasperated sigh into the small space between them.

"Okay, have it your way. I don't give a shit."

Lisa allowed her this small victory, and waited until Danesha finally offered, "I'll tell you what I like, I like my beautiful dark skin. It don't burn and it don't go yellow." She sank back into her seat and puffed out her chest with a self-satisfied smile.

Without blinking, Lisa turned to Eva-Lynn. *Please don't say your white skin,* Lisa thought, as Eva-Lynn blurted, "I like my nipple ring." In spite of herself, Lisa gasped as Danesha erupted with a surprised guffaw, which she rapidly tried to disguise as a cough.

"Good, and now it will be Eva-Lynn's turn first. Tell one thing you think you could grow to like about each other."

The silence that followed stretched on way too long as they sized each other up, blue eyes staring with distrust into charcoal gray ones. Lisa dug her fingers against her thighs, fully aware that if either or both girls refused, she was powerless to demand more than they would give.

Outside a screech of brakes sounded in front of their house, followed by the squeal of skidding tires. The noise seemed to break the suspension, and in a voice nearly too low to hear, Eva-Lynn said, "I like your iPod. I wish I had one."

Without missing a beat, Danesha said, "I want a nipple ring," at which even Lisa couldn't suppress a giggle.

"That's good. It's a start," she clapped her hands together and immediately both girls' faces hardened back into suspicion.

"This time say one thing you wish the other would change so you could get along better."

Eva-Lynn jerked back as if slapped, pulling herself stiffly away in case pigment could slither across the table. She didn't need words to say what needed and couldn't be changed. It was asking a river to become land.

Lisa didn't dare reprimand Danesha when she again slammed a palm down, sprang up, both hands tightened into fists, that, mercifully, she managed to keep by her side as she let loose a barrage of language worse than usual and trounced out of the room.

If possible, Eva-Lynn had paled further, and now turned to Lisa, wordlessly beseeching her for rescue. Lisa was struck by the conflicting emotions the girl continually raised in her. Most notably, pity and horror. "I'm sorry," Lisa murmured.

That night, the air around the dinner table was even more acrimonious than usual, with no one talking but the tension

135

ratcheted up to new levels. Afterwards, Lisa excused the girls from clean-up duty, and watched as they scurried away, she as relieved as they to be alone. Minutes later, strands of Diana Ross drifted out from Coreen's room, filling Lisa with a powerful sense of nostalgia and loss. Had Halloween really only been mere weeks before?

Lisa put her head on her arms, muttering, "Stupid, stupid, stupid." She continued to sit even as Danesha kicked on the door upstairs and shouted angrily at Eva-Lynn, who had locked herself in the bathroom and wouldn't come out. The bathroom was the only room in the house, besides Lisa's bedroom, that had a lock that worked.

Finally, it grew quiet and leaving the dirty dishes for tomorrow Lisa closed up the first floor, went into her own room and fell backwards onto the bed, trying desperately not to think or feel. Unbidden, a memory intruded. When she herself was fourteen, Lisa had been invited to a classmate's slumber party, where the entertainment was a fortune teller. Each girl was called into the den, one at a time, with her young heart pounding. There, a leather-skinned, silver-haired elderly woman solemnly took hold of the girl's palm, pulled it close to her rheumy eyes, then pronounced an indisputable future. "Lisa Harris, you will have a devoted husband and a houseful of beautiful daughters."

She laughed aloud at the bitter irony, even as she felt sudden tears sliding down the side of her face. It would be so easy, to pick up the phone and call Nate, to go back home, to leave all this behind. But then she saw again the pain in his eyes, heard his whisper, *We could try again.*

"Oh, fuck it," she groaned, forcing herself out of the bed. She splashed ice-cold water on her face and stumbled into the kitchen to clean up from dinner. Then, on impulse, Lisa instead climbed the stairs as quietly as possible and opened each of the bedroom doors to peek in on the sleeping girls, the light from the hall illuminating the shadows of their personalities.

Danesha's room, predictably, gave away nothing of herself, even after living here for months. She still had not hung any posters or pictures, had no rugs, knickknacks or splashes of color. For a short while, a framed photo of her brother had been on her dresser, but the past month the picture had lain facedown. The small stuffed teddy bear that Lisa bought for each of them was nowhere in sight. The room was never messy, no clothing draped over chairs or piled on the bed. Danesha could move out and the room would scarcely change.

Brianna's room was careful, neat, and quiet. She'd brought from home her own bedspread and matching curtains, their fabrics flimsy and muted. Her stuffed bear sat atop her pillow next to a stuffed frog from her grandmother. The frog had disappeared for about three days after Danesha accused Brianna of being "a boney black-ass baby embarrassment," then, at the end of that week, it had reappeared on Brianna's bed. A few posters of young, black singers were taped to the wall, looking like after-thoughts to adolescence. Her dresser was crowded to overflowing with framed photos of women with skin markedly darker than Brianna's. She was in none of them.

Coreen's room was bursting with colors, objects, messiness and an odd assortment of *things*. The room was a potpourri of her many prior lives. Each time she left a different relative's home, she simply added to a vastness of possessions. Clothes littered the floor and chair and crowded her closet. Her dresser was crammed with weaves, combs, hair grease, perfume, make-up, nail extensions, lotions, two boom boxes, an iPod, and a small television set. Each wall had two or three posters. The floor had several brightly colored rugs. Yet, for all the bright jumble, there existed in the room a void, as though too many identities had crowded out the central core.

Eva-Lynn's room was disquieting. There were no personal possessions save the opened, but not unpacked, garbage bag of clothes. She had no sheets, blanket or pillow of her own. Lisa had gone to Wal-Mart and bought her two sets of beige sheets and a cheap, but warm, comforter. The second set remained in its plastic wrap on the floor. She slept each night fully clothed atop the blanket, as though about to escape. Her only concession was she'd remove her shoes.

Lisa shuffled back to her own room, bypassing the dirty kitchen, then stopped at the entry, seeing it with fresh eyes. Her bedroom gave nothing away either. A framed photo of her parents and another one of Bonnie, both on her dresser. On her bookshelves, several novels she bought at a used book store but still hadn't read, as well as a couple of her favorites she'd taken with her as old friends. Otherwise, nothing of substance. No knick-knacks, no wall pictures. The only color, a navy blue comforter. Even her sheets were plain white.

She alone knew that inside a sock, which was inside another pair of rolled up socks, was the plain gold wedding band belonging to Lisa Rothman, waiting. And in a shoebox on a top closet shelf, pushed to the back where it was dark and dusty, was the well-hidden half-completed baby blanket. After a parade of scarves and caps, this blanket was the last item she'd attempted to knit.

She had several favorite photos of Nate, which she resisted looking at, stuck inside a collection of Shakespeare's works, surely a safe hiding place. And that was about all she'd allowed herself to bring. Everything else packed into boxes and stored in the basement of their—Nate's—house.

Back in bed, she thought again about the various rooms of the GIFT House. Not since living in a college dorm had Lisa realized the extent to which someone's personality could transform four walls and a floor. She was just drifting off to sleep when suddenly she opened her eyes wide with a startling insight. Her own room most closely resembled Danesha's.

CHAPTER TWENTY-TWO

For Eva-Lynn, life sucked at the GIFT House, but it was a thousand times worse at the school. "Stone" Charter? Were they fucking kidding? It was practically an invitation to smoke weed in the halls. But the coons musta not even realized 'cause as much as she'd tried to score something, so far nobody was selling her shit for shit. Yesterday they almost kicked her ass when she asked some big ugly bitch for something. And now today, that same bitch was staring at her in the shower that they had to take after gym class. You'd think the school could fork out for privacy curtains. Even at her old juvie school they had curtains.

"Oh, man, those are some ugly looking pubes," said the bitch whose name was something like Lauanna or Latwuanna or Layanna (where did they find these names, anyway?). The girl knocked her friend on the shoulder and they started whispering and laughing.

Eva-Lynn covered her pubes with one hand and crossed her other arm over her boobs.

"Never saw a blonde snatch before, did you, Sheena?"

The one named Sheena came right up and leaned down so close her nose was nearly touching Eva-Lynn's stomach. "Sure smells like someone forgot to bake this white pussy. What they call that? Soooshie?"

"And who threw you down the garbage disposal? All them cuts. Somebody sure don't like you."

Their laughter echoed even after they walked out, leaving her alone, finally. Jesus, she hated this stinking school. She hated their kinky hair and greasy smell, their yellow teeth, big black asses, huge nostrils. And they thought *she* was the ugly one? Even Lisa knew it. Eva-Lynn saw how she'd wrinkle up her hook nose and mutter some Jew word when she got too close to one of their stinking scalps. What'd they think? You wash your mud head once a month and spend the rest of the time smelling like roses? Soon as she could get into some money and the fucking temperature warmed up, she'd be history.

She dunked her head under the water, running her fingers through her hair. Last night after taking a shower at the GIFT House, the drain was covered with clumps of orange fuzz from the cheap-shit dye she'd used last week.

"This crown of glory, this is the proof that God has declared us the superior race," Grandpappy had said at the rally of the Knights of the Ku Klux Klan, holding her hair straight up pointing to heaven. She was six, scared and excited as she looked out at the rows of men preparing to go into the "nigga yards to do the Lord's work of purification" in the deep woods of rural Missouri.

It was cold, standing there without a robe or a coat, but she'd stayed as still as she could, knowing that Grandpappy freaked when she shivered, thinking it a sign of weakness. "Do we need further proof? Only the superior race would get hair of pure spun gold," he'd shouted as the men roared.

He'd bent down and kissed Eva-Lynn's head, then whispered, "Okay, little girl, now you go back inside with your mother, while your daddy, brother and I do our business." He squeezed her arms too tight, a reminder that she mustn't "let her fool head get too big"—that even though God had given her this golden scalp, she still was His servant.

The sound of approaching voices brought Eva-Lynn right back to now. She shut off the water, grabbed two towels, one to cover her body, the other her hair, and she hurried off to the locker room, nearly falling on the floor, slimy from all the coon grease.

"I'm jumping that honky punk-ass soon as school's over."

"I'll be there. Wonder what color she bleeds."

Eva-Lynn sank to the bench and pinched her arms to stop her shivering. Was that Danesha's voice? Were they talking about *her*? This place was nothing like her old juvie school, where at least there were other whites to stand up for her.

As the bell rang, she hustled into her clothes. She was still wearing the same jeans from the night she got there. Idiot Sheri hadn't even bothered to go through Eva-Lynn's closet, just dumped a bunch of T-shirts and one other pair of pants, her too-small boots and *one* shoe. Lisa had loaned her a sweatshirt until they could "go shopping together," but it gave her the willies wearing the fat lard's stuff. Better than coon clothes though. She gagged thinking how that first day she'd put Danesha's sweatshirt on. Surprised she hadn't noticed the stink before touching it.

"Anybody in here?" the gym teacher yelled into the locker room as Eva-Lynn walked out the back door. She'd be late for class, which meant Stoner would call Lisa and she'd have to go through a whole bullshit story, because if she told the truth—that she had to hide her white self—then for sure she'd get jumped tomorrow.

As the math teacher yakked on and on, she hid her face behind the text book, not that she'd miss anything if she took a nap. Bunch of losers who were even stupider than she'd thought. In ninth grade they were doing the shit she'd studied two years ago.

She reached into her back pocket and pulled out the picture of her twin, Jack. Same white-gold hair, clear blue eyes, even the same chipped tooth smile. Mirror twins, they called themselves—he was left handed and right footed and she was just the opposite. She stared at the photo, the last one taken of them together, and she felt like bawling as she kissed his paper cheeks. When she let herself, she missed him so much it hurt way worse than any slugging.

A year and a half ago, Sheri and Ray had split up; no more midnight fights, shrieks or slamming doors. For the six weeks Ray disappeared, Eva-Lynn and Jack felt like they'd gone to Disneyland. Then one day, sure enough, Ray was back, sitting at the kitchen table, sour and shaggy. "Come give me a kiss," he slurred. When Eva-Lynn shrank away, he whipped his palm across her face so fast she didn't know her lip was split until she spit bright red blood.

The next day, just for grins, Jack and Eva-Lynn burned down an abandoned neighborhood house. Jack had the gas can, Eva-Lynn brought the matches. They broke in through a cracked window, hoping to mess it up first, but finding it empty, they poured gasoline all over the living room, lit the match, and rushed out. When they spotted a neighbor standing on her porch, they told her they'd seen a nigger run out the back and she needed to hurry and call the cops.

That night Sheri opened the door to two police and a fat ugly woman carrying a stack of legal documents. Jack and Eva-Lynn were both removed from the house. Jack was sent to a juvenile detention home a hundred miles away. Eva-Lynn was placed in a home for "wayward" girls, where she stayed for one year. She spent five hours in classes, worked outdoor chores for two hours, had an hour of daily therapy. For the first time in her life, she met girls like her—"displaced," the therapist called them—girls who had never fit in their own skin, with secrets so frightening they whimpered and tossed in their sleep, but stayed tight-lipped silent in the day. Some of those girls even became her friends, which was kind of the first time ever. A couple of months in, Eva-Lynn earned enough privileges to take art classes, to go on field trips, and finally to go out with some of the others on weekend days. One time she returned with a pierced eyebrow and nose. After another she and her roommate both got a matching cross and bones shin tattoo. When the year was up, the only reason Eva-Lynn was ready to leave was to see Jack.

At first Sheri and Ray wouldn't tell her anything about Jack. Then she heard Sheri on the phone talking about her brother. She yanked the phone out of Sheri's hand and shouted, "You motherfucker, what happened to Jack?"

"Don't you go talkin' like that, girl. I am your mother. I tell you what I want." Sheri picked up a ketchup bottle and started beating Eva-Lynn's arms and shoulders.

Ray stormed in, his hand already raised in a fist, but before he could swing, Eva-Lynn rushed out the back door and started running in any direction that might get her lost. She was gone for three days, sleeping on park benches and eating out of trash cans, scared but too crazy mad to go back. When the police found her, they brought her home, made Sheri admit that Jack had disappeared two months ago and had not been found. They then gave Eva-Lynn's parents two choices: foster care or a new residential home they'd heard about in St. Louis.

"The GIFT House," Eva-Lynn said immediately. She had loved her girls' home and was ready to go live with kids away from useless adults. The next day, Sheri told her she wouldn't be going nowhere after all and to keep her butt inside and not let none of the neighbors see her neither. That lasted for a month, until one day Ray discovered that his basement stash was all drunk up, and he went ape-shit.

"You can't expect me to sit here every fucking day, *parched* like you call it," Eva-Lynn shouted back, too stoned to clamp shut her mouth. After that, the last thing Eva-Lynn remembered was Ray slugging her across the face and Sheri shoving her out the door. Eva-Lynn had stood shivering in the cold, then remembered the two tabs of ecstasy in her pocket. She popped them both under her tongue. Within minutes she owned the world.

She'd become an ace hitchhiker. The trick was to look like someone you'd wish you could fuck but wouldn't. She kissed the tip of her magic thumb as she climbed into the warm cab of the sky-blue truck. He took her almost the whole way to St. Louis. Just for grins, she gave the next driver the address of that house where her parents had almost sent her. She'd put it into the survival part of her brain where she kept the Youth Emergency Service and police hot-line numbers.

At first the trucker wasn't about to take her into "that neighborhood," which kind of freaked her, but it was pitch dark and freezing, so Eva-Lynn offered her best blow-job smile. It beat the streets and she could haul ass out of there in the morning.

Soon each bump in the road sent waves of puke up into her throat. She hadn't eaten since the night before and the ecstasy was fighting a gang war in her empty body. "Uh, uh..." she'd muttered as she unrolled the window and barfed yellow drool down the side of the door.

"Get the hell out of my car," he said. Or maybe she had imagined he had said that, so as soon as he slowed at a stop sign, she jumped out, fell to the ground, and sat on the sidewalk for a long time. When she did finally blink back to, she squinted and thought the sign said Clara Road, which was where she wanted to go. She staggered for a block, feeling weak and hungry and cold and really, really scared, and then she actually found the address, knocked on the door, and was told to come in by a skinny white dude and fat, dumpy white lady who already knew Eva-Lynn's name. She'd almost cried with relief. It wasn't a nigger house after all. Leave it to Sheri to get the fucking details wrong.

"Well, Eva-Lynn?"

She startled back to the math class, like leaving one nightmare for another. "Uh, I'm not sure. Could I answer the next question instead?" He smirked and she heard a couple of the coons laughing behind her. She slumped lower into her seat, trying to stay unnoticed.

After class, she snuck into the hall bathroom and splashed water on her face, moaning a little as it split her lip back open. The gold hoop dangling from her mouth made the throbbing worse, but she knew not to remove it now while white puss was trying to peek out. That piercing had been a mistake. She'd had a neighbor boy do it in exchange for letting him suck her tits. They were both high and forgot to light a match to the needle head before shoving it through her skin. The hole had festered up, leaving a big pock mark that had turned brown and puckered.

My beautiful angel, Grandpappy used to call her. Too bad he couldn't see her now. She'd give him an Aryan eyeful.

The bell rang the end of another worthless day. She pulled her sweater tight—thanks, Sheri, for still not bringing over my friggin' winter coat—and began the walk back to the GIFT House. It had gotten even colder during class and they were predicting a snowier than usual winter. For a moment she nearly cried, then she straightened her shoulders and began walking faster. She might be worse than nothing on most things—but she *was* a survivor.

CHAPTER TWENTY-THREE

"**Y**ou little bitch. I can't believe you did that."

Brianna froze. Danesha was so pissed her face had gone purple. Somehow she'd quit worrying on Danesha. First she'd stressed Devon wouldn't call or stop by again, the shitbum. Then she stressed that she'd given up her cherry for nothin', worse shitbum. But she'd quit stressin' on Danesha finding out.

Brianna straightened tall as she could and dropped her arms to her side. Sometimes the only way to play Danesha was to slam it back. "Why you always so much drama?"

Danesha stepped in so close Brianna could see the hairs up her nose.

"If you ever mess with my iPod again, I'll kill you," she hissed. "It keeps replaying the same fuckin' song over and over and you better fix it or...you don't wanna know."

For a moment, Brianna's mind went to nothing. *Her iPod?* Then she busted out a laugh. "Yeah, too bad." She turned and raced up the stairs, Danesha following fast. Brianna was able to slam her door shut with about one second to spare.

She stood against the wood, her heart pounding fast and hard, until she heard Danesha stomp off. They all knew one same thing. A shut door meant Privacy.

She crossed the room and opened the window, letting a strong wind blast her face. Two inches of snow covered the ground and Miss Lisa said more was coming tonight.

That was a close call with Danesha. She'd been lucky this time, but she'd best think on a next step, 'cause as Ma always said, *nothing* come without a cost. But it wasn't like she'd been all up on Devon's jock, it just happened. And anyways, he was "off-da-chain—don't nobody own Devon." That's how guys were.

Brianna leaned her forehead against the cold glass and watched her neighbor Flozie Pitzer limping by. Everybody on Clara Road knew Miss Flozie's story. How she'd lived her whole life in the same house her granddaddy built and how years before, she got her leg crushed in car accident. She'd re-learned to walk but wouldn't ever get into a car again. Every day Brianna would see Miss Flozie pushing her grocery cart up and down the street, moving slow as a legless rabbit, as Ma would say.

Oh, Ma! Brianna curled onto her bed into a corner, squeezing a pillow tight to her boobs, pretending herself inside Ma's arms and hearing Ma's voice and all her expressions for real. She rocked back and forth, heels digging into the rock-hard mattress. All the beds in the GIFT House had been donated and 'cause Danesha hollered for the best and Coreen too fat for a little single, Brianna got stuck with the lumpiest mattress. It didn't matter none. She spent most of her nights awake anyways, staring at the ceiling and thinking about how much fun it was gonna be living in Florida. Ma's boss had already given her a big promotion, though not enough yet for Ma to get a place of their own and bring Brianna down there to live on the white sand beach.

She snatched the piece of paper out from under her mattress. The paper had been opened and closed so many times it was starting to rip in the folds. She blew on it, giving it a "wish breath." She spread the paper on the bed and, though she knew behind her eyeballs nearly every word, she reread the letter.

My preshus Brianna,

Everything here is fabuloso. Your old mama is learning a little Spanish. You would be so proud of your Ma if you could see what a good job I'm doing at work. Everybody says so, even Auntie Billie, and you know she sometimes holds back those nice words for her big sister! I'm saving every penny I can. Of course, I had to buy me some new clothes. I was one silly joke trying to wear BLACK down here when everyone else in pink and yellow. I bought some of the cutest things, I can't wait to show you. Girl, your gonna love it here. I been trying not to get darker but Aunt Billie says I'm looking like Hershey. We'll get you some extra strong sun lotion.

Brianna held the letter close to her nose, trying to sniff the scent of Ma, but it just smelled like her own sour self. She was so hot lately, breaking into sweats sometimes like she had

146

fever. Nerves, Ms. Johnson said, from spending her first big holiday without her family. But Ms. Johnson was wrong. Ma was so disappointed that they wouldn't be together this Thanksgiving. She was everyday saving her money to bring Brianna down for Christmas, or for sure by Easter.

And now Brianna kinda almost had her dad. Twice in the past two weeks she'd lied to Miss Lisa, fronting like to go to the library, when really she walked down a block and then hitchhiked to the Central West End, standing in the cold, wishing her daddy to come down the street and hug her up. But yesterday the only white man she saw was the guy who gave her a ride when she hitchhiked home. He put his hand on her thigh and creeped her out so much she jumped out the car at a stop sign and ran the rest of the way, getting back so late Miss Lisa gave her a first warning.

Sounds of banging pots and pans and white people music was down in the kitchen. Most days Brianna didn't let herself go to that saddest place, but it was too hard not to on Thanksgiving. Miss Lisa was just so different than Ma, who loved being in the center of every room, singing with all the songs—rap and hip hop—dancing as she cleaned, sometimes just stopping whatever she was doing to crank up the volume and grab Brianna by the hand to make her dance along.

Aunt Billie's friend is letting me sleep on the best couch. They have two couches! You're wondering how come you can't sleep on the other one. That's where I gotta keep all my stuff. I'm so happy, Bri. This is a dream come true. Sometimes I can't even remember our old life. I hope that white lady (I forget her name) is treating you real good and you're making friends with those other girls. Remember your manners at all times. I won't call on account every minute costs money that I'm saving to bring you here with me so we can live ON THE BEACH. And you better grow some titties, cause I'm getting you a sexy swim suit when you get here! Maybe even sexy as mine!

After refolding the letter and hiding it away, Brianna tiptoed quiet-like across the room and listened with her ear to the door. There sure was a lot of banging going down in the kitchen, trying to sound like a big "family" meal. The only one who'd be gone was Coreen, and it was hard to feel envy for that girl. She'd told Brianna that last year on Thanksgiving she went to her daddy's place for a couple of hours and then her mom come and made Coreen leave and go to her uncle's, who didn't stay around, and Coreen had eaten dinner in front of the TV, babysitting her three little step-cousins and cleaning up everyone's messes. In the middle of the telling, Coreen'd laughed and said it was tight that everyone wanted her.

This year, Coreen was invited to four Thanksgivings. She'd packed a couple of sweaters and a pair of ratty looking khakis into a grocery bag and sat on the GIFT House porch yesterday, waiting to see who would pick her up for the weekend. She wanted Brianna out there with her, but it got so cold Brianna had to go inside and just stand by the window, knocking against the glass every couple a minutes so Coreen could know she wasn't alone.

After a while Brianna opened the door to go back out and sit some more, but when she saw Coreen's tear-red eyes she real quick snuck back in. There was lots Brianna didn't know about Coreen, but she did know that frontin' a happy face was about all Coreen took much pride in. Finally, more than an hour late, a noisy beat-up green car pulled up and Coreen got in and waved good bye, smiling like she was ready to star in someone else's show.

Brianna could hear Ma yelling in her ear that "she were raised better than this" and she'd best go help Miss Lisa. No biggie, she'd set the table or something, get through the night and be one day sooner to Florida. She opened the door and nearly fell over seeing Eva-Lynn just standing outside her bedroom, looking like she wanted to knock but didn't know how. That girl was so hella-lame. As always, she was wearing a stained, yellow Guns N' Roses T-shirt and wide-legged torn-up black nylon pants that Brianna didn't think even hobo white girls wore no more. In all this time living here, Brianna'd only seen Eva-Lynn in two pants and one other T-shirt, the one with a big tongue that was cracked and peeling off the shirt, some old white group called The Rolling Stoned or something, as if Eva-Lynn needed a billboard to announce her druggy self. That black trash bag musta had more clothes than that. But only shit wouldn't a gotten ripped off their lawn, so maybe this was the best Eva-Lynn had.

Brianna pulled shut her door behind her. "I'm gonna help Miss Lisa. You wanna come?"

Eva-Lynn wrapped her arms around herself, looking to cover the purple and green bruises that never seemed to fade.

"Yeah, I could," Eva-Lynn said, her voice sounding like cut glass. "You want to get high first?"

Brianna worked to show nothing on her face. Not like she were scared, she just hadn't done it yet. "Naw, not tonight. You know that turkey's gonna be too hard to swallow even if my throat ain't dry from weed," she croaked, grabbing hold of her neck with both hands.

Eva-Lynn snorted out a laugh, showing a real smile. "Yeah, you got that right. She's one thick-ass who sure can't cook."

Lisa was heartened by the laughter traveling down the stairs and more encouraged yet when Brianna and Eva-Lynn strolled together into the kitchen, offering to help and seeming to almost be in sync with one another. As usual, the cheer was short lived. Maybe the problem was that Coreen's empty chair was like a gaping hole. Or maybe it was the way Lisa couldn't stop herself from trying so hard to be the missing link in all their lives.

"When I was growing up we had a Thanksgiving tradition I'd like to honor tonight. Everyone game?" Without waiting for a response, Lisa grabbed Brianna's hand with one and Eva-Lynn's with the other, then dipped her chin to indicate they should do likewise to enclose Danesha, whose mouth dropped open.

"You shittin' me, right?" When Lisa refused to look away, Danesha finally deigned, with the slightest possible touch of her fingertips, to glance her skin against Brianna's, and, visibly shuddering, against Eva-Lynn's.

"Now, each of us needs to say at least one thing she is thankful for," Lisa said, resisting the memory of the last time

149

she forced a conversation between these girls. Silence descended around the table, but for once Lisa didn't budge.

Finally Brianna blurted, "I'm just glad cause next Thanksgiving I won't be here."

Danesha grunted. "So what, girl, you ain't my bestie neither!"

"I just meant..." Tears slipped down her face. "I miss my Ma."

Danesha's smirk had twisted into something unreadable. "Yeah, well, I'm *thankful* Jerrell stabbed Mama in the chest so I didn't have to."

"Oh, Danesha. Honey."

Her face went rigid as she shot Lisa one of her *don't you dare pity me* looks.

Eva-Lynn cleared her throat a couple of times, stared up at the ceiling. Her voice came out a squeak. "I guess I'm thankful that you were willing to take me in. You know, after what my parents musta said to you and all."

"What'd they say?" Danesha asked.

Lisa's heart lurched. She glanced to make sure the file lock was pressed in, and before Eva-Lynn could respond, said, "As for me, I am truly thankful for all of this." She pulled her hand from Brianna's and swept the room, then immediately re-linked fingers. "And I'm thankful for each of you."

"You sure must have left some shitty life to think this is aiight." Danehsa laughed, but her face looked curious.

Lisa's mind swept to Thanksgiving as a newlywed, sitting around the dining room table with Jeanette and Albert and her new husband, in her girlhood home. It was their first post-wedding visit to Minneapolis, and Lisa had been dreading the trip since accepting Jeanette's "invitation," a word that implied a choice.

Jeanette wasted no time. A slice of turkey was barely on their forks when she'd tilted her head as if mildly curious and asked, "So, Nate, are you thinking of going back to college? You two could live on Lisa's salary, couldn't you, while you get a degree? Then you could get a professional job?"

Lisa had shot up, causing a glass of red wine to spill onto the white cotton and lace tablecloth, passed down from her grandmother's trousseau some forty years before. Everyone watched in horrified silence as the deep red spread across the delicate fibers. For what seemed like whole minutes, no one moved, not even trying to blot out what was rapidly becoming a permanent stain.

Eventually, Albert began to chatter and Nate, sweet man that he was, joined in, allowing the sour mood to dissipate. The next morning, as they pulled away for the long drive back to St. Louis, Lisa noticed the corner of the tablecloth hanging out of the trashcan, as deliberate as Jeanette's curt wave. She'd grabbed Nate's hand and squeezed. They didn't speak until safely on Highway 35, when suddenly Lisa began to laugh with an energy that even she could hear bordered on hysteria. He'd looked at her intently, longer than was highway-safe, and Lisa had felt the warmth of acceptance and contentment that spread throughout her body.

She studied now the three curious faces, waiting for a response to Danesha's comment. The girls were hugely curious about Nate, kept asking where he was, who he was—all of them suddenly interested in Lisa's background (yep, be careful what you wish for). But, frankly, even if she were willing to say, Lisa didn't have an answer for many of their questions. She'd not heard anything from Nate since Eva-Lynn arrived. Nor had she called him.

In comparison, Jeanette called all the time, often several times in a day. After a couple of weeks without incident, Albert had suddenly become a constant worry. Yesterday Lisa had picked up the phone and before even saying "hello" Jeanette launched into a breathless monologue about how that morning Albert stole the keys from her purse and had scraped the passenger side of the car on the garage. "At least, thank God, he couldn't manage to get out of the driveway," Jeanette wheezed into the phone. They talked for several minutes during which Lisa tried, unsuccessfully, not to audibly cry. Then Jeanette had pressed—yet again. "I just don't understand how or why you're not coming home for Thanksgiving. Especially with everything going on here."

"Look, Mom, I feel awful about it too, but these girls have nowhere else to go. Imagine how terrible it is for them."

"Why can't that other woman stay?"

"Sheila?" Lisa hesitated, tempted to lie, but finally stuttered, "Uh...she well, she went home." At Jeanette's loud silence, Lisa tried, "This is my job," at which point Jeanette had blurted, "Well fuck your job," leaving Lisa stunned to hear the f-bomb dropped from her *mother's* lips.

What she didn't admit to her mom was that she too had wanted Sheila to stay with the girls so Lisa could go to Minnesota, or, at the very least, spend the holiday with all of them. But Sheila had made it clear she was off duty for the week and was visiting her own family in Chicago. Making Lisa feel even worse at a bunch of levels.

"Miss Lisa, you okay?"

Lisa snapped back. Brianna's face was pinched in worry, and all of them, bizarrely enough, were still holding hands or at least had fingertips pressed to one another. She forced a reassuring smile. "Sorry. I was just thinking about something else."

After a beat everyone dropped her hands. Lisa cut the turkey, butchering the slices as she struggled with a task that had always fallen to Nate, and before that to her dad. She tried to make small talk, however the girls weren't biting, everyone lost in her own sad musings. The turkey was surprisingly moist, but Lisa resisted taking seconds. She'd started walking again and was determined to slim down.

They'd passed the dishes around for the last time, when Lisa spoke.

"It wasn't a bad life I left, Danesha. In many ways, it was a wonderful life." Her voice cracked. She inhaled from deep within. "But it was a life that couldn't go on. It hurt too much. So I started over. You *can* do that, you know. When it hurts too much. You really can."

It wasn't enough—not enough information, not enough comfort. But it was all Lisa had to give. So they cleared the dishes, mostly in silence with everyone helping. Lisa was about to turn off the lights, the dreaded first major holiday over, when the doorbell rang, chiming loud and clear.

"Maybe it's Miss Vanessa!" Brianna said, racing toward the door. Lisa followed, struggling to fight back the jealousy that boiled up every time she witnessed what Vanessa effortlessly achieved—what still eluded Lisa—the girls' easy affection.

Lisa swung open the door.

"I was feeling a trifle lonely tonight. Mind if I have dessert with you?" asked Miss Flozie. She was leaning into the door jamb for support, mittened hands holding out what appeared to be a home-baked pumpkin pie.

Danesha was the first to sit back down, followed closely by a subdued Eva-Lynn. Brianna reached into the cabinet for another set of dishes as Lisa grabbed a long, sharp knife to dole out something sweet to each of them.

CHAPTER TWENTY-FOUR

Here she sat, alone in the principal's office, waiting for the teachers to come in and tell her which of her children had committed what terrible travesty. Lisa reached into her purse scrounging through the clutter of used tissues, loose coins and candy wrappers for a lozenge. Her throat was dry and scratchy, likely a condition that would persist throughout the winter. Apparently, the GIFT House didn't come with the gift of guaranteed warmth. Twice, the school had sent Ike Green over to caulk the windows, but still the wind whistled through her bedroom at night, creating a low-pitched whine that seemed to carry viruses on its back.

"Ms. Harris. It's always nice to see you." Ron Stone breezed into the room, placed a hand briefly on her shoulder, then stepped around his large walnut desk and sank into the green leather chair. "Even when..." his voice trailed off and his brow furrowed into a dour expression as two teachers walked in and were motioned to sit in chairs directly facing Lisa. They both looked familiar, but she was hard-pressed to remember their names or which of the girls they taught. Their frowns told Lisa she was about to find out.

"This is Mrs. Crawford and Mr. Hamilton, Danesha's English and European history teachers. We're expecting Ms. Johnson momentarily."

Right then Sheila opened the door and walked in. She, too, squeezed Lisa's shoulder as she passed.

Without any of the small talk preamble of Lisa's first visit to this office, Ron launched in, followed by a litany of angry comments from Mrs. Crawford and the drone of slow, stuttering accusations by Mr. Hamilton, the gist of which all pointed in one direction. Danesha was screwing up big time and was a single incident away from being kicked out of Stone High School. And who was responsible for getting the girl back on track? Of course—her house mom.

Lisa felt a wave of hilarity bubble up as they went on and on, voices rising with each example of the girl's "inappropriate, unacceptable, disrespectful" delinquencies, until, at one point, she choked back a laugh so suddenly it turned into a coughing spell that continued until actual tears were running down her face. "Excuse me, I'll be right back." She ducked out, heading for the bathroom, but yearning to sneak out the side door as Danesha, evidently, was still doing on a regular basis.

It was a relief to find the bathroom empty, disgusting as it was with soggy toilet tissue scattered across the floor, unflushed toilets, dripping faucets, the sour smells of the teeming waste cans—and suddenly her hilarity was gone. Lisa leaned against the wall, defeated by frustration.

Sheila came in. "I thought I'd find you here. Tough stuff to hear, isn't it?"

"Geez, Sheila. What am I supposed to do? I mean, I'm trying my best, but I'm just one person and—"

"Know what? You're the best these girls got. Pathetic, huh? So let's throw out the pity party and put energy into something useful." She clasped Lisa's elbow, and together they walked the bustling hallway back to Ron's office.

"Here's our strategy," Sheila said as they sat. "We'll call Danesha out of class. I've been informed that she just arrived from a rather extended lunch break. We let her know we are aware of what she's doing. She's going to have to sign a contract agreeing to certain specifications if she wants to stay in school. If she doesn't agree, then she'll need to be transferred to another school, one of the public high schools. And they'll take her—they have to by law—but then she can't stay in the GIFT House either. That's only for Stone Charter students."

Lisa gasped as Sheila's words sunk in. Danesha kicked out of the GIFT House? How many times had she fantasized about how much easier life would be without Danesha? Yet the actual possibility was... *unacceptable.* "Now wait a minute!"

"She has missed or been late to my class eight of the past twelve days. Next time I flunk her," sputtered Mr. Hamilton, slicing the air with his hand as if to slice through Lisa's clearly irrelevant opinion. "You make sure that's in the contract. I'm not fooling with that girl anymore. I don't trust anything she says or does."

"And she is missing three weeks of homework. I'm giving her one week to make it all up, or I flunk her," hissed Mrs. Crawford.

"And of course the next time she sneaks out, I'll have no choice but to call the police. I'm responsible for her during school hours," Ron chimed in, his voice less strident but his body language tight and the frown between his eyes pronounced.

Sheila was seated in one of the swivel chairs, calmly taking notes, as though at a board meeting preparing an agenda for reasonable adults.

The patterned stripes and swirls and checks on the chairs and couch were making her dizzy and suddenly, once again, Lisa felt the spasm of laughter deep in her throat. What was wrong with her today? This was not funny. Not even remotely. And less funny yet, was that they were all looking at her, waiting for assurance that Lisa Harris would get control over this demon of Stone Charter and transform the girl into the strong student everyone in this room knew she had the *potential* to become.

But she forced herself to nod, as if *sure, no problem, house mom in charge*, and waited quietly as Ron buzzed Danesha's science room for her to come down to his office. Only once had her mom been summoned to the principal's office, when, at age seventeen, Lisa was caught with a pair of boy's jockey briefs in her locker. The "trophy" underwear hadn't even belonged to her boyfriend, but to the brother of a classmate who deposited them there as a prank. She'd been plenty scared, though, knowing that what they hadn't found was a three-pack of condoms she had sneaked out of Albert's nightstand drawer—grossed out, but also desperate. Lisa was planning on finally "going to fourth base" that Saturday night. The visit to the principal's office preserved her virginity for yet another year.

She smiled at the memory, then realized that the two teachers were staring. She swallowed back the smile as Danesha came in.

The girl's eyes took in the roomful of adults and grew large and round before shifting downward. She didn't budge until Ron encouraged, and then Sheila demanded, that she shut the door and take a seat.

Lisa reached across and squeezed Danesha's hand. "You look really pretty." Danesha glanced up and for a moment her face smoothed into open gratitude before closing shut again as Lisa asked, "Where you been, all dressed up?"

"Yes, that's an excellent question," Ron said. "Where *have* you been, Danesha?"

"I ain't been nowhere," she muttered, then froze silent as Ron, the teachers and Sheila enumerated the list of transgressions, suspicions, and serious consequences. Danesha didn't try to defend herself, didn't provide an explanation, didn't offer an apology, didn't give any assurances for future behavior. She sat stiffly, looking straight ahead at absolutely nothing.

"Do you fully understand, Danesha?" Ron asked.

She nodded, just barely, but enough.

"You do realize you are on probation and one more, and I mean, *one* more slip-up at this school, and you're out. And that will mean out of the GIFT House too," Ron continued.

Again, no reaction beyond the slight downward shift of chin.

"Okay, then. Back to class. Miss Lisa will be bringing the contract home for you to read and sign. Meantime, you know what you need to do."

The chair nearly tipped as Danesha pushed it aside and rushed out, the two teachers close behind.

Lisa watched her retreating back, trying not to feel hurt that Danesha hadn't glanced her way for comfort or support. Danesha hadn't seemed particularly angry at Lisa either. It was as though she was no more, or less, important than any of the other adults in the room.

She could feel again that wave of resentment that Danesha so often evoked. Damn you! she wanted to shout. How dare you...what? Act like a stupid teen? Risk being thrown out? Not love me—or let me love you. A complex feeling, too complex to sort out, overwhelmed Lisa, exhausting her. As surreptitiously as possible, she glanced at her watch. If she hurried, she'd have just enough time for a nap before needing to prepare dinner. That, at least, she could control.

As she reached for her purse and stood to go, Ron motioned with his hand for Lisa to sit. "Ms. Harris, we're not through yet." Ron paused, waiting for Lisa to fully face him again. "I'd like to talk to you about some other concerns."

The phone was ringing as Lisa fiddled with the rusted-out lock—now why the hell didn't Ike, or even Nate, fix that?—and it was still ringing as she walked into the GIFT House, put down her purse and went out to check for mail. It rang yet again as she came back in. She waited until it stopped, instinctively knowing it was her mother and simply too wrung out to talk. She hung up her coat and put on the kettle to boil some water. When it rang yet again she answered.

"Lisa! Finally."

"Mom, it's been a lousy day and I'm just coming in. I have to cook dinner."

"I didn't call to chit chat. I *surely* know better than that by now." Jeanette allowed the sarcasm to carry its weight across the miles, pausing and wheezing into the receiver.

"I'm listening."

"Your dad," she stopped, sniffed loudly. It was the sound of sincere anguish. Lisa felt her chest tighten. *Not this too. Not today.*

"What about him, Mom?"

"I don't know what I'm going to do. Last night he found where I hid the key, undid the double bolt and left the house to go for a walk. No shoes, no coat, and I don't have to tell you what the weather is like. December in Minnesota, and there's your father out on the porch in pajama bottoms and a T-shirt. Luckily I heard the door open, I barely sleep anymore, who could? When I tried to grab him back, he..." she sniffed and wheezed again, louder this time. "He, oh, I know he didn't mean it, but he hit me. Not hard. Just a slap across my face. But your father? Of course he doesn't remember any of it."

Lisa stared blankly around the room, trying to wrap her brain around the words and coming up with only that same numbing disbelief she'd experienced after each miscarriage. *This can't be happening.*

Jeanette's voice was small as she asked, "Will you please come up? Even for just a couple of days. I understand this is your job, but, honey, I don't know what to do anymore."

"Yes."

"Because I'm here by myself and no one knows how it is, and I can't tell anybody, your father would just die of shame if anyone knew. I keep thinking if you or your sister could come then..."

"I said *yes,* Mom. I'll figure out a way to get away for a week or so. A couple of the girls are going home for Christmas, so that might work."

"You will? Oh, Lisa, thank you. It's been so long since we've all been together." A lengthy pause, then, "Now you won't call and tell me you can't leave those girls, right? Surely they can manage just as fine for a few days without you as they do with you."

An understatement so pitiful it was almost funny.

"You know, Chanukah falls the same week as Christmas this year. I'll have to dig out that old menorah. Remember how we always lit the candles and sang before opening gifts each night? You and Kate hated when I made you sing for your presents." Jeanette was nearly singing the words herself, no trace of wheezing in her voice.

"And maybe I can convince Kate to leave that *girlfriend* of hers and visit for the holiday. Wouldn't that be wonderful, dear, to have all of us together again? It will be good for you both to remember what's supposed to be most important..."

Lisa held the phone an arm-length away as Jeanette talked, one ear listening to her mother, the other ear hearing the echoes of Ron Stone's words.

Apparently, Danesha wasn't the only one creating issues at school. Eva-Lynn had called a classmate "the N word" and would have been beaten except a teacher overheard and publically reprimanded her enough to spare her a "pay-back slugging." For now. But Eva-Lynn was disliked by nearly everyone—students and teachers alike—and could Lisa please try talking to her about her attitude?

Brianna was also cause for concern, Ron Stone had continued. Her mood swings were frequent and extreme, ranging from misery to sudden, inexplicable, cheeriness. He was beginning to wonder if there wasn't, in fact, some sort of chemical imbalance that needed to be explored.

There had been no complaints about Coreen, for which Lisa was only marginally relieved. She was slowly growing to realize that Coreen's seeming lack of overt unhappiness was a mere cover. At night, Lisa could hear the soft mewing of stifled crying coming from Coreen's bedroom. Twice last week Lisa had tried to get Coreen to open up, and twice she'd failed. It was exasperating. The way she'd use so many words to say nothing, but when there was a true need for discussion, she'd utter a single syllable—"fine"—which inevitably was followed by a shrug. It was clear the Thanksgiving visit had been a total bust, but Lisa didn't know why, and it looked like she never would.

"It will be great to be home for a while, Mom," Lisa said as she watched an over-sized roach scamper across a tar-black scuff mark on the linoleum floor. The exterminator had been out twice but apparently Lisa was supposed to ignore the bugs and instead be grateful that she hadn't spotted any rodents in the house.

In the background the wind whistled through the cracks in the window sill.

CHAPTER TWENTY-FIVE

"Sit down," Sheila tried to control her irritation but knew it crept into her tone by the stricken look on Coreen's face. It had been a very long day of dealing with at least ten too many post-Thanksgiving, pre-Christmas problems—decidedly the least jolly time of her year—and Coreen's feigned denseness was trying her last nerve. The girl had been attending weekly counseling sessions for months. She knew the drill, yet each week she stood gripping the back of a chair until Sheila was pushed into commanding her to actually sit and begin to talk.

"So tell me about Thanksgiving. What did you do? Who'd you stay with?" Sheila had softened her tone, but it was too late. The mask was set and already it was obvious that this would be another wasted session. She could feel herself sigh with exasperation, though Coreen didn't appear to notice.

The girl's round belly peeked through the space between a too-short sweater and too-low jeans. The little beige cami she wore under the pink sweater had a long rip from the side seam to the front and a strip of ragged lace hung loosely over her naval like a single flattened curl. The jeans were unsnapped and the zipper lowered by an inch to expand for what looked to be at least five new pounds.

"Coreen, please. This is your time, dear. Don't waste it."

The mask loosened as the endearment seemed to reach Coreen's ears. She nodded several times, then eased herself into the chair. Her shoulders slumped forward, but she offered a full-tooth smile and her voice was strong and sure, the little actress firmly entrenched. "It was fine. I got to see a whole bunch of my relatives."

"Oh? Who?"

Coreen looked around the room, her eyes shifting and landing everywhere but on Sheila's face. With great effort, Sheila didn't press but gave her time to formulate an answer, knowing that the real answer with Coreen would be in what she didn't say.

"First on Thanksgiving day I went to lunch with my Mama's side and three of my brothers were there, but not Levontrez 'cuz he were with his daddy, but I saw him later and then me and my littlest brother went to our Daddy's for dinner and then we hung with our cousins 'cuz Daddy and Mellonie went to their friend's house and then me and Auntie Tiffany drove around near where she's staying next and then my sister, the one who's got Lil Travis, you know, I told you 'bout him, well then me and her went to where she stays 'cuz I said I'd babysit when she worked on Friday and then..."

And then and then and then. Sheila tilted her head as if catching every word as the next half hour repeated the first half, while scribbling notes in Coreen's chart. *Still using her sessions to talk about extraneous details in order not to have to admit to any of her feelings. Thanksgiving break spent being shuffled from relative to relative. Sounds like she stayed in four places in four days. Refusal to make eye contact belies assertion of being "fine" and while tone of voice is upbeat, body language shows otherwise.*

Sheila glanced at her watch, both dismayed and relieved to see they had only six more minutes. Of all the GIFT House girls, out-going, easy-going Coreen was still the toughest nut to crack. Sure the other three held their secrets closely guarded, yet they also admitted to their anger and their anguish: about Lisa, about Stone Charter, classmates, and mostly about one another. Every so often they'd even acknowledge deeper family issues. With Coreen, though, everything, always, was "fine," reminding Sheila of a fellow social worker's quip that the word was actually an acronym for "fucked-up, insecure, neurotic & exhausted."

"And how are things at the GIFT House? But before you answer, let me tell you that saying 'fine' is *not* an option."

Sheila was rewarded with a smile and several beats of silence before Coreen leaned forward and in a near whisper admitted, "Do you promise not to tell Miss Lisa if I tell you something?"

Instantly alerted though trained to keep her expression neutral, Sheila settled back against the seat and with a short nod assured the girl more than words could.

"Miss Lisa sometimes cries, you know, when she don't think we can hear her."

"Go on."

"Like at night, after we've gone upstairs, like if I sneak down, and lots of time she's sitting in the kitchen with no lights and I can hear her sniffing and stuff. She don't know I'm there but should I try to make her feel better? What's she got to cry for?"

Sheila felt a surge of alarm. This definitely was not what she wanted to hear, though certainly not a surprise. It was becoming ever more apparent that despite Lisa's best intentions, and despite the continuing hope that she would grow into the job, Lisa clearly found herself in a life she'd never intended nor thought through. None of which should have been evident to any of the girls.

"Let's start with the last question first. Everyone has a reason to cry sometimes. You know that, and this doesn't mean she's too sad to take care of you girls, which is what's important. But as for asking her, I think you need to rely on your own instincts. If you're comfortable, then definitely ask." She paused. "Coreen, do you think Miss Lisa will answer honestly if you ask her what's wrong?"

A shrug. "I don't want her mad at me."

"Why would she get mad?"

"You know, cuz I'm just a kid and all and..."

"And?"

"Nothing."

"Finish the sentence, Coreen. You can trust me."

"Never mind." She stared into space for several long moments and then visibly snapped back. "Okay, Ms. Johnson. I'll get going now."

Sheila reached out a hand as Coreen stood and gently pulled her back. "How does it make *you* feel when I ask you how everything is?"

"Huh?" And when Sheila didn't answer, Coreen smiled. "I get it. You trying to trick me, ain't you?"

"Actually, I'm trying to get to know you better."

"There's nothing to know. You can even ask my Mama, she'll tell you. I'm really fin...oops, I'm cool."

Sure, ask your mama or your daddy or your myriad relatives who pass you around like someone's stray puppy. It was time for Coreen to leave. Sheila had an appointment with another student that should have started several minutes ago. But she sensed something in Coreen, and she didn't want to once again throw back the onion because the layers wouldn't peel.

"Let's get back to Miss Lisa. Why do you think she's sad?"

Coreen snorted. "Wouldn't you be? If you had to be with all a us?" When Sheila didn't respond, she continued, "You know Danesha how she be. And Eva-Lynn and Bri don't never talk to her. She must hate staying with us."

"I find it interesting that you didn't include yourself in the list. How do you think she feels living with you?"

Coreen's face instantly assumed a placid blankness that was so immediate as to only be carefully rehearsed. "I guess it don't matter much either way living with me."

Sheila tilted her head in question.

She shrugged. "I don't cause no trouble, Ms. Johnson."

"Does that work for you?"

"Sure. Why not? "

Why not indeed? "What do you think might happen if you let others know when you're angry or sad?"

Again a shrug, this time of seeming genuine consideration, a long pause, and then she turned to Sheila, her eyes making direct contact, her voice emboldened by sureness. "I don't make no trouble for no one. And that's why everybody always wants me with them when I go home."

"Is it?" Sheila asked so quietly it was more a thought escaping than a true question, but Coreen heard and her face darkened.

"You trying to get me to say something you want me to say."

"No, what I'm trying to do is have you tell me what *you* want, Coreen. Can you claim it?"

Coreen pursed her lips together and slumped deep into the chair, curving her body so that she melted more than sat. She continued to say nothing, the clock's ticking the only sound in the room. It was, perhaps, the most honest exchange they'd yet shared, so that when Coreen stood and walked to the door, turned and said, "Ms. Johnson, I don't need nothing else," Sheila let her walk out without further challenge.

Sheila jotted a few notes about the conversation, closed the file and was about to stuff it into the drawer when she stopped. Though she'd scanned her notes briefly before today's session, she flipped back several pages to read what she'd written over the past several months. Mostly the same thing over and over. Coreen seems fine (there was that word again), not unhappy, doing pretty well in school, no complaints nor any real comments from teachers.

How could it be that this over-weight, chatty girl, whose skill lent itself toward theatrical drama, could continue to be so completely unremarkable as to barely be of notice? Yet, she alone commented on Lisa's emotions.

Emotions that were becoming evident to these troubled girls. Now that was *not* fine.

CHAPTER TWENTY-SIX

T he first robbery took place four doors down. A television, DVD player and some costume jewelry were stolen, the bedrooms ransacked.

Three days later and one street over, a fifteen-year-old daughter walked in while the burglars were there. She was grabbed from behind, a knife brought to her throat, and then a deep, long slit cut from shoulder to elbow, requiring twenty-two stitches. The girl was so shaken she could not identify the man except to note that he was dark-skinned, skinny, unfamiliar, and around age twenty.

The third house was a block away. Dishes thrown to the ground, framed pictures slashed into shreds, dresser drawers emptied. The house was in such dishevel it took several days before the owners could even determine what was missing and what was simply destroyed.

Through a series of coincidences Nate heard about the break-ins. A friend called to invite him out for beers after work. That friend brought another friend, who happened to be a cop. The cop started drinking and talking, telling about various "hot" neighborhoods he was forced to patrol, including one with a historically strong Neighborhood Watch that appeared to be "yet another new shit zone." "Three houses in less than a week. And a month or more before that, another house bombed to rubble. Seems to be some sort of gang initiation rite. They're not stealing much, just getting off on creating chaos."

At first Nate paid little attention to the conversation. It was December eleventh, fifteen years to the day since he and Lisa had first met. He was sure Lisa had no clue. She did well to remember their wedding anniversary. But for Nate it was one more pick at the scab.

The cop continued. "The pitiful part is once these things start, there's no stopping them. Pretty soon an area that was about as safe as any of 'em, which is like saying, 'well, at least it isn't Afghanistan,' becomes even more dangerous because people start believing they can't make a difference. You're not going to call the cops if you think someone is watching and will slam you for wagging your tongue. Not that anyone would call us anyway, with all the mistrust against the police. Like excuse the fuck me for trying to you safe." He paused, took a long swallow of his newest beer, and continued, "I tell them, 'Get a dog and keep your porch lights on.' Course, with two of the robberies happening a block away from that charter school, broad daylight, and still the shit-heads break in, their minds clouded by who knows what fucking drugs, no one feels safe no matter what. But if I lived there, I'd get me three of the meanest dogs ever born and I'd keep one in the front, one in the back and one inside."

Nate snapped to attention. "What'd you say about being near a charter school? Which school?"

He had tried to stay away. He'd said it was up to Lisa to make the next move, and this time he meant it. He wouldn't call and he wouldn't visit. Though that didn't keep Nate from making regular detours down Clara Road, just to make sure her car was still there and that nothing seemed out of the ordinary, or watching from a few houses away until he saw at least one of the girls leaving or coming.

But the situation had changed. Lisa wasn't safe. And that was a hell of a lot different than just running away from home and playing pretend mom.

He'd never been to the pound before and was unprepared for the feelings that overtook him as he walked up and down the row of cages, trying to decide which dog to adopt. The beagle with the torn ear and sad expression in his eyes. The snarling Rottweiler-shepherd mix that would scare anyone away, including its owners. The huge four-year-old Great Dane. He tried not to think about the fact that the ones he didn't select would probably be put to sleep.

A client who annually rented from Nate for employee family picnics had adopted an eighteen-month-old girl from an orphanage in Russia. He had described the experience to Nate, so focused on his own story he didn't appear to notice that Nate was visibly growing more and more upset. The client and his wife had entered the orphanage intending to go immediately to the crib of their new daughter and instead they'd paused in front of each of the sleeping babies who would continue to be without family. "We wanted to take them all and felt absolutely devastated when we walked out with only our one little girl in our arms," he'd said, his voice cracking at the memory.

Nate crouched down, leaning in close to the various cages, trying to judge from the dogs' actions which might be the best choice for a pet that would be gentle with its family while vicious with strangers. He'd nearly settled on a large mutt when a loud bark drew his attention to the last crate in the row. "Hold on there, fella." He walked to the end of the aisle and stared into the cage of a yellow lab/golden retriever mix, whose tail was wagging as he frantically scratched the metal bars with huge, oversized paws. *Take me*, the dog pleaded. *I'm the one you want*. Nate glanced back at the mutt, its tail now drooped between its legs. Then turned again to the golden-lab.

"Of course once we got home, we made ourselves forget about all those other babies. We had our own daughter to concentrate on now," his client had added, and then walked off in search of their little girl, leaving Nate with a mouthful of questions he wouldn't ask.

Driving to Clara Road, the seven-month-old golden-lab on the passenger seat with his snout out the window sniffing into the wind, Nate shook off the image of the mutt. He'd never owned a dog, not even as a child, yet his instincts told him that this was the right choice.

The dog began to whine and knock against the window as soon as Nate pulled into the driveway, as though sensing he'd arrived home. Nate slammed the driver's door shut and dashed across the lawn and onto the porch, nearly stumbling from that one damn step that was loose again. The doorbell, however, rang out loud and clear.

Eva-Lynn looked a bit better when she opened the door, less starved and not quite as rough. He hadn't known if she'd still be here, but he was surprised to find himself glad to see her.

"I'm Nate. I met you a couple of weeks ago. The first night you got here."

Eva-Lynn's face reddened with distrust.

"Hey, Mr. Nate." Coreen shoved in front of the other girl.

He pointed toward the truck. "Got a minute? I want to show you something."

He opened the passenger door slowly, intending to snap on the leash and walk the puppy to the porch. In a flash, the dog sailed out of the truck, raced around the yard in circles, then bounded up the stairs and leaped against Coreen, knocking her to the ground, where it stood over her, four legs planted on either side of her chest, licking her face with its large, pink tongue.

Nate held his breath, waiting for the screams or cries, but heard only laughter as Coreen tried to stand and Eva-Lynn flung herself to the ground, grabbing the dog into her arms, shrieking as the animal lapped her face and neck.

"Is this your dog? He's so cute," Coreen said.

Nate hesitated as he suddenly realized—what had he been thinking?—that Lisa would be beyond furious about this. "Uh, he's kind of mine," and then, because her face shone bright with an excitement that stung his eyes, he couldn't resist adding, "You like him?"

"He's so fyer!"

The door opened and Brianna and Danesha ran out to the yard as soon as they saw the puppy, who quickly worked his magic on them too. Nate stepped away, watched them as they chased and ran after the dog. As the last time he was here, he struggled trying to think of what to say to them, his whole body gangly and stiff. Then he realized it didn't matter. He might as well be invisible as the four girls pushed one another aside to hug her body closer to the dog's soft fur, acting as puppies themselves.

Only Vanessa seemed unimpressed, coming outside to see about the commotion, wagging a finger at Nate in mock warning. "You are really brave or really crazy, Mr. Nate." She watched for several minutes, a smile dancing across her face. "He's a cute one. What are you doing with him?"

Danesha lifted her head from the dog's face. "Yeah, Mr. Nate, if you don't keep him, could we?"

Again Nate hesitated, thinking through how to answer, when Lisa's car pulled into the driveway.

"Oh shit," Danesha grumbled as Vanessa bee hived back inside, muttering, "I don't even want to play my eyes on this scene," and as Lisa stepped out of the car and began strolling across the yard toward them, her arms full with a Home Depot sack.

Lisa's eyes and mind absorbed the scene in snapshots. The red truck. Nate. A dog. Nate's dog? Nate bought himself a dog? They'd always talked about getting a dog, but somehow it seemed like something they would do when their child was old enough to help take care of it.

Nate turned to her with a nonchalance that was obviously bogus and said, "Hi, Lisa, I've brought over a surprise...visitor."

Before she could respond, Coreen chimed in, "And if he don't want the dog, we do."

She stood still for several moments, confusion clouding her head as the same thoughts recycled through her mind. Nate. Here. Again. With a dog. His dog? *Their* dog? At which instant, the dog jumped full body against Lisa, causing her to drop the Home Depot bag, the bag containing metal locks and steel window guards, onto her foot.

"Fuck!" she screeched as a surge of pain shot all the way up her leg.

The girls couldn't move fast enough, suddenly the epitome of concern and caring.

"Are you hurt, Miss Lisa?"

"Want me to get some ice?"

"I'll carry that bag in."

At another time, Lisa might have been amused by their obvious fawning, but she was way too irritated for humor right now. She kicked the bag aside with her other foot, splitting the paper sack open and scattering the metal pieces across the lawn. "No, Coreen, if he doesn't want the dog, then the dog goes back to wherever he got it. No way are we keeping an animal around here."

"Aw, Miss Lisa. Look how cute he is."

"We'll take care of him."

"I'll walk him."

"I'll feed him."

Even in her haze of frustration, Lisa noted with no small irony that all four girls were talking as of one voice. And who was yet again the hero? The goddamned "Sunday father."

Nate was tilting his head and jerking one shoulder, trying to get Lisa to follow him out of the girls' earshot. But she wouldn't budge, so finally Nate was forced to tell all of them together about the cop's report of break-ins. Only Eva-Lynn seemed shaken.

"The police said the most effective way to keep burglars out is to get a dog. Makes sense, right?" Nate added.

"So the dog is ours?" Danesha yelped, as Coreen swept the large puppy into her arms, squealing, "Omigod!"

At this point Lisa yanked Nate to a separate part of the yard. "I don't know what you think you're up to, but this is not your job, Nate, and these are not your girls. You have got to quit coming around without my permission, fixing things, bringing gifts."

"You're not frightened? After what I told you? Be reasonable."

She wanted to shake him, make him understand that while he was *hearing* about the robberies, Lisa was *living* them. Too scared to sleep at night, every creak in the old house a stranger's footstep, every breeze a hand reaching from behind to muzzle or choke or rape. But, of course, he would only tell her to come home. Of course.

"Did you see what was in that bag? Window locks. But a dog? Are you going to walk him in this neighborhood at night? Are you going to scoop up his shit? Replace the furniture he destroys? Pay for his care out of your budget?" What she didn't add was that she'd actually, briefly, considered getting a dog and then ruled it out as too impractical and expensive. So instead she'd get the shit, literally, with none of the credit.

She fixed an icy stare on him, her cold eyes saying the words she kept inside her mouth. His response was to point with his chin. The girls were now sitting on the frozen, frost-covered ground, no coats on, the panting puppy in the middle of their circle, racing from one set of outstretched arms into another.

Lisa walked toward the center of the lawn. She leaned against the tree and listened to the excited chatter, her body fully aware of Nate just inches behind her.

"That's the dumbest-ass name. Only a hobo'd call a yellow dog Brownie," Danesha sneered.

"Well, it's not as bad as naming it Michael Jackson," Brianna said, pulling the puppy closer.

"I like Nelly. I once had a dog named Nelly but my mom got rid of it," Coreen whined.

Lisa turned to Nate. They locked eyes and each knew the other had similarly traveled back, standing next to a show-room crib, Lisa five months pregnant, the future full of promise.

"I like Sam."

"Too ordinary. What about Seymour?"

"You're joking, right?"

"Solomon?"

"Are you insane?"

She'd shared so much with this man, and here he stood, hoping to rejoin their two lives. Without letting herself think about it, Lisa touched her palm to his chest, to that place just above his heart where she'd always liked to rest her head. They didn't speak for long moments. Finally she said, "I get confused too."

"You didn't call. I tried not to care."

Lisa desperately did not want to cry. She stepped away, turning her back to his side, not rude, but no longer close. "You should have asked me about this first."

"I know. But I got scared for you."

She was diverted from having to respond by another shriek of laughter. To a girl, their faces shone with a carefree joy. She felt her shoulders slump; no point denying when she'd been bested. "I guess I'm supposed to thank you, Nate. I don't know if he'll protect us, but I think he'll be good for the girls. And," she offered a rueful smile, "he *is* ridiculously cute."

Nate wanted to hang around. Lisa wouldn't let him. He needed to understand—he'd gotten his wish, the dog was no longer his. She felt a pang as he waved from the truck, looking forlorn and alone, then she went back to the girls and threw in a suggestion or two of her own—all of which were quickly shut down—until they finally agreed that the dog would be called Dude.

The girls went to their rooms late that night, too excited to sleep. Lisa could hear them laughing with one another and calling out suggestions for their care-taking schedule—a schedule that likely wouldn't last a week. But that night, for the first time since Eva-Lynn's arrival, the GIFT House felt warm and close. A family welcoming its newest member.

Lisa found herself whistling as she closed up the house, locking the doors (sans new locks or window guards, having forgotten them on the lawn, only to have them missing the next day). She went into the kitchen, intending to make sure the small light over the stove was on and that Dude was comfortable in his new cardboard box bed. He thumped his tail and leapt out of the box and pressed himself against her legs. She'd never had a dog before. Jeanette had only allowed non-pet pets—baby green turtles, parakeets, goldfish, hamsters—the kind no one cares about until they die.

"Shhh, fella. Don't tell the others I'm in here with you." Lisa kneaded his knobby scull as he nuzzled his nose into her lap. He reeked of dried urine and filth, and his hair was matted in thick clumps. He badly needed a bath. How was she supposed to bathe this huge thing? And where? But he sure was sweet, with eyes that seemed, already, to trust the best in her.

Each time she tried to walk out, he began to yelp and whine. Finally, she did what seemed the only reasonable thing to do. She stretched out beside Dude and ultimately fell asleep with his head on her stomach, so that his crying didn't keep the girls up on a school night.

CHAPTER TWENTY-SEVEN

There were days now when she felt like she belonged. The shared experiences. The routine of day to day. The unexpected laughter. Continuing conversations.

And then there were days, still, when it was all so strange and out of her comfort zone that Lisa felt as if she'd stepped out of a plane into a foreign country.

Staring at the Stone lunchroom full of boisterous students, all of them strangers just months before, Lisa stood totally alone. Who in this whole packed room of people, who in this whole new life, truly cared about her?

"You okay? You look a little sick," Sheila said.

Lisa started, felt herself flush. Would she *ever* get used to the way Sheila so often just appeared, and how quickly and aptly she took the pulse of every situation?

"Actually, I'm trying to steel myself for the holidays," Lisa admitted.

"That's good, because I suspect most of our students feel the same thing and this way..." Sheila allowed her words to trail off as she hurried in the direction of two eleventh graders shoving one another in the far corner of the room.

This way *what*? Lisa wanted to scream across the deafening noise, knowing that even if Sheila heard the question, she wouldn't provide the answer. "They're your girls, Lisa," Sheila had said so many times lately that Lisa was beginning to wonder if Sheila had simply washed her hands of the GIFT House. If she had, then her timing sucked big time. With two more days until winter break, the tension among the kids—at the school and at their house—was palpable.

In addition to the pre-vacation restlessness typical at every school, many of the Stone Charter students faced the prospect of a Christmas without gifts or family or holiday meals. "Christmas trees in the shelters don't glitter much, and a holiday on the streets is the worst kind of bleakness there is," Sheila had told Lisa with the dull affect she acquired whenever the truth behind her words burned. In recent weeks, there had been a rash of suicide warnings and two actual attempts.

When Lisa received the letter to parents and guardians, she had immediately made an appointment to see Sheila. Sure, she knew what signs to watch for, but how would she recognize a warning when her girls were often withdrawn, depressed, humorless and angry.

"Just keep your eyes open, listen to your gut, and if something nags you, it's probably worth taking seriously," Sheila had advised.

So far, no one at the GIFT House seemed *unusually* troubled. Coreen and Eva-Lynn were going home for the Christmas weekend, and if things went smoothly, they'd stay there until New Year's Day. Brianna was even quieter than normal, and Danesha more brittle, yet Lisa's instincts weren't signaling alarm. Dude's presence helped to keep the mood somewhat elevated, but even he couldn't erase the general hostility that continued to color nearly every exchange between Danesha and Eva-Lynn.

"You bitch, get your honky ass out of there. This ain't a hotel," Danesha had screamed that morning, waking all of them up with her hot temper before the sun had a chance to rise.

As much as Lisa was tempted to interfere, to quell the outburst with a lecture about consideration for others, she, too, found Eva-Lynn's time behind the closed bathroom door excessive. And disturbing. Today, after they all left for school, Lisa had gone upstairs and discovered drops of blood all over the bathroom floor, bright red blood that didn't look menstrual. She would need to talk to Eva-Lynn or Sheila or both, as soon as the girl returned from the holidays.

Thinking about it now, Lisa felt her mood sinking further. She missed the easy camaraderie of Credit-Solutions, where her co-workers, while not exactly true friends, shared a holiday energy that made this time of year particularly fun. Worse yet, Bonnie was attending a ten-day work conference in Thailand and then staying on for the holidays, and they wouldn't be able to talk for the next three weeks. She shook her head, as if shaking off droplets of biting rain. She had a job to do today that did not include the luxury of self-pity.

She scanned the lunchroom once more, nodding to a number of kids she knew from tutoring, but with no sight of any of the GIFT House girls, she left for the school library. It was Holiday Shopping Day and Lisa had been assigned "store" duty. Throughout the month, teachers had collected new and gently used items from their homes. For the price of one dollar, each student could buy an admission ticket to select any two gifts for a friend or family member. Lisa's job was to help students pick something from each of the two tables—an adult gift and a children's toy.

Very quickly, she decided her real role would be as co-conspirator. She didn't argue with the girl who insisted that the two scarf sets she wanted came from the two different tables. She said nothing when an eighth grader opted for a man's leather wallet for his "dad," though Lisa knew he had no father on the scene. In a moment of what admittedly was misguided weakness, she even allowed Coreen ("Quick, honey, while no one's looking") to sneak a third item, as if it would make a dent in the child's shopping list for the who-knew-how-many relatives she would potentially see.

After an hour, Lisa took a break. She wasn't tired so much as emotionally wrung out. The students' raw desire both sickened and saddened Lisa. Her hands shook as she poured a cup of lukewarm coffee into a chipped mug in the teachers' lounge.

She walked to the edge of the room and looked out. The landscape beyond the smeared window was bleak, a barren, icy chill. When Lisa called home yesterday, Jeanette said the snow accumulation in Minneapolis had already broken the one-hundred-year record for December. Her mom's tone had actually been wistful, displaying genuine envy for Lisa's claim that so far it had yet to snow more than an inch or two at a time in St. Louis. But, now, staring outside at the mounds of littered paper that had clumped into a soiled mass beside the curb, Lisa longed for the frozen beauty of her hometown, where snow became the great equalizer of neighborhoods.

"Ms. Harris?"

Lisa sloshed coffee onto her fingers and floor. "Mr. Stone."

"You know what? It's time to make it Ron, please. And let me get that," he said, groaning as he bent to wipe up the spill. His face was flushed and dots of perspiration lined his brow. "Can I refill this for you?"

"That's all right. It wasn't very good," she said, then grimaced. "Oops, I didn't mean that. It's so nice of you to even have coffee for us."

His laugh sounded strained, followed by a thick cough. He looked paler than usual.

"You okay?" she asked, leaning closer.

"I've got to get through two more days. Then I can be sick." He plopped onto a metal folding chair. "This is always a rough time of year. I can't be gone."

Such a kind, devoted man. She wondered again why he'd never married. Sheila Johnson, too, was single. As were the majority of the teachers at Stone Charter. As—bizarrely—was she. It was inconceivable that less than a year ago, Lisa's world encompassed two-parent, two-child, two-car-garage families.

She sat across the table. "May I ask you something?" and not waiting for an answer, "doesn't it get to you?"

"I struggle every single day," Ron said. "I also work very hard to focus on the accomplishments. I wouldn't be able to come here if I let myself only think about the failures."

Below basic test scores. Chaos in classes. Huge discipline issues. What accomplishments? She wanted to ask, but before she could decide whether or not to push, he continued, his voice hoarse.

"Take your Coreen, for instance. She's now reading closer to grade level, when just months ago she was years behind. Clearly she's relishing the stability you're able to give her. Can you even begin to understand how miraculous it is in her life? To live in the same place for a full semester, and more importantly, to know that she will continue to live there with you through the remaining years of high school."

Lisa felt a nervous rush. Ron assumed she was at the GIFT House for the long haul?

"And that little Brianna. Almost overnight she's finally showing some self-confidence. She's even filling out. You must be feeding her well."

This time Lisa laughed outright. "Uh, thank you, but I'm not what you'd call a cook."

"Listen, I know the past couple of times I've come down hard on you. About Danesha. And about Eva-Lynn. I am concerned. But I hope you also realize that, for the most part, we are encouraged by your job performance at the GIFT House."

"You are?"

He heaved himself to a stand, swayed for a moment, visibly dizzy and weak. "Sheila says you're going home next week. If I don't see you, have a great holiday." He gave a thin smile. "Maybe I will leave a little early today."

She stood in the empty lounge, listening to the hiss of the wind through the cracked pane. Last week someone had thrown a rock at the top window, and the glass had splintered into an intricate web. Two weeks before that a nineteen year old tried to sneak a gun into the school for his little brother, to retaliate against a freshman in a drug deal gone bad. Two juniors, both of whom Lisa had tutored, reportedly had dropped out and disappeared. And *this* was better than the public schools. Brutal stuff.

She dumped the coffee down the drain, stared at the dark black granules that lined the bottom of her cup, then walked out, leaving behind the echo of her footsteps against the hard, cold floor.

Brianna and Danesha were both part of the second wave of shoppers. Brianna smiled at Lisa from across the room. Danesha refused to make eye contact, turning her back away. Lisa knew better than to offer either of them any help. In that way she was no different than any teen girl's mom—a public embarrassment. She tried to busy herself assisting other students, but couldn't help from sneaking glances to see what both girls picked.

Brianna immediately grabbed a gold spray-painted picture frame. She spent more time at the kids' table, fingering every item before finally choosing a palm-sized powder blue elephant. She brought the stuffed animal to her lips and held it there for several seconds, seeming to talk into the doll's ear before waving to Lisa and going to the check-out line.

Danesha wandered around the room, making a large circle eight as she passed each table over and over. Her shoulders were slumped, her characteristic haughty demeanor gone. After several minutes, she walked out without acknowledging Lisa and without a gift.

The afternoon hours sped by. Eva-Lynn never came in, but Lisa didn't register that until later. After a while, Lisa grew more comfortable, getting into the spirit of shopping by making suggestions to the students and sharing in their delight when they found the right gift. She was even able to forget that the items were second hand, someone's castoff. In fact, most of the students took longer and selected with more care than she herself had done yesterday when buying an electric rice cooker for her parents. She'd gone to the crowded mall with no ideas, stood for ages in a line full of cranky adults, sweating in her winter coat but too burdened by the bulky box to take it off. She'd put the rice cooker on her charge card without another thought, without really even knowing if her parents liked rice.

The last group of students was just finishing up when Danesha reappeared. Again she avoided Lisa's glance. She proceeded to the adult gift table and without hesitation picked up a large hand-held mirror. Lisa remembered unpacking it from the box of collected items and noting that it was cheap, ugly and more than "gently" used, with a grainy surface to the mirror and a stickiness on the pink plastic handle that wouldn't wash off. That mirror had been one of the first gifts set out this morning and had stayed put the entire day.

At the check-out station, Sheila was counting the student tickets. The money collected would go toward uniform shirts for the drum line. Danesha handed her ticket to Sheila and from across the room, Lisa could see it had been rolled and unrolled a number of times, the paper grown flimsy from sweaty fingers, its edges continuing to curl. Sheila smiled at Danesha, whose face remained impassive.

Lisa caught Sheila's eye as Danesha lumbered out and both shrugged. In the background strains of "White Christmas" could be heard, evoking the universal seasonal yearning for a simpler past, even when no such memory existed. Lisa resumed packing up the few remaining things—they would be delivered tomorrow to a nearby shelter—when she felt a tap on her shoulder. Danesha was standing there, both hands grasping the plastic handle.

"Here," she mumbled, thrusting the mirror toward Lisa. "This is for you." Before Lisa could say anything, before she could thank Danesha, or hug her, before she could tighten her fingers around the sticky handle, Danesha hurried off, back stiff, face cast to the side.

Lisa turned the mirror forward. The eyes that stared back were soft and damp.

CHAPTER TWENTY-EIGHT

In nearly every American Jewish child's life there is a defining moment when he or she becomes aware of being *different*. For Nate, it occurred at age nine on a Christmas tree lot with his new friend Peter.

"What kind of tree does your family get?" Peter asked.

Nate had coughed quietly, stalling.

"Don't tell me you guys have an artificial one. Those are so fake. My family gets a new one every year."

Nate had nodded a non-answer, which seemed safer than the truth. "Please, could we get a Christmas tree?" he later pleaded to his parents.

"Christmas is not our holiday. We have Chanukah instead," his mother had responded.

But Nate already knew what every Jewish child in America learns each December—Chanukah was a piss-poor substitute, and lighting candles and getting a present every night for eight nights did *not* make up for being outside the single biggest event of the country's entire year.

He'd cried in frustration. It was so unfair of his parents, who only went to temple twice a year, to deprive Nate of a holiday that was barely about religion anyway. Half his friends skipped the whole church part, just celebrating Christmas with gifts and trees, decorations and great cookies. What could be the harm in that?

But even his easy-going father stood firm. "Nate, we're special *because* we have our own holidays and customs. Someday you will appreciate the need to keep our culture separate."

Nate pulled his truck into the GIFT House driveway, clunking his tire against a large gouge in the asphalt—that needed fixing *too*—and sat for a few moments, missing his father with a sharp pain that still stunned him after more than twenty years.

As an only child, Nate had spent much of his childhood surrounded by adults. He had been especially close to his dad, from early boyhood going with his father on deliveries for his various businesses. Always, Nate sat up front, even when he was too small and they had to switch him from the back a block away from his mom's watchful eyes.

Because he was such a poor student, he'd mostly stuck to himself, grateful to have the excuse of working with his dad rather than joining in high school activities. When his dad died of a sudden heart attack, Nate knew he was also burying his best friend. The next several years were painful and lonely. Then he met Lisa and together they'd created a world for themselves in which loneliness no longer existed. Until…

He jumped from the truck and slammed shut the door as if to slam away his sadness. It was beginning to snow, large flakes that fell on his upturned face, blurring the glitter of elaborate lights brightening houses up and down Clara Road. Except on the GIFT House. He raced up the porch steps, noting with pride that they'd finally held firm since he'd snuck in a couple new nails last week on a day when no one was home. As usual, it took several persistent rings for someone to answer the door. Brianna stood in the entryway looking washed-out and tired, her eyes red rimmed as though she'd been crying. Nate wished he could hug her but before he could decide whether to reach out, Danesha pushed her aside, muttering, "Who the fuck…oh, Mr. Nate. Miss Lisa ain't here." As before, she leaned against the jamb, curving her hip to melt into the wood. When she smiled he noted the gleam of a gold tooth he'd not previously noticed. He felt a rush of dismay, which dissolved instantly as an oversized mutt came bounding to the entry, knocking the girls aside and jumping with force against Nate's chest.

"Wow, fella, you've gotten so big." Immediately, the dog slid to the ground and rolled onto his back, legs spread, tongue hanging out of the side of his mouth. *Love me, love me,* his brown eyes begged, and Nate was powerless not to do so.

"May I help you?" a husky voice asked.

Nate glanced forward at a pair of thick, dark ankles that stretched and spread over the rims of powder-blue terry cloth slippers. He looked up, past the wide calves, taking care to skirt his eyes around the hemline of a faded flower dress, beyond the wide waist, into the stern face of a middle-aged woman. Her frown turned her lips downward, but her eyes showed clear amusement as he stumbled to get up, stepping over the dog and the feet that blocked his way in the tight door frame.

"Hello. I'm, uh, Nate Rothman. I, uh...geez, this is a little awkward," he said, and then despite himself, laughed, which was echoed by the large woman.

She clasped his outstretched hand. "Of course I know who you are. The man who brought us Dude." Upon hearing his name, the dog inched his way back into the circle of legs and began to bark for attention. "Dude, hush and go lie down. Right now." His chocolate brown eyes met Nate's as if to say *I'm not done with you*, then he flipped his thick, furry head in a canine shrug. He padded across the room, circled several times, and flopped to the ground, groaning as he did so.

The woman overpowered the doorway with a commanding presence, though her face revealed a gentle strength that even he, a stranger, found difficult to resist. He glanced at Danesha and Brianna, at the way they both were looking to this woman for permission for something, and he recognized that Lisa would never be able to command this sense of respect, no matter how long she lived here.

"I'm Sheila Johnson, social worker up at the girls' school."

"Nice to meet you. How are you?"

"I'm blessed. You?"

He wiped his palms against his jeans. "I'm good. And actually, I've tried calling Lisa a couple of times, but I never got an answer. And I know she said for me not to come around without talking to her first, well, in fairness, I guess not to come around at all, but, see, I was thinking that if the girls want, well maybe this is silly, but I didn't know if Lisa remembered, with her being Jewish and all, if she remembered to get a Christmas tree. And if she didn't, then if it's all right, I'd be happy to take them to pick one out." He paused for breath. "Okay?"

All three were staring at him and in the corner Dude began to whine. Sheila darted a glance the dog's way. "Stay," she commanded as Danesha piped, "Jewish don't get Christmas trees?" and Brianna grasped his sleeve and said, "I'm ready."

"We were about to go ourselves. But this would be fine. Go get your coats, girls." As they ran up the stairs, Sheila turned to Nate, all smiles gone. "Mr. Rothman..."

"Nate."

"You do realize I know everything about you. I wouldn't have let you near this house if I hadn't checked you out thoroughly."

His mind darted back and forth. He'd smoked pot, but that was more than a decade ago. Everyone smoked pot back then, didn't they? And there was that one unpaid speeding ticket that a lawyer friend had bought off.

"I don't know what you're up to. If you're trying to win back your wife, don't go trying to do that here. But," and she leaned in, picking him apart with her dark eyes, "if what you truly want, coming round here often as you seem to do, is to help out these girls, fill in on a few repairs, and be a friend, then bless you."

He nodded repeatedly, suddenly realizing that in part, maybe in large part, that *was* what he wanted. He smiled in wonderment.

Sheila seemed to recognize something in his response—as if she knew more about him than he did himself—and for a moment he panicked that he might not pass this surprising test. Then she clasped his shoulder and squeezed. "Mr. Nate, let's go get us the best Christmas tree these girls have ever had."

The nearest lot was only a couple miles away and they arrived before the cabin of his truck had even begun to warm. He kept meaning to get it into the shop to have someone check out the heater, but he so rarely had a passenger anymore. And he didn't really mind being cold. Sometimes, on the worse days, it was all that made him feel alive.

Sheila followed behind in her car, but the girls begged to ride with Nate. Danesha had climbed in first. Nate sat as stiffly as he could, trying not to let his body touch hers as Brianna got in front and the three squished together. In her excitement Danesha had totally dropped her sexual persona, instead debating with childlike enthusiasm about what kind of tree they ought to get. Nate drove slowly, both hands loosely cupping the wheel, enjoying their interaction and again was struck by the connection they didn't seem to realize they shared. At one point he interrupted to ask about Coreen and Eva-Lynn, both staying with their families for the holiday week. Hesitating, he also asked about Lisa, and found out that she, too, had gone home for the holiday.

"Home?"

"To visit her parents," Brianna said.

"She seemed *real* upset about something. Not that she'd ever tell shit to us," Danesha added.

"Oh?" he asked, struggling to keep his voice even. "Do you know..." But the girls' attention was no longer his.

The lot was filled with cars and trucks and families, strings of bright lights and rows upon rows of pine trees in varying shapes, sizes and density. An assault of noises embraced him: children squealing as they chased one another, mothers yelling out instructions, fathers protesting as they heaved trees toward the cashier. The scent of freshly cut pine filled the air, again evoking for Nate a longing to be part of a bigger whole.

Sheila waved to him, motioning that she'd stay in the warm car, but clearly she'd be watching. Lisa had told him the rule was the girls could never, ever, be alone with any man. He slouched against the truck, then quickly straightened his spine, trying to appear as trustworthy as a *man* could be.

The girls skipped off, their steps fast and light, and were gone no more than a few minutes when Brianna reappeared from within the bundled forest.

"We found our tree, Mr. Nate," she exclaimed. "But we gotta hurry or it'll be gone." She smiled then, a smile of pure delight and amusement. "Well, maybe we don't gotta hurry. I left Danesha standing by it. I don't suppose anyone's gonna trip offa her."

He dipped his chin in agreement. Even from across the lot, Danesha's "don't trip offa me" attitude was apparent. The tree of choice stood out from those around it, the largest and widest in the row. By quick calculation, he could see that it was at least a half foot too tall to fit in the GIFT House living room, with branches of prickly needles that would sting each of them as they tried to walk past.

Nate started to shake his head "no," to suggest the tree several over, smaller, tighter and more uniform, his idea of what a Christmas tree should look like. But one glance at the eager expression on both girls' faces and he nodded yes as he pulled his Visa out of his back pocket, while signaling for the owner's son to help him carry the tree to Nate's truck.

Forty-five minutes, aching arms and a sore back later, Nate emerged from the bathroom, where he had tried in vain to wash away the sticky pine sap from his hands. He sank with a groan into the kitchen chair. Sheila placed a Santa mug beside him, filled to overflowing with hot cocoa. He inhaled the rich chocolaty scent and sighed with weariness and contentment, feeling at ease for the first time in the GIFT House. "Well, it's standing."

Immediately the girls burst out with strong opinions about how the tree should be decorated. Blinking colored lights. Frosted glass balls. Painted wooden ornaments. Sheila offered her own suggestions, drawn from empty pockets and a full imagination: paper ornaments, candy kiss foil bunches, strings of popcorn and cranberries.

"We need angels," Brianna said, "and a baby Jesus."

"No way, girl. I am not having a baby Jesus. And an angel is even worse. An angel is a joke and I ain't having no jokes on my Christmas tree." Danesha's voice was hard and shrill.

"But I want an angel," Brianna now said. "Angels protect us."

Danesha was out of her seat in an instant, her fist in front of Brianna's face. "You stupid bitch. An angel's no more likely to protect you than a pile of dog shit is gonna. Even my deadbeat ma knew that."

"Enough," Sheila's voice cut through Danesha's haze, razor sharp. "Danesha, go up to your room right now. I want you to write a letter of apology to all of us for ruining this moment. Come down when it's written and we'll talk about our Christmas tree then."

As she stalked out, cursing and mumbling under her breath, Nate dared to glance at Brianna. She looked smaller somehow, stricken and shrunken, her own face closed and her eyes brimming with unshed tears. "We always had angels. You can't have a Christmas tree without them," she whispered as the room grew silent.

Dude trotted over, the sudden quiet snapping him out of his nap. He nudged Brianna until she absently patted his head.

"Brianna, grab your coat and take him out for a few minutes, get some fresh air until Danesha comes back down. We'll work it out." Sheila handed her the leash, waited for the door to close, then turned to Nate. "Welcome to Christmas at the GIFT House."

"What just happened?"

Sheila shook her head, a frown pulling her lips into a sad grimace. "Too many memories. Too much emotion. This is the season of hell for these kids."

"Not just these kids," Nate muttered before he could stop himself.

She probed again with those deep brown eyes. "Pain and loss are color blind, that's for sure."

Interestingly, Lisa and Nate had discovered on their second date that their yearning for Christmas was a mutual childhood experience. And yet years later during the pregnancy with twins—the only one to occur in December— they were in agreement that they would avoid falling into the trappings of a holiday that was not their own. Their children would be raised Jewish, maybe even sent to religious school, something neither of them had experienced and now missed. Lisa had begun searching to join a synagogue compatible with their values and lifestyle. She lost the babies before she found one.

"What is it you're looking for, Nate?"

"Here? Or in general?"

"Are they different answers?"

He reflected for several moments. Outside the window Brianna was shuffling behind Dude as he marked his territory on the neighbor's tree. Her shoulders were hunched, her eyes cast down.

"Same as everyone. I want to be part of a family," he finally answered.

"Any family? Or a blue ribbon family?"

The snow was falling steadily now, covering his truck windshield and sticking to the branches. He thought about Lisa in Minnesota and winced. She hadn't even called to tell him she was going.

"I once thought I knew the answer to that. Now I don't know if I get a choice."

"I could grow to like you, Mr. Nate. You're honest. That's a rarity."

Her words settled as a balm. He took a long swallow of the hot cocoa, allowed its thick sweetness to fill his mouth.

"I've got a proposition for you. How would you feel about working a bit for the GIFT House? Keep up the maintenance, like you seem to want to do, maybe run some errands. And you could come visit, so long as you are never in the room with the girls unless Lisa or Miss Vanessa is here."

"You kidding?" he exclaimed, trying not to remember Lisa's clear message. *This is not your job, Nate, and these are not your girls.* He hesitated. "I'd love it. But you don't have to pay me. I'll just do it."

"You'll need to take a drug test. And sign a contract. You can donate the money back if you want, but we will have to pay you for our state records."

He looked around the room, noting the chipped corner of the mantle, the ceiling that needed painting against a seeping mustard yellow undercoat, the frost inside the windows. "I accept."

Sheila nodded as if pleased and then immediately, as a realization of what she'd offered and to whom crossed her face, she pulled in a deep breath.

"Listen, Nate, I suggested this job because the girls see you as a kind, caring man. Bu don't you dare get more involved here unless you mean it."

Brianna was walking up the porch stairs now. He could see her shivering in the thin coat. She bent low and kissed the top of Dude's head, and when she straightened, her face had lost a bit of its pinch.

"I understand," he said.

"Then do me a favor and shout upstairs and tell Danesha to come down. Whatever craziness seized that girl before is likely over. It's time to make us some popcorn and decorate this ridiculous tree." She laughed outright. "It's way too big for the room. Jewish folks can't be trusted to buy a Christmas tree, can they?"

He smiled back. "Next year's will be a better fit."

CHAPTER TWENTY-NINE

A nother useless nursery. A dusty crib, empty and stale, was backed into the corner. The zoo-motif mobile above it looked frozen, its giraffe and elephant heads crooked at the neck and bowed from disuse. The yellow-striped bumper pads were rigid, no warm body having softened them into pillows.

"I just can't bring myself to get rid of the crib," Jeanette muttered as Lisa dumped her suitcase on the twin bed and hurried out of the bedroom-turned-nursery-turned-spare-bedroom.

That was the first bad moment. The second one was worse.

Albert had been thrilled to greet Lisa, his normal reticence replaced by a near childlike joy. He'd clapped his hands together and shouted out when she walked into the living room. He flung his arms around her and engulfed her in a hug, pulling her cushioned body against his skeletal one. *He's fine,* she thought, hugging him closer.

They sat at the kitchen table, knee to knee, and Lisa felt her spine relax for the first time in months, as she and her parents sipped warm tea in the room that held so many of her favorite childhood memories. Unlike Albert, now alarmingly thin, Jeanette looked wonderful. After years of dying her hair brunette in shades that seemed to alternate between too purple to too orange, she'd let the natural gray grow in and had achieved a true salt and pepper blend that flattered a complexion clearer than Lisa's own. Even her wrinkles were flattering, adding character more than age. Most of Jeanette's friends, apparently, were doing Botox and fillers, a temptation Jeanette had yet to indulge. "It's like the Benjamin Button syndrome," she'd recently remarked. "Every time I see them they look younger than before!" Lisa wanted to compliment Jeanette but knew she would brush the praise aside, so instead Lisa squeezed her mother's hand, engulfed in a sense of easy love. This is what she'd needed, to come home for a while. Her sister Kate was flying up and would be here tomorrow and they would all be together for three nights of Chanukah for the first time in nearly a decade.

Albert turned to Lisa and asked, "How are the girls doing?"

She paused, not wanting to bring them into this room. "They're doing."

His brow knitted in confusion and he tilted his head. "What do you mean?"

"Oh, Daddy. I know they can't help it, I mean given what they've been through and all. But they're just so difficult." His face was free of judgment, so she went on, purposefully not addressing her mother. "Of course, teens are going to be challenging, no matter what. But these girls—"

"Teens? They're already teens?" He slapped his hand against his knee and let loose a deep grumbling laugh. "Where have I been? I thought they were still babies."

She sat up straighter. What had her mother told him? "No, didn't you realize I'm living with the girls to help them in high school?"

He leaned in close, caressed her cheek with his palm. "Oh, sweetheart, I have been working too much. And I've left you to raise those girls without me. I'll try to be around more."

"What are you talking about?"

Jeanette immediately scooted back, banging her chair against the table leg. "Albert, that's enough. This is your daughter Lisa."

"Mom, what's going on?"

"Come on, Albert. Let's get you to bed." Without answering, they both stood, and draping his arm against Jeanette's shoulder, they moved as one out of the kitchen and up the stairs to the bedrooms.

Lisa didn't budge, didn't let herself think, didn't let herself feel. Eventually Jeanette came back down and slid into the kitchen chair opposite Lisa.

"I'm sorry. I was hoping tonight would be one of his lucid nights. I never know when he'll turn on or off."

"What happened?"

"The girls he meant were you and your sister. He thought you were me."

She let the knowledge wash through her, felt her chin nodding that she understood, as though her mother's comment made sense.

"Look, it is what it is. And for now it's mostly bearable." Jeanette wandered over to the stove, turned the flame on under the tea kettle. "Want some more?"

"But, Mom, you were sitting right there."

Jeanette shrugged. "Not in *his* brain."

"Ohhh," Lisa said, more a whimper than a word. They drank their tea, catching up on neighbors and family friends, by implicit agreement avoiding all but the most benign topics, until Lisa couldn't hide her yawns. This time when she entered the spare bedroom the crib didn't loom as large and empty. Instead, it was the smell of urine that assaulted her.

Again, Jeanette shrugged when pressed. "Sometimes Daddy sleeps in here. Sometimes he doesn't quite make it to the bathroom. I've *told* you that," she added, her tone as cheerless as Lisa had ever heard from her mom. She placed her head on Lisa's shoulder, then brushed her lips against Lisa's cheek, patted her arm and turned to go. At the doorway, she paused. "I'm glad you're here. We need you."

Lisa sat on the edge of the bed, listening to her mother's footsteps, and minutes later to the sound of running water in the bathroom sink, the flush of the toilet, the groan of the mattress, her parents' murmuring and eventually the gentle snoring of her parents' slumber.

She continued to sit, not moving except to slump her shoulders forward as she finally admitted what she'd not let herself believe. Albert's brain was truly, progressively, irreparably disintegrating. Her sweet daddy was disappearing. She kneaded her eyelids with tight fists, fighting the creeping sense of sadness and shame. How could she have turned such a deaf ear to her mother's stories? For a moment she was tempted to tiptoe down the hall and nudge her mom awake to apologize. But she knew that unless she was ready to offer what Jeanette needed, there was little Lisa could say that would make a difference.

Suddenly she remembered another time, when she was a child and Albert had disappeared for a week. One day during that long week, she and Kate had gotten into a fight, and when Lisa told her to stop being such a big baby, Kate took Lisa's favorite doll and cut the doll's stomach wide open and yanked out the stuffing. What was left was a flopping piece of fabric that could no longer support a plastic head. Lisa took one look and went a little crazy. She could have smacked Kate with the doll's hard head, but she was smarter than that. She went running into the kitchen and wrapped her arms around Jeanette, crying with a sorrow that was both real and exaggerated. Her intent was for Jeanette to get off the phone (which she immediately did), to cuddle Lisa (she did) and to ask what was wrong so that Kate would get her comeuppance. Only instead, Jeanette pulled Lisa onto her lap, held her close and murmured, "I know you're scared about your Dad, sweetie. But I have great news. They caught everything before it spread. It's all going to be okay." Lisa had no idea what Jeanette was talking about—caught what? spread?—and all she really cared about was that her favorite doll had been destroyed by her bratty sister.

Weird, the vividness of the memory all these years later, Albert having not only beat the cancer but having never experienced a recurrence. Except he wouldn't be as lucky this time, and she was no longer a child, and the comforting arms belonged around Jeanette.

Lisa looked around the room, half expecting to see the doll's stuffing in the middle of the floor, then laughed aloud as she thought to herself, *you too much drama*, and with that she abruptly stood and just as abruptly her leg buckled, her foot fat and prickly with sleep. Lisa stomped a couple of times, remembering the day she had stamped her foot in frustration—was it only four months ago?—as she complained to Sheila about Danesha.

It was ten thirty. Sheila usually went to bed early, but there was no school tomorrow. She picked up the phone and dialed. As usual, the line was busy.

As she continued to redial, she studied the room through the eyes of a visitor. A neighbor had offered to loan a crib to Jeanette when Lisa became pregnant the first time. Lisa had already miscarried before she discovered that Jeanette had bought the crib outright, along with new bedding, a baby mobile and an array of stuffed toys and Discovery Toys rattles. Lisa visited her parents during those glorious weeks between ultrasound and losing the first of the twins. "Seems we'll need to get us another crib now," her dad had said, squeezing her close. "Let's not jump the gun," Jeanette cautioned, startling them both and sending a chill down Lisa's spine. Later, in a conversation that would haunt Lisa for years, Albert admitted, whispering into the phone out of Jeanette's earshot, "I can't help but blame your mother for pooh-poohing your pregnancy." "Oh, Daddy, we both know it doesn't work like that," she'd countered, while shaking her head in agreement at her end.

On impulse, Lisa dialed another number, this one so familiar her fingers danced across the buttons of the phone. Nate's voice answered. "You've reached Nate Rothman and I'm not home right now. Leave a message. Or not." She placed the receiver back, her hand trembling. *Nate Rothman. I'm not home.* Well, of course, he'd change the message. She would have been angry if it was still her cheery voice proclaiming that Nate and Lisa weren't there.

She redialed, listened until the beep, hung up and immediately dialed again. *Nate Rothman. I'm not home.*

They were married one week when they bought their first answering machine. How safe it had felt to record, *"You've reached the Rothmans. We're not here right now..."* She'd had to rerecord it several times because Nate kept interrupting, causing her to laugh as he farted, burped, erupted in song, until she'd shooed him out of the room and then had gone into their bedroom to find him sprawled on the bed, stark naked and waiting.

She dialed again. Where could he be this late? Surely not on a date? She pressed the buttons, listened to his irritatingly calm voice, hung up, dialed again. Then the GIFT House. Still

194

busy. Did *no one* miss her? She went into the hall bathroom and brushed her teeth, then dared to scrutinize herself in the full-length mirror, something she'd studiously avoided for months. She was too fat, startlingly round. Her face was so full it didn't even wrinkle where it should. Her roots were months beyond simple neglect. And her wardrobe was nearly as bad.

Despite having spent over an hour packing, she'd been unable to piece together a suitcase full of passable outfits. Since "outgrowing" nearly everything from before, she'd stopped going into the mall and had bought replacement clothes while shopping with the girls—at Wal-Mart and K-Mart. To Jeanette's credit, she'd clearly noticed but not commented on Lisa's cheap, ill-fitting "Faded Glory" (she couldn't resist the name) fourteen-dollar jeans and shapeless sweater, an unflattering shade of gold that was on the "40% Off Sale Price" rack.

Yet, Lisa had recognized the expression in Nate's eyes, the way he still looked at her with love and longing.

This time when she hit redial Nate answered.

"Hi, it's me." She forced her voice to sound calm, casual, as she slipped back against her twin bed mattress, feeling very much the twenty year old calling her boyfriend in the dark.

"Hey! Wow. I'm glad you called. How's your dad?"

"It's so awful. I don't think he even realized I'm his daughter." She felt her throat catch. The words made everything seem more real and more unreal.

"I'm sorry. You guys don't deserve this. I guess no one does."

She twirled her finger around the cord, allowing it to wrap itself into a tight cushion. He'd probably been working late, doing a holiday event. She used to hate that about his business. His hours were longest when everyone else was partying. "It's for our future," he'd tell her, compensation for her weekend and holiday nights alone.

Then she bolted up. "Wait a minute. How did you know I'm with my parents?"

"Danesha and Brianna told me."

"Huh? When did you talk to them? And why?"

There was a long pause as he weighed his answer, deciding, she supposed, between honesty and self. His voice, when he finally spoke, was so low, so hesitant, that it took a moment for the words to register.

"You're at the GIFT House? Late at night?"

"Don't be mad, honey."

"*Honey*? What the hell are you up to, Nate? And how can you be at the GIFT House when I called home. Your home."

"You called me?" He let out a slow whistle of pleasure. "I'll be God damned."

"You're not answering me. What are you doing there?"

"I can't believe it. You called me." He chuckled.

"Nate!"

"Sorry. I'm just..." his voice turned husky, "I'm just so glad to talk to you." The tender tone of a lover wooing back his woman.

Her finger slipped out of the phone cord and fell against her chest. She inhaled several times. This was a moment, an offering, the ability to go in any direction. Then she looked at the shadow cast from the crib rails, the way they elongated into prison bars.

"I can't do this, Nate. I can't share this new life with you."

The silence was longer and sadder this time. "Why is it your choice to make?" he asked, and left her alone in the dark with only the whining of the dial tone and the empty crib in the corner.

It was amazing what one could adjust to when she allowed herself to go numb. After the loss of baby Sam, Lisa returned to work. In time, she went out for drinks with co-workers. To the movies with Nate, to parties, to meetings. She began to scour the want ads for a new job and peruse catalogues for interesting classes.

She still had to turn abruptly from strollers and pregnant women. She had to leave the room or immediately get off the phone upon hearing news of another baby's birth. She routinely swallowed Tylenol P.M. in order to sleep through the night and indefinitely postponed her over-due Ob/Gyn exam.

But she was functioning and she was moving beyond. She even reached a point where she could feign enthusiasm as friends struggled with cloth versus paper, pacifier versus thumb, preschool versus daycare.

And all the while she and Nate assured each other that their lives were fine. They ate out whenever they wanted. They bought new furniture and planned vacations and shared stories from their work days. The white carpeting stayed clean.

But too often Lisa would squint at Nate as he undressed for bed and try to quell the queasiness she felt at the thought of faking passion or affection. And she suspected, with equal measures of dismay and relief, his feelings mirrored her own.

They'd also begun to bicker, not fights exactly, but a lot of prickly responses, furrowed brows, sharp tones. When they walked past one another, they held themselves stiff so as not to brush skin against skin. Every so often one or the other would try to talk about the distance between them, would dare to bring up the "baby thing," but words left them frustrated, sad and distant. There was no joy in their house. Yet life felt— mostly—bearable.

And then one day, Lisa came home early from work, sank into a corner in the empty nursery, began to cry and could not stop.

Dr. Leonard Berger was considered the best, having won local Therapist of the Year as well as having survived his own much-publicized family trauma. But even Dr. Berger couldn't bring Lisa out of the black hole in which she suddenly found herself.

Almost immediately she upped weekly therapy appointments to twice a week and counted the long hours in between sessions, though once in the therapist's office she often found herself at a loss for words. "What's there to say?" she'd snap.

"Try to figure out why having a child is so important to you."

She wanted to throw her purse at him. Men! He could get fifteen psychology degrees and thirty awards and he'd still never understand how it felt to be barren and damaged. To look in the mirror and see the failures of a woman whose body betrayed the most fundamental thing a woman's body should do—the very thing that young teens were doing every fucking day. To admit that the intimate joining of her egg and Nate's sperm repeatedly resulted in death. She was supposed to "figure that out?"

Initially Nate supported her therapy. He even offered to go with her. But as the weeks turned into months and Lisa, if anything, grew increasingly morose and unreachable, Nate became angry. "It feels like you're more connected to Berger than to me."

"Oh, please," she said, her voice so bitter she wondered that he didn't slap her, as she almost wished he would.

At work she found she could no longer muster professional concern. Mostly what she felt was a blazing jealousy when clients talked about not having enough money to feed their kids. Daily she had to bite back the words. *At least you have children.*

"It's too much pressure to pretend to my mom and to Nate that everything is going to be okay, that I'm going to just move on to the next stage," she told Dr. Berger.

"Then don't pretend," he said. And for that fucking advice, she owed him yet another one-hundred-sixty bucks.

Suddenly, she couldn't stop eating—trying to feed the monster or fill a hole or trying to look pregnant or any number of clichés and therapeutic "insights" that didn't mean shit when she was too miserable to care about making herself even more miserable. After a restless night of little sleep, she'd wake up groggy in the pre-dawn mornings and as she rose to consciousness her first thought was, *I hate myself.* And then she'd burrow herself back into bed, lie mindlessly in front of the television or trudge down to the kitchen and open the refrigerator.

Daily, sometimes hourly, she'd call Bonnie. In one of life's greater ironies, Bonnie never wanted children—had actively made sure never to get pregnant—but wound up with two step-sons whom she adored, especially when they were staying at their mom's house. Yet, Bonnie seemed to understand Lisa's pain, but could do little more than offer loving, if uncertain, reassurances, "You have to believe this won't last forever, Lis. Life will somehow get better again."

"I don't know who I am anymore," Lisa would wail.

"You'll figure it out. You will."

The chasm once known as their marriage had grown to a point where neither she nor Nate even tried. Sometimes she would watch him prepare for bed through slanted eyes. She knew she still loved him. She could even let herself imagine the emotion until he crawled into bed alongside her, and the heat from his body made her cold.

"Do you ever think about those babies?" she screamed on one particularly bad day. She watched the struggle creep across his face as he clearly mulled over the right answer. "Forget it!" she'd barked, stomping out of the room.

That day she indulged. Much the way an alcoholic takes a furtive gulp, she locked the door, took the phone off the hook and placed her hidden mementos next to one another. The plastic yellow ribbon that had been tied to the sapling she and Nate planted. The journal she kept while pregnant with the twins, filled with pages of large loopy handwriting and exclamation marks. And then Sam's footprint, the size of a thimble, the toes a connected box, the tiny arch, the ink-dot heel.

"Lisa, you have told me what Nate wants and what your mother wants, but what about you? Given the reality of your circumstances, what do *you* want?" Dr. Berger's voice echoed in the room as if the answer were attainable.

She'd always wanted children. Had always believed she'd have children and a loving husband. Long past the age at which most girls set their dolls aside, Lisa was still building little families with her stuffed animals and fixing Barbie and Ken up on blind dates. And there had been the summers spent as a camp counselor. "You're so good with kids. Bet you'll have a dozen of your own," she remembered hearing from the head of the camp. There simply was never any question for her. She had a vision and it was filled with diapers and car pools and photo books. She was a good and honest person leading a good and honest life and, therefore, had assumed her very reasonable vision would be reality. Because to think otherwise, to envision a future of days and days of nothingness—to be cheated out of such a basic desire—was unimaginable.

As she clutched each of the mementos, one more pitiful, more futile, than the next, she began to sob so hard that she didn't know how she could stop. This wasn't grief. She'd known grief. This was a hopelessness and self-loathing that made her nearly yearn for the simplicity and social acceptability of grief. And it wasn't about the miscarriages or Sam or even about her marriage. The pain she felt at the loss of her sense of self so overwhelmed any other pain that she truly believed Dr. Berger was wrong. It would kill her.

Nate found her on the floor in the closet. He pulled her onto his lap, wrapped his arms around her, whispered against her neck, "Lisa, how can this be happening? If I'd put together one-hundred people I know, you would have been the one-hundredth I could imagine having a breakdown."

The best she could offer was the dull retort. "Maybe that's part of why I'm going through this."

The next day she succumbed, much too belatedly, and went on anti-depressants. After nearly a year of subsisting, the cloud gradually thinned. Inch by inch, week by week, the meds kicked in. Finally, she was able to crawl out from under the crushing weight of intense emotions to clarify her issues. The therapy began to resonate. There were days she recognized herself in the mirror. And like a trite cliché, Lisa found the courage to honestly examine and then forgive her parents, her husband and herself for human frailties, to forgive her body for its imperfection, to forgive life for being unfair.

The realization that she would need to—and with hard work could—rewrite the script of her life, started to feel feasible. Some of what she'd learned a lifetime ago studying psychology in grad school made new sense.

Nate and Lisa began again to make love—this time, and every single time, using birth control.

CHAPTER THIRTY

The post-holiday airport atmosphere was a sharp contrast from the frenetic buoyancy of the week before. Travelers appeared flat as they stumbled through lines carrying bulky paper sacks filled with presents. Cheery Christmas music had been replaced with non-descript Muzak, adding to the deflated mood that Lisa had been trying to shake off since waking up that morning.

"Sit here, Daddy," she said, indicating the one free seat near the American Airlines ticket counter. She gave a gentle push on his shoulders, dismayed by the sharp bone where once flesh and muscle had bulged. Albert wobbled slightly. Lisa bit her bottom lip and turned away so he wouldn't see her tears.

"Where's Jeanette?" His voice was soft, and not for the first time, Lisa wondered if her father had Parkinson's disease. Her mother refused to acknowledge the possibility.

"Enough," Jeanette had snapped last night when Lisa tried to broach the subject. "Don't you think I've got enough to worry about without you adding a disease *de jour*?"

Her own nerves stretched to the limit after a week at home, Lisa had responded the only way she could. She turned her back and walked out, just barely resisting the urge to slam the door.

Now, as she looked at Albert slumping in the unyielding airport chair, at the vacancy in his eyes, the rivulet of drool on his chin, she felt a surge of remorse. However much sorrow she might be experiencing, what could she know of her mother's grief? To lose a partner by inches was beyond comprehension. Well, at least she hadn't experienced *that*.

She'd lain awake the entire night after Nate hung up the phone. Around three in the morning she'd crept downstairs, poured a large glass of bourbon from a dusty bottle into a crystal wine glass and had chugged the fiery liquid until it burned worse than her pain. She spent the rest of the week sleeping on the den couch. Neither Jeanette nor Kate commented, though they exchanged none-too-subtle glances throughout the visit.

Today when Lisa went back into the nursery to make sure she had packed everything, she stood for a long time staring into the crib. She didn't think about the babies or Nate or the dashed dreams. She thought about how, as children, she and Kate had never been close but they'd always been acutely aware of one another, in large part shaping their own personalities to be the anti-other—but still sisters. When young, they'd sometimes sneak into one another's rooms at night, during thunderstorms or when there was a new babysitter, and they'd share the bed until morning, head to feet, feet to head. During middle school, Kate went through a shoplifting phase and Lisa never tattled. In high school, the first time Lisa got drunk at a party she had called Kate to pick her up and cover for her. Then they'd entered their twenties, drifted further and further apart, and now could barely scratch out a conversation to fill the awkward silences until they could fly away to their separate parts of the country and unrelated lives. Sisters were supposed to be connected and the fact that Kate had a woman partner somehow made their own detachment that much more pitiful. Well, now they would need to stay in touch about their parents.

"Where's Jeanette?" Albert repeated.

"I told you, Daddy, she's parking the car. She'll be here any minute." Lisa bent over to kiss the top of his head, but he gripped her hand, stilling her motion. He held her eyes with an expression of intensity, blazing with an urge to be *seen*. "No, Lisa. You didn't tell me."

He was right! Maybe? Maybe they were all wrong? After all, didn't it often seem that when you went looking for trouble you found it? She sank into the chair and leaned her body into her dad's.

They sat like that, warming each other in a companionable silence, watching those around them. There was so much public emotion at an airport. The joyous reunions, the tearful goodbyes. Everyone had a story.

As a child, Lisa had often played an imaginary travel game on family road trips. As houses whizzed by outside the car windows, Lisa would create a family and situation for each one. This one was a newlywed, that one had six kids, this one was about to move. Kate considered Lisa's fantasy games "too dorky" and her mother was never one to stretch. "Don't we have enough on our minds without inventing other people's troubles too?" Only Albert would engage, offering his own descriptive scenarios. "Really, Daddy?" she'd ask, forgetting that what's imagined and what's real may appear as one but are rarely the same.

Lisa rested her head against Albert's shoulder and pulled his hand to her lips. She held it there for a few moments, not quite kissing him but letting her lips and nose taste and smell his essence.

"I love you, Dad," she murmured against his skin.

Again his eyes found and held hers. "Where's Jeanette?" he asked.

The plane was delayed at least an hour, perhaps more.

Annoyance seemed to swirl as dust motes off the bottoms of Jeanette's boots as she strode from the flight info board back to their seats. "Just ridiculous," she said.

The snow was falling at a rate of three inches per hour at the Minneapolis-St. Paul airport. But it was due to a three-inch *total* snow storm in St. Louis that the plane was late in taking off.

"Are they going to pay for my parking ticket too?" Jeanette hissed.

Lisa didn't bother to ask who "they" were, the nameless, faceless bane of her challenging existence.

"Mom, please don't wait. You and Dad need to get back while it's still light. I've got a good book and..." She pointed her chin in the direction of the window where large snowflakes continued to fall in thick white swirls.

"Oh, that," Jeanette tsked. "They'll have the streets cleared long before your plane leaves for that southern city of yours."

"Come on," Lisa said, struggling to modulate her tone. "I'll feel better if I know you're safe at home. And I ought to go through security and check in at the gate. Just in case they take off sooner."

Jeanette raised an eyebrow and Lisa laughed.

"Okay, but you belong at home."

"As do you."

Lisa inwardly groaned.

Jeanette patted Albert on the knee, as though to silence the man who'd yet to speak since she'd appeared. "You've been here a week and I still don't know any real details about this place where you're living and about those girls. And I want the real story, for once."

Lisa glanced at her watch.

"I'll leave after you tell me." Jeanette displayed a rare playful smile.

She started with the basics, their looks, a bit about their backgrounds, their grades, and then warmed into more personality particulars. As she talked, the girls evolved from adjectives into individuals, ones she took care of and cared for—and Lisa found herself powerfully missing each one. How was Coreen's visit home? Was she shuffled around as usual or actually able to celebrate the holidays with one parent or the other? And Eva-Lynn. Just how awful was that visit? Did Brianna hear from her mom for Christmas? Was Danesha mostly staying in her room or actually keeping Sheila company? And Dude, how was he?

Jeanette's eyes were intent upon Lisa as she spoke, sometimes tearing red, other times turning merry with recognition at some of the anecdotes. She waited, for once, until the stories wound down of natural accord before she offered in a whispery voice, "You should have adopted, you know. You still could."

Lisa took a few thoughtful moments before she responded, "Maybe I'm meant to do this instead?" She shook her head and giggled aloud. "Oye! Did I really say that?"

Lisa pressed Albert close as she hugged him goodbye, trying to squeeze some of her heft onto his bony frame. She and Jeanette wrapped strong arms about each other before reluctantly pulling back and away.

"We'll come visit. Perhaps go see that specialist you talked about for Dad."

Lisa offered a vigorous nod yes. "And I'll try to get home again this spring."

For the longest while Lisa watched as Albert slowly shuffled, pulled along with resolute briskness by Jeanette. She was seized by the realization that this stoop-shouldered, confused father was the best he would ever again be. She also suddenly realized—how had she never thought of this before?—that her parents quite likely would never get to be grandparents. For an instant, she imagined shredding the boarding pass to St. Louis, a confetti of unfulfilled dreams, and racing after her mom and dad, going home together, where they could all three take care of one another. Instead, she dug into her purse for her driver's license, her ticket and a tissue. Then she entered the long security queue for departing passengers.

PART TWO

CHAPTER THIRTY-ONE

January third, their first meal together since the holiday separation. Lisa put the platter on the table. The girls stared at what was supposed to be a roasted chicken but looked more like a burnt boot. Danesha was tempted to give her characteristic "what the..." response, but even she fell silent.

"Dig in, girls. Don't be shy."

Brianna reached for the bowl of cooked carrots, took a few and passed them on. No one else pretended. The full bowl reached Lisa, but she also passed.

"Ain't you taking any?" Coreen asked, shoving a forkful of chicken into her mouth. She quickly swallowed some water, but, still, they could hear the gulp of the food going down.

Danesha giggled, blurted, "Dang! Pass me some of that oven *dried* chicken," eliciting laughter from the other three.

"This is so nice," Lisa chimed, "to be a family all together again." Immediately, Danesha's face darkened into a scowl and an awkward silence took hold of the room.

Lisa struggled to cut apart her chicken. She gave a sheepish grin and explained that chicken had to be cooked thoroughly to avoid salmonella, a disease none of the rest of them had ever heard of.

Coreen wondered if it was something that only hit white people, the way sickle cell had ruined her cousin's life just because he was black. She wanted to ask Miss Lisa if next time she'd take the chicken out of the oven sooner for three of them and bake it long for Lisa and Eva-Lynn. But Miss Lisa weren't in any mood for a discussion so Coreen bit into another piece, this one drier than the last.

Brianna thought with a powerful wishing of how Grandmama fried hers up until it was so crisp on the outside you could hear it crunch all the way to the juicy tender flesh.

Eva-Lynn glanced out the window, noted the falling snow, and felt a rise of claustrophobia that made her want to vomit.

Lisa considered asking the girls about Nate's visit, but she wasn't sure she could bear watching their faces light up at the mention of his name. She looked at Dude, gently snoring in his corner of the kitchen, and remembered reading that chicken bones could be deadly for a dog. Grabbing a newspaper insert from the pile next to her chair, she wrapped up the gizzards, wings and innards for the trash.

"What are you doing? You're not thinking of trashing the best parts?" Danesha jerked the bundle from Miss Lisa's hands, remembering mama's slap when she herself had made this same mistake. Pinching them in her fingers, she removed the wings and put the rest smack in the middle of the table.

Coreen leaned forward. "Can I have the parson's nose?"

"The what, honey?"

"Parson's nose. This piece that looks like a little fat nose." Coreen giggled, "My daddy calls it the part that went over the fence last." As she twisted it off, Danesha muttered, "Figures you'd like the fat ass." Ignoring her, Coreen turned to Brianna, "What part you like?"

Brianna felt her eyes fill with tears and her throat thicken. "My part didn't even make it to the table."

"What's your favorite, Brianna?" Lisa asked, her voice soft.

Stupid, to cry over chicken. But suddenly she could hear Ma and Auntie Billie and Grandmama, could smell the greens—not frozen or canned vegetables like Miss Lisa's— these were heavy turnip greens, soaked in bacon fat and seasoned with lots of pepper, enough to make her tongue come alive. "The neck meat, that's the tenderest meat on a chicken," Auntie would say, shredding it off the little vertebrae bones and offering the purplish strips to Brianna. Wonder who ate the neck at their Christmas dinner in Florida. She frowned. "I don't really like chicken anymore."

They ate in silence, clanking their forks and glasses, avoiding each other's eyes. Mostly, they pushed the food around on their plates, except for Coreen, who plowed on with determination.

At least the holidays were behind them. A Christmas card and ten dollar bill that arrived three days late for Brianna. A drunken call and empty promise for Danesha. Eva-Lynn had come back with a split lip. Coreen said she couldn't remember what all she had done or where—and no one was curious enough to dig deeper. What Coreen didn't tell them was that on Christmas Eve there was a mix-up and instead of switching from her uncle's house to her dad's, she had spent the entire night outside a locked door, trying to hide in a dark corner at the top of the apartment stairwell as she watched two bums shooting up one floor below.

Lisa stared at her half-eaten portion, struggling not to think about her last dinner at home at which Albert had gaped at his chicken breast having no idea how to use a knife and fork, and then had tried to "eat" his coffee with his fingers. She stood abruptly, asked, "Everybody done?" and without waiting for an answer began to stack their plates, scraping all the food onto the top plate, plopping her chicken into the middle of Brianna's string bean casserole.

The girls watched in amazement, each face showing a kind of horror and fascination. It wasn't like it would taste any better *tomorrow*, but still.

My people would kill me if I did that, Coreen thought even as she did nothing to stop Miss Lisa from pitching Coreen's leftover tater tots into the trash. She'd been planning on sneaking the taters upstairs and having them in bed. Miss Lisa didn't let them eat anything outside of the kitchen 'cause she said the crumbs would attract bugs and mice. They'd all looked at each other the first time she said that. It was pretty funny to see her face wrinkled all up—as if just the words "mouse" or "roach" were full of germs.

"Uh, I don't think you wanna go and do that," Danesha said.

Lisa halted, standing stiff in front of the plastic trash can. *Now what?* In just a week's time away, she'd forgotten how draining it was to continually break some unspoken rule. She didn't have to wonder very long.

"In case you forgot while you was havin' your *white* Christmas, for us *po folks*..." Danesha paused, allowing the tension to build, "this here food is another meal, another day."

"Look, girls, I know our budget better than anybody. But if you don't want it tonight, are you going to eat it tomorrow?"

211

As if to answer, Danesha shoved her body between Lisa and the trash can. Coreen and Brianna inhaled, their eyes opening wide, barely breathing, waiting. Eva-Lynn leaned back; best goddamned show she'd seen yet in this coon house.

With deliberate slowness, Danesha plied the top plate from Lisa's hand. Bending at the waist, she began to retrieve from the garbage one piece of food at a time, a tatter tot, a bit of chicken, a mushy carrot. She flaunted a wild grin as she reached into the wastebasket one last time and grabbed a gooey dripping handful of string bean casserole.

"Hmmm, won't be goin' hungry at this here *special* home for *special* girls, fo sho." Danesha spun on her heel and sashayed out of the kitchen and upstairs to her room.

What the fuck! Had she really for ten minutes thought she'd *missed* this?

Welcome back to the GIFT House.

CHAPTER THIRTY-TWO

S he didn't mean to get all up in Miss Lisa's fat face. It was just so boring otherwise. And sometimes it almost seemed like Miss Lisa was asking for it, throwing food away while they was still eating. Even her own mama wasn't that big of a mess.

The phone rang and when Miss Lisa shouted up the stairs, "Danesha! Phone for you," she felt her breath stop. She still couldn't believe Devon had bust a u-turn on her, not calling for way over a month. *She* was supposed to be the one to run a game on *him*. Couple times a day his gold smile crossed her mind, so she'd started asking around without looking like she cared none and heard he'd skipped out of town. Where would he go when he musta known he weren't gonna be king of no corner outside St. Loser?

She walked into the hallway and stopped, her hand just above the phone, fixing her "never let 'em see you sweat" voice in her head.

"You skipped your session," Sheila Johnson stated as soon as Danesha picked up the line. "I'm waiting at the school. You need to be here in the next fifteen minutes or I'll have to count it as another miss." She didn't bother to say goodbye or wait to make sure Danesha would come.

"We're all just trying to teach you responsibility. Teach you follow through," Miss Lisa said as they drove the short ride to Stone Charter. The neighborhood was in that in-between hour when the drunks were still sleeping and the druggies hadn't sprung awake. Empty lots on empty streets. Could have been anywhere America instead of their sorry ghetto corner.

"I'll be back in an hour," Lisa said, skidding in the snow as she pulled away without her usual horn tap.

Long creepy shadows followed Danesha as she walked the empty hallway to the counseling office. Ms. Johnson waved her in, then put two fingers to her lip for Danesha to sit quiet while she finished her phone call. "Uh, huh. Mrs. Wallace, that's not good enough. If Dominique misses again, he's going to get suspended for three days. And that will go on his record.

Of course. I know how difficult things are. But he's got to come to school. It's not enough to show up once a week."

She placed the receiver down and offered a fake, adult smile. "Didn't mean to snap at you like that earlier. It's been a rough day." She sagged back into her chair, her fat self curling around the wooden arms. "Want to tell me what's going on that you're avoiding our sessions?"

"Ain't nothing going on." When Ms. Johnson wouldn't blink, giving her that 'don't bullshit me' look, Danesha added, "Talking here don't change nothing. What's the point?"

Ms. Johnson shifted her whole body. The chair legs squeaked and the table shook a little as she rested her elbows down. Most people that fat made Danesha sick, just the sight of all that extra skin. But Ms. Johnson's blubber was the kind where you could imagine resting your head in her lap and falling asleep.

"I hate living in the GIFT House." Ms. Johnson raised an eyebrow. Danesha continued. "The other girls are hobos and Miss Lisa don't know what she's doing and none of it matters anyhow cuz I got other plans."

"Care to tell me?"

Danesha held back her smile, trying to picture Ms. Johnson's hot jealousy if she knew that Danesha was planning on being the baddest ass black model New York had ever seen. Soon as she got a little more money and found a way to get there, get rich and bust Jerrell out of the joint.

"This school and that house ain't any place for me, Ms. Johnson. You can see that."

"Only thing I can see, Danesha, is that you're wasting what could be the first chance you've ever had to be in a stable place where you can worry only about you. No one else to take care of right now, but you."

"Nesha, fetch me another one of them purple pills, and some beer to wash it down with. My head is hurtin' somethin' fierce."

"Please don't, Mama. You'll just go to sleep and you promised you'd come up to watch me sing. I got a solo, and everyone else's mom is gonna be there."

214

The slap hadn't hurt nearly as much as the swelling made it seem like it should of. "Don't tell me what to do, girl. Maybe everyone else's mom ain't got a good for nothing son and daughter. Now I said get me my pill and then don't you even think about going to the church choir 'til you finish up those dishes. You think I like living with all that filth?"

"Danesha? Here, take one."

Only when she saw the box of tissues being shoved in front of her face did she realize she was crying. She pushed the box away and struggled to pull her lips into a scowl.

"How are things going between you and Eva-Lynn?"

She said the nicest thing she could think of. "I don't give a shit about her."

"Watch the language."

"Miss Lisa don't care."

"Doesn't."

"Huh?"

"Danesha, you're too smart to act this stupid. Even your teachers see how smart you are since you started going to class regularly. Which, by the way, is a very good thing and I'm quite pleased about that. But don't let anybody bring you down. You can be anything you want if you let yourself."

Ms. Johnson's face was so kind at that moment that Danesha almost told her the plan. Before she could say anything, Ms. Johnson leaned in too close and in a voice way too quiet said, "You're not making it up, Danesha. You've had it rough. But that doesn't mean that you can't make it better." She opened her hands and placed them on the desk, palm side up, pink against the dark black of the rest, a mirror of Danesha's own skin.

"You ever see a tapestry?"

Danesha wasn't sure if she had or hadn't.

"The design side looks like a perfect picture. Every thread in place. Turn the tapestry over and what do you have? In some tapestries you have the same picture, still pretty only muted. Do you know what I mean by muted?"

She didn't, but she nodded.

"But in most, on the other side are a lot of knots. A lot of threads not seeming to connect anywhere." She gave a soft dry clap. "Life is both sides, Danesha. We can take all those threads and work them until they create something appealing on the outside. Yet the other side is still there too—the knots, the ugly design. It's never just one or the other."

"That ain't true for me."

"Yes, Danesha, for you too. The GIFT House and this school can give you the tools to weave the other side. But you have to help make it happen."

The one good thing about Miss Lisa was that she never asked what they talked about in their "sessions." Probably some school rule or something. But as they pulled back up to the house, she made a point of saying that Danesha could come to her about *anything, any time.* Danesha was tempted to apologize for going all ham on her at dinner, except then Miss Lisa would want to hug her or something.

Danesha immediately escaped to her room. She fell onto her bed, stared for a few seconds at the white ceiling. When she was sure no one was outside her door, she pulled out from under the bed the stuffed animal Miss Lisa had given them when they first moved in. She hugged the little bear close, fingering the pink threads along its nose, its ears, its soft fat chest.

She must have slept. She jerked awake, startled to see the light blaring in her room, the outside pitch black and the house sleepy silent. Her eyes felt gritty and dry, her shoulder sore from sleeping on the stuffed animal. Danesha tossed the bear under the bed.

The creak of her bedroom door as she opened it seemed to scream down the hall. She tiptoed to the bathroom and tried to piss quiet so she didn't wake Brianna.

Back in her room, she gathered two pairs of jeans, a sweatshirt, two long-sleeved shirts, socks and all five of her underpants, and stuffed them into a pillowcase, along with her purse, a picture of Jerrell, and an old issue of *Glitter Magazine*, hidden under her mattress. She found a small, used plastic bag and filled it with the dried-out chicken, mushy string beans and tater tots. She changed to her Jordans, grabbed her coat. She looked around the room. There was nothing else that would matter.

The window slid open with barely a squeak. The cold air hit her like an icy fist. For a moment she thought again. She hadn't planned to leave yet. Then Ms. Johnson's pity face filled her eyes.

Danesha pulled both legs through, grasped the pillow case, and jumped.

Stunned, she stood on two solid feet. Nothing hurt. She glanced up and down the dark snowy street, thinking. And then she heard it. High sharp yelps followed by loud non-stop barking.

A bright light turned on the porch.

"Danesha? What are you doing out here? It's the middle of the night."

Miss Lisa stood barefoot and shivering in a short blue nightgown, arms wrapped around her sagging boobs, holding Dude on a long leash as he took a huge shit on the brand-new white snow. Danesha expected her to look pissed or maybe even worried but she seemed honestly confused, as if maybe Danesha had an okay reason to be outside about now.

She could outrun the house mom without breaking a sweat. But for what? So the cops could catch her by the second block. Instead, without answering, she turned and, pulling her bag close to her chest, brushed past Miss Lisa, past Dude, and back into the GIFT House. It was okay. Now she knew. She could jump from the second story window. Land safely. Run.

Next time she'd bring better food.

CHAPTER THIRTY-THREE

"**T**hanks for meeting me."

"Of course." Sheila probed silently, her eyes questioning.

Lisa rubbed sweaty palms across her jeans, picked up two menus and handed one to Sheila. "What do you like here?"

A laugh, then Sheila shrugged, admitted, "I've actually never been here before."

"Oh. I guess I thought...well, when I said we ought to grab lunch together, and you suggested this place, and..." Sheila was smiling but continued to appear as if waiting for an answer to an unasked question.

Lisa opened the menu and pretended to study the pages and pages of options, most of which were different than the ones offered at the Chinese restaurants she and Nate used to frequent. She couldn't seem to concentrate, her eyes glazing over the descriptions of dishes that sounded a lot like fried fast food over rice, no mentions of edamame or broccolini or black mushrooms or an alternative of brown rice. The heat was cranked up too high, the tables too close together, and the couple behind her was talking too loudly. Finally, she gave up, slapped the sticky plastic pages together. "Could we split a couple things? You pick?"

So Sheila ordered something chicken and something beef, both fried, of course, and suddenly Lisa thought she might truly throw up if she ate them, what with the crusted food and slick film on the cracked plastic tablecloth and the thick stench of grease now clinging to her clothes. Plus, it was so damned awkward with Sheila, out of the context of the home and the school. What a crap idea this had been. It was just that...

"Lisa? Are you okay?"

Sheila's face showed genuine concern and with that softening of expression, Lisa felt her own spine relax a bit. She sank back against the hard wooden booth and offered a rueful smile, then dared to say it aloud, "I've just been lonely. And I guess I hoped, I mean..."

"Well, damn," Sheila interrupted, "why didn't you say so? I

218

thought you asked me to lunch to spring some big surprise on me. I'm thrilled to get away from work for a while."

By the time their food arrived they were deep into conversation. They didn't mention Nate and to Lisa's great relief Sheila didn't dig further in response to Lisa's terse "*it was just okay,*" when asked about her visit home. Mostly they discussed the girls and various students, though in a rather light-hearted way. Lisa even managed to joke about Danesha, how she was pouting and slamming doors and, of course, blaming Lisa for being in a month-long "friggin' jack-shit prison cell."

"Omigod, I honestly didn't know someone could be that contrite and that pissed at the same time," Lisa said, but instead of the usual sense of ineptitude, she giggled over the image of Danesha with her pillow case of clothes, and cold tater tots and gooey string bean casserole leaking from the flimsy plastic bag onto the snow where Dude had just pooped.

"She was one desperate girl, thinking about running away with the leftovers from *that* dinner."

Lisa had eaten half her portion before she realized that everything was tasty in an over-salted way, though way too greasy. The beef a lousy cut of something fatty and cheap and the chicken, thankfully, fully cooked though both soggy and dry. "Hey, I could be a chef here!"

Sheila guffawed, quickly covered her mouth with a napkin, tossed it aside and grinned. "Okay, I admit, at the risk of breaking confidentiality, I may have heard a rumor or two that you're not exactly a *sous-chef.*"

Lisa laughed, but the reference to the girls' "confidentiality" stung, a sharp reminder of the many things Lisa didn't know about them. Or about Sheila.

"Can I ask you something, Sheila?"

"You can ask."

"Uh, how come you never married? Actually...have you ever been married?"

When Sheila hesitated, Lisa felt her gut tighten. It had been years since she'd made a new friend and tried to navigate the dance of timing. Had she crossed a line? Then Sheila snorted and before she could even respond Lisa found herself leaning closer in anticipation.

"Years ago, I did have myself a man for a while but when he proposed I sent him packing. I wouldn't be with him even if the Lord asked me to and that's saying a lot. Since him, well, you tell me, do you really think I want to give up all this blessed independence and freedom for some useless guy?"

"They're not *all* useless," Lisa said, seeing in her mind's eye Nate's expression of sheepish joy as he watched the girls tumbling with Dude that first day. Sheila's own face had re-arranged into a mock challenge, and when Lisa inhaled, grease filled her nose. Then, from who knew where, a bubble of laughter burst out of Lisa and she kept laughing so long Sheila joined in, until Lisa had to gulp tepid water from the plastic cup, which set her off into the giggles again. *This place is awful*, she thought. "This is nice, Sheila," she said.

Sheila concurred, "A good idea, Lisa."

When the bill came Lisa started to reach for it, but Sheila clamped her hand down on Lisa's as she whipped her wallet out with her other hand. "No you don't. We split, okay?"

"Of course." Lisa wanted to say something about "next time too," but suddenly felt like she didn't really need to. That maybe that was mutually understood.

She hummed to herself the whole ride back, turning down the now familiar streets, past "her" Shop 'n Save, the church the girls attended, the empty park, Miss Flozie's house—warmed in the cold car.

CHAPTER THIRTY-FOUR

Brianna hated to bake. Cooking was okay, especially with Grandmama Jones standing next to her, wiping flour off her face, liking to tickle her with fingers coated with sticky breading. But baking from scratch was to Brianna a waste of time.

Grandmama didn't think so. "Only two kinds of folks use box mixes, honey. White folks and lazy folks. And we ain't either."

Four times a year for each of their birthdays, no matter what else was happening, no matter how tight they'd already stretched the budget that month, Grandmama Jones and Brianna spent the afternoon baking up a three-layer German chocolate cake. The cake and icing took nearly four hours to prepare, especially with Grandmama stopping to give Brianna a talking-to about each step.

"You gotta make sure the water and melted chocolate have cooled before you add the eggs. Otherwise you'll have scrambled egg clumps in the dough."

You've told me that every time, Brianna would think, but there was never any point in correcting Grandmama. It would only earn her a sour look and a light swat on her butt.

"Here's a secret not many folks know. The harder you slam that egg against the top of the bowl the cleaner the crack. It's when you try to do it gentle you get all those little shell pieces. Nothing worse than a cake that crunches when it shouldn't of."

And on and on the advice went as they whipped the egg whites and folded in the chocolate mixture.

At some point, Ma would come out of the bedroom, complaining about all the racket and acting all surprised, especially if they were baking for *her* birthday, and she'd start saying how they shouldn't be making so much fuss over her. She'd poke her finger into the batter. Grandmama would slap her hand and hiss, "Girl, get those chocolate fingers outta our batter. Go away and let us do our work."

Hours later, they'd put the candles on, digging beneath the thick coconut pecan icing to place them into the top layer, turn the lamps off, light up all the candles with two to grow on ("one for good luck and another just in case the first one don't work, because in our lives we need all the luck we can ask for").

Ma would shut her eyes as she tasted the first bite, and every time she'd smile that stretched wide, lips-closed smile, hum a little, and say, "Best damn cake I ever tasted."

Grandmama would always take seconds, despite the frown from Ma and the warning, "Mother Jones, you know you got that high blood pressure."

Brianna didn't even like the cake all that much. Too rich. In fact, it kind of made her feel sick if she ate a whole piece. But she ate it anyway, for Ma, Auntie Billie, Grandmama and, especially on her own birthday. Too much loving went into that cake to let even a crumb go to waste.

That's what she was remembering as she leaned into the doorway, watching Miss Lisa open up the box and dump the brown powdery mix into the big bowl. Brianna stayed hidden during the prep time, less than five minutes, then she tip-toed back up the stairs, where she crawled into bed and stared at the walls, thinking that maybe she'd start doing some baking to make Grandmama proud.

An hour later, as she walked down the steps for dinner, she kept sniffing, but the house still didn't smell home baked like all her other birthdays.

"Tell me one thing about your day. Everyone gets a turn." Miss Lisa's voice was too high, too cheery, and as usual, no one said nothing 'til after a while each of them said something. You couldn't be a total jerk to someone who tried that hard. Even Danesha finally told (lied) about a B+ on her math quiz.

Danesha had been on strict probation since jumping outta that window, which made Brianna feel kind of unsure. She hated Danesha most days, but the thought of her being kicked out just showed that they didn't any of them have a true home. If Danesha could go, so could Brianna. Not that it mattered since she'd be leaving soon for Florida.

Right after dinner, Miss Lisa walked out of the kitchen, Coreen hopped up to turn off the lights, and then Brianna had to act surprised when Miss Lisa came back in carrying a near to tip over cake and sixteen burning candles (only one to grow on). It was hard to swallow the cake, not so much because it was rubbery and still a little doughy in the center, but because of a huge lump that was about to choke Brianna's throat. She forced herself to eat almost the entire slice, but right away started to burp up that too-sweet chocolate taste, the kind that stayed in her nose. "I'm sorry," Brianna said, her hand to her mouth, as she ran out of the kitchen to the bathroom and immediately puked her own birthday cake and most of the tuna casserole into the toilet.

Everyone was staring at her when she came back into the kitchen. She looked down so they couldn't see her crying eyes, and mumbled, "It's kind of a hard day."

"Oh, Brianna, of course it is." Miss Lisa squeezed her close, and for a moment Brianna let herself fall against the soft chest. "If you want to excuse yourself, you may," Miss Lisa whispered.

"Happy birthday, Bri," Coreen said, hugging Brianna. Even Danesha and Eva-Lynn kind of nodded in pity. Their birthdays weren't that far away either.

Brianna sat at her desk and tried not to vomit again as she hunted through her backpack for the algebra book. She had been late on the first assignment this semester. Another and Miss Lisa would get a call. Brianna didn't care so much about getting into trouble. But Miss Lisa's disappointment—the way her whole face sagged down like a dirty sock—was overwhelming. It was easier to just do the work. When Ma used to get upset, sparks would fly and the walls nearly shook with her anger. She'd shout so loud that her words seemed to echo long after she'd spanked Brianna and then slammed out of the room.

Ma, Ma, Ma. Did she really forget? Or maybe the card and gift would come tomorrow. Everyone knew how the mail could be, all the way from Florida. Plus, it wasn't that late yet, she'd probably still call tonight.

Brianna put her head down and let herself think about how it was going to be at that beach. If she squeezed her eyes shut enough she could see Daddy there too. Once she found him again, she'd ask. She bet he'd do it. He'd always loved her so much and had told her so every single time he saw her. Sometimes she pretended it was like one of them TV shows. A real family, at the beach, screaming with laughter as the freezing cold waves splashed over them, water running right off Ma's kinky curls, flattening down Daddy's silky hair, all of them brown and tan and copper in the hot yellow sun.

Brianna tried to ignore the knock at the door, but it was so soft that she was curious to see who wasn't sure about coming in. And then it was hard to know who was more surprised— Brianna when she saw that it was Eva-Lynn, or Eva-Lynn, who looked like she near forgot why she was standing there.

"Guess it sucks having a birthday here, huh?" Eva-Lynn asked.

Brianna didn't need to answer. Sometimes at night she could hear Eva-Lynn crying in the dark, and already she wore that shut-down look Brianna saw in her own mirror.

Eva-Lynn dug into her nylon parachute pants, reaching deep into the pocket, and pulled out a small package wrapped in newspaper comics. "I got this for you." She smiled sideways, showing her brown teeth and an open space in the way back. "It's not for your birthday, but it could be."

Brianna's hands shook and she nearly dropped the gift as she pulled off the paper and saw a jar of mashed peaches. "Why did you give this to me?" Her voice rose high, the way Ma's did when she was *really* upset.

Eva-Lynn shook her head back and forth. "I've been there. I got rid of mine. But I figured in case you keep yours, you're gonna need this."

Brianna slumped to the ground and put her head in her hands, her breath feeling like it would choke her throat closed.

"Hey, don't get all bent out of shape. I didn't really buy it exactly." She grinned. "It kind of found its way into my pocket."

"Why did you give this to me?" Brianna repeated, this time hearing her own whine.

"You ain't pregnant? Shit, I just figured. I've seen enough knocked-up girls." She grabbed the jar out of Brianna's hand and stood to leave. "Listen, man, I'm sorry."

"Wait." Brianna waved her back. In a whispery voice, she let herself ask out loud what she had not let herself know. "What made you think so?"

Eva-Lynn stared straight on at Brianna's chest. "And other things too. I hear you puking and crying all the time. And your face is all full. When it was me, I'd look in the mirror and think a fat moon was staring back. It was really creepy."

Brianna's whole body was shaking. She wrapped her arms around her middle, felt a fit of near-vomit, and made her arms fall to her side, away from that place she didn't want to think about. "I ain't had my period since the fall. But I thought maybe I was just stressed or something."

Eva-Lynn snorted. "You don't grow tits from stress." She pushed on her own flat chest. "Look, it's not a big deal. I ain't telling no one."

Brianna slid her butt until her back rested against the mattress. She took a look at the blonde, blue-eyed, chubby infant on the jar's label, then began to giggle. "Think my baby will look like this?"

"I guess it depends who the father is."

Eva-Lynn didn't even pretend to be curious. Brianna had the feeling that to Eva-Lynn one brown-skinned baby was pretty much the same as another.

"You think your Mom will come get you?"

It was weird the way Eva-Lynn seemed to see right through her, kind of a relief. So instead of repeating all Ma's reasons for not being here—the job, the money, the savings for the beach house—Brianna admitted, "I can't never tell what my Ma's gonna do."

"I can sure guess what Lisa'll say. '*Oh, Brianna, honey, a baby at your age?*'" Eva-Lynn paused, then added, "She *could* make you get rid of that baby, you know. If she's your legal guardian."

Brianna cupped her hand over her mouth. "I ain't gonna tell her. Not til it's too late."

Eva-Lynn was reminded of Grandpappy's words on their last afternoon together, the day they hiked through the woods in the burning August heat, just hours before he clutched his fist to his chest and collapsed. Her parents blamed her for killing Grandpappy, for not having the sense to not make an old man go walking in that weather, and in her sadness she'd shoved to the back of her brain his bitter words. But they came rushing forward now, "lesson of the day," as he liked to call them.

"The thing about niggers is they'll never let you down. Sure as the devil they've been cursed with, their babies will have babies and their men will go and get themselves killed or locked up behind bars." He'd laughed aloud then, his spit flying out and landing squarely on her cotton T-shirt, leaving foamy white circles and curdled stains. "Yes, siree, a nigger will never surprise you."

"Never, ever trust a white person," Grandmama had drilled into Brianna's head, as if she'd never met Brianna's daddy. "If a white person acts nice, it either means she wants something from you—to clean the doo off her toilet seat or wash up her windows—or else she's being nice to make up for some kinda guilt. The minute you see a white person trying to act friendly, go running, girl, before the whitey go running off and leave you worse than nothing."

The two girls stared at one another, silenced by the memory of words that were becoming irrelevant under this old, leaking roof.

Eva-Lynn smiled first. "Hey, babies are cool. I'm still sometimes sorry I got rid of mine. So I'll help ya."

I may not even be pregnant, Brianna wanted to say, but as she patted her bloated stomach, her arm brushing across boobs so sore she nearly cried out, she found herself nodding okay.

CHAPTER THIRTY-FIVE

There was no fucking way Eva-Lynn was gonna keep her baby. She was just past twelve, had her period three times, when one bored afternoon she let Jack's best friend Roger break her cherry. Ray had returned from his latest disappearing act and at night she could hear Sheri and Ray banging their fool bodies around in bed. Eva-Lynn had wondered what could possibly be so great that Sheri would let Ray back into their lives. After the fuck with Roger, she decided Sheri was as stupid as Eva-Lynn had thought. Three weeks later, Eva-Lynn began to barf. Two weeks after that, she made Roger pay for her abortion. The next week she and Jack burned down the neighbor's house and Eva-Lynn was sent to juvie.

Now, listening to Brianna puking in the bathroom next door, Eva-Lynn kept remembering her own short little pregnancy. Which seemed like a big deal at the time but turned out to be no more annoying than the rest of her sorry-ass life. She pushed her face into the pillow, then heard a low moaning in the doorway.

"Eva-Lynn?" Brianna was slumped against the wall looking like she might die right there. Ever since giving Brianna that baby food jar, the girl had been hanging onto Eva-Lynn like a bloated tick.

"Yeah? Come in."

Brianna nearly fell to the floor, closed her eyes and panted shallow breaths. She was scary thin and kind of green. Eva-Lynn didn't know brown skin could turn the actual shade of puke, but this one had.

A nigger camouflages itself better than a forest creature. Acting human while hiding the devil inside. Grandpappy's voice screeched in her head. "Go away," Eva-Lynn whispered.

"Okay," Brianna said, practically falling back down as she tried to get up.

"Not you!" snapped Eva-Lynn, and when Brianna turned even yellower like she didn't know whether to run or cry, Eva-Lynn shrugged. "Sometimes my dead grandpa likes to talk to me," she admitted, as much to shock Brianna as to try to clamp shut Grandpappy's voice.

Especially at night, in the dark, she'd feel him in her room. Sure that no one could hear her, she'd whisper-beg Grandpappy to understand and still love her even though she was living, for just now, in this house with these people. "What can I do? I have nowhere to go in the winter and there's no way I'm going back to that shit house ever again." Not after the Christmas when Sheri hadn't even bothered to buy her a goddamned gift.

"Who said for you to come home?" she'd said. "We didn't think you'd be here."

And Jack had stayed disappeared ("We've told the cops to call off their hound dogs. That boy don't want to be found? Fine with us.).

"I don't know if this is normal," Brianna said, wrapping her twig arms around her gut. A line of yellow barf had dried on her chin.

She definitely didn't look right. Too puffy and too skinny both, like pictures of kids in those countries where they died like flies and no one in the world gave a fuck. There were some pregos in the Girls' Home, but they were white and they turned pink and rosy. This had to be God's way of punishing Brianna for bringing another coon baby into the world. "Maybe we should hitchhike to a doctor. Just in case."

"No!" Brianna practically screamed it out, then as if anyone in the house gave enough of a crap to listen in on them, Brianna said so quiet Eva-Lynn had to stick out her own ear, "No one can know. Not until it's too late to get rid of it. I want this baby."

Jesus, the girl was crazy. Eva-Lynn didn't even know that Miss Lisa would make her suck it out or give it away. She had just said that to Brianna because it seemed what a prude like Lisa would do.

Tell the Jew yourself. No one needs another nigger baby. It's up to you, Grandpappy said. She shook off his voice. For now Brianna's pregnancy gave Eva-Lynn something to put her mind on. Later, if she was still here—and she'd learned not to predict nothing in her life—it might be kind of fun. She could practice on Brianna's baby and see if she wanted one herself next time. But there wasn't going to be a baby if Brianna kept on this way.

Brianna burped, then raced out, barely shutting the bathroom door before hurling. When the door opened, her eyes were dull, her skin greener. "Can you go to Walgreens and tell them about me, case there's something I can take?"

As half-assed as the idea was, Eva-Lynn didn't say no. Besides, she had to get the hell out of this hothouse before she started puking herself. "Yeah, I'll tell them 'my friend is pregnant' and let them think it's me," Eva-Lynn said, and only as she walked down the stairs did she realize that she had called Brianna a "friend."

Eva-Lynn stood on the porch and looked in both directions. She'd dressed in her usual costume—black hooded sweatshirt pulled down low over her forehead, a gray scarf wrapped around most of her face, gloved hands tucked into the pockets of the cheap-ass shiny yellow coat Miss Lisa had bought for her at Wal-Mart (on sale making her look like a walking lemon, as if she didn't stand out enough already. But at least it was warmer than nothing, since Sheri never did get her lazy butt over to drop off the one Eva-Lynn had from last year). She had to remind herself to shuffle, sway and slump—the cover-up didn't do shit if she still walked white. She was learning. She'd been called a honky bitch too many scary times.

More snow had fallen during the night, closing school for the third straight day. The weathercasters were creaming in their pants that they could be the headlines, a bunch of dorks standing in front of fake maps and waving their hands over purple lines and blue swirls. St. Louis totally freaked out at two inches of snow. When they got five inches last week the city ran out of salt and all the highways were shut down. Where she grew up, they went to school no matter what. Finally something good about St. Louis.

As she walked down the porch steps, she could feel the sting where her jeans brushed the cuts on the back of her calves. Stupid place to dig into, but she'd never tried it there before and wanted to see how it would feel.

The first time she'd cut herself it was an accident. Sort of. She was outside, behind the trailer park, pitching rocks at rusted out trash cans teaming with rotting garbage.

She and Jack liked to see who could knock the lids off the cans with the fewest number of throws. Jack was a natural, but Eva-Lynn had taken to practicing when no one was around and she had an eye for aim.

Eva-Lynn had scraped her finger tips against the rough edges of broken glass, pushing past cigarette butts and hardened clumps of molded food, until she found the perfect rock. "Jack, you are in deep shit now," she muttered aloud. Too bad he wasn't there to witness his undoing.

She squinted with her left eye, focusing on the underside of the lid, as she hurled her right arm back and thrust it forward, feeling the rock leave her palm, watching as it arced through the air and charged with force right on through the front window of the sky-blue trailer that belonged to Justin Long, meanest goddamned son of a bitchin' drunk in all of the Bootheel.

Immediately, Justin Long came swaying and swaggering out into the bright sunshine, squinting his bleary red eyes, hollering, "You little fucker, I'm gonna get you. I've told you hoodlums to stay away from here."

For a drunk, that man could run. He chased Eva-Lynn nearly three full blocks. But he was just an old fucking sorry-shit and as she rounded the fourth block, she looked back and saw him bent over, trying to catch his breath. She flipped him the bird and shouted out "Jackass," just as she went tumbling forward, her foot caught on a broken bike lying on its side.

She felt total numbness before the sting, then an intense throbbing from knee to shin. A thick stream of blood was pouring down her leg, soaking the top of her brand new green high-top sneakers she'd bought yesterday with her own money from four stinking months of babysitting the brats next door.

"Fu-uck," she shouted. She watched helplessly as the blood continued to soak and stain her shoes as she limped home, every step agony, until she reached her own house, a shabby two-story that was falling-apart-old, but at least it wasn't a *trailer*.

Sheri swung open the door. "Jesus Christ, girl, what happened to you? Don't you get any of that blood on my floor or your butt will be bleeding worse than your leg."

Eva-Lynn cupped the stream of blood with her hand as she climbed the stairs. However much her leg hurt now, blood on the carpets would make this pain seem like nothing.

She locked the door and sat trembling on the toilet seat as she stuck out her leg and began to push against the cut with damp tissue. It hurt like a motherfucker, but she wasn't about to let herself cry. She'd learned crying only made pain worse, not better.

A couple of rock pieces had dug into the wound. She reached up and pulled a clean straight-edge razor blade out of Ray's pack. At first she just scraped a little, picking with the corner of the blade to loosen the small rocks. Downstairs she could hear Sheri cursing and clanging dishes. She dug a little deeper. Then Ray's roar carried up the stairs, "You come help your mother," and she pushed the blade down into the skin, watching in amazement as a piss-load of blood came pouring out. She sliced lengthwise then. For a second, before it got all smeary, the blood made a perfect sign of a cross. And as her knee throbbed, the familiar pain between her ears and inside her chest dulled.

"Eva-Lynn!" Sheri's tone was reaching dangerous.

She dropped the blade into the toilet, flushed, and covered her knee with a bandage. She caught her eyes in the mirror as she limped out, shining with secret power.

A loud honk pulled her out of the memory and nearly sent her stumbling into the snow.

"Hey, Danesha! What are you doing outside in this weather?"

Leaning out of the cab of the red truck was Nate. "Oh, Eva-Lynn. Sorry. I didn't see your face," he said.

231

She flashed him her big smile. "It's cool. Glad it works."

He looked unsure for a second then seemed to understand. That was the thing about Nate—unlike Miss Lisa, who mostly had her head up her ass—Nate always caught on to what was going down around him.

"It's too snowy and cold to be walking in this. Where you going anyway?"

She thought fast. Nate was probably the one person she could tell. *"Don't trust a Jew neither. Next worse thing after a nigger."*

"Nowhere special. I just needed to get out."

He leaned his head far into the windshield as if measuring the snow and then wrinkled up his face. "So you think this is good weather for going nowhere special?"

She stepped closer to the truck and pushed her nose up to the passenger window. The inside of the cab was a shit sty of crumpled fast food bags, empty Coke cans and dirty napkins. She was surprised, expected him to be one of those neat freaks.

"Hey, move back while I pull in. I told Ms. Johnson I'd come by to see if you girls needed anything at the store. Maybe if Miss Vanessa and Miss Lisa are both there, one of them and you can come too."

Eva-Lynn watched as Nate hopped up the snowy stairs, slapped hands against his arms to keep warm, and finally entered the GIFT House. Immediately, she opened the passenger door and yanked open the glove compartment. A large screw driver, a map of St. Louis and a detailed record of his truck repairs going back to 2006. Not much under the seat either, except a shriveled apple core and more wadded up trash. Big whoop. She jumped back as she heard Nate coming.

"Miss Vanessa's there but Miss Lisa is up at the school getting ready for some program. Good thing I stopped by. You're almost out of milk and totally out of bread." He shook his head, mumbled, "Kind of amazed Lisa would be driving in this. She always..." He seemed to remember Eva-Lynn and changed his tone, like she hadn't noticed from his voice that the guy was totally stuck on fat-ass Lisa. "Miss Vanessa said since the weather's so bad, just this once you can come along to help me."

They drove a while without talking, the three miles to the grocery store taking forever on the slippery streets. Cool air blasted out of the heater and a wind blew a chill through the window. But Eva-Lynn felt warm sitting next to Nate, like they were on some kind of outing from her life.

With one eye she studied his profile. He wasn't bad looking. His nose was straight and narrow, not a Jew-beak. He had eyes that she'd seen change colors with his shirt, sometimes green, other times brown. Maybe he wasn't a full Jew? He was too skinny, and way too old, but if she'd met him while hitchhiking, she would have blown him if she had to. She shivered at the thought.

"Cold? Sorry about the heat. I keep meaning to get it repaired, but I'm too busy fixing stuff for other people. I guess it's like the shoemaker's son."

She nodded like she understood what the hell he was talking about. Lisa did that too—talked in expressions that made no sense and just reminded you that the biggest problem in their lives had probably been an ass pimple.

"So, you like living..." He stopped, swallowing the words back into his throat. That was another thing. Unlike Miss Lisa or Ms. Johnson, Nate didn't ask a lot of questions she wouldn't want to answer. But unlike Sheri or Ray, he gave a fuck, he just didn't push.

She decided she didn't have to have the same rules.

"How come you and Miss Lisa aren't living together if you're married?"

He startled, choked a little. He re-adjusted the rear view mirror, sat forward and tightened his fingers on the steering wheel, suddenly all eyes on the road even though they'd driven to Delmar, a major street that was mostly clear of snow and ice. He said nothing for a block, then answered, sounding so sad Eva-Lynn wished she'd kept her lips tight for once.

"It's complicated." He cleared his throat. "What has Miss Lisa told you?"

233

"She hasn't told us diddly squat. We ask but she just uses her mouth to eat. Except I figure stuff out."

He frowned like he was trying not to cry. "She was so beautiful." His tone was soft as a song.

"You love her."

He nodded, shocking Eva-Lynn with his no-horseshit. She turned to face him. If she squinted he kind of looked like how Jack might in a couple of years.

"I'm a twin. Did you know that?"

"No. I didn't."

They pulled into the grocery store lot, but neither moved after he turned off the ignition. Finally Nate said, "Then you know about love too, don't you?"

She couldn't stop her hand from shaking as she reached across the cab and squeezed his coat sleeve. "I can help you get her back, if you want."

She'd learned, living with Coreen, that a shrug usually meant yes.

Brianna's eyes were the first thing she saw over the top of the paper grocery sack. Eva-Lynn nodded her head up and down, mouthed, "You're cool." Brianna seemed to melt into her chair in relief. Let the girl think a pharmacist said losing weight was good for a baby and turning slime-green was okay. It probably *was* fine.

Miss Lisa had come back. At first she was big-time pissed with Nate until he unpacked the pound of Kona coffee, the gallon of Rocky Road ice cream and the Redbox rental of *When Harry Met Sally*. She'd laughed out loud and not even tried to hide her smile. Adults were so fucking weird, but looked like Nate knew his shit when he got those things instead of flowers. Good thing since they'd had to go to three places to find a Redbox in the city that hadn't been broken into. Fucking coons would steal Jesus off a cross.

Danesha grabbed the bag of cheese curls while Coreen unwrapped and started pigging on Snickers with one hand as she shoved a Butterfinger into her pocket with the other.

For once, Miss Lisa didn't say nothing when they all went upstairs with their junk food, leaving her alone on the couch next to Nate.

Eva-Lynn hurried first into the bathroom and nearly gagged. It smelled like barf and there was gooey food stuck to the inside of the toilet bowl. She sat and pissed on the goo. Without getting up, she pushed her sweatshirt sleeve past her elbow and stared at the pink lines crisscrossing her inside wrist and the newer red and scabby X's on her forearm.

"Tell me why you cause pain to yourself?" the three therapists at her juvie school had each asked.

"It doesn't really hurt when I do it," Eva Lynn told the first, being honest.

"It's kind of fun," she told the second, also the truth.

"It makes the pain go away," she told the third, sorry immediately that she'd said so much.

But yesterday, after being warned by tub-of-lard Sheila Johnson that if there were any more "hints of self-inflicted injury" Eva-Lynn would have to start seeing an outside counselor with Miss Lisa, of course she'd lied. "I won't do it again."

Miss Lisa had jumped up and nearly suffocated Eva-Lynn, hugging her so close their tits smashed together. "That's such a relief, Eva-Lynn. You'll feel so much better. And you'll see, you'll be *more* in control of your life that way."

Eva-Lynn felt proud of that moment, how she'd kept a completely straight face.

She reached into her pocket for the razor blade and placed it near the bend of her elbow, where the cut would zing every time she moved her arm. Then she heard a soft knock on the door.

"What! Who's there?"

A whisper, "It's me, Brianna. Hey, thanks a lot, Eva-Lynn. I'll see you tomorrow."

Eva-Lynn heard the soft, barely walking steps Brianna did, leaving Eva-Lynn sitting on the can with a razor blade in her hand pondering that someone who thought she was a friend wanted to see her tomorrow. She put the straightedge back in her pocket and flushed the toilet twice until the left-over vomit disappeared.

"You're welcome," she let her lips say to the empty hallway as she walked to her bedroom.

"*You stupid girl. What the hell do you think you're doing?*"

Eva-Lynn pulled the door shut, locking Grandpappy out alone in the hall for the night.

CHAPTER THIRTY-SIX

Her hair was flat in front, frizzy in back, flipping where it should have curled under, with ever-worsening deep brown roots and blonde-turned-green ends. She'd never found the wherewithal last month to get to the hairdresser in the Twin Cities, and once she returned to St. Louis, she once again avoided all mirrors. She was puffy, wearing the newest holiday pounds on her face so that her eyes slid into slits, and her teeth, five-minute bleached white, appeared too small. She had discarded more than a half dozen outfits, some of them twice, put a run in her only pair of black stockings and sloshed dots of black shoe polish on her good white silk blouse. Her heart was pumping, her palms were sweaty, her mouth dry. What Kona-coffee and chocolate-induced impulsive madness had taken over her senses and brought her to this?

She picked up the phone to call and cancel her date with Nate—a ridiculous notion, they were *married*, for God's sake—actually, they were separated, more absurd yet—when she heard an enthused rapping on her bedroom door.

"Come in," she said. All four girls burst into her room at once.

"Miss Lisa, we are here to save your butt," announced Danesha, as Coreen retrieved a carton from out of a Walgreens bag. "I know you white women don't care much 'bout your hair, but for Mr. Nate you got to."

"We couldn't choose between Starlet or Pure Diamond," said Brianna.

"I picked Starlet. I had that color once. Mr. Nate gonna love it." Eva-Lynn's usual drawl was pitched fast with excitement.

Lisa couldn't quite hide her horror. Coreen was holding a L'Oreal hair dye chart and the blonde color they'd selected was at least four shades lighter than she'd ever used. It was significantly lighter than her eyebrows, which would look like dark shelves under her bangs. Plus, she'd decided that if she ever did color her hair again, she'd go back to being a brunette. But they seemed so eager. So unexpectedly, poignantly eager.

"Okay. We've got two hours. Make me beautiful."

It had been at least eight months since she'd last had her hair dyed and she forgot how pungent the chemicals were. Within minutes of Coreen pouring on the mixture, Lisa's eyes began to water and her nose to run. Her scalp itched, then burned, then tingled as Coreen worked away, massaging the color in and instructing Brianna to "keep an eye on that clock, girl. Even one minute too long will ruin Miss Lisa's hair."

"Your hair is so soft it's weird," Coreen said, running the thin layers through her pudgy fingers. "Feel this, Bri."

"And she ain't got no kitchen," Danesha hooted, snatching up the underside of Lisa's back hair.

"Kitchen?" Lisa dared to ask, producing a burst of laughter before Coreen explained, "That nappy clump on our necks."

"Aw, shit, her neck's turning red and pimply. Does that always happen to you, Miss Lisa?"

Lisa lifted the hair dye box, squinted and read. *You must always perform a simple allergy test 48 hours before each and every color application.*

"Uh oh," Coreen said.

She felt her heart stop.

"I think your eyebrows may look really weird. Should we color those too?"

Never use on eyelashes or eyebrows. To do so may cause blindness.

"No!" she exclaimed, then, softer, "it will look more natural this way."

"Yeah, you'll be a tenner," Brianna said, giggling and squeezing Lisa's forearm.

With that squeeze, Lisa felt something inside her relax. And she decided to let go. Just let the girls do whatever they wanted, let them make her a tenner.

The results can be stunning, but be forewarned, this is a high-maintenance look!

She placed the box instruction-side down, closed her eyes, leaned her head back, and reveled in their chatter. *Remember this moment,* she told herself. *This is really happening.*

She did a double take when they were done, she couldn't help it. "Starlet" was too light, too brassy, and was not remotely flattering to her pasty complexion. She was reminded of a cheap blonde wig she and Nate had bought one year when they dressed for a Halloween party as a cheerleader and football jock. But when Coreen flinched, Lisa offered a toothy smile and with forced enthusiasm said, "I'm gorgeous. Now help me find something to wear."

The girls exchanged glances, then Eva-Lynn walked out and returned moments later with a bulging TJ Maxx bag. She handed the bag to Lisa. Lisa dipped in and pulled out a pair of denim shorts that couldn't have been more than five inches in length. Gulping, she asked, "Are these for me? Aren't they, like, way too short?"

Eva-Lynn grabbed them from Lisa's hands, flushing with embarrassment. "Oops, those are mine."

"But they're so short!"

Danesha laughed. "Miss L, sometimes you just too funny. If they was any longer they'd be pants. Anyways, look again."

This time Lisa retrieved from the bag a bright orange and yellow striped sweater with a slightly different shade of orange knit pants.

"It's gonna fit perfect," Eva-Lynn said, holding the pants up to Lisa's waist. "Size ten. That's what I used to wear before I got skinny. And it will stretch."

Lisa struggled to keep her expression impassive. She hadn't worn a size ten since her pregnancy with the twins. On a good day, she could squeeze into a *very generous* twelve, but increasingly was rationalizing that a fourteen was now the average size for an American woman. And *orange*? She was going to look like one of those over-sized Halloween pumpkins that stay too long on a porch.

She spread the two pieces out on the bed. They were actually much less tacky than she'd first thought and of a nicer quality. They seemed to be cut large too. Maybe they would fit.

She wanted to shoo the girls out of the room while she tried the outfit on, embarrassed for them to see her rolls of fat and blue-veined thighs. But it was obvious they weren't any of them budging. So Lisa swallowed her pride, tore off her shirt, pulled down her pants and squeezed her puffy self into the knitted outfit.

"Wait. Let me fix you up," Danesha said, shoving the sleeves to three-quarter length, standing up the collar, and blousing out the sweater's bottom into soft folds across her hips. She reached behind Lisa and yanked on the material that hugged her butt, pulling until it stretched to drape rather than cling, all the while seeming to be unaware that she was gently, affectionately, touching Lisa.

"You gotta know how to wear the clothes. I could teach you." Danesha's face shone with self-assurance. "Now take a look."

With more than a little trepidation, Lisa appraised herself in the mirror. Surprisingly, she didn't look terrible. In fact, the bright, horizontal stripes gave curve to her droopy breasts and the knit pants provided a girdle-like tightening to her thick waist and dimply rear. With the collar pulled up, it covered one or two of her chins. The hair was too "starlet-y," yet it definitely matched the cheesecake knit outfit. Some men were even attracted to that faux glamour. Not Nate. But surely some men. This time Lisa didn't have to fake her smile.

"Thank you. All of you," she said, her voice cracking a little. "I'll go shower now."

As she pulled the sweater over her head, she felt something hard and scratchy. "Uh oh, they forgot to take off the sensor."

"Aw shit," Eva-Lynn muttered, yanking the sweater from Lisa's hands. "Just wear something else."

"No, I love this. If it's from TJ Maxx, we have time to run up and get it removed. Find the receipt and we'll go right now."

"Forget it." Eva-Lynn scowled. She bunched the sweater into a knot and tossed it back into the bag.

"Hey, it's their fault, not yours. And we have time." Lisa shook her head at the swift change in the girl's mood. These kids had so little tolerance for everyday frustrations. She patted Eva-Lynn's arm, then suddenly stopped. "Oh no. Did you *steal* this?"

Eva-Lynn jutted her chin forward, defensive and embarrassed. "So?"

Danesha whooped in a burst of laughter. "Girl, you stole that sweater for Miss Lisa and left the sensor *on*?"

"So have you took a look in the mirror this morning?" Eva-Lynn snarled.

Too many conflicting words filled Lisa's mouth as she looked from one to another. A "real" mother would know what to do. Then she recalled a comment by Sheila several weeks before. "Not that I know from personal experience, but from my observation, parenting is one-third instinct, one-third luck, and one-third bad judgment. Unfortunately, you usually don't know which until it's too late to undo what you've done."

"Oh, what the hell," Lisa said, "I don't think the sensor even shows."

Danesha reached for the bag. "You take that shower." Her grin was sheepish and proud. "I'll get this off. And after that, no disrespecting, but you better let me do your make-up."

"I admit, I was a bit startled when I first saw you," Nate said as they finished their second glass of wine.

"Why startled?" she deadpanned. "You don't think this looks natural?" Lisa swung her head in exaggerated motion, allowing her blonde hair to sweep over her shoulders and holding the pose as he pantomimed shooting her picture.

He poured the remaining wine from the bottle into both of their glasses, picked up his by the stem, and swirled the wine around the bowl of the glass, the deep red liquid swimming precariously close to the lip. "You still look pretty, you know." Nate's voice was husky.

She'd forgotten this habit of his, to swish the wine so that it could "breathe," a gesture she used to find annoyingly affected and very un-Nate-like. But tonight it just made her sad.

"Do you believe me? You do know that you're beautiful, don't you?"

She looked at him as if for the first in a long time, seeing in the wavy curls of his dark hair and straggly eye brows, in the blunt shape of his fingernails and the soft hazel-brown eyes, in the poorly ironed collar and skipped belt loop, that he was the Nate of *Lisa and Nate,* the Nate before the miscarriages, the fights, his stubborn refusal to truly consider her wishes. This was the Nate who, when she canceled one of their first dates for "stomach issues," had dropped off a box of Dulcolax. "How can you not fall in love with a guy who wines and dines you with laxatives?" she'd joked the next day with Bonnie.

And, now, in this Nate's company, bizarrely enough she did feel beautiful. "Oh, Nate," she sighed, sloshy and loose-limbed from the alcohol. "Please don't."

He reached for her hand and pressed it between both of his own. "Please don't what, Lisa?"

She stiffened but before she could speak, he said, "Lisa, I'm not talking about..." he paused, laughed, "a really terrible dye job. I'm talking about *you*." He squeezed her fingers together, not loosening his hold even as she winced. "Tell me you don't feel it too."

There was no answer she was willing to give, not the truth and not a lie. Instead, she stared ahead, her emotions blanketed as though she were a casual observer of this woman waiting for the bill to be paid, their dinners barely eaten, who wobbled out of the restaurant, and climbed into the front seat of a tomato red truck that clashed horribly with her orange slacks. She watched the blur of familiar suburban scenery as he drove above the speed limit to their—to his—house.

He dashed ahead into the master bedroom, presumably to straighten the mess, and Lisa staggered down the hall to peer into the other three bedrooms. Nate had taken the smallest room as his home-based office when Lisa was pregnant with the twins. After that miscarriage, he suggested that he would move his office back to the largest extra bedroom and she had balked, assuming all the rooms would one day be filled. Now, opening the first door, she saw that he'd relocated to the bigger room. Like a fierce cruel slap, she was suddenly completely sober. She placed her forehead to the wall, struggling not to break down and sob. How had she forgotten about all those extra empty bedrooms?

Then his hands were on her shoulders, his body lean and hard as he stood behind her, so close she could fall backwards and not move. "Come with me," he whispered into her ear as he reached around and gently closed the door.

At first she was self-conscious when he traced his hand over her protruding midriff and the fat that rolled against her back. She tried to suck in her stomach, but his exploring fingers didn't pause long enough for her to hold any muscles tight. He hadn't forgotten anything. He knew where to touch, where to lick, when to push and when to hold back. And whether it was the familiarity or the strangeness, she abandoned restraint, erased all thinking, allowed herself to moan and whimper and demand more of him, until they both were panting and sweating and laughing. "Was that two or three?" he murmured at some point. Eventually, exhausted, sated, they slept.

She awoke with a start to a rising sun and checked her phone. It was not quite six-thirty. The girls and Sheila would still be sound asleep. In the dim light of early day, she examined the bedroom. Everything was in the same place as the day she moved out. The framed picture of them on the beach from their honeymoon was on the bed stand, next to the little red metal truck she'd bought when he expanded his rental company. On the dresser, closed with the brass key inserted, was the cloisonné music box he'd gotten for her on one of their vacations, though now she couldn't remember which one. Even the *mezzuzah* she'd hung for good luck on the door jamb was still there, a surprise since Nate didn't find comfort in Jewish symbols.

In the middle of the mattress, Nate was sprawled across the top sheet, completely naked, his penis thick and swollen. Unlike her, his body hadn't changed much except to be a bit thinner. Peering closer, she noticed that he now had a few gray pubic hairs. She was tempted to straddle his sleeping body, knowing he'd be receptive and eager. After all, Sheila had given her twenty-four hours off. "You need to figure out where your head and your heart are," Sheila had said, the words of a friend, not the employer.

She slid out of the bed for the bathroom, tottered for a moment on achy legs, and then felt it—the gluey rivulet of Nate's sperm, dribbling down her inner thigh. Instinctively, she plopped back onto the bed, rolled to her back, lifted her hips high, supporting her body weight with her elbows and heels. She held the position for about thirty seconds, allowing the sperm to swim back up, when suddenly it hit.

What was she doing? No! She would not do this. Again. Ever.

"No..." This time she cried aloud, but still he slept. She grabbed a handful of tissues and roughly wiped between her legs. She pulled on her underwear, her knit pants, sweater, shoes and coat. At the bottom of the stairs she called a cab.

She didn't leave a note. There was nothing new to say.

They were both in agreement—there would be no more babies, a commitment that was enabling the marriage to slowly heal. "Keep pushing forward," Dr. Berger advised. "You will be stronger for having come out on the other side."

The diaphragm, when used properly, is eighty-five percent effective, not perfect odds, but enough to have kept Lisa from getting pregnant every time she used it. And she used it every time they had sex, no matter what day of the month

Even one night when the full moon and balmy spring air caught them by surprise and they found themselves nestling bare skin to skin, when they made love slowly, languidly, the dark breeze cooling the sweat off their backs, even that night, when Nate asked Lisa, just this once, not to stop to get the diaphragm, she kissed him deeply and skirted her legs over the side of the bed, leaving him alone and naked as she snaked into the bathroom to protect herself. Afterwards, lying in Nate's arms listening to the steady exhalations of his quiet snores, she tasted the salty wetness of her tears on his chest.

Lisa no longer attached emotion or significance to her menstrual cycle. Which is why she only half-heartedly took a home pregnancy test.

"I thought you can't get pregnant using the diaphragm," Nate said.

"We've become statistics."

Lisa was panicked. It wasn't that she'd quit wanting a baby. Her therapy sessions had taught her that she would spend the rest of her life wishing for that. And she wasn't even afraid to have a miscarriage. She nearly assumed that she would. No, what she dreaded was the inevitability of having, once more, to feel—fear...and hope. Because wasn't that the bite of it all? Every goddamned time, there it was again. The hope.

A pregnancy doesn't just contain the desire for a baby in nine months. A pregnancy very quickly represents that baby's first step, first word, first day of kindergarten, first date, the walk down the aisle, the grandchild. The baby is the past, the present and the future. From the moment the test comes back positive, the dreams begin.

Nate was nearly boyish in his anticipation. "Another chance, Lisa. Can you believe it?"

They fell asleep holding hands that night. The next morning Lisa awoke to bright red blood and cramping.

"There is no viable pregnancy," the doctor explained during the ultrasound. At Lisa's stricken silence, he added, as if to console, "Before we had such early home pregnancy tests, a woman would never even know she was fleetingly pregnant. It would only be a late, heavier than normal period. In fact, I think you can view this that way...if it helps."

Her hormones were out of whack, her emotions even more so. How could this have happened yet again? Everywhere she went women were cradling infants, hugging toddlers, crossing streets holding the tiny hands of their precious children. And Lisa could feel herself sinking. It terrified her even as she felt helpless to prevent falling back into a hole. She made an appointment with Dr. Berger.

"What do you want and need, Lisa?"

But this time when he asked, suddenly, the answer was clear.

She paced the floor, waiting for Nate to come home. "I don't think I can live without children after all. Let's adopt," she announced.

Nate's whole body went rigid. "Why would we do that?"

"I need to have children, Nate."

"Then let's keep trying, honey."

She worked hard to control her frustration, to not shake him or bang her fists in anguish against his chest. "Nate, I will never, ever do that to my body again. I can't. But I can...we can...give a child a home."

Much later, when she reflected on the conversation, she realized that in part he was simply afraid. But at that moment, all she saw and heard was a close-minded man stealing from her the only possible option left.

"I love you, Lisa," he said, his voice squeaking with emotion. "But take in someone else's child? And pretend it's ours? I don't think I can do that."

"What do you mean, 'pretend, it's ours'? He or she *would* be ours. And it would be cool. We'd be helping out at the same time."

He couldn't seem to stop his head from shaking back and forth. "You know the kind of baby we'd get. Another race or someone from a foreign country. The child wouldn't look like us or seem like us. We wouldn't know if the mom had done drugs or been drinking while pregnant. And then it seems like every adopted kid I ever knew got all screwed up thinking that his parents had given him away. I just don't think I could love that child like a dad."

She must have looked as repulsed as she felt because suddenly his whole tone changed. "Listen, I wasn't sure I wanted kids at all. Then you got pregnant. And I came around for you. Right?" She nodded and his voice softened somewhat, "And I'm willing to try again to have our own or I'm okay if we don't ever have kids. But I know me and I know I can't accept someone else's baby as my own." His jaw was clenched so tight she wondered that he didn't spit out pieces of broken teeth.

Her mom suggested she go ahead and call an adoption services lawyer.

"Nate's adamant about not adopting. How can I do that? What if it's not the right thing?"

"I always say, 'untested, unknown.'"

"You never say that."

Jeanette tsked. "I'm saying it now. You watch, Nate will come around. He just doesn't realize what he's capable of yet."

Instead, when he heard, Nate was too upset to even fight. For days they circled around each another, more often than not one of them sleeping on the downstairs couch.

Then the lawyer called. He knew of a baby. Teen-age parents. White mother, black father. Due date in three weeks.

She met with the lawyer alone, who said the parents would not consider a single mother.

Lisa begged Nate. Literally begged.

"You refuse to try pregnancy again? So why is it any worse that I refuse to adopt?"

There passed between them the inexpressibly sad recognition that after all they'd been through, this, then, was the end. They no longer shared enough to save the marriage and save themselves.

He offered the house, but she couldn't bear the memories. She rented an apartment on a month-to-month lease. They told each other it was temporary. But almost immediately Lisa felt the tightness in her chest relax. Being alone in a studio apartment was less lonely than being with Nate.

She had barely settled in when she saw the intriguing ad in the St. Louis Post Dispatch. She'd nearly missed it, in fact was folding the newspaper to recycle when her eyes caught the words, Wanted: A woman to live with and care for four teenage girls in a residential home, to serve as foster mom...

With trembling hands she picked up her phone and called the number to set up an interview with Ms. Sheila Johnson.

She cried sad silent tears most of the cab ride from Nate's house. She should never have gone home with him. They had needed to talk, not have sex. She'd intended to air her frustration about his new agreement with Sheila. Or to vent about her dad to the one person who would truly understand her sorrow. Instead, she had nearly tried to make a baby.

"Nooo," she said yet again, this time as a soft moan. She pressed her face to the cold window, closed her eyes and tried to imagine, *could* she go back to him?

It had been glorious to be touched—not just sexually, though that was pretty great too—but to have her back and feet and legs and arms rubbed. And Nate's rough palms knew exactly what to do. She had fallen in love with those hands, with the small hard calluses that dotted his palms. They'd often joked that it was a good thing he had dropped out of college given how much she loved the rough feel of his manual-labored skin upon her body.

But there was also the moment when the girls burst into her room, when they'd laughed in unison, when they themselves touched her with their own hands, if not quite loving, at least closer than ever to something like what a mother must feel when her daughters are helping to make her beautiful. When they'd rubbed her kitchen-less neck.

And what about at the restaurant, where she had to actively work not to focus on the prices, where one entrée could buy half a grocery cart at the Dollar Store? Thinking about how the GIFT budget had again been sliced and how filling the pantry was becoming an ever-increasing challenge. She'd had to silence her mind in an effort not to resent Nate, casually spending his money—technically still *their* money— with barely another glance. Forcing her to remember how she too had lived before, could live again, in their big, beautiful, lovingly decorated home, all soft mauves and teals and cushiony furniture, carefully selected a piece at a time over the years of marriage.

Dully, she watched the landscape give way outside the window, like a reversal in time, back to the filth and disrepair of poverty. It was true—life *didn't* have to be this hard. What the fuck was she trying to prove, squeezed into a ramshackle house a fraction of the size, with four teenage girls and a ridiculously over-sized mutt, a house where there wasn't a single unused shelf or enough space to ever truly be out of sight of one another.

These girls weren't her daughters. They didn't look like her, or walk, or think, or dress, or smell or pray like her. On this, Nate was right. But sometimes at night she'd peek in on them sleeping and muse about their progress. This conversation or that, the quick hug when allowed, a shared laugh or tender exchange, and for those moments the differences would fall away and hope would reign.

While Nate rattled around alone in all those empty rooms.

The cab stopped on Clara Road in front of the GIFT House. As she got out she heard Dude at the inside window barking the specific high-pitched whiny bark he reserved for only the five of them. Lisa suddenly realized it was Sunday and she'd forgotten to do a new chores chart for the week. She forced Nate from her mind as she hustled up the porch steps.

CHAPTER THIRTY-SEVEN

"**Y**ou are such a stupid-assed schmuck."
"Gee, how do you really feel, Alan?" Nate fumed. He brushed the heavy hand of his business partner off his shoulder.

"Really, Nate. What are you waiting for? She's not coming back, and would you even want her if she did?"

He offered the blankest face he could though his damn right eye kept twitching.

"I'm telling you, there's a whole world out there just waiting for you." Alan licked his lips and gave a low, slow whistle.

Nate didn't attempt to swallow his groan. The guy was a complete caveman, as both of Alan's former wives had complained to Nate over beer and tears. Further, Lisa and Alan had never much liked each other. ("He listens to Rush Limbaugh," Lisa had denounced. "What else do you need to know?") But for all Alan's crassness, he was also a good friend. And Nate knew he not only meant well, but was probably right. It *was* time to let go. Nate had opened his heart to Lisa for the last time.

"You'll see, man, pussy's pussy," and at Nate's frown, "okay, I didn't mean that. But, really, Nate, there are other women. You gotta get there. I want my happy friend back."

Alan had probably never experienced what he and Lisa had shared—and yes, it *was* shared, and *still* existed, and it *was* unique. And then she'd walked out.

"I've got the answer for you," Alan said, grunting as he lifted a large crate of serving pieces onto his shoulder. "Help me with this and I promise to change your life."

They were setting up for the Soulard Mardi Gras party, a booking that had kept them working nonstop for the past three days and nights. In recent years, downtown St. Louis had become home to the second largest Mardi Gras celebration in the country. It was a major coup for their company to be selected as one of the suppliers of party rentals. Nate's whole body was beginning to scream, muscles he'd never before met were begging for rest. But he welcomed the work, welcomed the diversion and exertion.

"Okay," Nate said, bending to retrieve a bundle of purple, green and gold shrink-wrapped linens. "Change my life."

Nate stared at the computer screen so long the letters blurred into a wash of gray. He'd tried to answer as honestly as possible, though the temptation to either lie or exaggerate was nearly irresistible.

Which did he prefer? Curvy, athletic, full-figured or other?

He answered "other," and filled in "lean," feeling a rush of resentment that what he wanted, now, was lush, was Lisa. Nate had married a lean woman; he liked thin women. Yet, that night, he'd found himself sinking into her body and turned on with new vigor. Lisa Harris was both softer and stronger than Lisa Rothman, and it was a powerful aphrodisiac.

What was his geographic range?

In spite of himself, he'd driven by the GIFT House again yesterday, hoping in vain to glimpse any of them. He was tired of burned-out neighborhoods, ruts in the road, boarded-up windows, broken-down playgrounds. He was tired of driving, tired of searching, tired of begging.

He answered, "Within five miles of my zip code."

Which best described him? Definitely a social drinker.

His humor? Hard to remember.

He hadn't smoked in years and would not date someone who did. He refused to give his income nor cared what his perfect match earned so long as she was enthused about her work. He considered himself of average build (okay, he was a bit scrawny, but that was temporary), slightly below average in fitness (for now), and he considered himself average intelligence and expected the same. He left blank the level of education—he wouldn't want a woman who would want a man who'd not graduated from college.

Alan walked in without knocking, read over Nate's shoulder, and grabbed away the laptop.

"You shitting me, Rothman?" he kept muttering as he scrolled down. "You'll be lucky if they send you even one name, picky as you are. This is an online *dating* service and they've all got legs leading to the magic gash. You looking to get married or you looking to get laid?"

Nate shrugged. "I'm not sure I'm looking at all."

"Well, you can go buy some cheap hand lotion and get your palms nice and smooth or you can let me answer."

Nate shoved his chair aside and watched as Alan replaced specific answers with "any" and "all," stopping at the final, blank question. "You left this one blank too? What's the deal, Rothman?"

Nate turned away, but not quickly enough.

Alan cuffed his shoulder. "Man," he said, his voice growing rough, "let it go. This is killing you."

Nate walked out of the study, heavy footed, shoulders slumped, the epitome of everything a match was not supposed to be. His steps seemed to echo in the empty hall. He had an image of Lisa in her orange outfit, leaning into the door jamb, struggling not to break down. *Do you ever think about those babies?* she'd accused him during one of their worst fights.

He hesitated for a few seconds before turning the knob of the door. The room was bare—why was he surprised every time?—except for the tiny deep red Cardinals hat on the floor in the back corner.

He clenched his hands to resist the sudden powerful urge to shove a fist through the wall. *Well, Lisa, do you ever think about me?* For years he'd suffered through her hormonal mood swings, how she'd reach out to cry on him one minute and retreat into stony silence the next. He'd tip-toe around her, feeling like whatever he did never measured up. Console or give space, try to talk or pretend nothing was wrong. The Lisa he'd married had turned into someone he barely recognized. Yes, it was different for a woman, it was her body. And she had really wanted kids, way more than he did. But he lost those babies too.

He felt a warm presence behind him and turned into Alan's chest. Alan's hug was stiff and clumsy. Nate pulled away, shook off the useless pity and equally useless anger, and headed back to the computer.

He glanced one last time at their answers. He inhaled a ragged breath, thought of the GIFT House girls—he would *not* let go of them—then pressed his index finger against the capital X to mark the box. No Children. Let them wonder, was that his reality or his preference or just his pitiful past?

By the time Alan left, he'd downed three Budweisers. By the time he'd finished the vegetable beef soup straight from the can, five profiles had popped up. He read each one, studied their photos, reread their comments, then jotted down the name Lady Dragonfly.

CHAPTER THIRTY-EIGHT

L isa had packed a picnic lunch of all their favorite foods, including a large baggie full of Brianna's home-baked chocolate chip cookies. Ever since her birthday, Brianna had taken to baking something on a near-weekly basis, not exactly on Lisa's diet plan but too sweet, in every way, to resist. Last week she'd even attempted, with the help of Vanessa, to make sugar cookies shaped like Oscars, which they'd scarfed down, along with buttery popcorn and cheese curls, while all six of them watched the Academy Awards together.

"Here's a good place," Lisa said. She threw the blanket down, covering the damp ground. It was too cold for a picnic, but the sky was clear and sunny and on a whim Lisa had suggested an outing to Forest Park.

"Could we let Dude run around?" Danesha asked as she unsnapped the leash before Lisa could respond. Off he raced, running circles around the blanket three times before zipping away and rushing head wind into the lake.

"Omigod, does he know how to swim?" Coreen screeched, too late.

They all stood, a bit stunned, as he dunked his head and seemed for a moment to be sinking. Then he pointed his snout upwards, snorted twice and started to paddle in circles, lapping the water, nearly grinning.

All four girls ran to the edge of the lake, shouting out to Dude, clearly having way too much fun to come in. Lisa watched in amusement, feeling the veil of sadness lift off her shoulders for the first time since her date with Nate. Interestingly, no one had asked how the evening went, though it didn't seem to be about disinterest but actual sensitivity. She must have looked as disheartened as she felt.

"I'll get Dude back," Eva-Lynn exclaimed. She hunted around for a few moments, picking up and discarding various sticks until she found a solid smooth piece of wood. Bending a knee, closing one eye, slowly bringing her arm back until it stretched out straight, she whipped the stick in a perfect arc, sending it into the water, where it landed exactly just beyond

Dude's reach, toward shore. He immediately swam forward, retrieved the stick and was turning away to swim further out, when, with perfect precision, Eva-Lynn tossed another stick, again exactly in the spot that would lure Dude back to them.

"Dang, girl! You gotta sign up for baseball or something." Coreen shook her head in admiration.

"Here, do it again," Danesha said, this time handing Eva-Lynn a large misshapen branch.

She peeled away the bark, broke off a chunk, repeated the stance, and sent it sailing, this time bringing Dude to the water's edge, whereupon Brianna grabbed him by the collar and Coreen started clapping.

Immediately he loped forward and in Dude-like fashion shook his seventy pounds of wet fur all over the blanket and all over their food, sending the girls into peals of laughter even as they screeched and complained.

An hour later, back at the GIFT House, Lisa could hear from their tone that they were teasing one another upstairs as they rinsed Dude off in the bathtub, squeezed together into the tiny bathroom, laughing so loudly the sound carried down the stairs and into the kitchen. She could only imagine the mess they'd leave, tomorrow's project, but what were dirt on the walls and clumps of muddy fur in the tub compared to this incredible moment?

Quietly, in case anyone was in earshot, she whispered as soon as Bonnie answered the phone, "You won't believe the day we've just had. I think we are truly on our way to becoming a family. It suddenly feels like anything's possible."

"This is good, Lis. Real good."

They hadn't stayed long at the park; it was too cold, they were all too damp, Dude reeked. Originally, she had thought she might show them her walking route, maybe even go for a brief walk together. That didn't happen. Yet, it was an outing Lisa would travel back to many times and wish to relive once more. She couldn't know it at the time, that this would be the last sweet memory the five of them would create.

That this would be the day before the day.

CHAPTER THIRTY-NINE

"**I** believe you are about sixteen weeks along," the doctor said.

Lisa stared pointedly over his head, where a full-color chart outlined the stages of fetal development. At sixteen weeks, the baby was four and a half inches long, weighed three and a half ounces, had a heart, two legs, two arms, eyes and ears, a curved spine, the beginning of body hair and even tiny toenails.

"Dr. Mayer, are you sure?" Lisa swallowed a knot. She tried to keep her voice and expression neutral, aware she was betraying emotions that didn't fit the setting.

He cleared his throat. "We'll want to run some tests. But first tell me about the prenatal care to date."

The silence in the room was the answer. Lisa flashed to countless doctor's visits, the chalky horse-sized vitamins, the nauseating glasses of milk, the liver and spinach she'd forced down to give her baby and her body the much-needed, difficult-to-come-by folic acid. All those precautions.

Her body quivered with rage.

"Miss Harris? I asked if you'd be able to take Brianna to get an ultrasound. I think I could schedule it immediately in the lab downstairs. It's essential we get one as soon as possible. Given the patient's age and petite size."

Lisa thought about making a big show of thumbing through her datebook as though it were filled with important commitments, saying she couldn't possibly manage to take Brianna today, tomorrow or even for several more weeks. But she nodded dumbly, yes, of course. Then she looked, for the first time, straight on at Brianna. The girl was a child, how could she be having a child? She barely had breasts. No hips. She slept with a stuffed animal at night, sucking on its ears and leaving small pools of drool on the sheets and pillow cases that were still damp when Lisa stripped the bed to wash the linens.

But Brianna wasn't meeting Lisa's glance, nor was she responding to the doctor's questions. Her eyes didn't leave the chart, her hands cupping the—yes, now Lisa could see it—small swell of belly. Lisa could also read the girl's face, or perhaps she was remembering her own feelings at this point—the realization that she was having a *baby*. She pinched the skin on her empty left ring finger. "Dr. Mayer, are you absolutely sure?" she repeated. "I mean, she's so young."

Brianna shot her a look and tried unsuccessfully to hide a smile. She scooted closer and in a strong voice laced with self-confidence, said to Lisa, "It's gonna be okay. Ma weren't much older when she had me and it all worked out."

And where's your Ma now, you foolish girl? How dare you enter our program with the promise of breaking the cycle, only to repeat it when you've barely even started menstruating? How dare you imagine yourself a woman? How dare *you* have a baby?

Sam. He would be nearing two, learning to say new words every day, already comfortable with Mama and Dada.

Brusquely, she swiped away the tears that wet her flaming cheeks. The doctor's eyes penetrated with curiosity.

"Miss Harris, if you'd rather, I could have one of my nurses accompany Brianna to her ultrasound."

He had a kind face, with soft green eyes, a short graying beard, a one-sided dimple.

"Do you have any children?" she asked.

"Two girls, seventeen and sixteen, 'Irish twins.' And, phew, what a handful. Born just ten months apart...you'd think we would have..." He laughed, momentarily somewhere else, likely at home with his "handful" daughters.

The twins. Two black blinking dots on the screen, Nate with his head between his legs. *They* would be three and a half, in preschool. They would know their colors, would be able to cut shapes with blunt scissors, would recognize some letters of the alphabet.

She reached down to retrieve her purse. Then she felt small boney fingers gripping her forearm, pulling her back up.

"It'll be great, Miss Lisa. Babies are so much fun. And you can be the play-grandmama."

"Grandma," Lisa had first whispered into the phone five years ago, waiting with delight while her mother sputtered from "What?" to "Wow!" Then had come the day when she'd pulled down her underpants and seen the blood. Out of habit, she'd actually briefly thought, Oh! I just started my period, until, of course, she'd realized.

It was the same yesterday, when she'd gone into their bathroom to scour the tub out from the post-picnic Dude bath. As she emptied the trash into a clear bag, she noticed the two red lines on the white plastic stick. For a moment, she'd fantasized that it was *her* pregnancy test. Her pregnancy.

She'd confronted first Danesha, then Eva-Lynn, and finally, with disbelief, Coreen. It had never entered her mind to ask Brianna. She'd assumed Danesha was lying and had slammed her own door shut, frustrated at more levels than she could absorb. The tentative knock had later come from Eva-Lynn, who'd furtively stepped inside Lisa's bedroom and revealed the startling news.

"We'll need to call your mother. And Ms. Johnson," Lisa said as they pressed the elevator button to descend to the ultrasound floor.

"I wrote Ma a letter." Brianna's brow furrowed. "I didn't hear nothing, but she probably didn't get it yet. Don't you think she'll call when she finds out? Or maybe she'll hurry and drive back for me."

"Ma." What a joke. Though certainly what Brianna needed was a mother, any mother. But right now Lisa couldn't seem to be that woman either. Damn it! Why did it have to be *this?*

The doors opened to an empty hallway. Lisa stood against the long rubber stopper, neither in the elevator with Brianna nor on the floor of prenatal testing. She inhaled deeply several times, looking straight ahead at nothing until she gathered her composure. "Come on, Brianna. Let's go make sure everything is okay with your baby."

Lisa gripped the steering wheel with both hands to hide their trembling and to grasp control of something. Brianna kept her palms flat against her skinny little stomach,

258

humming low under her breath, every so often sighing in what sounded like pleasure.

They didn't speak until they pulled into the driveway, clunking the tire hard against the rut in the middle, causing Lisa to snap her clenched teeth. "Listen, Brianna," she said, her voice so tight that the girl's face paled as her eyes widened in fear. "What you did was wrong. And I don't mean getting pregnant. That goes without saying." She stared at the GIFT House porch stairs, at how they sagged in the middle from overuse and neglect. What was the point of any of this if they couldn't even fix a fucking piece of wood?

"How could you be so foolish, Brianna? Not to tell me? Not to see a doctor? Not to...not to even consider the option of..."

Then she stopped. Brianna's expression was so stricken that Lisa couldn't finish the sentence. "Go," she said waving her hand, suddenly exhausted. "Go inside. And don't tell the others. Not yet."

Brianna scampered out of the car and nearly leaped all three porch steps as one. For several minutes Lisa sat. She saw the light in the upstairs bedroom flick on, and shortly after, flick off. Must be naptime for the little mother. Sleeping for two while the other three were at school—or wherever the fuck they were. With Danesha, no one could be sure. And apparently Eva-Lynn was found in the bathroom stall more often than in class. Coreen at least went to class, made good grades, behaved at home and cared enough to pretend to be happy. So *maybe* one out of four?

Lisa had wanted to scream, to stomp her foot, to shake Brianna. As she watched the miracle of life appear on the ultrasound screen, she'd made herself go numb. *This is not about me*, she repeated in her mind over and over, her lips moving silently as if in prayer. *God damn it, this is not about me.*

CHAPTER FORTY

A s she picked up the phone, before she could even say
hello, a shrill voice blasted through the ear piece, so loud,
so piercing, so fast as to be nearly unintelligible and
completely unrecognizable but for a few telling words.
Brianna. Pregnant. Lawsuit.

Sheila's body went rock cold. There were few things that
terrified her more than having a GIFT girl get pregnant. How
well she knew the story, the ending written in the first
paragraph. And Brianna? Of all the girls, tiny, skittish
Brianna?

"Calm down, Ms. Jones," Sheila said to no avail, holding
the receiver far from her ear as the righteous harangue spewed
forth from one thousand miles away.

"Yes, yes, of course you've got a right to be upset... No, I
had no idea...Yes, I'll speak to Lisa Harris immediately...No, I
don't know who the daddy might be...I have no idea if she's
been to a doctor, Ms. Jones, I didn't even know until now that
she was pregnant... I understand that you are completely
shocked, as am I..." Though, of course, they weren't either of
them "shocked." It was a fact of both of their lives that a barely
fifteen-year-old mother was not an anomaly.

Sheila had to clamp shut her lips to keep from asking: And
whose fault is it that this child would seek such comfort? Just
who created the loneliness, the need to cry out, to be noticed?

But Sheila held her tongue because not to do so was futile.
She already knew what the mother was not yet admitting and
what Brianna, most likely, dared not yet consider—there was
no happy ending to this story. Lenore, herself a mother at
fifteen, had her first taste of freedom these past months, and a
needy, pregnant daughter was not going to fit prettily into this
woman's new life.

"Thanks to all a you, that girl of mine think she done
grown. Well, I got me a good mind to come up this minute. If
I'd saved me more money I would," screeched Lenore as her
way of saying good-bye.

Oh, Lisa, Lisa, how could you let this happen under your watch?" Sheila muttered into the empty room, though, hours later, when sitting across from Lisa, Sheila once again held her tongue. Sheila knew about the infertility issues—and she assumed that Lisa knew she knew, though, interestingly, they'd never talked about it. If Lisa didn't realize her background had been pieced together through dropped hints and expressions of grievous yearning, then the woman was a fool. And not only was Lisa *not* a fool, Sheila was even less of one.

She was prepared to tread lightly, to dole out empathy, until she looked closely at Lisa and saw in her crossed legs and studiously neutral gaze, an unmistakable, unexpected, judgment in the eyes of a woman who could, if she chose, walk away and never look back. Once, Sheila had driven out to the Rothmans' neighborhood, along the street of half-acre lots, two-car garages, custom-built swing sets. She'd wanted to see for herself what Mrs. Lisa Rothman had run from. And what had struck her then, and struck her now, was that Lisa quite likely wouldn't last. This was play time, a Peace Corps mission, until she could resume her real life

So when she spoke, Sheila's words were brusquer than she'd intended. "We hired you to keep these girls out of trouble. I thought we could trust you to do so. But maybe you just got confused and figured that rather than you save the girls, the girls would save..." And then she stopped because Lisa had turned so pale Sheila thought she might actually faint. Was it possible Lisa had not until this moment realized what had been obvious to Sheila from the first interview hour?

For a long uncomfortable minute, Sheila let Lisa squirm, even as she recognized that her anger was mostly misplaced. But she was sick of it. Sick of careless choices that repeated themselves over and over and over. Her people had survived slavery, racism and riots, and always the white man was their enemy. Until now. Now they were doing it to themselves. Drugs, drop-outs, deadbeat dads, babies proudly having babies. Yes, they had a black man in the White House, but in Sheila's narrow world, her efforts didn't mean squat if she couldn't even keep four girls from mimicking the same pitiful pattern they'd been entrusted not to repeat.

"Do you want me to resign?" Lisa asked.

"That's not going to do anybody any good, now is it?"

Lisa sniffled and wiped her hand across her nose in a gesture so patently vulnerable Sheila softened her tone to neutralize the sting of her words. "Look, Lisa, I'm not going to say I'm not upset. And I'm not going to say you don't have responsibility for this. It is your fault." She paused as Lisa slumped further, and then continued, "and my fault, and Brianna's fault, and possibly, depending on when and where this happened, Vanessa's fault, and, most of all, that wretched Lenore Jones' fault for leaving the girl in the first place." Sheila leaned back into her chair, laced her fingers behind her head, remembering how she'd originally turned down the request by Lenore to have Brianna stay at the GIFT House. Ironically, she'd been concerned that Brianna would just be settling in about the time Lenore snatched her back away. She should have listened to her gut. Because now. Now they were in a real bind.

"We've got to let her go, you know."

"I could help her with the baby..."

"You can't." And then, firmer, "By law. We're not licensed for pregnant teens. Lenore needs to get her daughter or she needs to sign Brianna over to a special home for pregnant girls. Either way, she can't stay in the GIFT House and once Brianna begins to show she can't go to Stone Charter. We've lost her, Lisa."

Lisa hid her face in her hands. Her shoulders shook and nearly inaudible sobs filled the otherwise quiet room. Sheila felt numbed by defeat, felt it all the way down to her swollen feet spilling out over her laced-up shoes. They sat that way for a while, each lost in her own thoughts, until Lisa raised her head, face streaked by tears. She picked up her purse and hugged it close to her chest.

"When?" she squeaked.

"We can buy a little time. Now that Lenore knows, it's up to her to make a decision. And either way she'll have to come up here, which could take her a bit. But it needs to be soon."

"Do I tell the other girls?"

"I imagine they know."

"She's so young. It's not right."

Sheila nodded her head. She kept nodding long after Lisa left, couldn't stop nodding until she turned out the lights to her office and pulled the door shut behind her, grateful, at least, that she was going home to an empty apartment.

CHAPTER FORTY-ONE

As she looked around the table at the four expectant faces, Lisa felt a sense of déjà vu so strong it left her light headed. She'd practiced what she wanted to say while cooking dinner, had practiced again while doing dishes. But saying it to the girls was so much more real here than the imagined scenario.

"It goes without saying..." she said, waiting to see if Danesha would mutter "then why you saying it?" giving Lisa a reprieve as the others reacted. But to a girl, they were uncharacteristically focused, their faces open and eager, ready for the news.

"As I said, it goes without saying that something has occurred. I can tell from the way you girls acted at dinner that you realize...I'm just going to blurt it out." She paused, a non-blurt moment, looking at Brianna, who offered a dip of her pointy chin in permission.

"Brianna is pregnant."

"Well, you a bum," Danesha said, her tone disapproving but her face bright with near admiration. And perhaps even a tinge of envy. "Who's your baby daddy?" she asked.

Brianna shrugged, looked down at her stomach, shrugged again. "Don't matter."

"Yeah it matters, Bri. He fine? Or," Coreen snickered, "a hobo?"

"Hope he ain't tall. Not much room in there for a tall baby," Danesha said, laughing when no one else was.

Eva-Lynn was sitting just outside of the circle, as usual, but she kept shooting Brianna chummy glances and several times Brianna looked to her as if for support.

"When you due?" Coreen thought to ask, and before she could answer Danesha piped, "You ain't getting out of doing dishes, you know."

Lisa watched, listened in amazement. No one seemed shocked or particularly dismayed. During Lisa's own ninth grade year a senior cheerleader had gotten pregnant and it was the whispered story for weeks until she dropped off the squad and out of the school.

Almost as if reading her mind, Coreen said, "Bri, they gonna let you go to school when you get big? With my cousin they made her do home classes 'til her baby was born."

They turned to Lisa. When she spoke her voice was so choked she could barely get out the words that needed to be said. "Actually, girls, this is terrible news. Brianna is going to have to leave the GIFT House and Stone school in the next couple of weeks."

Coreen's eyes immediately teared, and even the other two gasped.

"Oh no," Coreen wailed. She jumped out of her chair and hugged Brianna so tight that Danesha finally yelped, "Jesus, girl, don't squish her," as she stood and awkwardly placed an arm with exaggerated care around Brianna's bony shoulders.

Throughout, Brianna sat, saying little, her expression placid, her palms never leaving the tiny bump. If she felt sad or scared, it wasn't apparent.

Later, after all the girls had gone upstairs, Lisa lay on her back on the kitchen floor with Dude's head on her thigh, rubbing his fur so long the next morning her wrist and fingers ached. She kept replaying the same black and gray image, a film that refused to stop looping—stick-like arms, staircase vertebrae, puckered lips and a wide nub of a nose, the mimicry of Brianna's profile.

Right before Sam came out, she'd suddenly panicked. What if they were mistaken? What if she went into labor too soon and really the baby would have been fine? To her, on the ultrasound screen, he was perfect. And how, when she saw the webbed feet and sunken ears, she'd momentarily felt a giddy relief that he was so damaged he could not possibly have lived, even if she'd let him.

She shook away the memory. More pressing was Sheila's accusation that Lisa was only in this job to save herself. But for once Sheila was wrong. She *did* want to save these girls. Only, now what?

CHAPTER FORTY-TWO

Ever since spotting her daddy outside the donut shop, Brianna had snuck to the Central West End whenever she could—sometimes hitching a ride from strangers, other times copping a ride with kids from school. Two times she thought she saw him again, once with some hobo guy and once alone. She'd wanted to race into his arms, except something kept her just standing still.

But nothing was gonna hold her back now. It wasn't like she wanted her daddy instead of Ma, 'cept maybe Ma couldn't save enough money quick enough. And now that Brianna was gonna be a mama herself, she needed to worry less about herself and more about her Ra'Keem. That ultrasound couldn't tell yet, but Brianna knew she was having a big beautiful boy.

So for the second time this week, Brianna was hanging out on the corner of Euclid and Maryland outside the Coffee Cartel, with her hand on her stomach and talking in her mama voice, "Ra'Keem, you is my best boy," when she felt a fart bubble inside. She pressed hard against her jeans. "Ra'Keem, that you?"

"Girl, when you was in me you gave me the farts all the time,'til I found out it was you swimming in me. Imagine, Bri, me thinking you the shits when you was my own baby!" Ma one time told her, squishing Brianna into a big close hug."

This time the fart felt like a tiny bug flying in the dark. "Ra'Keem!" Brianna yelled and spun in a circle, punching the air all full of excitement. As she came to a stop, she looked up, and standing right there in shouting distance was...wow, it really was..."Daddy!" She ran without stopping to think and threw herself against his skinny body.

He immediately pushed her back and wrapped his arms around his chest. His pale cheeks had turned pink. His eyes were bloodshot, yellow where they should've been white.

"You sick?" she asked.

"Who are you?"

"Me. Brianna. Your girl."

His whole face went bright red, even his ears. "Brianna? You sure?"

She stood up as straight as she could, patting her hair backwards and down, like a done grown woman. She pushed out her new boobs and new fat hips. "Do I look so different?"

"Girl, you're beautiful." His voice was breathless.

But you said I was beautiful before too, she wanted to remind him.

He got real twitchy then, his body shaking, his eyes moving around.

"What, Daddy?"

He licked his lips and she could see how dry his tongue was, with a thick white coating. He glanced over her shoulder, began moving his head in rhythm to music only he could hear. She turned to see; swaying sideways and forward was the tiny light-brown woman.

He grabbed Brianna by the arm, his fingers shoving her skin into a pinch. She cried out a little and he let go. He leaned his face so close she could smell his breath, sour like garlic. "Listen, I gotta go, but give me your address and I'll come get you. We'll go to dinner." He shrank back against the brick wall. "But you gotta get out of here. Write it down, your phone number too—wait, you're not still living with your mama, are you?" and at her shake of the head "no," he smiled. "There's a bulletin board in there," he said, pointing to the coffee shop. "Just put a little *b* on the paper so I know it's you. I'll come by tomorrow." He walked away so fast he must've not heard her yell, "What time?"

On a napkin she did what he said, wrote down the address, phone number and the little b, a small letter for someone no longer a little girl. But of course he didn't know about Ra'Keem yet. She'd tell him at supper.

She hung the note on the bulletin board, moving around other slips of paper to put hers the most center, impossible for any daddy to miss. At the door she turned to make sure the note hadn't fallen to the ground or been moved to an edge, then she skipped outside to hitchhike back to the GIFT House where she would need to pick out what to wear tomorrow that would make her look grown, but still like the Brianna her daddy always loved.

"Girl, you ever getting out of that bathroom?" Danesha's voice was the high pitch of pissed off but not yet loud enough to carry downstairs. Brianna didn't bother to rush, rubbing the hair grease down to her scalp so nothing would frizz even though it was raining a little outside.

"Leave Brianna alone. Jesus! You've got to learn how to share," she heard Eva-Lynn say, and from the sound she could tell Danesha's response was a hard shove, then a harder one back. Brianna stood ready to swing open the door. If Miss Lisa heard them fighting she'd come upstairs and she'd see that Brianna was dressed in her best jeans and a velvet top she'd "borrowed" from Miss Lisa. There'd be lots of questions and then when her daddy showed up she wouldn't be able to sneak out. The shirt hung too big, even with her Ra'Keem boobies, but it was so buttery soft it made Brianna feel rich and spoiled like someone's favorite girl.

She added more of the purple blusher and put on a new pair of three-inch gold hoop earrings she'd bought this afternoon. She smiled at herself in the mirror. "Daddy, you're gonna be a grandpa." She watched how her own lips shaped the words. He'd probably want her and Ra'Keem to come live with him, which would make Miss Lisa and Ms. Johnson freak, but that was okay. She felt a sudden pain in her stomach at the thought of Ma, but Ma could move in too and her Daddy would quit liking that other woman. Brianna laughed out loud. "Oh, Ra'Keem," she whispered, patting her stomach.

Because of Ra'Keem, Ma was gonna come up from Florida after all. This afternoon she'd finally called Brianna. At first she was crazy, screaming over the phone that she was gonna whup Brianna's *"slutty black ass."* But then she said something about *"supposin' all of us could live together soon as I save me just a bit more money, but don't go holdin' your breath cause I can't say for sure when."* 'Course that was before Ma knew that Daddy could live with them too and they could put all their money together.

Brianna taped a note to her closed door, "My head hurts. Going to sleep," and tip-toed down the steps. Miss Lisa was talking with Coreen in the kitchen as they did the dishes. Brianna peeked in, careful to stay hidden behind the stairwell wall. They were standing close together, one washing, one drying, their big hips almost touching. Coreen was yakking on about nothing and Miss Lisa wasn't paying much attention, but Brianna felt a little jealous anyways. Maybe once Ra'Keem was born Brianna could be closer with Miss Lisa. She closed her eyes and then opened them, seeing a countertop filled with baby food jars and bottles, Ra'Keem in his little seat at the center of the room, his chubby face the same beautiful brown as Devon, his gold eyes real shiny and happy from all the attention and love, Brianna and Miss Lisa talking, talking, talking during Brianna's visit to the GIFT House. She blinked again and saw the empty, chipped gray counter top, the dirty green walls, the pantry full of drek discount food Miss Lisa would just ruin. She felt loneliness cover over her, then right away remembered. Daddy!

It was way colder out, but she couldn't go back in for a warmer coat. What if Daddy drove by and missed the house because she wasn't there?

She waited. Watching for every single car 'cause she'd forgotten to ask him what color his was. Miss Flozie limped by, pulling the rickety old grocery cart. A car full of boys from the ghetto high school down the block speeded past, the gun-fire exhaust sound making her jump. Then a nappy-haired boy jogged by wearing only shorts and a T-shirt, his naked legs reminding Brianna of the way Devon's strong legs had felt, all hair and muscle.

Dinner time passed. A couple stars came out in the dark cloudy sky. The air got colder. The lights in the GIFT House clicked off, one by one.

She waited. Watching. Knees pushing up against Ra'Keem.

She waited. Watching. Until her tailbone hurt and her hands like to freeze.

She waited. Until she was so cold that only by resting her head against her knees and curling her body so tight her bones seemed to clink together could she stop the shivering.

She waited. Head down. Not watching. Even when she heard the rumble of a truck, heard it idling in front, heard the door crank open. She scrunched shut her eyes, knowing he'd want to surprise her. And she held her breath. Waited. When she felt his hand on the back of her neck, felt the soft squeeze, she popped her eyes open. Daddy?

"Brianna what are you doing out here? It's cold. And dangerous."

She fell into his arms, let her frozen body push against Nate's warmth, let the tears come at last.

Chapter Forty-three

There was no way around it—today was going to be a bad day. Lisa knew it the moment she opened her eyes and saw that the sun was shining. She rolled over onto her back and groaned.

Last night, at the moment she turned thirty-nine, she was standing in front of the open freezer, spoon in hand, shoveling in mouthfuls of ice cream. Not the low-fat no-sugar stuff either, but the real thing—chocolate almond fudge with eighteen grams of fat and several hundred calories per serving. As the hand on the battery-operated clock clicked over to twelve, she tossed aside the spoon and began using her index finger to retrieve rounded creamy globs. Only when her finger throbbed with frostbite did she stop and instead call Bonnie.

Lisa had always hated her birthday and it had nothing to do with the number or being one year older. It was the pressure of this day singled out as special. Each year Jeanette insisted on making a big deal out of Lisa's birthday. Even when Lisa would ask for a simple family outing and a few books or small items, Jeanette felt compelled to invite classmates over as a surprise, to buy bouquets of helium balloons and large cakes and big presents. Nate had the opposite childhood experience. He grew up expecting birthdays to mostly be like any other day. The first year they were married he treated Lisa to exactly what she *thought* she wished for. At the end of the day, Nate half-heartedly said, "Oh, here," and handed her a very sweet, very loving, very cheap birthday card and nothing else. Still a newlywed, she struggled to hide her hurt feelings. The next year he bought her a parakeet she didn't want that thankfully died six months later. The third year he walked in with a large bouquet of helium balloons. Lisa burst into laughter, hugged him tight and could not imagine any situation in which she wouldn't adore this man.

She felt her eyes sting with tears as she folded her knees to her chest, trying not to dwell on the fact that her stomach was, impossibly, growling with hunger.

The house was quiet, too quiet. Lisa glanced at the clock and gasped. She was due at Stone Charter over an hour ago to volunteer in the library. Avoiding the mirror, she splashed icy water on her face and ran her fingers through her hair. She didn't need to look to know that her eyes would be red puffy slits and her brassy "Starlet" hair would be both flat and frizzy. She really should get to a salon, maybe that new one in Clayton she'd just read about called "Kink," which seemed apt. She squeezed into a pair of jeans whose waist was already too tight though less than a month old. That ice cream definitely was not sitting well this morning. She pulled on yesterday's drab olive green sweatshirt, noticed a splotch of chocolate on the right breast, shrugged, and left it on. As she passed through the kitchen, she glimpsed an envelope on the table, addressed to her in Nate's handwriting. It could wait.

Sure enough, Sheila gave her the once-over and a questioning rise of her eyebrows as soon as Lisa took off her coat. "Rough morning?" Sheila asked, her tone a mix of disapproval and pity. "Maybe this will help," and she thrust out a red envelope then hurried off.

In the two times Lisa had seen Sheila since finding out about Brianna's pregnancy there'd been a cool wall between them. Lisa knew she was going to have to address the issue, find out what was work related and what was personal. But not today, not when there were still so many hours to get through before it was tomorrow.

The library was crowded with students and not enough adults. Ron had recently implemented a reading incentive program and from the look of things it was either wildly successful or a total sham. As students finished books on their own time, they were given library passes to leave class and come take a computerized test for points on the book. Monetary gift and candy rewards were awarded each month to the kids with the most points. It had taken less than a day for the students to realize that all they had to do was pretend to finish a book to get out of their core classes and come surf the net while the harried librarian wasn't watching. Lisa's job, according to Sheila, was "you see someone not working, you bust him immediately."

A gaggle of girls was in the corner, their shoulders and heads close together, whispering and giggling. They weren't reading or testing. Three somewhat familiar looking boys and one very cute girl were in another corner, also not reading or testing. From where she stood, Lisa could see half the computer screens, all on the Internet. She heaved a deep breath and sank into the chair behind the librarian's desk. She felt something stiff as she sat, and, remembering, retrieved the red envelope from her back jeans pocket.

Good news! Things can only get better! the front of the card said. On the blank inside, Sheila had simply written, *Happy Birthday. Sheila.*

Lisa's eyes immediately welled with tears. She turned the card over and reread the front and inside. She brushed past the students, tears suddenly streaming down her cheeks, hurried into the bathroom and locked herself in the stall. The toilet was filled with unflushed pee and enough toilet paper to stop up the entire system. It reeked of old menstrual pads, a musky-sour odor that Lisa knew from experience would linger in her nose for hours. She leaned against the stall door and began to laugh-cry.

"There will be set-backs. Don't let them scare you, Lisa," Dr. Berger had said at her "termination" appointment. A set-back? Ya think, Doc? Just a failing job, failed marriage, fat body and responsibility for a pregnant fifteen year old.

She had no idea how long she stayed in that stall. Girls came in and left. Then a teacher, Lisa could tell by the clicking of heels. Another group of kids.

"Miss Lisa?" Brianna's familiar voice carried over the background noise. "You okay? Someone said you been in here a long time."

Sheepishly she opened the door. Brianna's face was twisted with worry. On impulse, Lisa pulled the girl to her chest and, for a moment, rested her cheek against the cornrow braids. "Oh, Bri." She hugged her tighter, pocketing the sensation for later, when Brianna would be gone. She forced her voice to be steady, "Thanks for the concern. I'm just not feeling one hundred percent today."

Her hand against Brianna's elbow, she walked over to the mirror, squeezing herself into the middle of the group. She dared to look and was startled—not by her piggish eyes or her swollen face, worse looking even than she'd imagined, but by her whiteness. Next to all that rich dark skin she was so *pale*.

Lisa was on her way back to the library when Sheila cornered her. "Got a minute? This is important," she said, steering Lisa toward an empty classroom. Perfect. First a birthday card, next a firing. *"Good news! Things can only get better!"*

"I've got something unpleasant to tell you," Sheila began, paused, inhaled deeply and paused again. *Just get it over with*, Lisa was thinking, so convinced of what was coming that it took several moments to realize what she'd heard. "Say that again."

"Yeah, you heard right. In the past twenty-four hours, Coreen's father has been arrested on assault with intent to kill, and her step-mother was evicted from their home. Her real mom, as I think you know, lost her apartment several weeks ago. She'd been living on the streets, but I put out feelers yesterday and she has disappeared." Sheila began to pace, bumping into empty desks and seeming not to notice. "We have to decide how much to tell Coreen. Everything at once or a little at a time?" She stopped still and at Lisa's blank expression, added, "You look like you're waiting for me to have the answer. I'm genuinely asking your input here. You know the girl better than I do."

Aware of the levels of irony, Lisa shrugged. "I don't really know her. I just live with her."

Sheila slowly crossed the room and sat next to Lisa. She sighed and for several moments it was the only sound in the room.

"Here's what I don't get, Sheila. Coreen has *so much stuff*. What's that about? Her family must have money."

"Let me tell you something about living in poverty," Sheila said, folding her hands as if a professor about to deliver a lecture her students might not want to hear. "You're a mother and you're three months behind on payment, so your electric has been turned off. It will cost eight hundred dollars to turn back on. You have two hundred fifty dollars to your name. You're not going to get those lights on anytime soon, but you *can* buy your kid two hundred dollar Jordans and make her real happy. What would you do?"

Lisa tried not to let her jaw drop. "That's crazy."

"Tell that to the mother or the kid. Just because they're poor, Lisa, the desire to make her child smile is no less important."

For their five-year anniversary, Nate had surprised Lisa with a diamond and emerald ring they could barely afford. When she asked, "Nate, why did you buy this?" he'd actually blushed and said, "To let you know how much I love you." Lisa looked at her ring-less fingers, struggling to stay in this room. "But our other girls have practically nothing. So what's the deal with Coreen's family? Or *families*?"

"We're talking about a girl who has flitted from place to place, adult to adult. Each time she moved she took something new with her, but think about what she didn't get and didn't take."

The room was suddenly filled with a burst of noise and commotion as the next class of students poured in, pushing and clowning around, even as they took note of Sheila's presence.

Out in the hall, Sheila squeezed Lisa's shoulder in a surprisingly friendly gesture. "Listen, it's your birthday. Let's both think on this and we can talk again tomorrow," and before Lisa could respond, she was gone.

Lisa turned toward the library then abruptly changed her mind. She scribbled a note, "*Not feeling well. Going home. Sorry and thanks for the card,*" and left it in Sheila's mail slot. As she passed near the side door she caught a glimpse of a mane of braids and large headphones sneaking out. Shit. Danesha was still pulling that crap? She hesitated, weighing her options, and assured that no other adult had also seen, Lisa slid out the door. Already, Danesha was out of sight. She gave a dismissive wave across the lawn to Ike Green, ignoring his unspoken invitation to a conversation. *Not today, Ike.*

The phone was ringing as she entered the GIFT House, and Lisa knew, as she picked up the receiver, that it would be her mother and that she would wish she'd not answered.

"Darling, I reached you. Happy birthday! My little girl is thirty-nine." Jeanette's forced cheer had lifted her voice a grating octave.

"Thanks, Mom. But, I'm just walking in, so could I talk to you later?"

"You're always just walking in. Or just walking out. I need to talk to you. Take off your coat, get some water or whatever you need. I'll wait."

Lisa rolled her eyes and suppressed a sigh. "I'm here. What's up?"

"Your father. He's getting so much worse..." There was a long pause and Lisa fought not to simply, quietly hang the phone back up. Instead she listened as Jeanette relayed the newest disturbing incident, this one involving Albert putting Jeanette's purse in the freezer, which took more than an hour to find, and she missed her dentist appointment. Lisa listened as Jeanette detailed how impossible her own life was becoming and how wonderful it would be if Lisa could come back up but this time for more than a visit and how and how and how. At one point, Lisa placed the receiver on the counter, rummaged through the refrigerator, picked the phone back up and Jeanette was still talking.

"Mom, I'm sorry," she finally interrupted. "I really do have to get going on dinner." *You, of all people—telling me this on my birthday.*

"You're making dinner? Tonight? Those girls should be preparing your dinner. Or Nate. Why isn't he taking you out?"

"The girls don't even know it's my birthday. And, Mom, please don't ask that. Nate and I are no longer together, so why would he ask me out?"

The long distance silence was loaded, but Jeanette only said, "Well, I'm sorry you're not here then. I'd make all your favorite foods for you."

For the third time that day, Lisa felt her eyes sting with misery. "Thanks. I know you would."

"You're going to look into that other thing?"

Lisa searched her mind. "Uh, remind me..."

"About seeing if we can get Dad into that dementia evaluation program in St. Louis. His doctor strongly recommended it. St. Louis, of all places. Isn't that something?"

"I'll make some calls this week."

The phone rang again as soon as she replaced the receiver. This time, it would be Nate calling to wish her a happy birthday, so she let it ring several more times before picking it up. They had not talked since she ran out the morning after their "date" weeks ago. She knew she was wrong, but couldn't bring herself to contact him to apologize. Surely he understood. Finally, she picked up the receiver, carefully keeping her voice casual.

"Hello?"

"Hello! This is the Children's Home Society. We're going to be in your area next week and we were wondering if you have anything for our pick-up."

The freshman science teacher called to tell Lisa that Eva-Lynn was flunking his class because she hadn't turned any homework in for three weeks. And a wrong number. But still no call from Nate. By the time the girls came home, got their snack, rushed upstairs to their rooms, she was both pissed and hurt. How could Nate not call? There was no way he'd forgotten. Okay, she shouldn't have run out. And maybe she should have called him since. But today was her birthday.

Then the doorbell rang. Dude hopped up from the corner and rushed barking to the front. He sounded less like a watchdog than an excitable puppy. She grabbed hold of his collar and answered the door, trying to slow her heart and her expectation. The florist's arms were full and she had to bite her lip not to squeal in delight. The card was addressed to Brianna, who must have answered the phone earlier to confirm the correct address. Lisa was surprised to find that her hands were trembling as she carefully pulled the paper

277

away from the flowers, dismayed that this should still matter so much.

One-half dozen tiny pink rosebuds were surrounded by baby's breath and filigree greenery. The bouquet was delicate and sweet, not quite Nate's usual style but beautiful and actually quite charming. *"Sorry about your dad. Your friend, Nate."*

Your friend? Huh? Even as a joke, Nate couldn't possibly mean *your friend.* And why would he send a birthday bouquet with a note about her dad? As she carried the flowers to the counter, she noticed the envelope from him, forgotten until now, stuffed into the corner. Again, she felt that mix of complicated emotions and was glad no one was there to witness how her fingers shook as she tore open the flap.

"What the fuck?" she muttered, pulling out a short yellow form that contained the vaccination records for Dude and a second notification for follow-up shots, now one month overdue. A scribbled note from Nate was clipped to the front. *"Sorry this got mixed in with other mail. Should have sent it sooner. That's why I delivered it in person last night. Brianna said you'd already gone to bed."*

"What the fuck?" she repeated, shouting it into the empty kitchen. Dude hurried over and shoved his snout against Lisa's thigh, whimpering for attention. Absently, she petted his head as she read the price list, her anger growing. It was going to cost close to one hundred dollars at the next veterinarian visit.

"Hey, who are those for?" Coreen asked as she, Brianna and Danesha wandered in. Lisa startled, suddenly realizing she'd frittered away an entire hour moping instead of fixing dinner. Now the whole evening would be off schedule, a potential GIFT House disaster. Sheila had drilled into Lisa's head enough times the need for routine among girls who'd spent their prior lives in chaos that Lisa had finally, herself, become a slave to the clock.

"Bri, they for you," Coreen said, her voice filled with awe. She retrieved the card from the clear plastic stand and read it aloud. Brianna grasped the bouquet to her chest and bounced out of the room, her head held high, her eyes shining. Coreen followed right behind, asking, "Why'd Mr. Nate send them to *you*? And how come he sorry 'bout your baby daddy? Did you tell him who it is? You gotta tell me!"

Danesha looked at Lisa for a moment, eyebrows raised. "Dinner ready?"

The meatloaf was burned, the frozen peas under-zapped, the frozen corn soggy. Everyone picked at their food except Brianna. She'd placed the flowers in a vase in the center of the table and was humming to herself as she ate twice her usual amount and then asked for more.

Lisa kept quiet throughout the meal. She didn't tell Eva-Lynn about the science teacher's call. She didn't ask Brianna if she'd heard any more from her mother. She didn't tell Danesha she'd seen her sneak out the school door in the middle of the day. She didn't bother to ask Coreen anything about her day. She did ask Brianna about Nate coming over last night and only then remembered that she had, in fact, laid down with a headache after dinner before waking near midnight to herald in her new age.

They all had mid-terms starting tomorrow, so they were off kitchen duty, leaving Lisa alone with her dirty dishes and self-pity.

She had just turned out the kitchen light and locked up for the night, when a quiet voice interrupted the darkness, "Miss Lisa, can I ask you something?"

"What is it, Brianna?"

"Do you think I should call Mr. Nate to thank him or send an email? I know my Ma don't do email, do he?"

"I think anything is fine," Lisa answered, summoning a shred of humanity she didn't realize she still possessed.

"Can I leave the flowers in here so they get more light? My grandmama once told me that's what they need."

Lisa nearly cried out "no!" but she numbly shook her head okay, brushing past little Brianna and her little baby bump. With the kind of tight control that made her stomach hurt, she closed her bedroom door quietly, not slamming it off its jamb like she wanted. She crawled into bed, placed the pillow over her face and pressed down.

Lisa opened her eyes to a pitch dark room. She sat up, feeling drugged and disoriented. The clock said eleven-fifty-five. Her birthday was nearly over. The next one would be the dreaded forty.

She trudged into the kitchen. The roses had begun to open while she'd slept and their cloying fragrance filled the room. She pushed her thumb against a thorn, slowly, deliberately, until a droplet pooled.

Brianna had repositioned the card so that it was dead center and higher by inches than the flowers. "*Sorry about your dad.*"

As she watched the drop of blood trickle down her palm, she suddenly realized. It didn't say anything about her "baby daddy." Nate was sorry about *Brianna's dad.* Since when did Brianna even have a dad?

CHAPTER FORTY-FOUR

Every day that she sat in another crunk class was another wasted day. Another day not getting Jerrell out of the joint so they could stay together in New York or California or maybe somewhere really far away like Africa or France.

"And, Danesha, who was it?"

"Huh?" then, fuck, there was that face again.

"What is it with you? Think you can just daydream all hour and pass my class? Fine. You can take my history class next year too, if that's what you want."

Hobo Hamilton was such an asshole pansy, but she could fake it for ten more minutes. "Sorry. Please repeat the question."

His eyes popped open in surprise and disappointment. She'd heard him brag, "I know if I give them a rope long enough they'll just hang themselves." Joke was on him. Rumor was old Mr. Hamilton was on Ron Stone's shit list and about to be fired. Then *he'd* be history.

Danesha swallowed her smile. Let him and all the rest of 'em think she'd "*finally* realized what her *priorities* were" so they'd quit trippin' offa her.

He repeated, "And which of the kings was dethroned by his brother in law?" She answered some bullshit, guessing between a Henry, William or James, and she must have pulled the right answer out of her ass because he moved on to the next bored victim, and finally the bell rang.

Danesha couldn't stop her head from turning to the side door window. She missed Devon. She missed the danger of skipping out with him and the way his fine gold eyes made her feel sexy. She liked watching his poker grow hard, knowing she had that kind of power even without letting him bone her. She'd need that to make millions of dollars as a super model. Not that Devon was any big challenge, but at least he was good for practicing.

After the trip to see Jerrell, she had only spotted Devon a couple of times and he always turned away, fronting like he didn't care none, even though she knew he did. And then, it was poof...he just disappeared. Still seemed like no one knew where the fuck he'd gone. But he'd be back and when he wanted her, she was gonna show him who ruled his corner. Yeah, that's what she shoulda told Hamilton, that it was King of the Corner Devon *dethroned.*

She walked to her locker, eyes to the floor so no one talked to her. It was pretty easy to do. She had no friends at school and really no one cared about her except maybe Ms. Johnson, but she was probably fakin' it too. She bent down and was leaning into the locker to grab enough books to keep Miss Lisa off her back when she felt a tap on her shoulder. She turned around, her nose smacking straight into a bump that was hard and not at all squishy as a normal stomach.

"Dang, Brianna. You're really prego, ain't you?"

Brianna right away covered her bony self, but instead of her usual wrapping her arms around her like one of them famine kids, she put her hands down low, like to holding a baby.

"Wanna walk home together?"

Danesha was about to nod yes when her eyes slid upward to the swollen boobs, all the way to Brianna's face, which was green-toned but also glowing proud. A rush of envy and anger went through Danesha. Even this mouse turd was going somewhere. Brianna'd be moving to Florida or some other place that had to be better than the GIFT House. She'd have a baby and would be able to get all kinds of food stamps and money and probably her own apartment.

Maybe she shoulda let Devon have her cherry.

Then she looked closer. Brianna was really one sorry mess. Skinny and scared, her whole life fucked forever. But not Danesha. She had it all in front of her, about to turn fifteen and get a legal work license. She didn't need any useless classes to teach her how to bounce and she sure as shit didn't want no baby now.

Brianna didn't talk much on the way home, she never did. But it was kind of tight to have someone to walk next to. Just as they turned onto Clara Road a chopped blue Chevy came cruising around the corner, bass thumping so loud and low

Danesha felt the rumble run her body. She stood still for a moment to put on her *I don't give a shit* face that she sometimes mugged in front of the mirror, and turned. But the passenger seat was empty and the only one in the car was Quinn. He slowed to a stop, unrolled the window, shouted over the music, "Yo, Danesha, ain't seen you 'round much. Need a ride? I got some news about a friend of yours you might wanna know."

She was about to climb in, when she noticed that Brianna's eyes were going crazy wild, searching all the empty seats in the car. "What the fuck you looking for, Brianna?" Danesha shouted, as Quinn suddenly flipped her the bird and hauled ass away.

Brianna kept walking faster than Danesha would have thought those skinny legs would move and got to the GIFT House and went right in. Danesha stood there, listening as the bass got softer and softer until she couldn't hear nothing, couldn't see nobody, and was left just standing alone, like she had nowhere to go and nothing to do. Well shit on that. She shoved open the door and went straight to the computer. She'd wasted too much time already.

"I need the Internet for homework," Danesha said and Miss Lisa barely nodded yes before shuffling her fat slippered feet back into her bedroom and shutting the door.

She googled a few key words and within seconds her ticket out popped up. **NO EXPERIENCE NEEDED! This is the chance for you to do what you love most... Model! An audition is not a time to be judged but a time for us to learn about you, your personality, your expectations, and what <u>you</u> want to do in the modeling industry.**

At MODELS & MORE we are here to meet you and evaluate your potential, as well as educate you about the business. We are looking for <u>all</u> experience levels and backgrounds.

Danesha stared at the computer screen and felt a model's smile stretching her mouth. Was it really that easy?

You think you've got what it takes? Call us TODAY!

And suddenly a memory came into her head. She was nine years old and wearing a brand new dress—red with a yellow ruffle at the neck and at the bottom of the short skirt. That dress had called out Danesha's name in the store window at J.C. Penney's, but Mama said no, said she was too young, she'd look cheap. Then that night, right after she and Mama had their plaits braided in, Mama shooed her off to bed. Danesha couldn't fall asleep on account of the braids tugging so hard. She got up to tell just as Mama was pulling out of a big white bag the red dress. Danesha had screamed out and Mama didn't yell none for her spoiling the surprise but just gave the dress to Danesha right then.

Jerrell had come home while she was twirling around to show Mama how it fit and he whistled a long whistle that made her feel beautiful. "You just wait, girl. You gonna be the most famous model in New York," Jerrell said, winking at Mama but looking dead serious at Danesha.

"'Cept we don't stay in New York, Jerrell. We in St. Louis."

He eyeballed her from front to back to front again. "Only now. Couple years, a tenner like you can go anywhere."

The next day, Mama let her wear that dress to school for her third-grade President's Day program. She kept pulling the skirt to cover herself, watching the clock. All the other mamas was already there, wearing their Sunday clothes on a Wednesday morning, none of them half as pretty as Danesha's mama. Only a couple men come. Most of the kids didn't have no daddy. Danesha didn't miss a daddy, never thought about it. She had Jerrell. But right now she and Crystal the only two with *nobody* visiting on this special school day.

Danesha walked past the cookie table. They couldn't eat until the end, 'til after the kids sang "Let My People Go" and "We Shall Overcome"—the two songs of praise Mrs. Taylor could play on her harmonica, the only instrument the school could afford since some hobo broke in last year and smashed the piano keys with a brick. After the songs, each kid was supposed to introduce his or her special someone, and then that person would say what was so fine 'bout the kid, and then they could all eat the cookies.

Danesha was getting that feeling in her stomach, to throw up or mess her pants. Mama had warned her next time she messed she would get the belt buckle. She'd never been whooped, but she'd saw plenty times how the buckle split open Jerrell's back, turning black skin pink and red. So far Jesus had been listening, 'cept suddenly not so much, 'cause then, standing in front of the plate of cookies, feeling a sprinkle sugar cookie drop from her hand into the front pocket of her red dress, Mrs. Taylor look up and see. Feeling her stomach rumble before the mess, Danesha knew Jesus had closed his ears. Then, at that same moment, there was a silence in the front of class.

The whole room had turned to stare at Mama. Full of curves, in brown, three-inch heels, skinny brown pants that made her long legs look longer, and a silky gold-colored blouse that hugged her boobs, liking to "suggest without promising." (So that was how come the Penney's bag so big.) Mama's outfit made all those others seem crunk and old fashioned, like someone's left-over grandma picked out their clothes. Every one of the women had on her "damn she looking good" jealous stares and the men was struggling to remember they in an elementary school classroom. Even the kids could see Mama finer than the rest.

Mama walked in a straight line (no wobbling today, thank you, Jesus, you didn't quit on me after all) over to Danesha, like ain't no one there asides her little girl. Real fast, Danesha put the cookie back on the plate and rushed to her seat. Mama stood right behind her, hands on Danesha's shoulders, as they all sang their songs of praise.

Thinking about it now, Danesha knew that even way back then Jerrell had it right. Sexy and beautiful would be the ticket to everything—if you knew how to use it. Mama had trashed hers. No way would Danesha do that drama. Once she got rooms of people mugging jealous, she'd never let go. She'd almost told that to Jerrell when he finally called her last week. Instead she just said the part he wanted to hear, "Devon is gone."

She wrote down the MODELS & MORE phone number and surfed a couple other sites, some across the river, others across the country, so focused that when the GIFT House phone rang, Danesha jumped and her hand shook as she picked up the receiver next to the computer, heard a shrieking, "Girl, every time I think about you I could strangle your neck!" then hung up at her end when Brianna's whiney voice yelled back, "Ma! It's you?"

"Yeah, it's me. And I'm getting madder and madder at you fucking up your life. And my life too. Even my fingers is screaming."

Brianna put her left hand on Ra'Keem as she took a look in the hallway mirror. "It's okay, Ma. I'm really happy 'bout this baby. I'm gonna be a good mama."

Nothing was said on the other end, and over the long silence Brianna could hear all the miles between them. "Ma? You still there? Please don't be mad."

When Ma finally spoke she'd turned all sad. "Oh, Bri. I wanted everything to be different for you."

"It will be." Brianna looked again in the mirror and suddenly saw Ma's face staring back at her—rounder and rosier than the old Brianna, the one before Ra'Keem. She stood up straight, pushing out her full boobs. "When you coming up?"

"You don't leave me no choice, girl. I was hoping to save enough for that beach house, but you gone and screwed that up. And I guess this baby gonna have a deadbeat dad too." Her voice was softer than her words, reminding Brianna of the way her hugs always felt tough and sweet both.

She thought about telling Ma how Devon didn't matter none, how he didn't even know she was pregnant, but then Ma would call Bri a bad name, and none of it mattered 'cause if Devon did know he might want to keep Ra'Keem for hisself, so it was good he never come by again. And anyways she'd seen her own daddy and they just had to find him once more. But instead of going into all that right now, she said, "I really miss you. Please hurry."

This next quiet seemed scary long 'til Ma said, "You know, I don't get paid on the days I don't work. And you gonna be sleeping on the floor, girl. Don't expect me to give up my couch 'cause you been fucking around."

"Wait 'til you feel how hard the mattress is here. That floor in Florida got to be softer. And now, Ma, you'll see my bedroom. I never really made it my room 'cause you was just waiting to send for me..." and then she stopped. She wasn't sure when Ma had hung up, but she was pretty sure it was right after Brianna started talking about what her life was like. "I won't do that to you, Ra'Keem," she whispered, feeling a bunch of things she didn't like to think about, even thinking for the first time for real how it might be bad for Ra'Keem not to have a daddy, but then shaking that off 'cause she'd be such a good mama he wouldn't miss a daddy.

She put the phone down and right off it rang again. "Ma?"

"I ain't calling for you, girl. We said everything already, I need to talk to that white lady, the one supposed to take care of you." Her voice was high-pitched again, and Brianna almost felt sorry for Miss Lisa as she yelled down the steps for her to pick up and was glad to leave that mad Ma to someone else.

"I'm getting you fired, lady. Fact, I might even sue you for everything you got!"

"Hold on, Ms. Jones. We need to talk."

"Talking ain't gonna get rid of my baby's baby. Who gonna raise that child? You?"

Lisa held the phone away from her ear and allowed the woman to verbally beat her up without responding except at one point to ask Lenore to quit screaming so loudly because it was hurting her ear, which enraged Lenore even more.

"You best be ready for a fight. You folks supposed to watch out for my girl, and you done her wrong," she shrilled before hanging up without saying good-bye or answering Lisa's repeated question. When exactly are you coming to St. Louis?

Lisa picked the phone back up to call Sheila and tell her about Lenore's threat. She also needed to relay an earlier, no less disturbing message, from a teacher who walked into the bathroom at school and saw blood spots all over the floor after

Eva-Lynn limped out. Thinking about it now just made Lisa's headache pound harder. She replaced the receiver and moved toward the kitchen, trying to fill her mind with nothing more complicated than dinner. The phone calls could wait.

"Miss Lisa!" Danesha visibly startled and quickly shut off the computer as Lisa walked in. She popped out of the chair, knocking a glass of water onto the floor in her haste. "My bad, I'll get it," she said, while Lisa stood in wonderment and watched Danesha not only wipe up the water, but go to the sink, rinse out the glass, dry it and put it back on the shelf before smiling a genuine smile, grabbing her backpack and scurrying up the stairs.

Lisa opened the refrigerator and stared at the still-frozen hamburger she should have defrosted hours ago. A large black roach scooted across the cabinet door as she scrounged around for a box of spaghetti. "Are you kidding me?" she groaned, then laughed bitterly. The bug man had sprayed for the third time just two days before, leaving behind a lingering stench of poisonous chemicals and very much alive, disgustingly huge roaches. "*Even the roaches are colored,*" she remembered saying the first time she'd talked to Sheri Fox, thinking then she'd heard the last of Eva-Lynn Fox.

Upstairs she could hear Dude whining to be let out. Heated words were being exchanged but through the floor it was hard to discern which girl was fighting with whom. Moments later, the sound of heavy footsteps told Lisa it was Coreen. Sure enough, she came stomping in and announced, "It ain't even my turn."

"Just forget it," Lisa snapped. She grabbed the leash from Coreen's hand and, ignoring her dismay, brushed past her and pulled Dude out the door, where she stood by and watched with grim satisfaction as he shit all over the GIFT House lawn.

She had just unhooked the leash and hung up her coat when the phone rang again.

"Mrs. Rothman?"

Lisa caught her breath. "Who is this?"

"Do I have the right number? Is Mrs. Rothman there?"

After a brief hesitation, "This is...she."

"Oh, good. You're a difficult woman to track down. This is Regina Gillespie. I'm the new director of Credit-Solutions. I've been going through our records and I'm wondering how my predecessor ever let you go."

Lisa struggled to find her voice but before she could react, the woman rushed on, "Listen, I know this must be coming out of left field, but I would like to invite you to meet—soon, tomorrow?—because we have an immediate job opening that I believe could be an ideal match."

She thought she heard a gasp, not her own. "Excuse me a moment," Lisa said, and without waiting for a response, she placed the phone against her thigh and shouted up the stairs, "Is anybody else on?" Hearing nothing, Lisa picked the receiver back up and managed to stutter, "Um, I have a full-time job right now. However...I guess I could come in and talk to you. Not tomorrow or Wednesday, but Thursday? Around one?"

As she hung up she felt a wave of dizziness and grasping the side of the table she sank into the nearest kitchen chair.

Upstairs, the receiver clanked back into the cradle.

CHAPTER FORTY-FIVE

A s she opened the door, Lisa was greeted by four grimacing faces and a palpable electric tension. "Okay, girls, what's going on?" she asked, shoving aside Brianna's latest batch of cookies and placing the two bags of groceries on the table. "And where's Miss Vanessa?"

"She gone already," Brianna said, casting a furtive glance at the others.

"She *what*?"

"They was kicking her out of the place where she stay, so she had to leave right off," Coreen piped in, but before Lisa could react, Danesha grabbed hold of Lisa's arm and hissed, "Miss Vanessa don't matter. Here's what matter. Ask the bitch. She'll tell you."

Lisa searched each miserable face to determine which "bitch" was culprit. Eva-Lynn had gone starkly pale, her lips pulled tight. Must be her.

"Did you know?" Danesha glowered, her eyes glinting to a dangerous shade of gray.

"Know what?"

"Ask her. The KKK Nazi." Danesha shook a fist at Eva-Lynn. "I ain't living with this shit. She go or I go."

"So go," blurted Brianna, startling everyone. She hooked an arm through Eva-Lynn's and pulled her close.

"Whoa, girls!" Lisa struggled to step between all of them, maneuvering past the grocery bags and empty chairs. "Everyone sit down and calm down. Now."

Danesha sat, though she held herself stiff, a cat ready to pounce. They glared at one another, no one speaking. After a few beats of tense silence, in itself oddly more disturbing than the outbursts, Danesha pulled from her jacket pocket a copy of an old newspaper clipping.

Lisa caught two words in the headline, just enough. She slowly asked, "Danesha, where did you get that?"

"Did you know about this?" Danesha screeched.

"Answer my question first," Lisa said, stalling.

Danesha tilted her head toward the open file drawer and Lisa's heart sank. She must have forgotten, at five a.m., to lock the drawer after scouring Eva-Lynn's papers for previous incidents of cutting. How could she have been so careless?

"Did you know?" Danesha's voice was pitched feverously high as she thrust out the article, her hand crumpling the paper into a wad.

How to answer? How to explain that of course she was deeply disturbed after reading the article from eight years ago that exposed the strength of the rural Missouri white supremacy group, as then headed by Grand Dragon Ray "Pappy" Fox, father to Ray Fox Jr., grandfather to twins Ray Jack III and Eva-Lynn Fox. That she, too, recoiled, her own Jewish blood pumping faster with repulsion and dismay. That, in fact, *every one of them* had backgrounds that still, at times, freaked Lisa out.

Instead, she leaned across the table and tried to hug Danesha, sensing in the child as much fear as anger.

"No! Don't." Danesha thrashed her arms, slugging an elbow into Lisa's ribs. "You knew, didn't you? Are you one too?" Tears were streaming down her face and her mouth was twisted into an ugly scowl.

"Some things are too complicated to explain." It was as much clarification as she dared.

"Too complicated? Like leaving us for another job? Well, fuck this shit." Danesha whirled around and stood threateningly over Eva-Lynn. "I *hate* your stinking guts and all your stupid-ass cuts bleeding all over everybody's business."

Eva-Lynn shot up, her expression grim and defiant. "Yeah, so what? I hate your stinking guts too! I shoulda listened to my Grandpappy. He warned me about your kind before he ever knew I'd be living in this trash house."

*No! You don't hate each other, not anymore. You were just brought up to think you do...*words that Lisa wanted to say, should have said, but instead stood rock still silent, watching unfold a scene she would later replay over and over in her mind.

291

Danesha clenched her hand into a fist, growled, "Don't you say your Nazi grandpa's name in front a me again, that mother fucker. If he weren't dead I'd go out and kill him. But since he ain't here…" and with studied and deliberate care, her face so tight as to be nearly unrecognizable, Danesha calmly pulled her right arm all the way back, seemed for a precious moment to reconsider, then swung it forward with a whooshing fierceness. The thunk against Eva-Lynn's jaw resonated and was the only sound for several astonished moments. Then, at once, everyone was shouting, screaming, crying.

"My jaw! You broke it," Eva-Lynn shrilled, blood from her split cheek and lip filling her cupped hand.

"Oh quit your drama, Nazi bitch. It ain't broken. You couldn't talk if it was." Danesha's voice had turned eerily calm.

Brianna's own jaw had dropped open, and she was gasping, as though for breath, as she popped up and without hesitation shoved Danesha as hard as she could, sending the bigger and stronger girl stumbling backwards in surprise. Immediately, Brianna hurried into the living room and curled tight, wrapping her arms around her stomach as Danesha rushed forward.

Coreen jumped between the two. She grabbed Danesha's shoulders with her thick, powerful hands. "Stop it. What's wrong with you?"

Danesha shook Coreen's hands off her, turned to Brianna. Curling her lip, she taunted, "Go ahead. Stick up for her until the next time this white bitch punches someone out for calling her a nigger lover. You didn't know that did you? Maybe you was too busy being a thirsty slut with all them boys."

Brianna arched her back, allowing her baby bump to protrude. In a voice unrecognizable, she fired back, "Not boys, Danesha. Devon. Uh ha, girl. Didn't know *that*, did you? Didn't you wonder why he quit on you? Can't blame him wanting some sweet meat 'stead of your sour self."

The words hung suspended as Danesha froze in place, her face sagging and then she roared, and with bitter force shoved Brianna, propelling her against the mantelpiece. Brianna fell with a thud, cracking her head against the unyielding brick.

Blood spurted from her forehead, flowing unchecked down her face as she grabbed her middle and moaned. Shrieking was stilled, replaced by stunned silence.

Danesha spun on her heel and stomped out of the room, slamming the door of the GIFT House firmly behind her.

CHAPTER FORTY-SIX

Later, Lisa suspected that she must have been in shock. The drive to the hospital, the emergency room visit, the events that subsequently unfolded all seemed to happen in slow motion, every movement, every word, distinct and exaggerated. She felt strangely composed throughout, as if she had grown taller and thinner and sharper. All her senses were on alert and at the time she heard every beeping monitor, every nurse's question. She saw the same CNN newsfeed over and over and downed from the same pot multiple cups of tepid bitter coffee.

Yet, afterwards, she had no memory of actually driving the two bleeding girls in her car to the hospital, though Coreen said that Lisa honked her way through several red lights and then spoke calmly and slowly to the emergency room attendant who seemed more concerned about insurance cards than head wounds and a possible miscarriage.

Coreen pushed Brianna in one wheelchair through the air-pumped door while Lisa pushed Eva-Lynn. At no point was Danesha's name even mentioned.

The doctors allowed all four of them to be in the same room until it was time to stitch up Eva-Lynn's cheek and Brianna's forehead. Lisa insisted on staying with Brianna, even though Coreen clearly would have preferred otherwise. But if a miscarriage was in process, Lisa would need to be the one grasping the girl's hand.

The attending doctor looked to be about ten years old, though he immediately put Brianna at ease with his calm demeanor. "Now this may sting a bit. Have you ever had stitches before?"

Brianna shook her head back and forth. "What about my baby?" she asked, barely above a whisper.

An expression of disapproval knitted his young brow tight. "We've ordered an ultrasound but you've got a pretty good head wound here that we need to tend to first. After all," he continued in a tone obviously part of his training, "wouldn't want a pretty face like yours to have a scar, would we?"

Brianna scowled and briefly Lisa worried—given the bold side she'd witnessed an hour before—that Brianna might respond in a way that would offend the doctor, prolonging the time until they could get down to the ultrasound lab.

But all she uttered was, "Ra'Keem," and then bit her lip and turned her bleeding forehead toward the doctor as she squeezed shut her eyes.

On the other side of the curtain, Eva-Lynn was trying to remember if this was the fourth or fifth time she'd had stitches. The first time, she was only two when the ring on Ray's pinky clipped her chin at a bad angle because she turned her face. It left the faintest scar, but in many ways was her favorite. The first badge.

"I'm beginning to stitch now, Eva-Lynn. Tell me if you feel anything at all, because I can give you more numbing agent." The doctor's voice was deep like someone tall and good looking, though he was skinny and short, with red hair and a gray mustache.

Eva-Lynn kept her eyes closed as the doctor worked. He hummed a little, a soft familiar tune that made her remember how Grandpappy used to hum when he pitched hay. Grandpappy. What would he say if he could see her now? He'd twist her arm until her shoulder and her elbow were nearly touching, all in the name of loving her enough to teach her the kind of lesson she'd need if she wanted to get by in this God forsaken world. She shuddered.

"Hold on there," the doctor said. "Don't go moving around like that."

Eva-Lynn snapped her eyes open. The doctor was leaning close to her face, his arm frozen in place, a sharp needle between his thumb and forefinger. She motioned for permission to move, and at his nod, she shook her head, trying to cut Grandpappy out of this room.

"Ready?" the doctor asked.

She closed her eyes against the needle and the pulling of thread, not really pain but pressure, different than a razor. It felt less real.

"We're nearly finished. You doing okay?"

She didn't nod. Most adult didn't give a shit about an answer. She'd found that out each time in the E.R. when they asked lots of questions but sent her back home anyhow.

"Well, young lady, that should do it." He handed her a small mirror. Take a look."

The cut was clean, the stitches neat and even. This one might not even scar.

"Wait twenty-four hours to get it wet. Then just watch to make sure it doesn't get too red or swollen. The stitches should be removed in eight days. You'll need to see your pediatrician or come down to our clinic between two and four in the afternoon." He looked to Miss Lisa, now in the room taking notes. She squeezed Eva-Lynn's hand tight. That's when tears came to Eva-Lynn's eyes, which Miss Lisa right away apologized for, thinking she'd pressed too hard. All of a sudden Eva-Lynn wanted to thank Miss Lisa, thank them all (except that fuck-face Danesha) for taking her in. But instead she just squeezed back.

Though neither girl felt dizzy, hospital regulations required that Brianna and Eva-Lynn be taken by wheelchair down to the floor below, where all four were told to wait until, finally, the ultrasound technician came and wheeled Brianna away.

Blood splatters had dried on the mantle and surrounding bricks. She'd sent the three girls up to their rooms. No one asked about Danesha, and Lisa didn't say anything either. She got a bucket of soapy water and started scrubbing until the spotted bricks gleamed so clean, she wound up washing down the entire mantle.

What she later remembered with astonishment was that she would wash bricks before she picked up the receiver and with a trembling finger punch in the number.

"The worst has occurred," Lisa said without preamble.

"Are all four girls alive?" Sheila asked.

"Yes."

"Then," Sheila said, "whatever it is, it isn't the worst. Now tell me what happened."

As she hung up the phone, Lisa stared at the unpacked bags of groceries, mindlessly watching droplets of thick melting chocolate drip to the floor. It had been a stupid, impulsive purchase. But she'd splurged, somehow imagining— was it only four hours ago?—that a quart of Häagen Dazs double chocolate would bring them all together.

Finally, she snapped aware and before giving in to the numbing release of cleaning the ice cream from the floor, she again picked up the phone and this time called Nate.

CHAPTER FORTY-SEVEN

It was their third date and as he laughed with a lightheartedness he hadn't thought he could ever feel again, Nate realized that he was actually growing fond of "Lady Dragonfly." Patty Klemen was everything Lisa was not. She was brash and uninhibited. She was spontaneous. She'd even passed the Alan test. "Finally, Rothman, the kind of girl you ought to be with."

On impulse, he grasped hold of her hand and brought it to his lips. They'd hugged a few times and had kissed a quick good night at the end of both of the other dates. As his lips grazed, then lingered on her palm, he heard her give a startled gasp. She met his eyes, questioning, and he found himself nodding yes, an unspoken promise that tonight would be a turning point.

He held on with his right hand while he reached for his wallet with his left. "Two tickets for 'Play It Again, Sam,'" he said, winking at her as though they shared a secret. Like Nate, Patty loved old Woody Allen movies and last week she had snorted aloud so many times during the Tivoli Film Festival showing of "Bananas," Nate found himself laughing at her delight. When was the last time that had happened?

Patty went to find them two seats while Nate got in line for popcorn. And then his cell phone rang.

As he dropped Patty off at her door, he offered a half-hearted apology, explaining again about an emergency and promising they would see the movie another time. But already his head was elsewhere. And by her downcast eyes and pouty lips, he sensed she would not be sitting by the phone waiting for it to ring.

At the GIFT House he found the door unlocked and Lisa curled up on the kitchen floor, cuddled against Dude. He kneeled next to her and allowed his arm to drape lightly against her shoulder, pulling with gentle tugs until she folded herself into his hug. Her shoulders shook with soundless cries for several minutes. Finally, she lifted her face and her distress shifted to something unreadable.

"You were on a date?" She didn't wait for a response before adding, "That's nice." Her voice was carefully modulated, as if he would be fooled after so many years of non-fight fights.

He nodded as noncommittally as he could. "You said you needed my help?"

"Is she someone special?"

"Lisa, I hardly think..." he stopped himself.

She pulled her hair up and away from her face, a gesture he had once found sensuous, and cocked her head to the side. She even offered a half smile. "Well, I'm glad you're finding companionship. I mean, I hadn't realized we were going to start dating, but if you have someone, Nate, I guess I'm happy for you."

Matching her sugared tone, he responded, "Thanks for the good wishes." Immediately, her eyes filled with tears, setting off in him a boomerang of emotions. He inhaled several times, trying to tamp down his own feelings as he took hold of her hand, thinking of the last hand he'd held just thirty minutes before. "Lisa, what happened tonight?"

Briefly, she caught him up on the essentials: the newspaper clipping, the fight, the emergency room and, ultimately, the reason she'd called—Danesha's disappearance.

"How long has she been gone?"

Lisa looked over her shoulder at the kitchen clock and paled. "My God, it's been almost five hours. In this neighborhood. Oh, Nate, I didn't even realize. I've been so preoccupied with the others..." her voice drifted off. Her bottom lip, he now noticed, had dots of dried blood from having chewed it raw, reminding him of the weeks leading up to their decision to separate, when he'd wake up to blood-spotted pillowcases.

Outside a car pulled up and moments later Sheila barged into the room. As usual, one glance and she appeared to assess the entire situation. "First thing, where's Brianna?"

"Upstairs. On bed rest. She had some cramping, but it's stopped and the ultrasound looked good. They're concerned about how tiny Brianna is. Of course, the trauma didn't help anything. Or," Lisa shrugged, "hurt anything. However you want to view it."

"And Eva-Lynn?"

"Quiet. Scared. You know," Lisa shook her head in quick bursts of amazement, "I think what scared her most is that she seemed almost to have forgotten her past. Catching up with her like this unglued her more than I would have believed."

"Miss Vanessa?"

Lisa hesitated, tempted by unexpected loyalty for the well-intentioned, if unreliable, young woman. But the truth would come out, so better now. "She wasn't here when I arrived home from the grocery store."

Sheila's eyes sparked with anger. "Tell me I didn't hear that," she said, then waved her hand in dismissal. "Let's deal with Danesha."

Together they searched her room for clues and went through her backpack. The only thing they found of note was an assortment of teen fashion magazines hidden under the mattress.

"Where's she getting the money to buy these?" Lisa asked. "And why hide them?"

Sheila didn't even attempt a guess. Another subject for later.

They called neighbors; no one had seen her. Minutes passed and the tension grew as it seemed increasingly unlikely that Danesha would simply come slouching sheepishly into the house. Nate was the one who thought to check the computer. He punched in several keystrokes and immediately gasped. "What the hell?" he exclaimed, slumping back into the chair as Sheila and Lisa peered over his shoulder and groaned. "NO EXPERIENCE NEEDED! This is the chance for you to do what you love most...Model! You think you've got what it takes? Call us TODAY!"

Nate grabbed his cell phone, jacket and keys. "I've got a buddy who is good friends with a cop. He won't make us wait twenty-four hours to get the police looking."

At the door, Lisa rested her head against his chest. She kept her arms at her side and her back stiff, but her face nestled so close she could hear his heart beating.

"I'll bring her back." And he opened the door and walked out, hopping over all three porch stairs.

CHAPTER FORTY-EIGHT

It took twenty-two hours for Lisa to hear any news from Nate. She didn't sleep, she barely spoke, she nearly didn't even move during the entire time of waiting. *Please God please God please God*, she repeatedly muttered, a mantra with no beginning or end, not even a specific request, because to do so might invite the unbearable thought of an alternative.

For a while, Coreen sat alongside Lisa on the couch, jabbering until she grew silent and then stumbled back upstairs to her own room, where she fell into a deep sleep that lasted until early afternoon.

Eva-Lynn crawled into bed with Brianna and they whispered and napped, whispered and napped. At some point, Lisa became aware of this and briefly wondered at the mystery of this friendship but then allowed her mind to once again go blank and her lips to mutter in prayer, feeling very much a hypocrite, but not daring to not pray.

No one mentioned school that morning and no one bothered to eat breakfast. Sheila called every couple of hours, and each time the phone rang, Lisa's heart felt as though it stopped, sped up, and stopped again, a cliché she would not have believed could actually be experienced, though it was.

Mid-day she interrupted Bonnie at work. "What if we can't find her?"

"Don't go there."

"But what if?" Lisa stared at the kitchen table, still bearing remnants of sticky ice cream. "By the way, I am so done with chocolate ice cream. If you ever hear me say I bought some, please shoot me."

"Mint chip from now on. And, Lis, just try to stay positive."

At hour fifteen, the screech of brakes outside the GIFT House startled Lisa out of her stupor. The doorbell didn't ring so much as it seemed to shrill with sharp, angry blasts. Lisa opened the door slowly and stared into the fuming face of an older, prettier, darker version of Brianna. "Lenore Jones," Lisa mumbled as the woman barreled past and raced into the house, yelling, "Brianna, get your sorry-ass butt down here and let's go."

"Ms. Jones, don't do that, please," Lisa said, crossing the room and blocking Lenore from the bottom step.

"Excuse *me?*"

"Brianna is on bed rest."

Lenore turned slowly and deliberately scanned half-slit eyes over Lisa, from the brassy Starlet blonde hair to the wrinkled shirt to the muffin of flesh oozing over the too-tight jeans. Lisa stood, buzzing with anger at Lenore's smug judgment, as if being thin made up for parental neglect. It took every ounce of self-control for Lisa not to clench her fist and swing, understanding with frightening empathy the energy behind Danesha's outburst. Then she heard Brianna from all the way upstairs, exclaim, "Ma!" with such obvious delight that Lisa said with resignation, "You can go on up. Bri's room is the last one on the left. Next to the bathroom."

As she watched Lenore's slim back, Lisa felt a sudden clutch in her chest. This was it; Brianna was leaving. She swallowed back a sob. Right now she had to stay strong. There would be time enough later to cry.

She thought to call Sheila, who was already on her way over, so that by the time Lenore and Brianna—followed behind by a tearful Eva-Lynn and Coreen—reached the kitchen, Sheila was there with all the paperwork finalized for Brianna's release.

The girl's face shone with excitement but she kept wrapping her arms around herself, reminding Lisa of the early months when Brianna seemed too frightened and forlorn to even speak.

"Look at my daughter. If this face scars I'm gonna sue your asses," Lenore said, jutting out a hip as if to add heft to the threat. "Fact, I'm gonna sue you anyways. Now give me those papers and let's get the hell out of here."

"Oh, Brianna." Lisa swept the small girl into her own arms as tight as she dared. "I'm so sorry," she murmured against her ear, scratching her cheek against the stiff braids and inhaling Brianna's scent to bottle the memory for later.

By this point, Eva-Lynn and Coreen were both openly crying. Brianna hugged each of them, clasped Dude to her chest. Lisa watched and thought about the times she'd been tempted to give the dog away—the mess, the barking, the expense—and how there was no way she, nor any of the girls, would do so. Again she felt a bubble of anger so intense that she had to clasp her hands together so she didn't shove Lenore across the room.

Brianna whispered into Dude's scrappy ear, kissed his snout, and then walked with Lenore toward the porch. All her belongings had been packed into one medium-sized duffle, which Lenore carried, though clearly begrudgingly. At the door, Brianna paused and slowly, almost languidly, crossed the room and once more, without tears, hugged Lisa close.

"It will be okay. I'll come visit, me and Ra'Keem, and we'll go shopping together," she said. And then she was gone.

The small crowded kitchen immediately felt empty.

Sheila flicked her hands, palm-side up. "That's it. I'm sure we will never hear from Brianna again."

"No!" wailed Coreen.

"As her mama says, Brianna thinks *she done grown,* probably done with any kind of real schooling too. She and that baby of hers." Sheila nearly spat the words.

Both girls stomped back up the steps and minutes later Sheila left, leaving the instructions—*call me the moment you hear anything*—as Lisa resumed her vigil in isolation.

At some point around hour seventeen Lisa realized that she'd totally blown off her job interview with Credit-Solutions and that she might be fired from the GIFT House.

At another point, she pondered. If Lenore did sue, would Lisa be liable for negligence and sent to jail?

But mostly Lisa didn't think. She just prayed.

CHAPTER FORTY-NINE

A t seven in the evening, Nate finally called.

"You found her?" Lisa asked, daring to allow hope to raise her voice.

"We did," Nate said, as simply and as powerfully as he'd ever said anything to her before.

"Can I speak to her?"

Before Nate could answer, she heard the phone being grabbed and a breathless, "Miss Lisa, I'm so sorry," followed by a sob that caught in Danesha's throat and was swallowed by a terse, "Mr. Nate said to tell you we'll be there in about an hour."

"Where are you?" Lisa asked before realizing that Danesha had already disconnected.

She stumbled into the kitchen, where Dude immediately wakened and romped in circles while she called Sheila. Then she went upstairs. First she told Coreen, visibly relieved, but whose eyes filled anyway. "Bri was my best friend," she cried, and as Lisa hugged her close, Coreen's whole body sagged in sadness. "How come no one ever sticks around?" she whispered, to which Lisa could say nothing. She wrapped her arms tighter as they clung to one another, offering and receiving a genuine comfort that Lisa would never have believed possible—particularly on this night, in this house, with this girl. In the deepest recesses of her awareness she recognized that Coreen's true emotions were for once being laid bare. Yet Lisa did not have the emotional reserve to take full advantage of this moment of progress, only later reflecting that once again Coreen had received short shrift.

Eva-Lynn's response was more complicated. She went ashen when Lisa told her that Danesha was an hour away from returning. Lisa sat in the desk chair as Eva-Lynn continued to lie in her bed and stare wide-eyed at the ceiling.

"Listen, I think..." but before Lisa could continue, Eva-Lynn interrupted, "It ain't my fault you know."

Treading lightly, Lisa reassured, "I know," though she wasn't sure exactly what she was letting Eva-Lynn off the hook for. And whether or not it was deserved.

The three ate together, the two empty chairs creating a huge vacuum. They made small talk to avoid the silences. It struck Lisa that the five of them had, in fact, finally created a small circle of family.

As Brianna headed south and Danesha headed back, Lisa dozed. The sound of the door opening startled her awake and she jumped out of bed and raced into the living room.

Nate held back and allowed Danesha to enter first. She appeared exhausted. Gone was the usual haughty demeanor, replaced by hunched shoulders, hair yanked out of her braids, her face filthy and streaked with tears over black smudges of eye make-up and remnants of too-red lipstick.

"Oh, Danesha!" Lisa said, crossing the room with outstretched arms. Danesha fell into Lisa's embrace. Lisa's mind traveled to the last and only time Danesha had allowed her to hold the girl close. She had not pressed for information that time, so thrilled to be able to hug without rejection. That would have to stop.

She locked eyes with Danesha. "Things are going to change around here. No more running away, no more secrets. If you can't do that, you can't stay," she said firmly.

Danesha didn't nod in agreement, but she lowered her chin, in itself an admission.

"I love you," Lisa blurted, startled by the true depth of emotion behind the words, so that she found herself repeating, "I do. I really love you." She glanced over the top of Danesha's braids and mouthed to Nate. "Thank you."

There was so much unresolved between them, so many uncertainties and complexities. That too would have to change. But first she had to ask. "So tell me, where did you find her?"

Danesha sat stone-faced, offering no apology or explanation as Nate relayed the details of having followed up on the web site phone number, which lead to Sauget, Illinois—the strip club capitol of lower Illinois—to the address of a different "modeling" agency another twenty miles away, where Danesha was sitting in the basement of a run-down building waiting for her third "interview" in which she was to have modeled specially selected outfits.

Sheila had quietly come in halfway through Nate's story. Lisa expected her to jump in with accusations and threats. When she didn't, instead continuing to stand on the sidelines, Lisa cupped her hand under Danesha's chin, forcing the girl again to meet her eyes, and asked, "What were you thinking?"

Danesha's expression tightened in defiance, but her tone was unexpectedly soft and discernibly sad as she admitted, "I been thinking 'bout my mama."

"Oh, honey," Lisa said, dropping her hand into her lap, and then, since no one else had responded, voiced the one question she did not want to ask. "Danesha, do you want to go back and live with your Mom?"

Behind her, Sheila cleared her throat in disapproval. Clearly, this was not an option to be casually tossed about. But Lisa needed to know.

Danesha hesitated as if truly considering the suggestion. She stared past Lisa, seeming to see nothing. When she spoke, her voice was husky. "Don't you see? My mama could have ruled the world she was so hella-fine." Her face twisted into a bitter scowl, evoking the many days when Danesha had been completely unreachable. "She threw it away. But just 'cause she a fool don't mean I'm gonna be."

"Seems to me you been acting the fool, though, haven't you?" Sheila said.

"They woulda hired me."

"But why do you need the money?" Lisa asked.

Danesha simply shrugged. The GIFT House answer to everything and nothing.

"Yeah, well, whatever you think is that important best be shelved for the next several years, girlfriend," Sheila said, her tone stern but also laced with genuine caring.

Her head shot up. "You the one told me I could be anything I want," Danesha said, and for a glimmer of a moment her face was stripped bare of the defensive veneer

307

and she looked like what she was—a young girl trying to figure herself out.

"That's true. But I know that you know the difference between sense and...*non*-sense," Sheila said.

A very tough hour later, Lisa was locking doors and turning out lights. She started to walk down the hall toward her bedroom, then turned instead.

It had been an exhausting evening even once Sheila and Nate left. The awkward reunion between the three wary girls, with so much left unspoken for now. And the days and weeks ahead loomed large and difficult. There would be multiple incident reports and meetings about the fight, the emergency room visit, the runaway, Brianna's departure, Lisa's role. Vanessa would likely be fired and there would be a search for a new assistant. Danesha was on lockdown probation for at least a month, which would turn her surly and unpleasant. And now they would need to fill in the fourth spot with a stranger—who would bring to the GIFT House a near-empty suitcase and overflowing baggage.

And what about her own job security? And Lenore's threats?

But that was the tomorrows, time enough to shuffle the woulda-shoulda-coulda cards. For tonight, Lisa walked slowly, quietly up the stairs. Brianna's door stood open and the room already seemed as if it had always been vacant. Then Lisa noticed something in the corner. She finally allowed herself to cry as she bent to retrieve the small stuffed pink teddy bear. Bringing it to her lips, she kissed it and brushed the soft fur against her face. Nate, too, had cried when he heard about Lenore and Brianna, and Sheila's prediction. If only Brianna had realized how much they all cared, would she have resisted the lure of King of the Corner Devon? Gone, no one knew where. And fifteen-year-old Brianna carrying his baby. She placed the teddy bear on the empty bed and walked out, pulling the door closed behind her.

Coreen and Eva-Lynn's doors were shut tight, but Danesha's was ajar by inches. Peeking in, she thought at first that the girl was awake, until she heard the steady rhythmic sound of a gentle snore. Daringly, Lisa tip toed into the room and glanced her lips against Danesha's cheek.

"I was so scared," she whispered into the warm ear. "Please don't ever do that again."

In the dark, Danesha's mouth stretched into a smile.

CHAPTER FIFTY

Danesha returned to school where she was greeted by her classmates as a hero for having hitchhiked across the state-line. According to Coreen, Danesha ducked the compliments and attention, keeping her head low and offering little information. Lisa found some small comfort in that.

Sheila had set up an appointment for the day after Danesha came back, then called to cancel. Lisa didn't hear from her until several days later, when she popped into the kitchen unannounced minutes after the three girls had left for school.

"Sorry. I must have had the flu or something. I couldn't drag myself out of bed," Sheila said, sinking into the nearest chair and heaving a loud weary sigh.

"Why didn't you tell me? I would have gone to Walgreens for you. Or made chicken soup." Lisa grinned and in a self-mocking tone added, "What's the point in having a Jewish friend if you can't call for chicken soup when you're sick?"

The non-response spoke volumes. They each busied themselves glancing around at everything but each other, until Lisa summoned the courage to ask, "Am I going to be fired?"

"Do you want to be?"

Lisa almost shouted, "No!" then surprised herself by taking a step away. For the first time since finding out about Brianna's pregnancy, she realized that she might actually have the choice of whether or not to stay. She felt her shoulders sag with the weight of the past many months and flicked her hand, resisting a shrug but not committing to a response.

"Until you can answer that, I can't either."

"I don't know where else I'd go."

Sheila's jaw went rigid. "Don't you dare stay for any reason other than you want to keep this job and live with these girls."

It was tempting to lie, to at least buy some time, except Lisa was too dispirited to give it that much energy. She nodded in tacit agreement, but when Sheila continued to probe with her dark piercing eyes, Lisa sunk her face into her hands. Despite herself, she began to cry, quietly, though obviously.

Sheila gave her the space to come back. When Lisa opened her eyes, it was to the face of a woman who still cared.

"There have been a series of set-backs, Lisa. No denying that. And life is not about to get any easier. Among everything else, we need to address that blood discovered in the school bathroom last week. You know what that means, right?"

"Eva-Lynn is continuing to cut herself. What else could it be?"

Sheila leaned forward, resting her elbows against her thighs. "She wanted it discovered. A girl of Eva-Lynn's cunning does not leave droplets of blood by accident. Not to mention the fact that her family background is now GIFT House knowledge. How many group and individual counseling sessions you think it will take to deal with all of that? "

A shade of dingy mustard paint was seeping through the ceiling white. Maybe she would ask Nate to fix that. And the chair leg that had splintered. One of the girls could get hurt if it broke.

"There's more," Sheila said, then went on to tell Lisa that the previous night she'd tried to reach Brianna and found out that Lenore Jones' phone number had been disconnected. When she called the home in Florida where Lenore had been staying, Sheila was informed by Billie that "she and that pregnant girl of hers ain't welcome here. I don't need to be livin' with my sister when she spittin' mad. I 'spect they'll end up in Arkansas or some such."

This time Lisa didn't try to hide her tears. It was the second time that she'd cried openly in front of Sheila and it was oddly liberating. Outside the sounds of a siren pierced, a sound so common Lisa rarely noticed anymore. Police, ambulance, fire— flashing red lights were no stranger to this neighborhood.

In a voice so husky that Lisa thought perhaps Sheila's own tears had simply been swallowed, Sheila continued, "I'm going to change the subject. Tell me, now that you've lived here for a while, which of the nearby garbage bins could you easily access for thrown-away food?"

Startled, Lisa laughed, then immediately tried to cough the sound back. "Uh, I don't know. Should I?"

"Could you pack you and the girls and find another place to stay in the next hour? Would you know where to get a gun right now? Which rummage sales have 'bag sales' and when?"

"Sheila! Why are you asking me all this?" She didn't even try to check the whining tone.

Another siren wailed past, and Sheila waited until silence descended before continuing. "I ask because these are the questions a person living in poverty and chaos could answer without a thought. I'm not talking about skin color. This is also Eva-Lynn's world here. She doesn't always know it or want it. That's part of her pain. But, Lisa, this will never be your world."

"I'm a social worker. I've worked in debt counseling for the poor." With a wry smile, "And I did major canvassing for Obama. Both times."

"Of course you did," Sheila said dismissively. "That helps these girls how?"

As Lisa leaned away in hurt confusion, Sheila grasped her hand and squeezed. "Just know it. Accept it, that you're *deciding* to live differently than you *could*. But choose, don't let it choose you."

Then, as if an afterthought, when clearly it was anything but, she said, "I have to say one more thing. We've already told you many times that one of the hard truths of this job is you can't save them all..."

Lisa finished the sentence for her. "I should have been able to save four."

They met each other's eyes for an intensely awkward moment and Lisa felt compelled to defend herself. Before she could say anything Sheila spoke up. "Lisa, I owe you an apology. I realize that what I said about you just trying to save yourself was unfair."

"No, you were right. Initially I came here for me, not for them. I don't think it's true anymore. But..." she hesitated. The timing was all wrong. Yet, if she didn't voice it now she'd have to later. "Here's a different concern. Let's say I stay and I guide these girls to be the best they can be. Help turn their lives around. What happens in three and a half years? They leave and then what about me?"

Sheila's mouth twisted into a scowl and she was silent so long Lisa stood, paced once around the room and sat back down before anything was said.

"Look, by law I'm not supposed to tell you this just yet, however, I feel like you need to know. So we're not having this conversation." Sheila moved her chair so close to Lisa their knees brushed against one another, immediately putting Lisa on alert.

"Okay," Lisa said, wishing that she had the courage, instead, to voice what she really felt. No more complications, please.

"Danesha hasn't been told any of this, but several weeks ago her mom began making noises about trying to get Danesha back. When the DFS made an unscheduled house call, they found mom strung out on crack and refusing to go into rehab. Pretty clearly she was wanting Danesha to take care of her, maybe even score some money somehow. Not only has mom's request been denied, there's chatter that her parental rights could be terminated."

"What would that mean?" Lisa asked.

"Danesha would become a ward of the state."

Her eyes again traveled to the ceiling, to the creeping mustard yellow that turned the entire room dingy and uncared for. "Would. . . would she have to leave here?"

This time Sheila clasped both of Lisa's hands and squeezed them between her own. "Yes, she would. *Unless* we can keep her in the custody of the GIFT House, with you as the long-term foster mom," Sheila leaned even closer, "with the potential for eventual adoption."

"Whoa!" Lisa gasped, grabbing hold of the chair for support. "Sheila, are you asking what I think you are?"

Sheila tilted her head in question, those probing eyes digging as if trying to see all the way to Lisa's inner core. "I'm just saying, the answer to your question about three years from now is a series of more questions. Some of which only you can decide how to answer." She stood, pressed the wrinkles out of her skirt, pushed in her chair. "You know by now that things can change day to day, hell, hour to hour. But I wanted you at least to start considering all the possible options." She paused, then, "And, Lisa..."

More? "Yes?"

"No matter what, I hope you'll stay."

After Sheila left, Lisa collapsed onto the sagging couch and just sat, staring forward, lost in a kaleidoscope of flash points. Crying in Dr. Berger's office. Nate's staunch refusal to adopt. Her parents' growing needs. Nate on a date with another woman. Whatever the hell a "bag sale of a rummage sale" was. And, oh my God, adopting Danesha as her own daughter? Danesha?

She sighed, a loud, sad, confused sigh, filling the room with the complexity of emotions. Lisa pulled herself off the couch. Shaking her head free of thoughts and memories, she wandered through the empty house, looking for chores to distract herself. In the kitchen, still in the drying rack, sat an empty cookie sheet, little dark circles staining the Teflon coating, remnants of a young girl's efforts to sweeten all of their lives. Lisa opened the cabinet to put it away, and stopped, clutched the baking sheet to her chest, inhaled, and placed it back in the rack. She needed to be able to see it every time she entered the kitchen, at least for several more days.

As she got out the vacuum cleaner, she noticed a penny on the carpeting, smack in the dead center of a particularly dark stain. Absently, she picked up the coin and began tossing it in the air. Maybe she'd let the penny decide—heads she'd finish out the year and then leave, see what easier life could await her, one where she might feel successful. Tails she'd stay, fully commit herself to these girls, even consider...

She flipped, caught it, slapped her hand down, and then remembered Albert's favorite decision-making technique. Toss a coin with the promise that it will absolutely determine your choice. In that moment—*before* looking at the coin—admit which side was hoped for. Therein was the truest emotion.

Lisa placed the penny on the table, without looking.

CHAPTER FIFTY-ONE

K *eep it simple and don't engage,* Ms. Johnson had advised a couple of times during the three-hour drive here. She'd even offered to come in, but Eva-Lynn knew *that* would be a total disaster.

"You too good to sit down?" Sheri muttered, lighting one cigarette from another. Her hands were shaking so it took several tries before the new one lit. She inhaled with a loud breath, coughed, then stabbed the old butt hard against a chipped ashtray, shoving gray ash onto the beige carpeting. She flopped against the vinyl recliner, while pointing a yellow-stained finger to the couch where Eva-Lynn was supposed to sit.

Eva-Lynn continued to stand, noticing all the tiny, disgusting details, like she was the social worker yanking a pair of twins from a shit-sty "home." She didn't want to relax, didn't want to get sucked in. "I'm just here to pick up my things, Sheri. You didn't pack none of my spring clothes."

"*I* didn't? Near's I remember, girl, you didn't pack shit and you lucky I sent anything over at all. So don't you go running me down for..."

"Sheri! You promised." Eva-Lynn hated the way her throat caught with a whine that slipped through.

Sheri glared hard until Eva-Lynn finally sat on the couch, then smiled like she'd just won a big fucking battle.

"Where's Ray?"

"That shitbum. I kicked his ass out last week."

The wallpaper was peeling in new places. Stuffing was coming out of the back cushion. "So when's he comin' back?"

Sheri took a long, hard drag on her cigarette. She turned her face upward and exhaled a perfect smoke ring that floated toward the stained ceiling before breaking into nothing. Without warning she began to cry. "What if he ain't coming home this time?" she choked out.

"You say that every time."

"Naw, it's different." She pushed her fists against her leaking eyes, swiped away the tears, shook a cigarette out of the pack, lit it from the burning tip of the one in her mouth, inhaled, and blew a series of rings, one right after the other. "It's been a nightmare since you left. I reached my limit and..." she smiled a bitter, yellow-toothed sneer, "I guess I pushed him past his. The fucker."

Eva-Lynn stood abruptly. She'd heard it all before. The tears were new, but that didn't mean shit. "I gotta get my stuff. Ms. Johnson will be back for me in a couple of minutes."

"Already? I thought we could go out for some chicken or somethin'. I'm all alone now, you know. A girl supposed to help out her mom."

She shook her head, trying to clear out the scream that was pushing loose. *Don't engage.*

Sheri followed close behind as Eva-Lynn walked down the dark, narrow hall to her old bedroom. Nothing'd been touched since Christmas. The bedspread was still on the chair, the towel she'd thrown into the corner had dried into a stiff mound, next to a muddy pair of blue jeans she'd dropped to the floor. That December day seemed long ago. She'd promised herself then, and she promised now—as she stuffed T-shirts and shorts into a plastic garbage bag, walking past Sheri and her unwashed self—she would never, never allow herself to want or need Sheri or Ray again. Never.

She let Sheri stand with her on the porch, even kept her mouth clamped as Sheri ragged on about what an SOB Ray was and how that fucking no-good twin of Eva-Lynn's had yet to call his own mother and how it was time for Eva-Lynn to get her sorry ass back home and Sheri was gonna make that happen. Eva-Lynn tuned out the roar, until finally Ms. Johnson's green Dodge pulled into the driveway.

"That a nigger?" Sheri sounded stunned.

"Good bye, Sheri," she called out as she hefted the bulging garbage bag onto her shoulder and walked away as fast as the bulk allowed.

Sheri ground a cigarette onto the porch, lit another. "You watch and see, girl. You're coming home to take care of me," she shouted as she went inside, letting the screen door slam shut before they'd even pulled out of the driveway. Someone needed to burn the place down. But it wouldn't be Eva-Lynn.

Ms. Johnson didn't ask, so Eva-Lynn didn't have to answer. At one point she told Ms. Johnson about Sheri's threat to bring her home and was promised that they would fight to make sure it did not happen. She then asked if she could please, please, please be emancipated from her parents, but Ms. Johnson said what Eva-Lynn already knew. Not until she turned eighteen.

"I swear, the minute I can I'm gonna legally disown them." She stared forward so Ms. Johnson didn't see her lips quiver with trying not to cry. "Will you help me?"

A smile crossed Ms. Johnson's face and she squeezed Eva-Lynn's hand, the skin so dark against Eva-Lynn's that it creeped her out a little, which made her feel like a piece of shit.

"We'll help with whatever you need at that point," Ms. Johnson said. "You won't be alone."

They didn't talk much the rest of the ride back, but it was an okay quiet as they listened to the radio, each lost in her own thoughts. She was proud of herself. She'd kept her cool. Kept it simple. She picked at a scab on her arm from one of her deeper cuts but when she saw Ms. Johnson watching, she flicked the dried brown skin away and sat on her hands.

It would be a relief to get back to the GIFT House.

CHAPTER FIFTY-TWO

"Come with me. I have a surprise for you," Lisa said, grabbing Coreen with one hand and Dude's leash with the other. She drove for nearly twenty minutes before she would answer any of Coreen's questions. After a while, Coreen fell silent, simply staring with her mouth slightly agape as the landscape out her window changed from urban to old suburban to nouveau riche. As they pulled into a lush, tree-lined parking lot, Lisa turned to Coreen and laughed aloud at the girl's stunned expression.

"This is the world's best dog park. I've wanted to bring Dude here for months. Put on his leash and let's go." She walked to the nearby sidewalk, waiting as Coreen let the dog out of the back seat and locked the car doors.

It was an unseasonably mild afternoon for March, yet the park appeared empty. As they began the first quarter mile of the loop, they passed a small, gleaming playground area with brightly colored equipment that, even to Lisa's untrained eye, met every imaginable safety standard. On one side of the asphalt path was a repaved tennis court and on the other side an empty two-hundred-year-old Historic Registry log cabin, its upkeep considerably better than the houses on Clara Road. The field in every direction was sloping and well-manicured, spreading out to the width of a school soccer field.

"This place is ratchet," Coreen said. "And they don't charge us? To come here? Dang!"

Lisa smiled to cover that place in her heart that hurt. For years, back in her running days, she'd jogged this path and barely even noticed. Certainly, she'd never considered the space an anomaly.

"You've been to parks, Coreen."

"Not like this, Miss Lisa. I never seen so much grass before," she said, then giggled. "Well, you know, this kinda grass. Just fooling."

"Not funny," Lisa said, knowing she should press but deciding that today was a day for enjoyment, not for hard truths. There'd been little enough joy in any of their lives

318

recently, but coming home today from a lengthy meeting about Eva-Lynn with Sheila and the school nurse, Lisa had been eager for once to get out, *out*, instead of crawling into bed or cleaning the house. Both Danesha and Eva-Lynn had after-school tutoring and the impulse to take Coreen to the park had suddenly seized her.

At the top of a hill and off to the right was a large lake, and just beyond was a fenced area, a park within the park. "Okay, here we are," Lisa said, leading Coreen and Dude toward a locked gate with a combination keypad just above the handle and just below a sign warning that only paid-up dog park members were allowed. For grins, Lisa tried a couple of easy combinations and when neither of them turned the red light green, she slipped her hand through the slots to push down the inside handle and open the door.

"Miss L!"

"I know, I know," she said, winking, suddenly recalling the sensor left on the shoplifted orange outfit and that torn feeling between doing what's right—setting an *example*—or doing what's wrong for the right reasons. Again she laughed. "Don't you ever pull a stunt like this. But it's our day together and we don't want to disappoint Dude."

Lisa reached to unhook the leash from Dude's collar and off he ran, heaving a discernible canine sigh of relief at the ability to run farther than the eye could see, freely and safely.

"Come on, let's explore," and without waiting for Coreen to object, as all the girls typically did when asked to exercise, Lisa began walking at a brisk pace. Coreen quickly followed. The dog park was at least a half mile round, with grassy hills (free of debris or glass), park benches (free of rust or gang graffiti), and even two dog-bone-shaped plastic kiddy wading pools, turned upside down from the winter (swimming pools for dogs!).

They circled the perimeter twice, Dude running ahead then racing back to keep them in sight, but when another owner entered with her two Golden Retrievers, obviously recently groomed and pure-bred, Lisa motioned to the nearest park bench as Dude took off. Coreen sank onto the bench with obvious relief.

"I'm too thick, huh?"

Lisa pinched a roll of her own waist. "For a while I was power walking several times a week. I definitely need to get back to it. In fact, let's do it together. Go for an hour after school each day." But even as she said it, she recognized that it wouldn't happen. With Vanessa fired and no replacement yet, Lisa could not leave the other girls, and she knew there was no way they would be interested. Plus, there wouldn't be time after school to go all the way to Forest Park and how much fun was walking a neighborhood where the threat of danger lurked on every corner?

Coreen's brow furrowed in an expression Lisa couldn't quite discern. Yearning? Anger? Awe? "Miss Lisa, this is tight and all, but this park, just for *dogs*, is bigger than, like, our whole block. That ain't right."

How she wished that just once an answer came surely and easily. "I can't argue with you there."

"How'd you know 'bout this place?"

She gazed beyond the fence to the lake where a gaggle of geese pecked at the winter grass. She'd always been a little afraid of them, giving wide berth to the hissing adults as she ran past the babies every spring. "I used to live nearby. I jogged the path a bunch and always thought if I had a dog I'd come to the dog park too."

Coreen's eyes opened wide in such astonishment it was nearly comical. "You lived near *here*?" Then she leaned closer. "Hey, did you know that one of your eyes is a different color?"

"No way!" Lisa teased, and immediately Coreen laughed out loud, a hearty carefree sound that carried in the fresh clean air like music itself.

Lisa scooted closer so their arms brushed. For a while neither spoke, content to sit in the calming aura of a peaceful setting on a spring-like day, no sirens or car horns or shouting, just the occasional bark of a playful dog. Lisa thought back to the last time she and Coreen had sat, just the two of them, on the porch step waiting for Danesha to return with news of the neighbor's house fire. And yet again, that memory slipping to the forefront, the minutes before Nate pulled up in his red truck, offering a true alternative, but one in which she could not live with these girls.

She patted Coreen's knee and asked, "How are you doing, sweetie? I mean, really."

"I miss Bri."

"Yeah, I do too." Lisa hesitated, then offered, "I'm really sorry about the bad news with both of your parents. I can't imagine how you feel. Your dad arrested, your mom homeless. But I'm here if you want to talk."

Coreen shrugged. "It don't matter," she said, her face closing down and shut as tight as a locked file, as tight, Lisa realized, as her own face must look when the girls asked about *her* life.

"It does matter. You and I both know that. But fortunately you have a lot of other relatives who love having you around."

Coreen stared off into the distance. "I like when I get to be with Auntie Tiffany and even Aunt Nadia, but she's got lots of kids." She turned to Lisa. "You know what? Before I came here I thought it cool to stay in so many places with so many people, changing every year. That's crazy, ain't it?"

Lisa's nod felt like an implicit lie. Yet maybe it wasn't. After all, even if Lisa left, Coreen could stay. Coreen was—as Lisa was slowly growing to appreciate—the "reason the GIFT House existed."

"Well, like I said, I'm here if you want to talk about your parents or Brianna or anything. It's not good to keep all those feelings bottled up inside."

Coreen grabbed Lisa's arm and squeezed so tight Lisa groaned aloud. She relaxed her grip only slightly. "Miss Lisa, I gotta ask a really big favor of you."

Lisa felt her chest tighten but forced her expression to be open and encouraging.

"Will you promise me something?" Coreen's voice had a tone of urgency.

"I can't promise without knowing what you're asking," Lisa said, and when Coreen didn't back off, added, "But I promise I'll listen with an open ear."

"I need you to believe in Jesus. He's your Savior too."

Lisa lurched away, pulling her arm back and tucking it against her side as if the mere touch with Coreen would cause an unwelcome conversion.

Coreen stood, paced away from the bench, stopped and with her back to Lisa, said so quietly that at first Lisa was sure she didn't hear correctly. "Because otherwise you're gonna go to Hell. And..." She turned to Lisa front on, not bothering to wipe away tears that now streaked her cheeks, "I don't want that to happen to you."

"Oh, Coreen. Come here. Sit."

Coreen plopped down and allowed Lisa to wrap her arms around the girl and hug her close. What she thought was that it might be time to introduce the girls, especially Coreen, to some Jewish basics, maybe even try to have a Passover Seder at the GIFT House next month. But what she said aloud was a promise she didn't remotely mean but which seemed necessary. "Let me think about it, ok?"

Coreen immediately brightened. "Hey, guess what? The drama teacher asked me do I want to be in the spring musical. Said I could maybe get a solo. I'd have to stay after school every day for a month."

"Wow, that would be great."

"Really? I mean, 'cause of my chores and all. Danesha will be pissed."

Lisa almost said that Danesha would be pissed no matter what, but held back her tongue. "We'll work it out."

"Except, what if I don't get a part?"

This Lisa could answer. "You for sure won't get a part if you don't try." Coreen's expression was so doubtful she immediately added, "This is really important for you, isn't it? The acting and singing. And you're good. You should pursue it."

"Ms. Johnson says it's a way for me to deal with my stuff."

She met Lisa's eyes and held them, the opaque blankness gone, her shoulders pushed straight back and up, rather than the usual guarded forward shrug. Lisa realized, as on the night that Brianna left them, this was an honest exchange—here on this park bench in sloping green beauty. Lisa considered the constraints of cement and noise and fear—how they shut a person down. She shuddered with unimaginable images. Jeanette living on the streets. Albert behind bars. Growing up in constant fear.

"I love you, Coreen."

Lisa watched as Coreen visibly struggled to repeat the words and when, instead, she simply smiled, Lisa got a glimpse into a possible future. If she was willing to put in the time, to truly do what she could for these girls who had been placed in her care, the words and the feelings *would* come. From Coreen. From Eva-Lynn. Even from Danesha.

Yesterday she had driven to Danesha's house, to a street of boarded-up abandoned houses, gunshot holes, pumped-up cars with sub-woofers blaring, men drinking from paper bags, women listlessly sitting and smoking on small uneven porches. She'd driven fast, resisting the urge to duck her head. When she'd arrived at Danesha's mother's address she stopped and unabashedly took in the scene. The place was even more ill-kempt than those around it, a rusty chair holding up a screen door that was falling off the hinge, bars on the windows, paint peeling in long strips from the porch rafters. Clearly this was not a house of love.

She'd felt shamed. What had taken her so long to come here, to try to better know this damaged, yet promising, fourteen-year-old girl? It was now too late for Brianna, too far for Eva-Lynn, impossible to visit any one meaningful place where Coreen had stayed. But at least with Danesha, Lisa finally had drawn the courage and wherewithal to take this next small step to a deeper understanding.

As she'd driven back to Clara Road, she'd recognized at a whole new level what the GIFT House, and even what Lisa herself, could offer. She appreciated that it wasn't nothing. In fact, potentially it was not only life-altering, but maybe even life-saving for these girls. As it was for Lisa herself? And with that thought, she realized that she was actually truly consciously crazily and with butterflies of excitement in her gut considering what Sheila had intimated during their recent conversation.

She turned back to Coreen, slouched jelly-like against the bench, obviously more at ease than just minutes before. "Well, my dear, much as I'd like to stay longer, we better head back. Danesha and Eva-Lynn are due home in an hour and we could run into rush hour traffic." She whistled for Dude, who came forward reluctantly, reminding Lisa of each of the girls.

It was a short drive to the highway. As they stopped at the red light on Ballas Road, Lisa looked to the left, where two short miles away was her former—Nate's— house. The house she still half owned.

Nate. He had not returned either of her calls since the night he brought Danesha back to them, and then yesterday she'd finally caught him by calling from the school phone. "You avoiding me?" she'd quipped and when he didn't respond she stuttered, "Uh, listen, I just wanted to thank you again for helping us out. I mean, especially since you had to break plans and all." A pause and then, his voice just slightly warmer than chilly. "You're welcome. But I won't be doing that anymore, Lisa. I've decided to live my life. And I suspect, even if you don't know it, you've already made your choice about your life too."

When the light turned green, she went right.

Pulling into the GIFT House driveway, Coreen again grabbed her arm. "Miss Lisa, how could you leave all that?"

The comforting reply was obvious. That she'd given it up for the girls. That she had no regrets. That it was a sacrifice worth every hill and every leaf. But Coreen's face was still so open, her eyes searching with a genuine curiosity that deserved an answer as honest as the question.

So, Lisa answered. "I don't know."

Coreen continued to sit and suddenly it hit Lisa that if she expected the girls to fight old patterns, and especially if she asked of Coreen to peel back the layers, then she, too, needed to offer a more forthright Lisa. No, it wasn't the Minnesota way, the sharing of one's difficult emotions, but maybe it could become the GIFT House way.

"There was a baby," she paused, talking around the lump,

"several babies. When I lost them I think I lost my way. I came here hoping for an answer."

Coreen was clearly startled by the frank response. "Did...did you find the answer?"

Such a simple question from a girl who was anything but.

"I believe I'm getting closer."

CHAPTER FIFTY-THREE

Lisa squinted, surveying the scene to determine if a stranger would identify the oddness and pathos. A rail-thin, stooped-over elderly white man, a short, gray-haired white woman, three adolescent girls of dramatically different skin tones, and of course, herself—a middle-aged, pasty, pudgy, starletty blonde.

As she'd entered the parking lot in the borrowed Stone Charter van it had struck Lisa that this was the second time this month that she'd introduced GIFT House girls to a place that belonged to her past. She and Nate had been in a Wednesday night league at the Strike 'N Spare bowling alley years ago. The place had changed little, unlike Lisa Harris Rothman.

"Whoa! Mrs. H," Danesha squealed, her voice carrying over the rumble and growl of rolling balls and scattering pins.

Jeanette strutted back toward them, a smile plastered on her face, all traces of asthma gone. To her back, ten pins lay sprawled on the ground. "Haven't lost the ol' touch," she said, hitting high fives with each of the girls before collapsing onto the stiff plastic chair to record her score on the overhead.

Lisa shook her head in amazement. In the few hours they'd all been together something nearly magical was occurring. Her mother and the GIFT House girls were completely taken with one another, particularly Danesha.

Yesterday, the school bus had dropped the girls off at the exact time Lisa pulled into the driveway with her parents in tow. Albert had stepped out of the car and immediately slid to the ground. Danesha and Coreen had hurried over and helped pick him back up, then, without Lisa even asking, had grabbed an elbow each and steered him up the uneven porch steps and into the house. Jeanette nearly fell all over them in gratitude, and as they shed their jackets, backpacks and purses, the undressing seemed to shed their characteristic suspicion. By the time Lisa came out of the kitchen to announce that she'd made hot tea, Albert was safely settled onto the couch, and Jeanette was holding court, telling the story of the eight-inch April snow storm they'd just left.

The bowling excursion was Eva-Lynn's idea. Coreen and Danesha had never been, and when Jeanette heard that, she insisted they go as a group. All three girls were game as soon as they realized it would be a night off from chores or homework.

"No, no, you've got it all wrong." Jeanette struggled up from the deep plastic seat and moved directly behind Danesha. She positioned Danesha's feet on the second row of dots, gently glided her hand to pull Danesha's arm straight back, and then pushed it forward with a slight twist inward of the wrist as the girl released the ball. They stood close together, watching as the ball very slowly rolled straight down the alley, curving into the gutter just a foot away from the pins. Jeanette raised an eyebrow and a palm.

Danesha's face darkened for a moment, then, surprisingly, cracked a smile. "You pushed my arm wrong," she said, but there was neither anger nor accusation in her tone.

"I pushed it right, you moved it wrong," Jeanette responded. Lisa felt a chill run down her spine. She'd never before realized how alike they were—self-righteous, defensive, resolute.

"I'll be damned," she muttered aloud.

"Uh oh, Miss Lisa's cussin'," Eva-Lynn said.

"Demerit," Danesha chimed in.

"That's okay, Miss Lisa," Coreen said, sliding down the bench so that their thighs touched. She leaned her head on Lisa's shoulder. Lisa placed her cheek against the bristly plaits, a stale odor filling her nose. Lisa had nearly grown used to the fact that, with plaits, the girls sometimes went three and four weeks without washing their hair. "Doesn't your scalp itch?" she'd asked Coreen when she first put it together. "That's why we do this," Coreen said, banging her head with the palm of her hand, a familiar gesture Lisa had noted but never understood.

Sitting close, Lisa found herself drawn to the smell. It was certainly more natural than the floral scent of her own head.

"Holy shit! You thuggin' blood, girl," Danesha shrieked, jumping up with arms raised above her head as Eva-Lynn knocked down all the pins in a powerful throw that brought her third straight strike.

Eva-Lynn tried to swallow her smile, but it snuck out on her face. Eva-Lynn was a natural bowler, which should not have been a surprise. As she had told them on the drive over, "When you live near a trailer park you throw rocks and you throw bowling balls."

As Coreen walked over to select her ball, Lisa patted the empty space next to her. Eva-Lynn ignored the invitation. Since returning from her brief visit home, Eva-Lynn had been jittery again. She had a fiery look in her eyes and carried the restlessness of a brooding storm. Several times Lisa had stumbled upon her alone in the living room, looking out the window, fists clenched by her side.

Tension continued to permeate any room in which Danesha and Eva-Lynn shared space, though after weeks of group counseling, the degree of hostility seemed to have lessened as they established a new rhythm sans Brianna. And tonight, watching them interact and even cheer one another on, Lisa once again allowed herself to hope that those two might eventually cross the divide.

Coreen selected a purple sparkly ball, a ten-pounder. She stood on the dots at the edge of the line, studied the lane for a few moments, leaned down and with two hands pushed the ball forward. It rolled so tenuously it appeared as though it might just stop midway, but it continued its path slowly, slowly, until curving and plopping into the gutter, the third such for Coreen. She walked over to wait for her ball to make its way back for another try. As she stood sideways, Lisa noted the obvious improvement in the girl's appearance. The day after their dog park outing, Lisa and Coreen had put themselves on a diet. Each week they would weigh one another and support each other. Lisa had lost three pounds so far, suddenly no longer always hungry. More dramatically, Coreen had already dropped six pounds, and she now carried herself as if she were even lighter than that. It wasn't just the diet or the fact that she and Lisa were in this together. Being one of three instead of one of four suited Coreen more than Lisa would have imagined. Which, she thought, feeling a tightening in her stomach, was about to end.

A new girl would be moving in next week to finish up her ninth grade at Stone Charter and presumably live in the GIFT House until graduation. LaTara Chapman had been staying with an uncle and step-aunt for several years. The uncle had been hotlined to the Division of Family Services numerous times, but his physical and verbal abuse always stopped just short of LaTara's removal from the home. Until last week's "lesson" that resulted in a broken wrist from the whooping for LaTara having missed the bus that morning. Lisa had nearly gagged reading the file of a girl forced to transport her bloody pads in her backpack because, as the uncle freely admitted when he gladly signed the release form, the "sight of her menstrual just reminds me of the unclean pig she is."

Lisa shook away the image. There would be time enough to stress about LaTara's issues, not to mention the inevitable increased upheaval from her presence in the GIFT House.

"Your turn, Mr. Harris," Coreen said, after pushing her predictable follow-up gutter ball.

"My turn for what, little lady?" Albert asked.

"Albert, come on. You've been sitting here all night. Focus." Jeanette's harsh tone made Lisa cringe. The specialist at the Washington University Dementia Center of St. Louis that afternoon had confirmed what they already knew. Albert was in the early to middle stages of Alzheimer's. The doctor had recommended that they put Albert on one of the new meds, keeping him as engaged as possible, and returning to St. Louis in three months for another battery of tests. "It will be a fine balance of allowing Mr. Harris to preserve his dignity while helping him adjust to his increasing limitations," the doctor had advised. He had taken Lisa aside and recommended, "I understand they live in Minnesota, but you're going to have to figure out a way to keep an eye on your mother. Too often the caretaker collapses under the weight of this terrible disease."

"*What's* my turn?" Albert now repeated, with an uncharacteristic sharpness causing Coreen to shake her head in confusion and glance to Lisa for unspoken help.

"Daddy, you go bowl. And I'll be right back," Lisa said, walking quickly away before anyone could see the sudden tears

329

that threatened to spill down her face. She stopped briefly by the bar, barely resisting the temptation to go in and sit in a dark smoky corner.

"Lisa? Is that you?"

"Greg," she almost said, but caught herself in time. "You have the wrong person," she mumbled and beelined for the bathroom door. She leaned against the wall and heaved deep breaths, trembling. Greg Gartner had bowled in the same league, two lanes over. One time she and Nate had grabbed beers with him, and Greg had nearly cried over a pitcher about how lonely he was since his wife walked out. Nate had held her hand under the table and repeatedly squeezed their fingers together.

Lisa dipped her head in the sink and splashed cold water on her cheeks and eyelids, then ran chilly fingertips over her ears as if to silence the sounds of Albert's confusion. She felt a hand gripping her shoulder and turned to face her mother, now seeing Lisa's despair. "I know, honey."

"I'm so glad to have you here, Mom, even for a few days." Stepping closer, Lisa allowed her head to rest against her mother's soft shoulder, her eyes closed, relishing a moment of easy togetherness. Then her mom did something totally unexpected. She pulled Lisa so tight their bodies melded one to the other. Lisa grabbed on, as if to a lifeline. Jeanette smelled like Mom. She felt like Mom. And Lisa almost let go. Almost let herself begin to cry in a way that might not end. But Jeanette spared her. Gently, she pushed Lisa back, walked over to the sink and ran her hands under water for long quiet moments. With her back to Lisa, she said, "I keep feeling guilty about the kind of wife I was to your Dad."

"Mom! You've been wonderful."

"Lisa, you have no idea. I used to pressure your father to be so much *more*. Albert this, Albert that. You know how he was. Always gone and barely there when there. Now I just wish he knew my name." She paused, and in a voice that seemed to trail off before it began, "He's not the only one losing memory."

"What are you telling me?"

Jeanette swiped the back of her hand across her nose and carelessly wiped her hands against the fabric of her skirt, so un-Jeanette-like as to be alarming. "It's such a horrible disease. More and more I can't remember who Albert was. I try to imagine us dancing but can only picture him shuffling. I try to hear his laugh, but only hear his muttering. Do *you* remember your father...*before?*"

Albert before. A whisper of a parent, a man who loved his daughters, yet shied away from showing outward affection. A constant and a shadow. He'd never once raised his voice to either of his girls, but he'd rarely spoken at all. It was Jeanette whose energy dictated the dynamics of the house. Her demands, her voice, her opinions, her very presence—in itself reassuringly solid even as it allowed less room for self. A mother like all the rest, Lisa had thought before meeting the kind of women who didn't deserve the title.

"Okay, dear, let's change the subject. I have to admit, it's not so bad here."

Lisa felt herself exhale, having not realized she was holding her breath. She flashed a grateful smile for the gift and again found herself wondering, what kind of parent would *she* have been? If she'd learned anything from this job it was that having a baby and being a mother did not necessarily coincide.

Her last baby, if it was briefly a baby, would have just been learning to walk. She rubbed her empty left ring finger. Would the counting go on for the rest of her life? Would, on any given day, if asked, Lisa forever know the exact ages of each of the five lost babies?

Yet, she also now knew the birthdays and ages of Danesha, Coreen, Eva-Lynn, and, of course, Brianna. She could attempt to bake their favorite cakes with the icing of choice. She could name their best teachers, favorite CDs, could even probably buy the exact right pair of jeans for each of the girls. She didn't always know when to push or when to retreat—but did any "parent?"

Looking at her mother's red-rimmed eyes, Lisa accepted there was a new, perhaps more important question. What kind of daughter was Lisa going to be?

As if reading her mind, Jeanette quietly said, "I'm going to need you." There was no judgment or command in her mother's tone.

"I know," Lisa said. "Maybe you guys could move to St. Louis?"

"Good lord, I can't imagine that. Our whole world is in Minnesota." At Lisa's crestfallen expression, "Of course, the doctors here seem to know more about Daddy's condition..." She squeezed Lisa's hand, linking their fingers together. "I sure hope you and your sister will start talking with each other more. She can be your people now. A sister to share this with."

Instead of feeling the usual pressure, Lisa realized that Jeanette was right. She had vowed to do so after the Chanukah visit. It was time to make the effort.

"You know, dear, Nate needs you too."

"It don't think so, Mom. We still love each other, yet we're like two speeding cars heading in different directions. Maybe that's okay?"

"That story is definitely not over. But that's another conversation." Jeanette paused, weighing the wisdom of her own thoughts, then offered, "And as if you're not being pulled in enough directions, these girls obviously need you, perhaps most of all. You don't see it yet, the way they look to you for guidance."

"Seriously?" Jeanette nodded and Lisa couldn't keep herself from asking again, "Really?" With Jeanette's smile, Lisa shook her head in wonderment, which was quickly canceled by a surge of panic. "Oh, Mom, am I making stupid choices with my life?"

Jeanette placed her index finger against the small of Lisa's back, gently pressed and said, "I wish I had an easy answer for you. I see that you're healing, sweetheart. How you continue to do so is something you'll need to figure out on your own."

Suddenly Lisa was transported back. She is twelve years old, in a gymnastics class, trying to marshal the courage to do her first solo back flip. She's been assured repeatedly by her teacher that she is ready. Yet, she stands paralyzed in place, knees bent, arms straight up, eyes forward, lacking the faith to let go. Then she feels the press of her teacher's finger on her lower back that triggers for her the confidence to fling herself up and head-long backwards into the air.

"Look, Lisa, it's no secret that this is not what I imagined for you. But I will accept whatever you choose." The words were clearly sincere, another gift, but Jeanette's tone had gone brusque. *Enough emotion already.* "Come on, we better get back. I'm sure the girls and Dad are wondering what's happened to us."

Before she could stop herself, Lisa took the plunge, even knowing that putting it out there would give it weight. "Mom, I have to tell you something crazy Sheila told me. I need your advice ..." She halted, took a deep breath, suddenly afraid of Jeanette's response—in either direction. Bonnie's reaction had been completely predictable. "That could be the craziest thing I've heard from you yet. You've got to do it!" But what might her own mom say? What did she want her to say?

And then, as if just thinking about Bonnie caused Lisa to be "saved by the bell," Danesha burst into the bathroom. "Miss Lisa, you okay? You been gone a long time and we was worried."

Don't cry, Lisa thought. She clamped down on her lip and nodded.

Danesha stared at her for a moment, with eyes bold and wise. "Your daddy bowled a strike," she said.

Lisa smiled. "You shittin' me?"

"Miss Lisa," Danesha bellowed, "you ain't allowed to cuss. We already told you that."

She wanted to grasp the girl close. But she knew better. Instead, she matched her mother's steps as she allowed Danesha to lead the way back to their lane.

Sure enough, Albert was standing with a broad grin on his face.

"Hey, it's your turn, Miss Lisa," Coreen shouted.

"Here I am," she answered.

ACKNOWLEDGMENTS

Every writer should have a dream agent like Allison Hunter, whose warmth, enthusiasm, intelligence and persistence never wavered as she continued to believe in this book. Huge thanks to Lonnie Whitaker, editor truly extraordinaire, and to Louella Turner, a publisher who exceeds what I ever could have hoped for. The expertise of all three of you has been invaluable.

This book has had many readers along the way whose feedback and support helped to shape a manuscript into a novel and then into a better novel. Much gratitude and love to you all: Debbie Taryle (reader of several drafts), Barb Bogard, Linda Wendling, Janet Goddard, Perry Pattiz, Karen Kriger Bogard, Jonathan Bogard, Daniel Bogard, Susie Dykstra, Debra Finkel, Lise Bernstein, Dr. Diane Rosenbaum, Cheryl Silver, Patti McCarty (Bonnie owes her life to you) and Robert Bogard, editor, photographer and draft cover designer.

Many thanks to the UMSL MFA program for developing the novelist in me, with a special thank you to my teachers, whose voices still echo as I write: David Carkeet, Mary Troy, Howard Schwartz, Jaimee Wriston Colbert, and David Haynes.

I owe this story to the entire Lift For Life Academy "family" and to the Clayton Pathfinders. You gave me the opportunity to do the work I was always meant to do and were the genesis of these characters.

Lastly, thank you to my biggest supporters, Shelly Feldman Bricker and Robert Bogard. Your love and encouragement have always sustained me in everything I do. And to my children, Daniel, Jonathan, Tenzin, Karen and Gompo, and my grandchildren, Gavi, Yaeli, Noa and Namkha, for the joy you bring to my life every day.

About the Author

Denise Pattiz Bogard is an award-winning author who has been writing professionally for more than 30 years. Her fiction and non-fiction have been published in *The Oklahoma Literary Review, Lady's Circle, Newsweek, Teacher Magazine, St. Louis Magazine, The St. Louis Post-Dispatch, P-D Magazine* and the anthologies *Are We Felling Better Yet? Women's Encounters with Health Care in America* and *Winter Harvest*. Denise earned her MFA in creative writing from the University of Missouri-St. Louis. She is the founder and coordinator of St. Louis Writers Workshop. Previously, Denise coordinated the writing program at Lift For Life Academy charter middle and high school in downtown St. Louis, taught media writing at Webster University and was a co-founding partner of the public relations agency, Bogard & Finkel Communications. Denise lives in St. Louis with her husband and is the mother of three and grandmother of four.

CPSIA information can be obtained
at www.ICGtesting.com
Printed in the USA
BVHW04s0940020818
523279BV00020BA/886/P